Laura Lamont's Life in Pictures

"*Laura Lamont* might be the most anticipated debut of the year. It's easy to understand the hullabaloo; Straub's style is clear and engaging, and her plot balances the glamour of the Hollywood golden age with trenchant thematic links to issues of contemporary working women. The result is a delightful, entertaining read with substance."

—*Minneapolis Star Tribune*

"Delightful . . . Mesmerizing."　　　　　—*The Miami Herald*

"Straub vividly recaptures the glamour and meticulously contrived mythology of the studio-system era."　　　　　—*USA Today*

"[With] effortless prose and precise observations . . . Straub's novel explores themes of identity, career, and motherhood through the filter of one woman's life experience . . . An entertaining narrative."

—*San Francisco Chronicle*

"At once a delicious depiction of Hollywood's golden age and a sweet, fulfilling story about one woman's journey through fame, love, and loss."　　　　　—*The Boston Globe*

"Straub makes masterful use of the golden age of Hollywood to tap contemporary questions about the price of celebrity and a working mother's struggle to balance all that matters."　　　　　—*People*

continued . . .

"Sinking into this book is like settling down to watch a Criterion Collection print of a Greta Garbo film—it's elegant, clean, lovely to spend time with, and refreshing in its simplicity of storytelling. . . . Straub ultimately delivers a novel that feels timeless."

—*Los Angeles Review of Books*

"[A] timeless tale with true heartfelt warmth throughout . . . one of the most entertaining novels this fall."   —*Matchbook Magazine*

"Bighearted . . . A witty examination of the psychic costs of reinvention in Hollywood's golden age."   —*The Washington Post*

"The novel's engaging concept plays to our cultural longing to peer behind the movie screen, and Straub keeps her narrative moving, filling it with vivid details."   —*The New York Times Book Review*

"Straub's brisk pacing and emotionally complex characters keep the story fresh. . . . This bewitching novel is ultimately a celebration of those moments when we drop the act and play the hardest role of all: ourselves."   —*O, The Oprah Magazine*

"Straub keeps the dramatic twists coming."   —*The Daily Beast*

"Will appeal to any girl who has left a small town behind to follow her dreams to the big city."   —*Marie Claire*

"Straub imbues her writing with surprising insights and wit. . . . Straub's writing reminds the reader how good literary fiction can precisely capture the human experience."   —*PopMatters*

"Fantastic . . . A stunningly intimate portrayal of one woman's life."

—*Entertainment Weekly*

continued . . .

"With a precise balance of glitz and dirt, Emma Straub's *Laura Lamont's Life in Pictures* captures the scope of great, sweeping cinema. Straub ultimately earns a reader's desire to follow the character of Elsa Emerson/Laura Lamont through most of her life by stripping the character's gleaming, diamond-laden exterior and showing her guts . . . It deserves its own soundtrack and spotlights."

—*Paste Magazine*

"At once iconic and specific, Emma Straub's beautifully observed first novel explores the fraught trajectory of what has become a staple of the American dream: the hunger for stardom and fame. *Laura Lamont's Life in Pictures* affords an intimate, epic view of how that dream ricochets through one American life."

—Jennifer Egan, author of *A Visit from the Goon Squad*

"Emma Straub is a magician, full of brilliance and surprise."

—Lorrie Moore

"An exquisite debut novel that brings Depression-era Hollywood to life with startling immediacy. Laura Lamont is a memorable character, and Emma Straub illuminates her inner life with uncanny authority." —Tom Perrotta, author of *The Leftovers* and *Little Children*

"I absolutely loved this tale of one woman's incredible journey from small-town girl to movie star. Straub brings Old Hollywood fully to life, in all its glamour, excess, ruthlessness, and beauty. I didn't want this marvelous novel to end."

— J. Courtney Sullivan, author of *Commencement* and *Maine*

LAURA LAMONT'S
Life in
PICTURES

EMMA STRAUB

RIVERHEAD BOOKS

New York

RIVERHEAD BOOKS
Published by the Penguin Group
Penguin Group (USA) Inc.
375 Hudson Street, New York, New York 10014, USA

USA | Canada | UK | Ireland | Australia | New Zealand | India | South Africa | China

Penguin Books Ltd., Registered Offices: 80 Strand, London WC2R 0RL, England
For more information about the Penguin Group, visit penguin.com.

The Library of Congress has catalogued the Riverhead hardcover edition as follows:

Straub, Emma.
Laura Lamont's life in pictures / Emma Straub.
p.   cm.
ISBN 978-1-59448-845-0
1. Motion-picture actors and actresses—Fiction.   2. Fame—Fiction.   I. Title.
PS3619.T74259L38   2012   2012011330
813'.6—dc23

First Riverhead hardcover edition: September 2012
First Riverhead trade paperback edition: July 2013
Riverhead trade paperback ISBN: 978-1-59463-182-5

PRINTED IN THE UNITED STATES OF AMERICA

10   9   8   7   6   5   4   3   2

Cover illustration and lettering by Christopher Silas Neal
Book design by Michelle McMillian

This is a work of fiction. Names, characters, places, and incidents either are the product
of the author's imagination or are used fictitiously, and any resemblance to actual persons,
living or dead, business establishments, events, or locales is entirely coincidental.

While the author has made every effort to provide accurate telephone numbers and Internet addresses
at the time of publication, neither the author nor the publisher is responsible for errors, or for changes
that occur after publication. Further, the publisher does not have any control over and does not
assume any responsibility for author or third-party websites of their content.

FOR MY HUSBAND,
A GOLDEN STATUE
IF EVER THERE WAS ONE

You can take Hollywood for granted like I did, or you can dismiss it with the contempt we reserve for what we don't understand. It can be understood too, but only dimly and in flashes.

—F. Scott Fitzgerald, The Last Tycoon

Gold rushes aren't what they used to be.

—David Thomson, The Whole Equation

I can be an actress or a woman, but I can't be both.

—All About Eve

LAURA LAMONT'S
Life in
PICTURES

1

CHERRY

Summer 1929

Elsa was the youngest Emerson by ten years: the blondest, happiest accident. It was John, Elsa's father, who was the most pleased by her company. His older daughters already wanted less to do with the Cherry County Playhouse, and it was nice to have Elsa skulking around backstage, her white-blond hair and tiny pink face always peeking out from behind the curtain. Elsa was a fixture, the theater's mascot, and the summer crowds loved her.

The Cherry County Playhouse, so named because of the cherries Door County produced, was housed in a converted barn on the Emerson property in Door County, Wisconsin's thumb. The barn was two hundred feet off the road, which had been renamed Cherry County Playhouse Road in honor of Elsa's parents' efforts and because there was no real reason not to. From May until September, tourists from Chicago and Milwaukee and sometimes even farther afield drove up and stayed in the small wooden rental cabins for the entire summer. After days spent on Lake Michigan or Green Bay, they would pile into the old barn and sit on wooden pews cushioned with calico pillows sewn by Mary, Elsa's mother. John directed and often starred, his booming baritone carrying into the surrounding trees, all the way to the road. The older girls, Hildy and Josephine, who had been such promising Ophelias and Juliets in their early teens, had instead taken jobs at the Tastee Custard Shack down the road and could most often be found handing over cones of frozen custard. Elsa was nine years old and happy to participate. She tore tickets, swept the stage of errant leaves and clods of dirt, and doted on the barn cat, who hated everyone, especially children.

The actors and crew members all moved onto the Emersons' land for the entire summer. The boys from fancy schools on the East Coast, the ones with drama programs and crew teams, and all the delicate young women moved into the main house; the men with sturdier constitutions slept in tents and cabins scattered around the property, which gave the whole place the feeling of a summer camp. Elsa loved cuddling up to the beautiful young women, who would do her makeup and brush her hair for hours on end, all for the low cost of listening to them talk about their sordid and endlessly complicated relationships with men back home.

Hildy, Elsa's second-oldest sister, was nineteen and had few interests outside of her own body. She would sometimes borrow her mother's sewing machine to make new dresses, but would give up halfway through and leave the fabric limping off to one side like a wounded animal. Hildy was given to the dramatic, despite having forsaken the theater.

"Mother, I could not possibly help you with the dishes. My headache is the size of Lake Michigan," Hildy said. It had previously been the size of the kitchen, the size of the house, and would soon be the size of the entire state of Wisconsin. Elsa sat underneath the long barn-wood table and watched Hildy waggle her knees back and forth.

"Excuse me," Mary said. "There is no room for talk like that in this house." Elsa could hear Mary's tired hands shift to her hips, where they would roam around, pressing into the sore spots with her wide, blunt thumbs. Mary woke at dawn and made breakfast for the entire cast and crew—that summer, it was twenty-seven people, all of whom would groan loudly if given the chance. The girls' mother ran a tight ship. Elsa often thought that her mother would have made an excellent homesteader, as she seemed happiest when conditions were tough and the going was hard.

Hildy rubbed her temples. She had always had headaches—all the Emerson women did, blackout, knock-down headaches that crowded the sides of their skulls and didn't let go for days. One of Elsa's chores was dampening a washcloth and placing it over her mother's and sisters' closed eyes, then tiptoeing out of the room. Elsa couldn't wait to be a woman, to feel things so deeply that she too needed a dark room and total silence. She'd asked her sister about the headaches once, when she could expect them to start, and had been laughed out of the room.

"Honestly, Mother, honestly." Hildy was the most beautiful of the three Emerson sisters, though Elsa was so young that she hardly counted. Josephine was the oldest and the most like their mother, with a wide, flat face that hardly ever registered any expression whatsoever. It was what their father called A Norwegian

Face, which meant it had the look of a woman who had seen fifteen degrees below zero and still gone out to milk the cows. Josephine was inevitably going to marry a boy from one of the cherry farms down the road, and no one thought that they would be anything more or less than perfectly fine.

But Hildy was better than fine. Elsa loved to look at her sister, even when Hildy was having one of her episodes and her blond hair was wild and matted against one side of her head from all her flip-flopping and thrashing in her sleep, and her pale pink skin had flushed and broken out into a crimson red. When she wanted to, Hildy could look like a movie star. It hadn't come from their mother—that was a fact—neither the raw good looks nor the knowledge of what to do with them. Hildy pored over all the magazines she could find, *Nash's* and *Photoplay* and *Ladies' Companion*, and practiced putting on the actresses' eyeliner in the mirror for hours every day until she got it right. When Hildy was feeling light, as she put it, and the headaches were gone, she wriggled through the house in castoff costumes, and Elsa thought she was as beautiful and lost as a landlocked mermaid.

The first play of the summer was an original, which the audience never liked as much as one it knew, but John thought the story was relevant and so said to hell with it. They would do *A Midsummer Night's Dream* in August like they always did, and that would satisfy the fogeys. The new play, *Come Home, My Angel*, was about a wounded soldier returning from war to find that his girlfriend had married his best friend. In the end, the soldier shot himself, but the couple was happy. It was dark, but sometimes people liked that. John had found exactly the right actor for the wounded soldier, a young man from Chicago who looked hurt all the time, but never without looking handsome. His name was Cliff, and he was a brooder. Hildy was in love with him the second he walked into the house. The feeling, if feelings could be judged by noises coming from Hildy's bedroom in the middle of the afternoon when no one else was around, was mutual.

The Tastee Custard Shack couldn't compete with Cliff's sturdy biceps, and so Hildy was once again home for the summer, running lines with the actors and helping her mother with the sewing. Elsa quickly won a new job as well—she became the messenger, and would deliver hastily handwritten notes to and from the young lovers, dashing between the barn and the house, running up and down the stairs. She was filled with urgency, and would sit, panting, once she arrived, her ragged breath proof of her dedication. Hildy would draw her close and set Elsa on her lap while she read the newest missive, sometimes reading bits out loud, but only if it was something she thought Elsa was old enough to hear. That meant that there were long pauses in between when Hildy just read to herself, sometimes covering her mouth with her fingers, or sticking a knuckle in between her teeth. During those sessions, Hildy hadn't forsaken the theater at all, only reduced her audience to one. The point was still the reaction, the tailoring of the performance to the crowd. Later on, it was clear to Elsa that Cliff had practiced this particular art before, but at the time, neither she nor Hildy could see it, and the girls were desperate in their hope that Hildy's own juvenile attempts at love on paper would match up.

"'. . . and then, at last, the sweet and creamy skin of your upper thighs . . .'" Hildy read aloud. Cliff was slowly working his way up her body, and Hildy stopped there. She lay on her stomach with her knees bent, her pointed toes waving back and forth with pleasure. Elsa sat in the small chair at the foot of the bed and tried to imagine Cliff without his shirt on. His hair was so dark that it was almost black, with curls the size of quarters. "Oh, my God, Else," Hildy said, and grabbed Elsa's wrist. "Oh, my God." Then Hildy flipped over onto her back and snapped her fingers for Elsa to bring her a new sheet of paper, on which she immediately began her response. Relationships with the cast and crew weren't forbidden—it had simply never been an issue. The girls had always been just that, girls—their parents seemed not to have noticed Hildy's swift ascension into womanhood. Though Josephine was older by a year, she had not transformed the way Hildy had, and seemed to still be plodding her way through life without a sudden influx of feminine hormones.

It was warm in Hildy's room with the door shut, and there were pockets of sweat behind Elsa's knees. Even so, Elsa loved summertime best of all. In the off-season, Door County emptied out and got so quiet that Elsa sometimes forgot that there were other people living in other houses, that the kids at school went home to other families. Everything was cold and tight. Her entire world got bigger in the summer—when the ground went from white to brown to green, when the birds started talking to one another at dawn, when the trees all around the house would sprout new leaves and flowers and just beg her, beg her to climb them. Elsa knew every inch of the land her parents owned, every rock and root. Hildy and Josephine were too old to have any interest in running around with her, too wrapped up in their own teenage lives, and so Elsa had to do it all herself. She counted butterflies and fireflies and made bouquets for the weddings of her dolls. But when the actors arrived—that was the best of all. Even though Elsa loved her parents, her father in particular, she sometimes wondered when one of the actors would see her and recognize her as his own, and she would be rescued. In her daydreams, there were never any brooms or washcloths; there was only the theater, with a full house, everyone clapping for her.

Cliff was living in the cabin, which was about fifty feet from the main house, on the other side of the barn. He had requested it, though John had offered him a room in the house. When pressed, which of course never took much pressing at all, Cliff said that he wanted to live as the character would live, apart from everyone else. He wanted to spend the summer in isolation. Elsa's father had built the cabin himself the previous summer, nailed together each wooden plank until the planks came together and were entire walls. Josephine had helped, her thin hair pulled back, her pale eyes squinting in the sun. Unlike Hildy, Josephine never worried about whacking her thumbnail with a hammer, or being out in the sun for too long; she just kept her head down and worked. The cabin was of a modest size—just one room, with a basin sink and no toilet—but it was private, and the door faced away from the house, into the woods, which meant that Cliff could come and go as he pleased.

Elsa was wary of Cliff. The first time she delivered one of

Hildy's notes she knocked on the cabin's door and thrust the note toward him with her arm outstretched over her head, so that she didn't have to look him in the eye. Once he plucked the letter from her hand, she turned around and ran into the trees, as if she were a nymph or a sprite and could vanish into the leaves just by wishing it so. The second time, though, Cliff grabbed her by the wrist, not hard, but insistently, and made her come inside.

It was strange to be in the cabin when it was occupied. The place was the same, of course, all the knots in the planks in the same places they'd always been, the same view of the barn on one side and the trees on the other. But the whole cabin was different now that it was where Cliff lived. In just a matter of days, the room had taken on his smell. Elsa breathed it in, flaring her nostrils like a dog.

"Be careful," Cliff said. "If you keep doing that, your nose will stay that way." He winked. Elsa backed up until she hit the folding chair at the small dining table, and then tucked herself in against the wall. Cliff watched her, an amused look on his face. He was wearing a plain white undershirt, and Elsa could see the curly hair under his arms, bits of it snaking out from under like the climbing ivy that her father cut off the house every year. As though he could hear Elsa's thoughts, Cliff lifted his arms over his head and stretched from side to side. She knew he was testing her, seeing how long she could last. Elsa thought of the tabby cat who lived in the barn and how fast she ran out of there every night when the audience showed up.

The room smelled like dirt, like Elsa's undershirt after she'd been running around all day, like her father's coffee. Elsa crossed her arms on the table and squeezed her elbows. Cliff unfolded

Hildy's most recent note, and paced back and forth while he read. Every so often he chuckled. When he was through, Cliff folded the note back up and slid it into his pocket.

"Your sister is a wild one," he said. "But I'm sure that's no news to you." He stroked his chin with his thumb and pointer finger. The room seemed small, smaller than usual, as if Cliff's body was too big for the space to hold, but Elsa knew that wasn't true. Her father was always taller than the actors, and he'd made sure that the cabin was big enough for him.

"Hildy likes you," Elsa said. "She told me." Her face burned. Hildy wasn't wild, not really. Elsa wanted to tell Cliff the truth about her sister, about how she'd sometimes lock herself in her room for days, how she would often cry for no reason, and her pretty face would crumple into something red and ugly. She shouldn't have told him anything—Hildy wouldn't have wanted her to. Elsa had just needed something to say, something to prove that she knew a fact that he didn't.

"Did she say that? I think she about more than likes me," Cliff said, coming closer. He leaned down, so that his face was only a few inches away from Elsa's. She could see the tiny beard hairs starting to push through his skin. There was a bump in the middle of his nose—he'd broken it once; Elsa had seen that kind of nose before. Had someone punched him? She felt her pulse begin to speed up inside her body, until all the blood was shuttling back and forth and up and down and she could hardly keep her mouth closed. "Don't you think so?" Cliff straightened up and laughed. "I don't blame her, do you?" He looked back at Elsa, who had drawn her knees up to her chest, thereby turning herself into the smallest ball possible.

"Sure," Elsa said, not really understanding. She recognized the smell in the cabin—it wasn't her father's coffee Cliff smelled like, it was her father's beer. You couldn't get beer just anywhere, but in Wisconsin, the rules were looser. The deliveries came once a month, late at night, not that anyone was watching so much anymore. She loved that smell, slightly sour, like her mother's bread when it was rising, but it was different coming out of Cliff. Elsa let her legs down to the floor one at a time, and slid out from behind the table.

"Leaving already?" Cliff asked, and jerked back his head in laughter. The sound wasn't at all soft, like laughter should be, but hard, like a barking dog that knows no other way to get attention. Elsa tiptoed toward the door, in hopes that Cliff wouldn't follow, and he didn't, but instead let her go without moving an inch. She could hear him laughing as she ran back to the house.

The season always started on the first Thursday in June. Elsa accompanied her mother and Josephine to the grocery store and the old tavern that now served only lunch and dinner and the Lutheran church and the restaurants with the best fish boil to drop off flyers they'd made at the kitchen table. Everyone in town knew the Emersons. Mary had taught school before starting the playhouse with her husband, and so she was always patting some young person on the back of the neck, as roughly as a cat picking up a kitten by its scruff. This was why Hildy never went along on these trips; she found it so deeply mortifying to see their mother socialize. It was better when she was at home, behind the scenes.

Hildy told Elsa this a thousand times: that their mother talked too much, which Elsa thought was strange, because their mother hardly ever talked at all. Elsa often felt like she and her sisters had two entirely different sets of parents. It was one of the things she wondered about, late at night, after everyone else was asleep. Josephine seemed not to notice, and just sat patiently in the truck, staring out at God knew what, while Elsa twirled around their mother's stiff body, holding on to one hand and then the other and dancing in place until everyone noticed and told her what a good dancer she was, and how beautiful.

Come Home, My Angel was up every weekend, four shows a week. The *Door County Courier* came on the first two nights, and wrote a review that heralded the "vision of John Emerson, Door County's preeminent theatrical director, for bringing Clifton Parr to roam the boards this summer. Parr delivers a masculine edge to his character's wounded body and pride. Ladies in the audience will swoon." Hildy ripped the review out of the paper before anyone else could see it, and read it to Elsa in the privacy of her bedroom. "They're damn right he'll make audiences swoon." She twisted her hair around her finger, a coquettish tic she'd picked up from Suzanne, the actress playing Cliff's former love. "They'd just better stay away after that," she said. "Or I don't know what I'll do." Suzanne was married to one of the other actors, a half-gimpy guy named Walter, otherwise Hildy wouldn't have spoken to her. After three long summers away from the theater, Hildy was once again in the audience every night, though Elsa knew it was that she wanted to make sure no one else got any fresh ideas about Cliff, and not about seeing the same thing over and over again. Josephine had covered her shifts at the Tastee Custard Shack and was gone until ten o'clock every night, which meant that it was only Mary and Elsa cleaning up after each show.

"It's going to be tonight," Hildy whispered to Elsa during the show one night. Cliff was off changing into his bloodstained costume. They could see him through the stage door, which wasn't a door to anywhere but the outside of the barn, where actors waited for their cues. Cliff pulled down his suspenders and lit up a cigarette. He was talking to Warren, one of the other actors, the man who played his rival. Offstage, in real life, the actor couldn't have held Cliff's cuff links. The inferiority was laughable—Warren was short, he was slight, he was blond like everybody else in Door County. How could anyone choose him over Cliff? That was why they got along. Elsa understood that much about human nature: No one in the theater liked to be around people who were better-looking than they were.

"What's going to be tonight? He dies every night, you know." Elsa had already seen Cliff shoot himself twice. After the big, loud *pow*, which always scared her, there were a few moments when the whole audience held their breath, wanting to make sure that even though Cliff was limping, collapsing, heaving, he was actually okay, and would stand up again in time for the curtain call. Elsa hated those few minutes, when no one was breathing, but only until those minutes had passed, and the audience erupted into applause, shattering the worried quiet. After that, that silent pause was her favorite part of the show. The theater was made for holding your breath, and for forgetting what was real and what was fake. It was better than the pictures, where everything was so far away and perfect.

"Not that, Else. Me and Cliff. It's really serious. You know about that stuff, right?" Hildegard got to be Hildy, but Elsa only got to be Else, as in Someone Else, a human afterthought. Hildy bit her fingernail. It wasn't like she could talk to their mother, or to Josephine, who would rather talk about the procreation of cows and cherry trees. She certainly couldn't talk to their father, who would lock her bedroom door and throw away the key. "I think tonight's going to be the night. Don't tell anybody, okay?" Hildy's blue eyes looked as wide as full moons. She was nervous.

"Okay," Elsa said. Hildy had had boyfriends before, boys from town, but next to Cliff they seemed like pictures from a magazine, easily ripped into pieces. Elsa didn't like the idea of Hildy alone in the cabin with Cliff, who seemed so strong that he might snap her in half by accident. By the barn entrance, their mother flickered the lights, and the audience got quiet again. Outside, in the dark, an owl gave a series of long hoots, as though it were the ringmaster announcing another round. After the show, Hildy told their mother that she had a headache and didn't want to be disturbed. Elsa watched as she went out the door of the barn and turned right instead of left, heading straight for the cabin, where she was going to do something that couldn't be undone, even if Elsa never told anyone. The truth would still be there, pulsing like a heartbeat. After her parents went to bed, Elsa sneaked back downstairs and sat by the window until Hildy came home, her teeth chattering and a wild look in her eye. She reminded Elsa of a spooked horse, one you couldn't touch behind the saddle without fear of being kicked in the gut. When Hildy saw her sister sitting in the dark, she tucked a hand behind her back.

"What is that?" Elsa asked.

"Shh, go to bed! What are you still doing up?" Hildy asked, though the look in her eye told Elsa that she knew the answer.

"What's behind your back?" Elsa scrambled out from behind the kitchen table and grabbed at Hildy's hands.

Perhaps thinking that a struggle would make more noise than a whispered explanation, Hildy handed the thing over. It was a ball of wadded-up fabric—her underwear, the faded blue rosettes the same as Elsa's. Elsa quickly handed them back, but not before seeing the bloodstains that Hildy would no doubt try to rinse out before their mother saw them.

"Did it hurt?" Elsa asked.

Hildy shook her head. The kitchen was completely dark except for the moonlight coming in through the windows. Elsa couldn't see the expression on her sister's face, but she knew enough not to trust her denial.

"Go to bed," Hildy said, her voice low and gravelly. She closed her eyes, despite the darkness, as though Elsa would be able to see inside Hildy's head if her eyes were open. Elsa understood: There were a lot of things Hildy would want her to ignore. Whatever had happened in Cliff's cabin, whatever had made her bleed. Hildy didn't want to find her sister waiting for her. She didn't want to stand in her parents' kitchen with no underwear on and a new place open inside her. She didn't want to feel different, to be different, to be something less than she was before. Elsa wouldn't sleep with a man for the first time for nearly a decade, but she would always remember the look on her sister's face that night. Hildy was only pretending to look outward, into the world. Inside, she could only think about her own body, and the change that had just occurred.

"Good night," Elsa said. "I'm glad you're home." She wanted to kiss her sister on the cheek, and to say something more, something better, but those words didn't come. Elsa and Hildy climbed the stairs together, both stepping on only the quiet planks, silent as ghosts.

It wasn't even July when things started to go wrong between Hildy and Cliff. At the breakfast table, Hildy was even crankier than usual, and Josephine had to go into town every morning to buy whatever the actors had finished the day before. John was so engrossed with the opening rehearsals for the next play that he didn't even notice until Mary pointed out Hildy's behavior.

"Hildegard," John said, his hands clasped together on the table. "Is there something going on? Would you rather be back at the Tastee Custard Shack with your sister?" Josephine's unblemished work record was the gold standard, the measuring stick for all three Emerson girls. Next to their sister, both Elsa and Hildy looked like layabouts.

Hildy stared at her father, hiccuped once, and let one low moan escape into her napkin. "It's Cliff," she said, and began to sob so vigorously that her shoulders rocked back and forth with a force that could power a steam engine. Their mother was so startled by Hildy's histrionics that she got up and walked out of the room, uncomfortable as she was with great showings of emotion. Elsa, her father, and Josephine all sat still for a moment, wondering what to do. In the end it was Josephine who stood up and hooked her heavy arm around Hildy's shoulder and made shushing noises until her sister's wailing subsided.

Cliff had been honest with Hildy from the start. Well, maybe not from the start, but after the flowery love notes had stopped and the actual visits had begun, first in his cabin and then in her bedroom, in the barn, on the stage, in the hayloft, in the still-freezing-cold waters of the bay, on the rocky beach, on the kitchen floor, and in any number of undisclosed locations, he'd started to see other women.

Cliff's conquests around the theater were legion; it was Suzanne, whose marriage was less solid than Hildy thought; it was Fay, who helped Mary with the costumes; it was Virginia, who played a teenage girl and had the flat chest to show for it. Elsa knew how proud her sister was of her breasts, two giant mounds that had appeared under her nightgown four summers ago. The only woman around under the age of thirty whom Cliff hadn't slept with was Josephine. They weren't even halfway through the season—John couldn't replace Cliff, though he said he'd like to be rid of the lug; they were stuck with him. Once Hildy stopped crying, which took an entire day, her headache came back, and she went straight to bed. Elsa was her meal delivery service, which meant that she got an earful at least three times a day.

"Have you seen him?" That was how Hilly would start, without even a hello or a thank-you, after Elsa had carried a tray piled high with sweet rolls and juice and cold cereal up the stairs.

There was only one window in Hildy's bedroom, and she kept the shade down, which meant that Hildy's summery skin, which had started to freckle and brown in spots, had once again returned to its natural state, the color of fresh milk. The skin under her eyes had darkened, though, to a mossy green, like a bruise. When prompted, Hildy counted her number of sleepless nights on both hands. Elsa wondered what she did in her room for so many hours, if not sleep.

Hildy piled up all the pillows on the bed, each one made of some fabric scraps and sewn and stuffed by their mother. They all sat behind her, so that when Hildy leaned back against the wall, she looked like the princess and the pea.

"No," Elsa said, and put the tray down on the floor next to Hildy's bed.

"Then I'm not hungry," she said, and began to examine the skin on her arms with great interest, as if each beauty mark might give her the answer. She scratched her forearm, and Elsa saw fat red lines where her nails had been.

"*Okay*," Elsa said. She sat down next to the tray and started picking at one of the rolls. "Of course I see him—there's nowhere else to go." She wished that it weren't true, that she could ignore Cliff all day and night, but the fact was that she liked the play, and the rest of the actors, and the way the grass smelled just offstage. It didn't seem fair that Hildy was asking her to choose.

Hildy reached down and snatched the roll out of Elsa's hands. She took a big bite and brown sugar clung to her lips. "Go on."

"That's all, Hildy! He dies every night. What else do you want me to say?" Elsa turned away from her sister and scanned the rest of the room, overflowing as it was with stockings and shoes and pieces of lace that Hildy was forever meaning to do something with. The room was a fort made of girlish things. Maybe it wasn't Hildy's fault that she was so dramatic—maybe it was that she'd always had this giant room to use as her stage. Elsa's bedroom had been a closet, and was big enough for only her small bed. John had taken the door off its hinges and replaced it with a heavy sheet that slid back and forth on wooden rings. Whenever Mary cooked anything smelly, bacon or stew or an unidentified roasted thing, it clung to that sheet for days, and to Elsa's pillowcase, and all her clothes. If Hildy or Josephine ever got married, she could have a proper room, with a door made out of wood.

Hildy unpeeled the outer layer of her sweet roll and stared at it. Her narrow wrist twisted back and forth, sending caramelized bits of sugar and dough onto her quilt. She was bored. "Oh, come on, Elsa, you must know more than that. You're not a baby."

In fact, Elsa had seen Cliff bend Virginia-the-pretend-teenager backward over her favorite tree stump, a ten-minute walk into the woods, and kneel down on the mossy ground in front of her and stick his face up her skirt. But she couldn't tell her sister that, not in a hundred years. "I think you should find another boyfriend."

"Sure, because they're so easy to find! Else, in case you haven't noticed, we live way out in the middle of nowhere, and the only interesting people who come here are people who then turn around and leave." Hildy's voice got higher and higher. "I really thought that he was the one who was going to get me out of here."

She threw the piece of sweet roll she'd been playing with back toward the tray, and Elsa watched as it knocked over the glass and sent orange juice seeping out onto the floorboards. Hildy started to cry, but it wasn't until Elsa was on the other side of the door and halfway to the kitchen to get a rag to clean it up that she heard Hildy start to make even bigger, scarier noises, like she was being attacked from the inside out. When Elsa made it back up the stairs, Hildy was curled up like a cat and facing the wall. She didn't flinch when Elsa picked everything up and pulled the door shut behind her with a good, solid thunk.

It was news to Elsa that someone would want to get out of Door County. True, she'd never been anywhere else except for Green Bay and a few other small cities farther south in Wisconsin, but Elsa thought that Door County was the most beautiful place on earth. Whenever she read a book about a little girl, and they showed a picture of where she lived, Elsa thought, *Wow, that looks just like home.* The house her parents had built was the perfect size for a little girl, with rooms and hallways and closets and endless places to hide. There was a cellar full of jars of jam and summer tomatoes. There was an attic full of Hildy's and Josephine's old things, the clothes that Elsa hadn't grown into yet. There were the woods and the lake and the bay and the boat and the cherries! How could Hildy want to go somewhere else when there were so many cherries right here? Elsa thought Hildy must have made some mistake when she was thinking about leaving. Sure, Elsa liked to imagine the actors scooping her up like a caravan full of Gypsies and carrying her off into the night, but those daydreams always ended with her coming home the next morning, to her sisters, and the theater, and her father. It was all playing pretend—

wasn't that what Hildy was doing too, when she had her headaches? Surely Hildy didn't want to stay away for good.

◦

The play was doing well—some people came back two or three times. Without Hildy squeezing her hand every time Cliff was onstage, Elsa got to move around more. She watched from the last row, from the front row, from the grassy backstage. There was a crowd scene toward the end, where Cliff's character imagined the wedding he and Suzanne's character would have had. The actors all decided that there should be a flower girl added, just for Elsa. *Wouldn't she like that, being onstage?* After all, they said, to her and to John, Elsa knew every inch of that barn. She could toss paper flower petals out of a basket, easy. She could turn around and look at the audience and smile. *Don't you think so, John?*

Her father loved the idea so much that he made the cast reblock the scene the very next morning. Elsa put on her fanciest dress, navy blue cotton that was tight around her chest and then flared out to her knees, with a white sash around her middle—it had been Hildy's, a costume from years ago, no one could remember what play—and waited backstage for her time to go on. Suzanne was running her lines over and over, mumbling them under her breath. She did it every night, Elsa knew, talked through the entire show before she went out onstage. She was the most direct match for Cliff: similarly tall and dark haired—they could have been siblings. Elsa watched Suzanne's mouth, her red lips opening and closing with each silent syllable. There was power in pretend. That was what Hildy didn't understand—for Suzanne, getting into bed with Cliff was probably just another exercise, a way for her to better understand a woman who thought she'd been widowed by the war. How had she loved that man before he went away, when he was all bravery and hope? Suzanne didn't love Cliff. It wasn't a competition. Elsa would try to explain that to Hildy later.

John hustled backstage from his spot along the side of the theater, in the very last row, to give Elsa some words of advice. He crouched next to her and whispered, "Honey, you're going to be great. Break a leg." John kissed Elsa on the forehead, and then wiped off the moisture he'd left behind with his thumb.

"I just turn around and smile at the audience? Then throw my petals and walk to the back of the stage?" Elsa knew her part, but wanted to say it a few more times to make sure she had it right.

"That's exactly right, Else. Let me see your smile. Pretend I'm the entire audience." John sat back on one knee and held his arms open wide. It was dark, and Elsa could make out only parts of his face. She saw his eyes, little wet pools, and his teeth, tall and white.

Elsa closed her eyes and pictured a chapel with wooden pews and a high white ceiling. There was going to be a wedding, and she could smell dozens of roses. They were clustered at every aisle, and the bride—oh, the bride! She held half a dozen in her small, gloved hands. Elsa felt the patent-leather shoes pinching at her toes, the anxiety of being first into such a magical space. She opened her eyes and smiled at her father, who wasn't her father anymore but a chapel full of people who had come to this place for the blessed event.

That night, when the audience stood on their feet to clap at the end of the show, Elsa came out onstage with the rest of the actors and knew that she had done it. They were all clapping for her. The sound of the applause was the most beautiful song she had ever heard—no matter how many times she'd heard it before, it had never been like this. So loud! So happy! Even Josephine had stayed to watch the show, rather than clomp back to the house and wait for it to be over. The people were on their feet, and they were smiling at her. Elsa knew that she was the one who had invited them in. She couldn't wait to tell Hildy. Cliff and Suzanne walked forward for their bows, and after he turned to rejoin the rest of the cast, Cliff caught Elsa's eye and winked. A part of her stomach clenched, but once Cliff was back with the rest of the cast, and Elsa couldn't see him anymore, she was high again, as light and full of air as an escaped balloon vanishing over the treetops.

❧

Hildy!"
Elsa opened the door to her sister's room without knocking. It was just before breakfast, when the cast and crew were all still sleepy eyed and pleasantly quiet. Mary was out in town, running errands, and Josephine was at work, plugging cone after cone into the stream of soft, icy custard. Elsa couldn't wait to tell Hildy about her triumph, her conversion! It was that clear to Elsa that she now knew what she wanted to do. She was an actress. Elsa said the word to herself in the mirror—*actress, actress, actress*—just to see how it looked coming out of her mouth. It looked like gold.

The door swung open with a creak. Instead of moving quickly into the already dented wall, though, the door stopped short and swung back toward Elsa. She pushed it open again, until she saw that Hildy's bed was empty.

"Hildy?" she said. The room felt abandoned, which didn't make any sense. Elsa would have seen her sister if she'd left the room—Hildy would have made noise in the bathroom; she would have complained about not having strawberry jam, only blueberry. The door was hitting something before it was hitting the wall. A tiny sliver of Elsa's brain knew what she was going to find when she looked on the other side of the door, but the other part (the larger, more hopeful part) knew that that couldn't be true. She stepped around, putting each foot in front of the other slowly and carefully, as though the floor were covered with poisonous snakes and any step she took might be lethal. Elsa stared at the ground, which was why she saw the stool first, a rickety wooden one for household chores that their mother had long since abandoned. Then Elsa saw Hildy's toes poking out from her nightgown. Then she saw the rest of Hildy, all the way up to her neck, which was strapped to a crossbeam of the house with a leather belt of their father's. Hildy's eyes were open, and Elsa looked at them for what felt like several hours before letting out her first truly bloodcurdling scream, the kind of noise that could mean only that something had gone horribly, horribly wrong.

❦

Cliff was gone by dinner. He agreed that losing the rest of the summer's paycheck seemed fair, and hightailed it out of town before John and Mary could change their minds about involving the police. It was a family matter. Hildy's moods had always been as unpredictable as the undertow of the ocean, as deep and dark, but this was something else entirely. Elsa watched as her father and Josephine limped around the house, sometimes unable even to get out of bed. She herself tried to be good, as good as possible, as if behaving perfectly would change what had happened. She washed her own dishes and cleaned her room, did the laundry, swept the floor. Her mother didn't even seem to notice, offering only a small thank-you when Elsa made her breakfast in the morning, cracking an egg into a frying pan all by herself. Josephine wrote a sign that hung on the barn door, canceling two weeks of shows, maybe more. No one knew for sure when everything would be back up and running, so the actors and the crew all hung around, walking the grounds slowly with their heads pointed toward the grass, their hands clasped behind their backs. They were all playing at mourning. What else could they do? Get on a train and leave? There was nowhere else to go.

The house was quietest of all. Elsa often thought about an old, ramshackle place two farms over, a house no one had lived in for at least her entire life. It was probably noisier in there, what with the birds roosting in the bedrooms, the raccoons burrowing through the kitchen cabinets. As a family, the Emersons tried not to make a sound. Mary cleaned the dishes with a rag, and nestled them carefully in the drying rack so that the plates didn't knock against each other. Josephine concentrated on keeping her lips closed all day long, and succeeded at least three days in a row, communicating with only nods and shrugs and shakes of her head. John slept in the barn on the pile of pillows that were stacked in the corner. Elsa sometimes hid there during the day, letting the calico and burlap and tiny scraps of old sheets rub against her skin. She nestled her body in against the wooden floor and then pulled the pillows over her until she was buried in them up to her shoulders. She never wanted to let anything touch her neck ever again, for fear that she might strangle too, by accident. But no one said the word *strangle*, no one said the word *suicide*. John said *accident* and Mary said *fine*. It was sad enough already without adding that on top. How were people ever supposed to come back, to laugh? Years later, Josephine admitted that one of her first thoughts was, *At least Hildy didn't do it in the barn*, and then covered her face with her wide fingers.

The plays were put on hold for three weeks, until it was nearly August, the busiest time of the summer. The entire peninsula was crazily in bloom, with berries and pies and girls on bicycles, their short hair flapping behind them like miniature flags. Eventually Suzanne and her husband approached John about taking over, in the interim, until he was ready. Too afraid to feel the loss of the theater on top of the loss of his most beautiful daughter, John acquiesced, and *A Midsummer Night's Dream* began as scheduled. The Emersons sat at their kitchen table in silence and watched the people file into the barn. They heard the laughter and the other happy sounds swelling out of the barn's open windows. Josephine's face was as solid as stone, and she parted her lips only to insert a fork or a spoon. Elsa thought Josephine could probably kill a bear with her teeth with one hard *snap*, and she started to cry. Mary fixed her a drink, something warm to help her sleep. It coated her throat and that was enough—Elsa imagined the thick liquid formed an impenetrable barrier between her and the outside world. She became unbreakable, a human fortress. John was staring out the window at the barn and at the actors, in frilly new costumes, talking and laughing on the grass.

"People are going to ask you about your sister," John said, still looking out the window, but Elsa knew he was talking to her. She stayed quiet, waiting to hear the rest of the sentence. "And you're going to have two choices. You can either tell them the truth, which will make them uncomfortable and awkward, or you can pretend that everything is okay." He turned his face back toward Elsa for a moment, and then jerked his chin down to his chest, as if examining the bottom of his coffee cup. "People won't know how to react if you tell them the truth."

"Like in the play?" Elsa watched her father's hands, his large fingers clasped together around his mug.

"Just like in the play," he said. "You're an actress now." Despite it all, Elsa could swear that there was some pride in her father's voice. It was good for all of them to remember that there were actors in the world, people whose job it was to pretend. For Elsa, there was no other option after that moment—she saw her future as clearly as she saw the water of Green Bay. Even if she wasn't happy on the inside, the outside could be something else entirely. There was always another character to play.

No one ever moved into Hildy's room. Sometimes it was offered to one of the actors, a new recruit off the train who'd never been to Door County, and she would say yes, nodding at her unbelievable luck, but by dinnertime she would have heard the story and chosen to sleep in the cabin with three other girls. Elsa was seventeen and as tall as Josephine, who never did marry the cherry farmer. Instead Josephine moved into a small apartment in Fish Creek that she shared with a friend from school, a pretty nurse. She came home every weekend to help with the shows, and carried enormous vats of food for the actors. Josephine was as strong as their father, and never wore any perfume, so she smelled like him, too, musky and clean at the same time. It was the ninth summer since Hildy. That was what they said, since Hildy. Not since she died, or anything even more specific, and therefore worse. Just since.

That summer, Elsa was Gwen in *The Royal Family*, though she felt she could have played any of the parts equally well, and had memorized the entire thing from start to finish. The play was about a family of aging actors, each of whom was more narcissistic and self-obsessed than the last. Gwen was the family's ingenue, the starlet in training, and got lots of funny, screwball lines. Elsa's favorite was "Name me two seventeenth-century stockbrokers!" It always got a laugh.

The young man John cast as Perry, Gwen's hapless fiancé, was Gordon-from-Florida. He had a last name, but no one knew what it was. Florida was a funny place to be from, not that Elsa had ever been. She still hadn't left Wisconsin for longer than a one-day trip into Chicago, when her father was so nervous about her safety that he wouldn't leave her side, even waiting for her outside the ladies' room in the restaurant where they had lunch. All she knew about Florida was the boll weevil and the ocean. Gordon's parents grew oranges, which he found about as exciting as eating oranges, which he hadn't done since he was a child, thanks to overexposure. Gordon had run away at seventeen, the previous year. He still had a slight suntan, as though those seventeen years of beachy sunshine had soaked into his skin and would never fade, no matter how much he wanted them to. He saw the Cherry County Playhouse as a perfect halfway mark in between Florida and California. Gordon was planning on taking the bus to Los Angeles as soon as the summer was over, trying his hand at motion pictures.

They ran lines at the picnic table behind the barn. As a character, Perry was very stiff, but Gordon was doing a good job of making him likable—attractive, even. It was still cool out, and they both had sweaters on as well as sunglasses. That was what Elsa loved about Door County: Even on the prettiest days, you could never forget you were in Wisconsin. There was a clarity to the air that she was sure didn't exist in other states; it didn't seem possible. She had the feeling that Gordon-from-Florida had no idea where he was, and couldn't find it on a map even with a couple of flashing arrows.

"I think Perry's a dope," Gordon said.

"Why? Because he's a stockbroker?" Elsa picked at her lunch, cheese sandwiches Mary had made, with fat slices of brown bread and a swipe of mustard.

Gordon pulled his face to one side like Groucho Marx. "Because he doesn't know how lucky he is to have Gwen." He waggled an imaginary cigar, and shot his eyebrows up and down.

Elsa laughed. "Is that right," she said, without adding a questioning lilt to her voice. She knew it was right, just as she knew from the moment that Gordon-from-Florida walked into the Cherry County Playhouse that she would walk out with him at the end of the summer, walk all the way to California if she had to. John and Mary would fill their house with surrogate children: all of them alive, all of them equal. Girls and boys from Egg Harbor and Ephraim and Sturgeon Bay would arrange the pillows on the benches and pass out programs, and Elsa would be on the other side of the country. It wasn't that she was in love with Gordon-from-Florida, whose last name, she would have to learn, was Pitts. Instead, it was that Elsa looked at Gordon and saw a kind and perfectly normal face. Gordon looked like he could wind up a leading man, which made Elsa feel like she might be in love, after all—wasn't that how it happened? A girl, a boy, and a long bus ride? If it were a play, Elsa thought it would have a happy ending.

"I think Gwen knows just what she's got," Elsa said. She slipped off her shoe and found Gordon's foot under the table. She was playing the part of a love-struck girl. Elsa thought of Hildy and the way her body had undulated with pleasure at the sight of Cliff. Elsa wiggled on the bench. She would get better at it; she would practice.

Gordon drank his lemonade and stared at the table. His cheeks turned from tan to peach to nearly purple. He wasn't brawny like Cliff. Gordon was the opposite—small features on a small face, everything crammed together toward the middle. By the time he looked up at Elsa, his cheeks pulled wide into an unguarded smile, she knew that she would get exactly what she wanted, because he wanted it too.

They waited until the season was over—it was the end of August, and flowers spontaneously burst into blossom over and over again. Mary and Josephine made batches of fried chicken, and after the ceremony in the barn, everyone in town came to eat corn on the cob and to celebrate little Elsa Emerson becoming Elsa Pitts, riding off into the sunset on a cross-country bus. There wasn't any worry about Gordon turning out like Cliff, because Gordon was no Cliff, anyone could see that. Josephine pulled Elsa aside and enclosed her in a long, silent bear hug, her thick arms clasped at the elbows around Elsa's back. Neither of the girls cried, at least not after raising their faces from each other's shoulder and blinking into the sunlight. Mary gave Elsa and Gordon each a hard, quick squeeze and went back inside to start the dishes.

John drove the couple and their meager suitcases to the depot in Chicago, where they boarded a creaking bus and waved enthusiastically at him through the tinted windows. Elsa watched as her father hugged himself in the parking lot, the first time she'd seen him cry since Hildy, now nine years gone. On the bus, Elsa and Gordon settled into their seats. They kissed on the cheek and then stared straight ahead, both anxious to see the ocean and the mountains and all the stars in the sky, which would surely light their way.

An hour into their cross-country ride, Gordon was fast asleep with his head against the bus window. Elsa snuggled up next to him, but found his shoulder too pointy to rest against. A few rows in front of them, a mother and daughter were having a quiet discussion about the daughter's upcoming wedding. They were talking about flowers: peonies, zinnias, all showy, big blossoms. Elsa thought of her mother's face at the wedding, as clear and calm as if she'd been watching a bird hop around the yard through the kitchen window. For a split second, she had the urge to get off the bus while Gordon was asleep, to slip off in Minneapolis or Colorado or Wyoming and just vanish into the night. Who would miss her, really? Not Gordon, not her mother. Josephine smiled only at her roommate, the first in a series of plainly pretty women, this one with a long, dark braid down the middle of her back. But then Elsa thought of her father. She couldn't let him lose two daughters. Elsa was going to do great things in California—she was going to do enough for two whole lives. That grassy patch behind the barn was going to have a big, brass plaque one day: ELSA EMERSON, MOVIE STAR. Her father would stand next to it and point it out to tourists passing through. It would be almost like having her home. Elsa stayed in her seat. She balled up her jacket and wedged it under the back of her neck. Gordon was snoring slightly, not unpleasantly. Elsa watched his chest rise and fall for a few breaths, and then she turned back toward the front of the bus and closed her eyes. She didn't care about the mountains; they would still be there in fifty years, or a hundred. All Elsa cared about was arriving. She was going to step off the bus and into the waiting arms of the world.

2

LAURA LAMONT

Summer 1938

The bus station in Los Angeles looked like all the bus stations before it, except turned inside out, with no ceiling, no roof, only sky. The buses pulled into slots poking out into a long, gray street. Elsa hadn't known it was possible for the sky to be overcast in California. Gordon was asleep on her shoulder, as he had been for the last several hours, and she slid him back onto his own seat. The bus stopped, and all around them passengers leaped up, grabbing their satchels and suitcases and heading for the door. Elsa waited, staring out the window. She could have woken Gordon, but she wasn't ready. The buildings on the other side of the window weren't tall, but they were endless; over the tops of the squat, white buildings across the street, there were rows and rows of roofs poking into the sky behind them, and behind them, ad infinitum. Elsa didn't know which way was north. It was after dark, nine o'clock. If Gordon never woke up, then maybe she would never have to get off the bus, and it would slowly turn around and take her home.

"Hey, we're here!" Gordon's mouth was next to Elsa's ear, his breath warm and stale. He pushed his body against hers and craned his neck, looking around to all sides. "I guess the buses don't pull up in Hollywood, huh."

Elsa didn't know what Hollywood looked like, or whether it was actually even a proper neighborhood, or just an idea, like heaven. She'd been afraid to sound too disappointed. "Well, sure," she said, and hoped that that was noncommittal enough.

"Let's go. My friend Jim said he was going to pick us up—I just have to give him a call," Gordon said, stretching in the now-empty aisle. They were the only passengers left on the bus. Even the driver was outside. Gordon moved aside to make room for Elsa. She smoothed out her skirt and dusted off her hat, which had been sitting in her lap since they left Chicago. It was her nicest hat, a brown felt cloche with a feather pointing toward the sky, and she just knew it wasn't going to be good enough for Los Angeles.

"I'm coming," Elsa said. She put her hat on and followed her husband off the bus. It was still funny to think of him that way— as her *husband*, which felt like such a heavy word in her mouth. Elsa found that it was amusing to say aloud to strangers, who wouldn't find it odd at all that she was married. The idea that she was married still seemed like a great big joke, a fiction she was able to pull over her head like an oversize sweater.

Gordon's friend arrived an hour and a half later. Everyone else had vanished into the night, hopping into waiting cars or humping their bags down the street into an unknown future. Only Gordon and Elsa were still sitting on their suitcases on the empty street. A car pulled up and a young man stuck his head out the passenger-side window.

"Hey, Gord-o!" he called out, and whistled. Gordon jumped up, sending his suitcase toppling to the ground, and ran over to the still-moving car. Elsa stayed put. After the car stopped, its brakes screeching into place, she watched the two men embrace with a firm clap on the back. Gordon had already forgotten about her, Elsa was sure. He would have been just as happy to throw himself into the backseat of his friend's car, pour some whiskey down his throat, and enjoy the sunrise on the beach. She watched him talk and laugh for a few minutes without even turning around—Jim was an actor too, of course, and Gordon wanted to hear everything. They'd been friends as children, which wasn't very long ago, no matter how you counted, even though Gordon and Elsa were married, as Elsa was barely seventeen and Gordon only nineteen. Maybe by the time she was twenty, it would all be old hat, being married and living so far from home, but she doubted it. Elsa looked down at her left hand. Gordon had found the band somewhere in town—he wouldn't say where—which meant it hadn't come from the jewelry store in Sturgeon Bay. She wasn't even sure it was real gold. Elsa liked the feel of it, though, the small metal reminder that she really was someone new. It was enough for her to get up off the narrow edge of her suitcase and walk over to Gordon and his friend.

"Hi," she said. "I'm Gordon's wife."

For the next week, Elsa and Gordon stayed at Jim's apartment, sleeping on a stack of blankets on the floor. Elsa still got confused when people talked about Hollywood, because she still wasn't sure if they were talking about the neighborhood. Jim's apartment was as small as her parents' bedroom, with a shared bathroom in the hall. When Jim was out, Elsa and Gordon had sex on the blankets, because it seemed like one of the only things they *could* do without any money or a car. By the time they got their own place, Elsa was already pregnant, though she didn't know it yet.

⤙⤚

At a year old, Clara had only blond wisps of hair, but enormous green eyes like a cat's, almost perfectly round. Between her two parents, Gordon had more experience onstage, and therefore he had signed up with Central Casting and went to most of the calls, where he and all the other men of his description would line up outside the gates of the studios and wait to be seen, one by one. Gordon promised that Elsa could go when she was ready—and after all, someone had to stay home with Clara. Though each job made Gordon a little money, it was by no means enough to hire someone to watch the baby. Their rent was late as often as it was on time, and Elsa found that most of the acting she did was in telling the landlord that the check was on its way.

The house was in Los Feliz, on the east side of Los Angeles, a few blocks from where the Disney animators had been working on *Snow White*, and close to a handful of studios. Elsa and Gordon didn't mind being far from the ocean. "I never went to the beach when I lived in Florida," Gordon said, to anyone who would listen. "Why would I go now?"

Being in Los Angeles wasn't so different from sitting in the grass behind the Cherry County Playhouse—everyone was an actor, even the waiters in the restaurants and the mailman. Every woman she met lived at the Hollywood Studio Club, which was where Elsa would have wanted to live if she weren't married. Certainly all the men lining up for the open calls listed in *Variety* seemed like men Elsa had known all her life. She often thought how much her family would enjoy it, and wrote to them telling them so, but Elsa knew that the one member of her family who would have jumped on a train to come and join her was the one who had been dead for almost a decade. Her mother wrote back with details of the landscape—the flowering rhododendrons, the magnolia's short window of glory, the small, sharp waves on the lake—but said little else. Her father wrote about plays and actors and always told Elsa how much she was missed. Josephine never wrote at all, but sent packages filled with crumbling cookies on Elsa's birthdays, which Elsa knew was expensive, and therefore thoughtful. Even though the playhouse had always made the Emersons enough money to live on, they were by no means rich, and it felt extravagant to receive a tin of cookies when so many people were out of work in Los Angeles. Elsa spent most of her time walking up and down her street, pointing out the palm trees and the cockeyed succulents growing crookedly out of the ground. Every few blocks there was a normal tree, one that wouldn't look out of place in Wisconsin, and Elsa would pause underneath its branches and explain to baby Clara all about where they'd come from.

Elsa loved being around other actors, even at the giant casting calls that reminded her of docile, herded cattle. The listings were in the paper, and then all you had to do was show up at the gates of the studio, where a waiting crowd had already formed, other anxious young women with big smiles and bigger dreams. She tried out to be a dancer in a Western, a girl in a crowd, barely in the frame. Elsa loved to walk back and forth, pretending to be someone else. The auditions themselves felt like performing in a play, with all the women acting for one another, and Elsa felt invigorated by the camaraderie. She didn't seem to be what the studios were looking for, though, and went to six open calls without getting chosen once. Gordon tried to be supportive, but he was usually so busy hustling up his own work that he didn't spend too much time worrying about Elsa.

In the almost two years since their arrival, Gordon had been in three films. Twice he was an extra, and moved through the back of a shot, where he could be seen only from behind, and at a great distance. Elsa told him he was very convincing, and they'd celebrated with a steak dinner at home, a luxury they couldn't afford. The third was a bit part as a corrupt prison guard in a Gardner Brothers film, and Gordon had had to walk back and forth in front of an empty cell for two hours, whistling and dragging a baton along the bars. There was one moment when the camera zoomed in on his face, and Gordon no longer looked ordinary. His cheeks were drawn; his eyes were dark. In the ten seconds that the lens lingered on him, Gordon's prison guard conveyed much more than the script had required. It was as beautiful as a violin solo, an Irish poem. In the Vista Theatre, Elsa had put her hands to her face when her husband appeared on the screen and cried with happiness. His forehead was ten feet high! Gordon-from-Florida! She called her parents to describe every moment, and her father asked her to repeat it again and again, the lead-up scenes, the camera cuts, the fade-in. Every actor they knew told Elsa how excellent Gordon had been in the film; they stopped her on the street to say so. The part couldn't have been better if they'd let him speak.

Early in their marriage, which was to say within the first six weeks, the couple had engaged in lovemaking with relative frequency, encounters during which Elsa shut her eyes and concentrated very hard on the pleasure she knew she was meant to experience. Gordon's member was small, or rather Elsa assumed it was, having never seen one before. She knew for a fact that she felt little more than a gnawing tickle when he moved around on top of her, and that seemed proof enough, though she wouldn't have wanted it to be larger. Once those playful weeks were through, and Clara had taken root deep inside, Elsa had put sexual intercourse out of her mind and left it somewhere on the shelf, in between dental work and inoculation shots, as something to schedule, if done at all. The evening after the opening of his film, however (for that was how they thought of it, *his film*), Elsa invited her husband into her half of the bed, which was divided from his with an elaborate setup of pillows, some of which she had brought all the way from Door County. Gordon was so thrilled at the invitation that the coitus itself lasted less than a minute, and Elsa rolled her husband back over to his side with the satisfaction of a job well done. It was during this celebration of Gordon's cinematic achievement that Elsa conceived their second child.

❧

The fourth film Gordon was cast in, *No Angels Here*, was also a Gardner Brothers film. The producers were so impressed with his prison guard scene that they called him into the main office and had him sign a contract for one hundred and fifty dollars a week. Exclusive! Gordon Pitts was going to be a star in the Gardner Brothers galaxy, a real contract player; that was straight from the mouth of Louis Gardner himself. Elsa wanted every word repeated, every motion, every gesture, and Gordon happily obliged, telling the story over and over again, whenever an opportunity for virgin ears presented itself.

"Louis—you know, Mr. Gardner, but he said I could call him Louis—invites me in, sits me down. The office is huge—huge! Ten-foot-high palm trees in pots. Practically a jungle. Louis invites me in and sits me down. He says, 'Mr. Pitts, we think you've got something special.' Goddamn!" Gordon paused. This was his favorite part of the story. Gordon's least favorite part of the story, which he never repeated in front of company, and had in fact told Elsa only one time, drunk and sobbing, was that the entire meeting had lasted just three minutes, and that Louis Gardner had been present for only two of them. The truth of the contract itself was that it was for a bit player, which meant work but not glory. Gordon chose to see that as a stepping-stone rather than a stop sign, however, and simply forged ahead in his bragging.

They were sitting in their favorite local watering hole, Loopy Pete's. Pete himself had yet to materialize, but Elsa and Gordon spent a great deal of time with Raoul, the bartender. Elsa was fairly positive that Raoul had heard the story before, but she tried to be a dutiful wife, and so enjoyed being out of the house, and detached from the baby, that she let Gordon continue uninterrupted. The bar was nicely dark, made of mahogany wood and polished brass. It was the sort of bar that Elsa's father would have found too posh, too expensive, though the drinks were cheap enough that Gordon could afford three, two for himself and one for Elsa. With his salary from Gardner Brothers, they had enough money not to worry. That was a big part of the studio's promise, Louis Gardner had made clear—his actors were taken care of for as long as they were under contract, which, by law, could be terminated every six months, at the studio's discretion.

"That's great, Gordon," Raoul said. "Congratulations." He wiped off some glasses with a towel.

Gordon swiveled around on his bar stool, looking for another listener. When he didn't find one, there being only a handful of people at the bar, and most of them old and devoted drunks, Gordon turned back to Elsa and took her hand.

"It's really happening, baby," he said, and lifted her hand to his cold lips. He turned away from the bar and Raoul, who Gordon claimed always looked at Elsa with a wolfish gaze. Gordon wanted to be the only wolf in town.

The Gardner Brothers contract was for seven years. They controlled every part Gordon would have until he turned twenty-seven. Gordon was to report to the studio every day, Monday through Friday, and to sit in his dressing room when he wasn't needed. There were acting classes, diction classes, a place to eat lunch, and bicycles to ride around the back lot when there was nothing else to do. To Elsa, it all sounded just like an enormous version of her father's theater. Gordon didn't want her to come visit just yet, not until he was settled, but the studio was all he could talk about at home. Elsa could picture every inch of the lot: the grand metal gate on Marathon Avenue, the winding pathways, the buildings dressed up in hollow bricks to look like buildings in other cities. California could be anything: They could even make it look like Wisconsin by tossing shaved pieces of soap into the air and letting them fall down on the actors' heads as snow. It was magic.

The first film Gordon spoke in was *Country Boy, City Girl*, which starred Gardner Brothers' reigning on-screen lovers, the youthful and wholesome Johnny and Susie. They'd both been stars since they were teenagers, and had been paired up in so many movies that it was strange when Elsa saw one without the other in the lot. It was like seeing a person with a wooden leg or an eye patch—something was missing. Off-screen, Susie and Johnny were seen dating other stars and starlets, but they weren't allowed to marry, or to disgrace themselves in public. America wanted them sweet, and so did Louis Gardner. This was in the contract, as it was in Gordon's. Though her husband railed a bit about the number of points he'd had to agree to—he couldn't pick his own roles, or work for any other studio, unless Gardner Brothers had arranged the swap—Elsa was secretly delighted by the power of the studio. She understood: This was a factory. Instead of making cake plates or dungarees or drill bits, they made movie stars. It all boiled down to an equation, one too complex for Elsa to imagine, but Mr. Gardner, he knew just what to put in. If Gordon did what he was told, they would get everything they'd ever wanted.

Gordon's part was as Susie's friend at the newspaper where she worked as a secretary. His job was to be less appealing than Johnny at every turn: slightly slicker, slightly rougher, and always less handsome. Of course, Gordon wasn't actually less handsome than Johnny, who was half a foot shorter than Elsa, and could star in films only with Susie, because she was even shorter than he was, and even then he had to stand on a box. But such was the magic of moviemaking—when Louis Gardner decided that you were a star, you were a star. This was the system, and Elsa was a believer.

ittle Clara was an Emerson, fleshy and pink. The Pitts, though Elsa had yet to meet the rest of her husband's family, were smaller, darker people; according to Gordon, they tended to emerge from the womb with a full head of hair. Clara was a year and a half now and still had only blondish wisps around her crown. She'd gone from crawling around the house to scooting on her bottom, and finally was taking confident steps on her own, which Elsa watched with great interest. Clara gripped the arm of a chair or the lip of a table and raised herself from the ground, legs wobbling. She was getting stronger. Elsa sat on the sofa, a beat-up Chesterfield they'd bought used, and ran her hands back and forth over the leather. It was December, and even outdoors she was wearing nothing more than a shawl pulled around her shoulders. Clara's feet were bare, and stuck to the wooden floor with each step, making a little *thuck-thuck-thuck* noise. Weather in Los Angeles never ceased to amaze her, though Elsa knew it was a bore to discuss. Sometimes Elsa wondered what her parents had done with her bedroom—whether they'd asked some poor girl from Sheboygan to sleep there, or whether they'd finally turned it back into a closet. She hadn't asked. She didn't miss her bedroom, or the pervasive cold, but she did miss the snow, that thick white blanket that hid everything below the waist. Each winter Elsa thought about going home to surprise her parents for Christmas, but it was too far, and too expensive for them all to go, even with Gordon's steady paycheck. Elsa might have gone on her own, just her and the baby, but Gordon didn't think it was a good idea, too many nefarious characters lurking around the bus and train stations. She understood—they would go eventually, the whole family. It would be better that way. After all, the only thing she'd accomplished so far was procreation, which she could have done in Wisconsin. Elsa liked the idea of going home with something more behind her name, something that even Hildy would have been impressed by. She thought of her sisters often, and Hildy most of all. On the days when Clara wasn't feeling well, and Gordon was gone, Elsa would often imagine Hildy knocking on the door, having been transported to Hollywood instead of heaven, the result of some wonderful glitch in the cosmos.

The house was small—one bedroom in the back, a larger room up front that was both kitchen and living room. The single bathroom was big enough for only one person at a time, but they didn't need anything bigger. Elsa had made curtains to block the sun from the windows in their bedroom, but the hems were all uneven, and bits of thread hung at either end. Gordon didn't seem to notice, but it was all Elsa saw when she was in bed. Her mother and Josephine would have been horrified. The living room was better—a sofa, a coffee table. Gordon liked to check books out of the library and stack them beside the sofa, though Elsa rarely saw him read them. On good days, Gordon came home early and read out loud so Clara could listen, and she rolled around on her stomach while her father pronounced words she didn't know, happy as a bumblebee in springtime. Elsa sat back and watched them, thinking about her own father and his musky gentleness. She was pleased that Clara looked so much like her side of the family. On bad days, Gordon hardly came home at all, and the baby cried so hard and loud that Elsa was sure the neighbors would call the police. Sometimes it got so loud and lonely that she would cry too, and she and Clara just sat in the middle of the floor together, howling, their faces wet and purple.

She hadn't made friends, not any real ones. They'd been in town for only a couple of months when she realized she was pregnant, and Gordon had ideas about what she should do, what was best for the baby. Elsa stayed in and dusted shelves with her fingers. What had her mother done all day? She had done everything that had to be done, so that her father could concentrate on the theater. That was what Elsa would do. The truth was, though, that their house was too small to sustain an imagination, and Elsa spent most of every day staring out the window and taking walks around their neighborhood when Gordon was on the lot, which was five days a week. Gordon had friends coming out of his ears: Every day he'd tell Elsa about someone new, an actor from Kansas with a lisp he'd met in the Gardner Brothers barbershop, a girl from New York who danced in the background behind Susie and Johnny but never got to speak because her accent was so thick. Sometimes Elsa would find Gordon's wedding ring in his pants pocket when she was doing the washing. She asked him about it only once, and his response was so immediate— "Baby, it was for an audition!"—that she let it drop. Elsa couldn't fault Gordon for trying.

In three months the second baby would be born. Clara loved to stroke Elsa's growing belly. Sometimes Elsa lay on the floor with Clara and turned herself into a landscape with mountains and valleys and streams for Clara to cross. When she was hungry, Clara looked just like Josephine, impassive and serious. When she was full of joy, having seen a dog or a butterfly, or when she took

her first crazy-legged steps across the wooden floor, all Elsa saw
was Hildy.

❧

Country Boy, City Girl was wrapped. Louis Gardner and Irving Green, his second-in-command, were throwing a party
for the cast and crew, and Elsa was invited. It was her first trip to
the studio in Hollywood, despite the fact that Gordon had spent
the last two months sitting around his dressing room, his part already finished, or just gabbing away with the other actors in the
commissary.

Elsa had only two dresses that would still wrap all the way
around her body.

"Blue or white," she said to Gordon. "Blue or white?"

"Blue," he said. "The white one will make you look like a
beached whale." He made an elephant noise. Beside him, Clara
giggled. In the end, it wouldn't matter anyway. Elsa knew that
either dress was going to look shabby next to the dresses the actresses would be wearing. Being so massive actually gave her an
excuse to look less than perfectly done-up, Elsa thought, as if to
say, *If I weren't pregnant, I would have worn nothing but diamonds
and sequins.*

Elsa put her hands where her waist had once been. Her belly
was hard, like a shield. It wouldn't be long before she had her body
back, she knew. With Clara, it had taken only a few months before
all the parts zipped back to the way they'd been before. She was
impressed with the elasticity of the female body, the wisdom her
cells possessed. They grew this way, not that. She expanded out, not

up. Elsa knew she was having another girl, even though the doctor hadn't said. Elsa could feel it deep in her center of gravity. It was her fate to be surrounded by women for the rest of her life, by sisters. Late at night, Elsa sometimes thought that if she had done more to stop Cliff, and been better to Hildy, she would have had boys.

"The blue it is."

Elsa squeezed herself into the blue dress, coaxing the zipper up along the side. They dropped Clara off at a neighbor's, promising to bring back details of the Gardner Brothers party, and set out at eight.

Gordon nodded hello to the man at the gate, and they drove into a large parking lot. As they walked from the car to the party, Gordon pointed out spots around the studio that had been used in movies.

"You see that wall over there, with the columns in front of it? That's where *Claudine Claudine* was shot, the whole thing, supposed to be Rome." Elsa squinted. It was dark; the wall looked nothing like Italy, not that she'd ever been. It was almost better that way, that things didn't look the way they were supposed to— that was why they were *actors*. A real actor could perform *King Lear* with an empty stage, could perform *anything* on an empty stage; that was what her father would have said. Gordon guided them around a corner, and then down a narrow alley between two enormous buildings, three stories high with no windows—the soundstages.

"The party's on stage twelve," Gordon said. "It's this way."

They rounded another corner, and it was easy enough to see where the party was. The two-story-high sliding door was open, and light spilled out onto the narrow space between stages twelve and fourteen, across the way. A crowd of people stood outside smoking cigarettes, and Gordon greeted them all warmly, kissing all the women on the cheek. Elsa knew their names from their screen credits: Betty Lafayette was a curvy brunette from New Orleans; Dolores Dee was a blowsy blonde who'd been playing ingenues for the last five years; Peggy Bates had a squirrelly face but a real, honest laugh, and was so nice that it seemed rude to take note of the squirellyness.

"Hey, gals, this is my wife, Elsa Pitts," Gordon said, introducing her around.

Dolores took one look at Elsa, stubbed out her cigarette, and headed back inside.

"Don't worry about her," Peggy said, pumping Elsa's hand up and down. "You're a blonde. Dolores hates all other blondes—it's just what she does. Obviously Susie gets all the nice-blonde parts, and then all of you have to duke it out for the rest. But hiya! It's so nice to meet you."

"Okay," Elsa said. The baby stuck an elbow in between her ribs, and Elsa smoothed the spot with her free hand.

"Are you pregnant?" Peggy asked, though the answer was clear. Elsa cocked her head to one side. "I'm sorry. Of course you're pregnant. My mother told me it was rude to just assume, though, and that one should always ask."

There was music coming out the open door, and Gordon was craning his neck to see who else was inside.

"Come on, Else, let's go in," he said, not waiting for her before walking through the door.

"Nice to meet you," Elsa said to Peggy, who was doing the Charleston in the middle of the street with another short-haired girl, an unlit cigarette dangling from her lips. Peggy waved her off with both hands.

The party was on a soundstage that had last been used as a ballroom, with walls that ended abruptly despite the lack of a ceiling, and several tons of lighting strung on wires overhead. Elsa had never been inside a proper soundstage before, and tried not to gape. The walls were padded and covered with chicken wire to keep the noise locked inside. Bales of hay lined the fake ballroom walls, and the cigarette girls were dressed to look straight off the farm, with gingham blouses tucked into their short skirts. Everyone they passed clapped Gordon on the back. Elsa kept her hands clasped beneath her belly, making sure that the actors all knew that Mrs. Gordon Pitts was pregnant, not obese. The room was warm, despite the presence of large electric fans, and Elsa's throat felt dry.

"I'm going to find something to drink," she said, touching Gordon on the arm. He nodded, already scanning the room.

"I'll meet you over there," Gordon said, and set off in the opposite direction.

Elsa smoothed out her dress, which was not all that bad, considering her girth. It still clung to her bosom in a way that was flattering, and flared out around her knees. Pregnancy was good for her hair too, and Elsa ran her fingers along the side of her head. She'd pinned it up all day, and there were perfect waves still in place, shiny with a swipe of Gordon's pomade.

The bar was on two levels of hay, with cowpoke bartenders at the ready. Someone was going to put down her cigarette and set the whole place on fire. Everyone had on bolo ties and blue jeans. Elsa felt overdressed. She rested her hands down on the hay. Surely they had cows in California, and dairy farms, and people who looked like her family, but Elsa had never seen them. She was sure that anyone who looked at her face would know straightaway that she was a country girl, no question about it. Gordon had slipped into Los Angeles like a hand into a glove, his Floridian past vanishing well before the Gardner Brothers wiped his slate clean with a squeaky new biography. They thought he looked like a New York City boy, maybe half-Italian, with his dark skin and his soft voice. He was going to be the next Valentino. Next to her husband, Elsa felt about as cosmopolitan as a bovine.

The intimidation factor at a Gardner Brothers party was high: Everyone on the guest list looked like a movie star, and half of them were. Elsa saw Susie herself holding court in the middle of the dance floor, the whole party spinning and dancing around her as if she were the tiniest human maypole. The other half of the party guests were waiting in the wings, like Gordon, and wanted nothing more than to shake hands and light cigarettes and maybe even dance with the actors who had already made it big. Elsa recognized all of them, her memory snapping photos of everyone who walked by, even the ones who thought they were nobodies and clung to the sides of the room like barnacles. The unfriendly (and maybe already sauced) Dolores Dee was swiveling her hips on the dance floor, paying attention to only her internal rhythms. Moving around the actors and actresses were the poised hairstylists and the well-painted makeup artists, the strapping dolly grips and the men who built things with giant saws and pieces of wood. Elsa wanted to go home and take off her heels. Her already large feet had swelled up another whole size, and her toes were hanging out the peep-toe of her shoes, looking more monstrous than peep-worthy. She scuffed the bottom of her shoes on the concrete floor.

"We have horses who do that on command," a small, thin man with glasses said. He stood to Elsa's right and held out a glass. "Cheers," he said, "to the baby."

Elsa accepted the drink, which had a lime bobbing gamely near the top. It tasted like bubbles, with a healthy dash of gin.

"Thank you," Elsa said, and extended her free hand. "I'm Elsa Pitts."

"Ah, the young, fertile wife of Mr. *Gordon* Pitts, I presume." The man shook her hand and looked her up and down.

Elsa took a sip of her drink and the sourness opened up the back of her jaw. It felt as good as pressing a bruise. "I'm sorry," she said. "Do I know you?"

"Irving Green," he said. "I work here."

It was only then that Elsa noticed the small audience surrounding them; a growing ring of actors and other hangers-on had positioned their bodies so that Mr. Green, should he wish, would be able to see them. If he could see them, he could talk to them. If he talked to them, they might get a bigger part, a devoted publicist, their face on the cover of a magazine. Irving Green was second only to Louis Gardner himself, and from what Elsa heard, maybe even more powerful. He was younger than the other producers, no older than thirty-five, and had the look of a boy who had always hated the sunlight. His skin was so pale it was nearly green, as if all the blood vessels underneath were desperately close to the surface. The word on the lot (according to Elsa's husband) was that Gardner was a softie compared to Green, despite his physical frailty. The studio lore was that Irving Green never put his name on any of his movies, because doing so would make everyone else look bad by comparison. Elsa stood up straight and tried not to move. But she hadn't sought this out, she reminded herself. He had come to her. She felt embarrassed at her own ignorance, embarrassed that she had looked so out of place that he'd felt the need to speak to her.

Elsa had seen photographs in magazines and should have recognized him. Irving Green was slighter than Gordon, but with an intense gaze, dark brown eyes that focused on Elsa without looking away. He had dressed for the evening without a nod to the country theme, which made Elsa feel more secure in her own choice of dress. His round glasses sat high on his nose, which was disproportionately large and leaned slightly to the left, as though a strong wind were blowing through the room. Irving's pitch-black hair swooped backward, slick as oil. Elsa thought he looked like a Greek statue, and when Irving smiled, he displayed two rows of crowded, imperfect teeth. Here was a man with all of Hollywood's glamour at his fingertips, and all he had done was put on an expensive suit. Elsa admired his lack of vanity.

"Sir, it is a pleasure to meet you." She clutched her sweating glass with both hands. Soon it would start to drip, and the drips would appear on her silk dress, and Elsa would be convinced that she'd ruined her first impression.

"Have you ever thought about acting?" Irving said, staring at her steadily through the tinted panes of his glasses. He was warm too; Elsa could tell. There were beads of sweat clinging to his hairline, tiny perfect drops.

Elsa shifted on her heels. The actors nearby were pretending not to listen. Off in the distance, she heard Gordon shouting into another man's ear. They were drunk already; she could see it from across the room. Louis Gardner was at the party too, she guessed, walking through, the two producers creating waves and wakes wherever they went, like twin tropical storms. Elsa said, "My parents have a small theater in Wisconsin. It's all I've ever known." She wanted to tell him about the first time she walked on a stage, how she could hear everyone in the audience breathing, and how it meant that she could be anyone she wanted, instead of just herself. Elsa answered his question. "I think about it all the time."

Irving took in this information and nodded. "I bet you were the prettiest girl in town."

Elsa laughed, but Irving stared at her so directly that Elsa began to color. She quieted down as quickly as possible. Even after her death, Hildy was always the most beautiful girl in Door County. Elsa couldn't imagine a time when that would no longer be the case. "I'm afraid not, Mr. Green, but thank you for the compliment."

He nodded. "Here's what you should do. Do you mind if I tell you?" Irving didn't wait for her to respond. "Have the baby. Take a few months, lose thirty pounds. Not so much that you lose the milkmaid look, though. It's your trademark—Miss Wisconsin, all sweetness and light. And Elsa Pitts isn't gonna cut it, is it?" Irving looked at her hard. Elsa blushed. He stared for so long that Elsa began to sweat even more. She reflexively put her hands around her belly, as if to protect the child from whatever was to come. Then Irving snapped his fingers so loudly that it echoed through the room, over all the chatting and flirting. Elsa was surprised that such a sharp, loud noise could come out of such a small person.

"Laura Lamont," he said. "You want it? It's yours. Come see me when you're ready." And then Irving walked away, leaving his full glass teetering on a bale of hay. Elsa watched as he walked into the crowd and was immediately swallowed up by actors calling out his name. Louis Gardner was in the crowd too, as short as Irving but twice as stout, with white hair and a slight stoop. Elsa saw Irving speak to Louis, saw her name come out of his mouth. Both men were looking at her for a brief moment, and then Irving gripped Louis on the arm and vanished farther into the fray.

Gordon scampered over to Elsa's side less than a minute later—the news had rippled through the party like fire in a dry field.

"What did he say?" Gordon asked, nearly panting with excitement. "He liked that last scene I did, with the horse, didn't he? I *knew* he was going to like that."

Elsa took a sip of her drink. Her husband's hairline was receding more and more quickly every day, and when he pointed his face toward the ground, Elsa saw the soft brown peaks, higher than they'd ever been. There was music playing—a band off in the opposite corner. Elsa heard a fiddle. Inside, the baby moved, shoving an elbow into her side.

"Mr. Green? He was very nice," Elsa said. She sounded like her mother, as cool tempered as if she'd been hypnotized. "He gave me a new name." She laughed at the idea of it, but of course it happened all the time. It was the easiest way to shed one's skin: by losing one's undesirable, ordinary name, which had been given by silly parents without a thought to the future. She's already lost one name and gained another, less attractive moniker. Why not do it again?

"He did what?" Gordon came so close that his mouth was almost touching Elsa's ear. The pretend friendliness in his voice was gone—Elsa could see it now. Gordon had wanted his boss to like his wife, of course, but he hadn't wanted this.

"He told me to lose some weight." She shouldn't have been so flip. Elsa held her dress against the bottom of her belly again, feeling the entire circumference of her body, as massive and sturdy as a Roman column. She wanted to remind Gordon that when they met, they were both actors in a play, and that she hadn't always been someone's mother.

"Oh," Gordon said, clearly relieved. "He is tough. I told you that, didn't I? He's tough."

"He sure was." Elsa set her drink down, and shook her head when the bartender asked her whether she'd like another, though she could think of nothing she wanted more. "The baby's really moving around," she said. "I think I'd better go home."

Gordon nodded solemnly, and did his best to look concerned as he walked her to the door. At the entrance to the lot, girls with tap shoes clicked by on their way to convince the assembled that there were no problems left in the world that the movies couldn't fix, as though they needed encouragement. Gardner Brothers understood more than the other studios that glamour was the order of the day: the illusion of happiness, of opulence, of tap-dancing girls in top hats and lipstick.

Elsa thanked the neighbors for watching Clara. She scooped her daughter's sleeping body up and held it to her breasts, the only available space above her belly. Clara's head was sticky, as it often was in the night, as though all the energy she had accumulated during the day could not be contained by her small body, and was seeping out her pores. Elsa let her lips run back and forth over

Clara's faint eyebrows as she carried her home. *Laura Lamont*, Elsa thought that night as she turned over in her sleep, *Laura Lamont*. The bed was full of bodies present and future: Elsa and Clara, Laura Lamont and Clara's younger sister. There were so many people yet to arrive. Elsa kicked all the covers to the floor; their combined body heat was more than enough to keep her warm.

The signs of labor were clear and sharp. Though Clara had been born at home with the help of a local midwife, just like Elsa and her two sisters, Gardner Brothers had their own doctors—indeed, their own *hospital*—on the lot itself, and they insisted. Elsa didn't like the idea of hospitals. They were at once too clean and too full of illness. When Gordon wheeled her into the waiting room, all Elsa could hear were men lighting cigarettes and chatting as though they were at a cocktail party. Their wives had been taken away, as she would soon be taken away. Elsa's mother would have been appalled. The taller doctor took the wheelchair from Gordon and told him to wait in the lounge. Elsa's contractions were already only three minutes apart, and they had little time to waste on good-byes. She felt Gordon's tentative mouth on her face and was glad that she was going alone.

The Gardner Brothers' doctors had names, Drs. Ames and Crowley, though Elsa thought of them only as instruments of Louis Gardner and Irving Green. If they could have sucked the extra thirty pounds off her body at the same time, they would have. Dr. Ames was the tall one, stretched out and slender, with thick, dark-framed glasses.

"Mrs. Pitts," he began, helping her shift into the hospital bed. "I understand you gave birth to your last baby at home?"

Elsa nodded, trying to ignore the giant motions happening inside her body. She would have screamed if she didn't think everyone in the entire hospital could have heard her. The Emersons were quiet people. Even here, in the hospital, Elsa wanted to be nothing but a polite patient, the kind of woman the doctors would recall later as having been a dream to deal with. "That's right," she said, so wanting to agree with what was going on.

"Well, then I think you're going to like this," Dr. Ames said. He had a large needle in his right hand. "For the pain."

They had both signed forms, Gordon and Elsa, agreeing to the treatment prescribed. Elsa had never taken more than an aspirin in her life, and she felt woozy as soon as the metal point went into her arm. "Gordon . . ." she said, though Gordon was through many doors and walls, and even if he'd been sitting right beside her, he couldn't have done a thing.

The doctors were right—whereas with Clara there had been pain, Elsa felt none. Dr. Ames took a seat on a low stool at the foot of her bed. The room was cool, with all the metal surfaces ringing like tiny bells whenever someone hit them by accident. The rails on the side of her bed, the sanitized instruments ready to be used. Elsa thought of her childhood doctor, who would come to the house with his big black bag. Hildy would always tease Elsa by playing with the doctor's stethoscope, putting it against her heart and then Elsa's. "Mine is louder," Hildy always said. "I can't hear yours at all. You must be dead." And then Elsa was in Hildy's bed, with all those pillows and dolls and pieces of fabric that Hildy had stolen from their mother's sewing basket all strewn around. Strips of lace waved from the ceiling. And then she was back in the hospital room, strapped down to the bed by her neck. She looked around, wanting to be reassured. Her parents were standing at the foot of the bed, and it was Josephine who sat on the stool before her. Why hadn't Elsa seen her there before? Josephine looked serious, as usual, with concentration that bordered on the absurd.

"Why are you looking at me like that?" Elsa said, her voice loud now that it was just her family present.

Josephine didn't answer. She reached toward Elsa's body, her hands extending under the sheet that hung from Elsa's knees. Hildy's room looked different now; how long had she been away from home? Elsa couldn't remember; the room itself seemed as foggy as her brain, as though the winter storms had broken through the window, and there was a layer of snow covering everything. Even her body was dusted with it, thin and white as a sheet. Elsa tried to reach down and brush it off but found that she couldn't move her arms. Her parents were standing on either side, holding her arms down on the bed.

"Mom! Dad!" Elsa said. She was glad to see them. A baby cried somewhere in the room—Clara. It was Clara. Elsa felt tears come to her eyes as she thought of her daughter, her sweet little girl. Her father would enjoy Clara's company. This summer they would go, whether or not Gardner Brothers approved. She would tell Gordon that it was not a request, it was an order. Elsa felt so tired. She opened and closed her eyes and watched Hildy's room disappear.

The doctors were gone, and a nurse was wheeling by, pushing a cart down the hall. Elsa thought about calling out. Her head felt thick and heavy, the way it did when she drank too much, a fly trying to swim through honey. If only the world could be quiet and clear, the way Green Bay looked on a calm summer day. When the nurse came back, she would wheel in the baby, another girl. Gordon had insisted the next daughter be named after his mother, and so she was. Florence Isabelle Pitts was as dark as her sister was light, with a large tuft of dark brown hair. She was larger than Clara had been at birth, a smidge over eight pounds. The first time Elsa got to hold Florence in her arms, she was two days old, and they were on their way home. Gordon, who'd been sent off almost immediately after Elsa was wheeled in, waited by the door of the waiting room, a lit cigar in his mouth and a bunch of flowers in hand. When Elsa saw him, both she and the baby began to cry, out of something like relief. The air around Gordon smelled of a lit match, and hope.

After Florence was born, Elsa made herself a promise—she would do just what Irving Green had told her, and fast. Gordon bristled at first, but then decided that it was better for him to have a wife with a shapely figure, and let it go.

There were exercise classes at the studio: dance, tap, calisthenics. Elsa dropped the girls off with on-lot child care and went five times a week at nine. At first, Clara cried when Elsa left the day-care room, accustomed as she was to their long days at home together, but after a short while she got used to the women there, and the other children, and quite enjoyed it. There were blocks to stack and letters of the alphabet to learn. Florence was too small to mind being passed around, only three months old, and cooed happily no matter who was looking after her. Though she loved her daughters enormously, Elsa never felt quite as free as she did the moment after dropping them off and walking out the door. Her arms nearly floated up, away from her body, suddenly so unencumbered. That the services were free was the fresh whipped cream and berries on top.

Elsa's favorite class was ballet, which was taught by a Frenchman named Guy who wore all black, with a scarf knotted tightly around his neck, the silk corners flapping against his collarbones as he demonstrated the movements. Elsa liked to be in the last row, near the corner, though the dance studio was lined with mirrors and there was no hiding from the teacher's critical eye.

"Aaaand, left toe *point*, left toe *sliiide*, left toe *point,* left toe *sliiide*," Guy said, marching across the room with his eyes trained on one set of slim ankles after another. Elsa checked her work in the mirror—no, she was on the wrong side again. "This is a simple *rond de jambe*, ladies! *Rond de jambe!*"

Elsa quickly straightened her left leg and drew a circle on the lacquered wooden floor with her pointed toe. The other women in class never seemed to have any problem remembering their rights and lefts.

"Damn it!"

Elsa turned her head, while trying desperately not to lose Guy's count. She was still fairly new, and he'd been kind enough to ignore her pathetic efforts thus far, but Elsa had seen him snap at some of the other women. She didn't want that kind of attention. Elsa didn't harbor any illusions about being a good dancer—Busby Berkeley and his legions of dancers practiced at a studio that bordered Gardner Brothers, and Elsa heard that they brought in an entire orchestra for their rehearsals. Elsa just wanted to stay on her feet. Along the back wall, two women over, Elsa saw a redhead struggling even more than she was. The woman had tied her hair up in two pigtails, which flapped against her cheeks like dog ears with every clumsy *rond de jambe*. She too was on the wrong leg. Elsa smiled, and the woman smiled back and then stuck out her tongue, exhaling extra hard.

"And now the *oth-er* side! Right toe *point*, right toe *sliiide*, right toe point . . ." Guy walked over to Elsa's side of the room. She watched him approach in the mirror. When she was looking at him, she couldn't look at herself, which made the steps seem somehow closer at hand. She felt her leg lock into place, as strong and sturdy as steel. Elsa made eye contact with Guy in the mirror— *See! It's not so hard!*—and immediately lost her balance, falling clumsily to the floor. He sneered, disgusted, and walked back toward the front of the room. Elsa watched his narrow, perfectly straight back recede into the more talented sector of the class. In the front row, the women hadn't missed a beat. Little Peggy Bates, the chatty girl she'd met at the party, was in the crowd somewhere, hoofing away like a professional, and Dolores Dee was in the second row, her buxom frame swaddled in a baby blue leotard. Elsa was mortified.

The redhead scooted over, shoving the leggy women between them out of the way, and helped Elsa up.

"I thought he was going to yell at you," she whispered. "God, I'm so scared of everyone in this class. I feel like such a bottom-feeder."

Elsa didn't know quite what she meant, but she dusted off her pants and said, "Me too."

"Hey, look," the redhead said, and fell down in exactly the same way Elsa had, with one leg outstretched like a drunken flamingo.

"Out, out, out!" Guy shouted, and pointed toward the door, cursing in French. The twenty-five other women in the room may have tittered to one another quietly, but not one turned around to watch Elsa and her new friend skulk out the door. It was a room full of actresses, after all, each of them loath to admit that she wasn't the center of attention.

❦

Lillian Hedges was her given name, though Gardner and Green had already changed it twice. "First I was Lillian Fleur," she said, in between bites of a roast beef sandwich at the commissary. Elsa looked about for her husband, and was relieved not to find him hovering. She knew better than to look for Irving, who had a private dining room in his office suite and was never seen inside the regular commissary's walls. At the next table, two men were dressed like Civil War soldiers, ready to battle with their lunch.

"That's pretty," Elsa said. She was trying to be on a strict diet, but it was hard when eating with a new friend. Lillian ate like a longshoreman, not caring whether she sent bits of food sputtering out from between her teeth. Talking to Lillian made Elsa realize how much she missed talking to her sisters, and the easy comfort of another female body so near. Elsa picked at her salad, spearing a single piece of lettuce with her fork.

"Sure, but it wasn't *me*," Lillian said. She dabbed at the corners of her mouth with a napkin, and then let her shoulders collapse forward. "Gosh, do I look like a *fleur* to you?" She let out a great big whoop of a laugh. Several people at adjacent tables turned, but Lillian seemed not to notice. One of the Civil War participants was so startled that he knocked his musket to the ground.

"So what's the name now?" It had been two hours since Elsa dropped off her daughters at the day care. They would be fine a little longer than usual. If Gordon asked, which he wouldn't, she would just tell him that she'd decided to stay for another dance class. Getting her figure back was important, he agreed. It just didn't look right for an actor like him to have a heavy wife. Gordon seemed to have conveniently forgotten that Elsa wanted to act too, that they'd made this journey together, that she wasn't just along to clap at his name on the screen. Elsa folded another lettuce leaf into her mouth. She missed talking to her sisters—even Josephine, who had never had much to say at all.

"Ginger Hedges." She gestured to her hair. "Because of the red."

"So he does that with everyone?" Elsa felt embarrassed—she'd imagined herself special. Surely Irving Green didn't approach every woman he saw with swollen ankles and offer her a new life in Hollywood. Making actors into stars was one thing, but making a pregnant woman into an actor, that was something different.

"Gardner does, sure," she said, and Elsa felt a swift sense of relief, for what she wasn't quite sure. In her imagination, Irving was the harder nut to crack, despite not having his name on the side of the building, and she was glad to have his attention all her own for another moment.

Lillian—Ginger—had an elastic face, and she didn't miss an opportunity to widen her eyes and stretch her cheeks. She leaned forward and cupped a hand around her mouth. Elsa watched as Ginger's white blouse dipped perilously close to her roast beef sandwich.

"You never know who's around here. These publicists will eat your brains if you say too much." Lillian's rubbery face relaxed, and Elsa saw that she was older than she was—maybe by as much as ten years. Lillian was probably already thirty, ancient and adult. "Really. They can change anything they want to."

"Oh," Elsa said, unsure of how else to respond. How had Gordon made it through unscathed, with a name like Pitts? Maybe it was different for men, who could be any number of things: lumpy, foreign, scarred. Women had only two speeds at Gardner Brothers: beautiful and serious or beautiful and funny. Elsa wondered which one she was supposed to be—probably the latter, as it was easier to fudge the beauty part if you were making people laugh.

When they finished eating, Ginger took Elsa on a tour of the back lot, and she understood, at last seeing it in the daylight, why Gordon was always so reluctant to come home. Some of the sets were always up, as though the studio were going to decide on the spot what to shoot that day. A musical! A romance! A Western! There were whole city blocks built to look like New York and anonymous small towns, picket fences and all. There were alleys that led to nowhere, and shops with papier-mâché objects in the windows. The wide, empty streets never had any cars on them, but were instead filled with people practicing their lines or teaching one another dance steps. Her father would have loved it.

"So are you an actress or what? I didn't ask," Ginger said. They were standing in front of an ice-cream parlor. Elsa recognized it from a Susie and Johnny movie the previous summer—Susie had climbed up on the roof and sung a song. When she was through, she'd slid back down the striped canopy into Johnny's waiting arms. There was something magical about being inside a place like this, a place where glamour and imagination mattered more than what you'd been called since birth. "I know you're not a dancer." Ginger was kidding her again, but Elsa was still thinking about her first question.

"Yes, I'm an actress," Elsa said, except that the moment the words were out of her mouth, there on that spot on a street that existed only in the movies, she wasn't Elsa Emerson anymore, at least not all of her. "I'm Laura Lamont."

"Well, okay, then!" Ginger linked her elbow with Elsa's, and they walked all the way back to the day-care room that way, in sweetheart position: a pair.

After that afternoon, she was always two people at once, Elsa Emerson and Laura Lamont. They shared a body and a brain and a heart, conjoined twins linked in too many places to ever separate. Elsa wondered whether it would always be that way, or whether bits of Laura would eventually detach themselves, shaking off Elsa like a discarded husk. She thought of the butterflies that floated around her mother's garden all summer long, their gracefulness belying the fact that they had so recently been another organism entirely. Change was possible, as long as one was willing to stick that first wing out of the cocoon.

3

THE NURSEMAID

Fall 1941

The studio lawyers made everything easy: Within two years of her initial contract, Elsa was divorced and Laura had never been married. Gardner Brothers represented both Laura and Gordon, though it was easy to see whom the bosses favored. Who was Gordon but a sidekick, a bit player? Louis Gardner arranged to help Laura find a bigger house, perfect for her and the two girls and one nanny. It was so easy to change a name: Clara and Florence became Emersons, as they should have been from the start. Elsa couldn't believe she'd ever let herself or her daughters carry the name Pitts. The lawyers never charged Laura for their time: It was all in the contract. No one in the papers asked the questions Laura thought they might: *If you've never been married, where did these two girls come from, the stork?* Questions that did not follow the script were simply not allowed. The divorce had been Elsa's idea, which was to say it had been Laura's idea too. She found that there were certain activities (feeding the children, taking a shower) that she always did as Elsa, and others (going to dance class, speaking to Irving and Louis) that she did as Laura, as though there were a switch in the middle of her back. The problem had been that neither Elsa nor Laura wanted to be married to Gordon, who wanted to be married only to Elsa. Before the girls were born, Gordon seemed happy enough for Elsa to be an actress, but not when she was the mother of his children.

Clara spent her days in the on-set school with all the other kids, though Florence was only a baby and stayed home with Harriet, the nanny, who was the first black woman Laura had ever really known and charged as much per week as the lead actors at the Cherry County Playhouse. Harriet was exactly Laura's age and had a kind, easy way with all three of the Emerson girls. The new house was on the other side of Los Feliz Boulevard, on a street that snaked up into the hills. Sycamore trees hung low over the sidewalks, and Laura loved to take long walks with Harriet and the girls, pointing out squirrels and even the occasional opossum. Griffith Park wasn't technically Laura's backyard, but that was how she liked to think of it. She went to every concert she could at the Greek Theatre and at the Hollywood Bowl, which wasn't often but often enough, and far more often than if she had stayed in Door County, Wisconsin. She sat outside, under the stars, with all of Los Angeles hushed and quiet behind her; Laura felt that she was once again sitting in the patch of grass outside the Cherry County Playhouse, and every note was sung just for her. One evening, a secretary found Laura on her way from the day care to dance class, and stopped her in her tracks. Irving Green had a box at the Hollywood Bowl, and wanted Laura to be his date for the evening. It was never clear how Irving came to possess all the pieces of information he did, just that he was very good at finding things out and holding them all inside his brain until he needed them. Laura said yes, which neither pleased nor surprised the secretary, and Harriet stayed home with the girls. Irving and his driver came to pick her up at six, before dusk, and they sat in near silence until they reached their destination, which gave Laura ample time to examine the inside of the automobile, which was the first Rolls-Royce she'd ever seen up close. When they arrived at the Hollywood Bowl, ushers quickly showed them to their seats, which were inches from the stage, so close that Laura could have reached out and grabbed the first violinist's bow if she'd had the urge. A few minutes in, an usher hurried over to Irving's side, whispered in his ear, and they ducked out again. Laura fussed nervously, sure that everyone in Los Angeles was staring straight at her, wondering why she'd been chosen as his date at all, and sure that he probably wasn't coming back. When Irving returned a few minutes later, he said only, "Garbo," as if that were all that was necessary, and it was.

"I've been meaning to ask you," Laura said, in between movements. The seats around them were empty; the Bowl wasn't always full, she knew from her time in the cheap seats several hundred feet from where they were sitting, but even so, Laura imagined that Irving was behind their seclusion, that he held unseen power here as on the lot. "Why 'Brothers,' when it's only Louis? Isn't that misleading?" She blushed at her wrong choice of words—she hadn't meant *misleading*, which implied that Louis, their boss and Irving's mentor, was hoodwinking the audiences. She'd meant secretive, or goofy, even, something that she hadn't communicated. Laura was nervous whenever she was alone with

Irving, whether it was in his office or the few times she'd seen him walking purposefully around the lot. There were things everyone on the lot knew about Irving, things Laura had overheard: He'd been sick as a child, and there was something wrong still, a weakness in a ventricle (so said Edna, the costume assistant) or a lung (so said Peggy, a devoted gossip). Laura didn't think she'd ever be bold enough to find out the truth. Eating together was the worst: Irving hardly touched his food, swallowing tinier bites than Laura knew was possible and pronouncing himself stuffed. The desire for him to like her was so strong she could barely think. Laura thought of the first time they'd met, and how silly she'd found all those actors pretending to examine their shoes when all they really wanted was his attention. Now she was just as guilty. He was a father figure to all of them, and most of the actors weren't afraid to get scrappy with their siblings.

"Oh," Irving said, "that. I told Louis I thought it sounded better."

The orchestra began playing a selection from *Così fan Tutte*. Strings soared up into the sky, and Laura felt as if the entire park were filled with bubbles. She laughed and turned her head toward the sky, as if the stars would laugh back at her.

"That's rich," Laura said. "That's rich."

Irving reached over and put her hand in his, never turning his eyes away from the stage. His skin was soft and not nearly as cold as she imagined it would be, and even though Laura's hand began to perspire, Irving didn't pull away. Laura knew that from the cheap seats, the Hollywoodland sign was visible on the hills behind the dome of the Bowl, and she felt it there, flashing in the darkness like an electric eel. They sat quietly for the rest of the concert, ostensibly listening to the music, though Laura could hear nothing except the sound of her own heart beating wildly within her chest. Garbo may have been on the phone, but Laura was there, right there, sitting beside him, feeling the bones in Irving's surprisingly strong grip.

The first starring role Irving gave to Laura was in a film with Ginger, *Kissing Cousins*—they played sisters, which made them both squeal with excitement. Laura was blond and Ginger was red, which meant that Ginger was the saucy one, and Laura was the innocent. The sisters were from Iowa and had moved to Los Angeles to be stars. It was a simple story, with lots of flirting and costume changes. Laura's favorite scene involved the girls dancing clumsily around a café, threatening to poke the other patrons' eyes out with their parasols. She loved being in front of the camera, loved the weight of the thick crinolines under her dress, loved the elaborate hats made of straw and feathers. Acting in an honest-to-goodness motion picture was the first thing Laura had done that made her think of Hildy without feeling like she'd been socked in the jaw—Hildy would have loved every inch of film she'd shot, every dip and twirl, and that made Laura feel like she would have done it all for free. Of course she would have! Every actor and actress on the lot would have worked for free; that was the truth. Gardner Brothers didn't know the depth of desire that was on its acres, not the half of it.

There were differences between acting onstage and on-screen; Laura felt the gulf at once. At the playhouse, choices were made on a nightly basis, always prompted by the feelings in the air, by the choices made by the actors around you. There were slight variations, almost imperceptible, sometimes caused by a tickle in your throat or a giant lightning bug zipping across the stage. On film, choices were made over and over again, a dozen times in a row, from this angle and that, with close-ups and long shots and cranes overhead. The movements were smaller, the voice lower. Laura beamed too widely, sang too loudly. Everything had to be brought down, and done on an endless loop. She and Ginger skipped in circles for hours, it seemed, their hoop skirts knocking against each other like soft, quick-moving clouds hurrying across the sky.

Kissing Cousins was a modest hit, and though the critics called it "a lesser entry into the Johnny and Susie canon, though without the star power those two pint-sized powerhouses might have lent," moviegoers responded to Laura's sweetness on-screen. She got fan mail at the studio: whole bags of letters from teenage girls who wanted to know how she got her hair to do that, what color lipstick she liked best. One boy wrote and asked her to marry him. She kept that one; the rest she passed along to the secretaries at the studio, one of whom was now devoted just to her and Ginger, the new girls in town. Irving and Louis had her pose for photos—a white silk dress, gardenias in her hair—that could be signed and sent out to her fans. The dress was the most expensive thing Laura had ever felt against her skin, and she wore it for as long as possible before Edna asked for it back. Laura had fans: a small but growing number. Irving Green and all the imaginary Gardner Brothers brothers made sure of it.

On top of the dance classes (Guy, chastened by the girls' new-found success, left them alone in the back of the class, and they did improve, slowly, at both the *ronds de jambe* and the poker faces necessary to survive the class period), Laura and Ginger were now required to shave their legs on a regular basis and to visit the beauty department for eyebrow and hair maintenance, which they were not to attempt on their own. Ginger had to use a depilatory cream on her faint mustache. Laura felt sheepish about all the primping, though she enjoyed the attention. She was most comfortable in a pair of pants and tennis shoes, walking through the dry Griffith Park trails, with all the city laid out below her, still full of nothing but possibilities. It was the opposite of her parents' land, at least at first, where Laura knew every knot on every tree. There was still nature to discover in the world, an endless laundry list of sun-seeking plants and trees.

Ginger moved in a few houses down, and on the weekends the two women would often meet in the street, Clara running around their legs and Florence staggering back and forth between them. It was as though they were any two women in the world, generous with gossip and cups of tea. It wasn't until some of the other neighborhood women began to gather on their front steps across the street to watch these interactions that Laura and Ginger moved their dates inside. It wasn't a bother—who wouldn't have noticed if two movie stars took a walk down the street together? Laura understood. This too was her job now, being Laura Lamont off the set as well as on. The children called her Mother or Mama, her parents and Josephine called her Elsa in their letters, Harriet called her Miss Emerson, and Ginger called her Laura, which was what she called herself. The trick seemed to be commitment: Elsa Emerson was a good Wisconsin girl. Laura Lamont was going to be a star.

Gordon stayed in their old house, a fifteen-minute walk down Vermont Avenue. He saw the girls infrequently; at the beginning it had been once a week, but it was now no more than once a month, and never without supervision. Those were the lawyer's rules. Laura would have been more generous, but the agreement was not up to her.

When he rang the bell, Clara ran into the kitchen and hid behind Harriet's slender legs.

"It's okay," Harriet said. "He does anything funny and I will knock him sideways." She cupped Clara's head with her palm.

"He won't, though, will he?" Laura said. "I just don't know."

"Probably not," Harriet said. "But if he does, sideways." She nodded confidently, as if only just truly agreeing with herself. "You should answer that, before he changes his mind."

Laura picked up the baby and answered the door.

The rumors were everywhere at the studio. It was no crime to drink to excess; everybody did it, even Johnny, the boy wonder, who was so popular at the Santa Anita racetrack that he had his own viewing box. But nobody did it as often as Gordon. Sometimes Laura overheard other people talking about Gordon in the commissary, some young man dressed like a gondolier or an Indian chief, new faces who didn't know she and Gordon had ever been married. The word was that he'd started doing other things too. There was a group of jazz musicians who had played a couple of parties on the lot. People said they'd seen Gordon with them out at night, places he shouldn't have been. *But then why were you there?* Laura wanted to ask. *How do you know so much, then?* But she didn't. Gordon Pitts was just another star in the Gardner Brothers galaxy now; why should Laura Lamont care about him? Sometimes she had to remind herself that the woman Gordon had married no longer existed. In some ways, she really had let Elsa Emerson stay on that bus—when her feet hit the California ground for the first time, something inside had already shifted. Gordon wanted to be an actor, yes, of course he did, but not the way Laura did. He saw it as a fun job, a step up from working in the orange groves or at the grocery store. It was being far away from home that mattered most. There was nothing frivolous in Laura's decision to leave Door County, no matter how quickly it had come about, even if she hadn't quite been aware of it at the time. It was just something she had to do. Gordon could understand that about as well as he could understand how to engineer the Brooklyn Bridge. Some things were beyond his ken.

With Gordon at her door, though, it was harder to dismiss him. She saw the dark skin under Gordon's eyes, black and pouchy. His shoulders rounded forward, as if the weight of the visit were already pulling him toward the ground. Laura stepped out of the way, inviting him in. Gordon shuffled past Florence and gave her toe a pinch. She howled, her tiny mouth a perfect circle of misery. Laura felt the sound deep inside her chest.

"Sorry," Gordon said. His voice was low and scratchy, as though he'd been up all night talking.

Laura tapped a cigarette out of her pack and sat down in the living room, facing the still-whimpering Florence outward, toward her father. She gestured for Gordon to sit opposite her, and held her unlit cigarette over the baby's head. It felt funny to have an ex-husband, a person out there in the universe who had shared her bed so many nights in a row and was now sleeping God knew where, and with God knew whom. Laura always assumed that she would be like her mother, and sleep alone only when her husband's snoring got too loud. Instead, she was only twenty-two, and already groping around in the dark alone.

"Harriet?" Laura called into the air. She and Gordon sat in silence waiting for Harriet to come and take the baby away. Laura watched Gordon's face as he stared at Florence. She'd just woken up from a nap and still had her sleepy, cloudy expression on.

"Is it true?" Gordon asked.

Harriet walked in and plucked Florence off Laura's lap. She gave Laura a look that said, *Just holler*, and retreated toward the girls' bedroom. Laura appreciated Harriet's loyalty. So often it was just the two of them with the girls, a female family of four, and Harriet was protective of all of them in equal measure. Even though it had been only a few months, their time together had been so concentrated, so intimate, that Laura felt that Harriet knew her better than Gordon ever had. Laura waited until they were gone before responding, and even though she knew what he was referring to, Laura said, "Is what true?"

The living room wasn't finished yet. There was a long, low sofa, and two high-backed chairs to sit on, and a coffee table, and a couple of lamps scattered around the room, like a half-built set, a facsimile of a lived-in space. There was an untouched chess set that the girls were always grabbing at, lamps that hadn't been plugged in. Laura wondered whether her house would ever feel the way her parents' house did, like no one else could have lived there and found everything. She wanted secret drawers and hidey-holes. Maybe when Clara was older, or when Florence was older—

they were so close in age, like Josephine and Hildy. They would do everything together, the three of them, a package deal. She had a flickering thought about Irving, and whether he liked children. She hadn't asked—why would she? It seemed presumptuous, when he had so much else to do.

"I mean about you and Irving Green." Gordon could barely spit out the words.

Laura lit her cigarette, sure that the thought had registered on her face. Some thoughts burned too brightly to conceal. Laura tried to shift her attention to her cigarette, to the feel of the paper between her lips, and the bits of tobacco that landed on her tongue. "What about me and Mr. Green? He's my boss, just like he's your boss, Gordon."

"He pays for this house, doesn't he?" Gordon stood up and started walking the length of the room with his hands clasped tightly in front of him.

"He pays for your house too!" Laura tapped the end of her cigarette against the edge of the ashtray.

"But you're sleeping with him." Gordon stopped. He had his back to Laura and was looking out the wide window onto the street. The jacket Gordon was wearing had a small hole in one sleeve, and Laura couldn't stop looking at it. All he had to do was ask—either her or the girls in wardrobe at the studio—and the hole would be gone in five minutes. Had he not noticed? Or did he notice and not care? The first time she'd gone in to meet with Irving, when her life with Gordon was still held together with pins, Gordon had stared at her getting ready, wearing a dress borrowed from Ginger, and then he'd told her she'd lost too much weight. Gordon had never wanted two actors in the same house, not really. He wanted a wife who sat on a kitchen chair and stared at the clock while he was gone. Sure, that was what most men counted on when they married, but Gordon had sworn up and down that he was different. No matter what whispered hopes they'd shared in the earliest weeks of their marriage, Gordon wanted to be married to another actor the way he wanted to be married to a gorilla—he just didn't. It would never have worked; that was what Laura told herself. Their divorce wasn't her fault, no more than Gordon's drinking was.

Even so, Laura felt sorry for Gordon, staring at the hole in his sleeve. She perched her cigarette in the ashtray, its small smoke signal still reaching for the ceiling, and walked over to her husband. Her former husband. The lines were blurry—if they'd never been married, were they ever really divorced? There had been so many papers to sign, so many layers of confidentiality promised. Laura couldn't keep them straight. It wasn't as though Gordon wanted custody of the girls—that was never a question. The girls belonged to Laura. She sometimes thought that she could have willed them into being all by herself, without a man's help, if given enough time. And it wasn't as though Gordon really loved her, either. They'd both imagined more for themselves, a real Hollywood-type romance, with flowers and kisses underneath a lamppost. But he had believed her all those years ago, when they were sitting at her parents' house, and she'd decided that he was the one. Gordon-from-Florida had bought every line. It wasn't the loss of his own profound love that he was mourning, it was the loss of his belief in hers. Laura walked over to Gordon and put her arms around his waist, laying her body against his spine. He hadn't known she was playing a part. Laura had always thought that, over time, the act would soften into the truth.

"I'm not," Laura said. Louis Gardner had a wife, Maxine, and two plain-looking daughters, both of whom were enrolled in secondary school at Marlborough. Maxine always looked uncomfortable in furs and dresses with sequins on them, but Louis would drag her out anyway. People at the studio said horrible things, compared the three Gardner women to farm animals, though the girls were nice enough. Louis had been married for twenty-five years already, and Maxine predated any success. They'd worked at silent-film houses together in Pittsburgh. Laura couldn't imagine Louis as a young man, without any of the trappings of power he surrounded himself with now. She imagined him like a paper doll, always the same, no matter the year, with little tabbed suits and ties to fold around his body. That was the kind of marriage she could have had with Gordon, if she'd been content to stay home. Irving Green had never been married—he wasn't so much older than Laura, only in his early thirties, still a young man, despite all his success. He'd been too busy to get married, Laura thought. Plus, he'd never met the right girl.

"It's okay," Gordon said, without turning around. "I would too."

Somewhere in the house, Florence wailed. Laura felt the nubby wool of Gordon's jacket against her cheek. His body stiffened— the babies had not been his idea, as they hadn't been hers. The girls had arrived, as children did, whether or not they were invited. Was that it? Maybe it wasn't the drinking, or the fact that he and Laura had little in common except their shared desire to leave their hometowns and live big lives. Maybe it was that there were children, two tiny people who had not existed in the universe before. Laura felt sorry for Gordon; she could feel how badly he wanted to bolt, how unnatural it all felt to him. Some people couldn't take care of a dog, let alone a child. Gordon seemed more and more like he was one of those people, doomed to always have empty cupboards and no plan beyond his evening's entertainment.

Gordon shrugged out of Laura's arms and walked himself to the front door. It was his last visit to the house, and more than ten years before either Clara or Florence saw their father in person again, and by then they needed to be reminded who he was.

Irving Green had an idea every thirty-five seconds. Laura liked to time him. Sometimes they were about her career, but sometimes they were just about the studio—he wanted to bring in elephants for a party, and offer rides. He wanted to hire a French chef for the commissary, to make crepes. Had she ever had a crepe? Irving told Laura that he'd take her to Paris for her twenty-fifth birthday. They hadn't slept together yet; Laura hadn't lied. But she would also be lying if she said she didn't see it coming, cresting somewhere on the horizon. She'd heard things about his previous flirtations, including Dolores Dee; there were so many pretty girls around, how could she expect to have been his first temptation? And Laura wasn't interested in being anyone's fling. Before anything happened—before Paris, before sex—she would be a star, a real one, and there would be a firm understanding of exactly what was going on. Elsa hadn't become Laura to become someone's wife, and Irving had promised, though not in those exact words. What he'd actually said had more to do with what he wanted to do with Laura once she *was* his wife, and they were living in the same house. It made Laura blush even to think about it.

Irving had a part in mind, a movie about a nurse and a soldier. Nothing like the last movie. Ginger was a comedienne; that was what the studio had decided—let her stick with the funny stuff, the Susie and Johnny business. She did pratfalls and made goofy faces. Laura was something else—she was a real actress, Irving was sure. The movie was a drama about love torn asunder by war. No dance numbers, no parasols. He told Laura that she would have to dye her hair a good dark brown, the color of melting chocolate. As if she had a choice, Laura said yes, and started that night painting her eyebrows using a darker pencil.

He wanted to watch the hair girls do it. The hairdressers were used to Irving sitting in on important fittings with Cosmo and Edna, the costume designers, but it was unusual for a simple dye job, and made Laura even more nervous. Florence was so young—what if she didn't recognize her? What if Clara hated it? When Laura told Ginger what they were planning to do, Ginger screwed up her face and shook her head. "Nope," she said. "You're a blonde, inside and out. This is just weird." But Laura didn't have a choice, and didn't struggle when Irving led her to the chair by her elbow.

"Dark," he said to the girls, who were already mixing a bowlful of nearly black goo. "Serious."

"Scared." Laura had never been anything but a blonde. Dark-haired people stood out in Door County like people who were missing a hand. Almost all of the natives were blond and fair, Norwegian or Swedish blood pumping strongly through their American veins. If she went back now, her mother and father would pause at the door, their hands still on the knob, unsure of whether or not to let her in. She locked eyes with Irving in the mirror. Bright, naked bulbs ringed his face like a halo, which seemed funny. Irving wasn't an angel; he was a businessman, the first she'd ever really known. Even though Irving was physically small and slight, with his famously bad heart ticking slowly inside him, Laura never thought of him that way—he had the confidence of a lumberjack, or a lion tamer, or a black bear. Laura trusted him implicitly. If he wanted to dye her hair himself, she would have let him.

"This is going to be good for you," Irving said. "You have to do it, Laura. I know it, trust me. This is going to be what sets you apart. Think about Susie—that's a blonde, all surface, all air. You're something different. You're better." He looked to the girls and nodded. "Do it."

Laura shut her eyes tight and waited for them to start. The dye was thick and cold against her scalp, the way she imagined wet cement might feel. It didn't take long, maybe an hour. One of the girls, a tiny blonde with rubber gloves up to her elbows, told Laura to open her eyes. First she held out her hand, and Irving took it, giving her fingers a quick squeeze.

"Look at yourself," he said. "Laura Lamont, open your eyes." His voice was gentle; he liked what he saw.

Laura blinked a few times, and focused on the stained towel in her lap, her free hand clutching at her dress. She looked up slowly, and by the time she made it to her own face in the mirror, she knew that Irving had been right. Her skin had always been pink; now it was alabaster. Her eyes had always been pale; now they were the first things she saw, giant and blue.

"Wow," she said, turning her head from side to side. "Look at me." She covered her mouth with her hands, embarrassed at her own reaction.

Irving was already looking. He bent his knees to crouch beside her chair.

"Look at you," Irving repeated. He kissed her on the forehead, and then on the mouth, and the girls pretended to be occupied in the back of the room. Irving's lips were stronger than Laura anticipated, and pressed against her with the force of a man who had kissed many, many women before, and had no doubt in his own abilities. She closed her eyes and made him be the one to pull away. Once Irving straightened up and ran a hand over his hair, the hairdressers still tittering and chatting and washing things in the backroom sink, he helped Laura to her feet. Five-foot-seven when barefoot, Laura was taller than Irving by a few full inches, more in her high heels. Irving didn't seem to mind, and so neither did she. In fact, Laura never thought about their difference in size ever again. It wasn't every man who could make a woman forget that she was the larger in the pair, who could make a woman feel sexy when every part of her body was heavier, but Irving was that kind of man.

Laura pulled the hairdresser's cape off her shoulders and set it down on the chair. She couldn't take her eyes off herself in the mirror.

"So," she said, shifting her gaze from her own reflection to Irving's. "Tell me about this part."

The script was based on a novel written by a macho writer Laura had heard of, but never read, a writer her father loved. *The Ballad of Bayonets* was a period piece about the revolutionary war. Irving and Louis Gardner were betting on the audience's desire to see an earlier war, one that was well resolved and in the past. Men around the studio were starting to enlist—several dolly grips and best boys, several actors, even some big names—Johnny made a big show of telling the press he would enlist if he could, but he had flat feet and a bad ear. Some of the other studios were making war pictures too, and Laura kept her mouth shut around Irving, even though she worried it might all be in bad taste. Her contract was for twice what Gordon's had been, and Irving assured her it was only the beginning.

Her character was a woman named Nellie Smith, and she fell in love with a wounded soldier she was nursing back to health after the loss of his right leg. Clara loved the idea of her mother as a nurse, and so Laura had two child-size versions of her nurse costume made for the girls. Clara wore hers to school every day, and Harriet reported that she rarely took it off when she came home, choosing instead to run tests on all the other children in the neighborhood.

Three days into the film, the actor playing Laura's love interest fell ill with appendicitis and had to be taken to the hospital. ("Isn't that the point?" Ginger had joked. "That he's supposed to be sick, and you're supposed to take care of him?") It was Irving's idea to replace him with Gordon.

"Gordon Pitts?" Laura asked. "My Gordon?"

"He's not your Gordon anymore," Irving said, already holding the telephone in hand. His voice was hard, definite. There was no argument Laura could make that would sway him, she knew, but she tried anyway. She knew as well as Irving did that Gordon played broken better than anyone else on the lot.

"What about Johnny?" She knew it was a long shot. Johnny'd been out of Gardner Brothers' favor as of late, thanks to a gambling problem he'd acquired while filming *Las Vegas Is for Lovers*, a romance about mistaken identity and shotgun weddings that culminated in a scene with Susie and Johnny racing from one chapel to the next, a herd of angry mobsters trailing behind them.

Irving held up a finger. Someone was on the other line. "Get me Gordon Pitts," he said. "I don't care what kind of hole you have to go down to find him." And that was that. Laura stood in the doorway as Irving called the director and wardrobe. Everything would need to be taken in.

"There," he said when he was through. "That should make it more interesting."

❧

Gordon was late to the set every single morning. More than half the scenes were just the two of them, which meant that more often than not, Laura would arrive, get dressed, have her makeup done, and then sit in a canvas folding chair for an hour, watching grips carry things back and forth across the set. A flock of extras gathered nearby, all smoking in their knickers and bonnets. Peggy Bates had a real part, another nurse in the unit, and Laura was surprised at how calm she seemed after they called "Action," how her nervous energy could be boxed up and put away. Nurses made Laura think about her sister Josephine, who had always hung around with nurses, and could have sewn together a wound without flinching.

The first day of shooting, when Gordon finally arrived a half hour late, he ambled over to the director, J. J. Rush, and began to apologize. J.J. wasn't known for his patience, and Laura couldn't help but watch as Gordon's already stooped shoulders seemed to lower several more inches to the ground as J.J. laid into him. All the extras stomped on their cigarettes and scurried off to their proper places. When Gordon turned, his eyes swept over Laura and onto the rest of the set, only to backtrack—was it really her? When he realized he had already seen his former wife, Gordon stopped moving. Laura tried to stifle a smile when Gordon clomped up to her.

"What did you do to yourself?" Gordon pointed at Laura's head, in case she couldn't tell what he was blabbering on about.

"Don't you like it?" Laura put a hand under her hair, which the girls had curled into (she was fairly certain) historically inaccurate ringlets.

"You sure look different," Gordon said. He narrowed his eyes, taking her in as if for the first time.

The whites of Gordon's eyes looked yellow. Laura had to resist the urge to back away. "Thank you," Laura said, though she was sure he hadn't meant it as a compliment.

The first scene took place in Nellie's farmhouse, somewhere in Virginia. Laura sat on the bed until there was a knock on the door. Gordon's wounded soldier was on the other side, and she helped him in. They both still needed lines every so often, Gordon more often than Laura. The script girl moved so that she was closer to him. If necessary, J.J. said, they'd write all his dialogue out on cards. It had been done before. Laura wished that Gordon would pull it together: He was a good actor; she believed that. She never would have married a bad actor. When they had acted together in Door County, Gordon had had something better than average, a darker bloodline that ran much closer to the bone than most of the summertime boys. It wasn't so different than it was for her, Laura imagined, watching Gordon murmur his lines to himself in between takes—there was a part of Gordon, buried deep inside his body, that he was trying to reach. The only real question Laura had was whether Gordon could stay close to the good part of himself, the actorly part, when this other, larger beast was trying to take over. Gordon coughed, and kept putting all his weight on the leg that was supposed to be shot and broken and infected. Everyone turned away and waited for him to finish.

"Sorry, J.J., I'm sorry," he said, still hacking away. "There must be something caught in my throat." When the script girl started rolling her eyes, Laura knew he was in trouble. Gordon coughed something up and spit it into his handkerchief.

The bonnet itched. The shoes were flat and square, like something her mother would have worn. Laura was nervous that everything she thought showed on her face. The camera got so much closer than it ever had before. When it was her and Ginger in their matching dresses, the camera was never less than ten feet away, skimming over the surface of their youthful exuberance. Now the camera's lens hovered over her like a lover, its open, round eye coming ever closer.

"Is Irving here?" They were in between shots, and Laura couldn't breathe. There were too many layers of clothing, and Edna, the assistant costume designer, had wound too many ribbons around her neck, which began to feel as if it were being strangled. She started tugging at them, and wandered off the set, out of the three walls of the farmhouse, and onto the concrete floor of the soundstage. Several voices shouted at once, and the quick feet of grips and assistant cameramen ran off to find him. Laura stared at the ground, unable to move. A strand of her hair had fallen out and clung to her sleeve. She picked it up by its end like a worm in the garden and tried to fling it off, but it wouldn't go. "Can someone call Irving Green, please?" Edna hurried over, her legs moving as quickly as her narrow skirt suit would allow. There were pins sticking out of the hem of her skirt, and a little cushion strapped to the back of her hand. She knelt down next to Laura and loosened several items at once, her tiny, birdlike hands moving furiously. Laura moved onto her hands and knees, as though she were playing with Clara and Florence on her own rug at home and not surrounded by grown-up people who might think ill of her if she began to vomit. Her neck, it was her neck. She should have remembered to tell them she couldn't have anything on it; she should have told them that her neck was off-limits, nonnegotiable, no matter what the costume designer said.

"Laura, what's going on?" Irving arrived quickly, relieving

Edna. He'd been in his office bungalow, where he almost always slept and ate all of his meals. If nothing else, Irving Green was an easy man to find. Despite his presence, which did calm Laura a bit, the room was too warm still, and her entire body felt damp and feverish. Laura held out her hand, and Irving helped her stand up. The extras all pretended to look away, but Laura knew how strong the impulse was to get Irving's attention.

"I don't think I can do it," she said softly, so that only he could hear. "I couldn't breathe." Laura pulled at her collar, trying to free up her heart, which was booming against her jaw, and felt as if it were about to burst.

"Why, because of Gordon?" He sounded so disappointed, as if she had let him down personally. He had expected more. Irving adjusted his glasses, and then leaned down to pick up the bonnet that had been tied tightly under Laura's chin, and the ribbons that had been so tight around her throat. "That's too much, don't you think?" Irving craned his neck, looking for Edna, who was still nearby. He wasn't talking to Laura anymore. Edna came over with a pair of scissors and snipped a few more things off, opening up Laura's costume so that her neck was free. Edna's small eyes focused on parts of Laura that only the camera would see. Hair and makeup rushed over to fluff Laura's ringlets.

"No," Laura said, although she wasn't sure whether she was telling the truth. She looked at Gordon, who kept readjusting his hat. He did look sickly. The casting had been good; as usual, Irving was right. "I've never had to be serious before. In front of the camera, I mean." In the theater, there were always people sitting right in front of you. Even with the few meager lights that her father had rigged in the barn, Laura could make out one person's nose, or another person's laugh. The audience had been right there with her, and she could react. What choice did she have now, to react to Gordon? Just looking at him made her sad. No, Laura thought, no. She could do it. When the nurse looked down at the soldier's gangrenous leg, its oozing and bleeding mess, she would see her husband and her own broken heart. Gordon hadn't broken it—no, Laura doubted that he would even know how. She had broken it herself when she'd climbed aboard that bus in Chicago, when she knew that she was hitching her wagon to Gordon's only temporarily. When she watched her father hold his own elbows and not turn away until the bus was gone, maybe not even then. Her father probably waited in that depot for hours, wanting to be there if she changed her mind and decided to come back. That was what she would see when she looked at Gordon; she would be Elsa, saying good-bye to her former life, her happy childhood and her sad one, all at once. Laura thought of Hildy's body and put her hands back to the collar of her dress, pulling it down and away from her face. She could heal Gordon's leg with her bare hands if she had to.

t night, someone would drive Laura home. Gardner Brothers had a fleet of cars, and Irving insisted. It was pleasant not to have to drive: Laura enjoyed waving good-bye to whoever was around and then folding herself into the backseat of a waiting car. Once inside, she could shut her eyes and lean her face against the leather headrest. She hadn't been in such nice cars before, and after the first few trips, Laura stopped telling the drivers where to go, because they had obviously already been informed. It was an odd feeling, that strangers knew who she was and where she lived, and that they cared, but Laura could get used to odd.

Harriet put the girls to bed and waited for Laura to have dinner, though Laura would never eat much. They sat together at the small kitchen table and whispered about the days, as if speaking in their regular voices would wake the girls up.

"Florence walked like a mermaid all afternoon," Harriet said. "Every time she took a step, she said, 'Squish, squish, squish.'"

"Oh, no," Laura said, her eyes widening with pride. "She's an actress."

"Some spice cake?" Harriet got up to clear their plates.

"I shouldn't."

Harriet brought over two plates with tiny slivers of cake. "Just a smidge. Hardly counts."

Laura nudged a bit of cake onto her fork and put the bite on her tongue, closing her lips around the fork. In every house Laura had ever lived in, the kitchen was always her favorite room, the place where conversations actually happened, rather than where they pretended to. It didn't matter how tired she was, and how long her day would be tomorrow. It was nice to be at home. Across the table, Harriet ate her piece in two swallows. "Let me get you another," Laura said. "They were awfully small pieces."

Harriet leaned back and hooked her hands behind her head. "I won't say no to that," she said, and laughed.

The filming went on longer than expected, nearly three months. Gardner Brothers rented an abandoned lot in Echo Park for the battle sequences. Laura appeared in only the final one, when she waded through the dead and dying men strewn about the field in search of Gordon's soldier. She found him dead, his healed leg having swiftly delivered him to the front lines of the war. When Laura collapsed over Gordon's body, she smelled his sweat and his foul breath, and the tears that she shed were real. When the film was released, the studio leaked photos of the final scene, and Laura's mascara-streaked face, to the "Facts of Hollywood Life" column in *Photoplay* magazine, which screamed that the two actors were in love. Only the people on the Gardner Brothers lot knew the truth, and they weren't talking. It all seemed so silly, so backward: When Laura and Gordon really were married, no one had cared, but now that she wanted nothing to do with him, everyone wanted to take their photo and whisper behind their backs. When Irving asked Laura and Gordon to sit next to each other at the premiere, they did so. Gordon sucked gin out of his flask throughout the entire film, clinking glasses with all the well-wishers. Laura couldn't stand to be next to him, but when the spotlight found them, she let him kiss her on the cheek. His lips were dry and cracked, no matter what the makeup girls put on him. Whatever he was putting inside his body was stronger. The girls were at home with Harriet; Irving was in the balcony with Louis Gardner and his stout family. *The Ballad of Bayonets* showed on screens all over the country, in movie houses large and small, and Laura Lamont was a star, through and through. The newspaper photographers snapped her photo when she left the theater alone, her white stole dragging behind her like a child's security blanket.

The announcement went out on the wires the morning after the opening: Gordon Pitts was so moved by his role that he had chosen to enlist in the United States Armed Forces, and he would be shipping off to basic training that afternoon. Louis Gardner was quoted as saying that he was proud of Gordon, as he was proud of all his employees who had chosen to serve their country. Such bravery! Such selflessness! Hearts were stirred from Santa Monica to Pasadena. Laura went to Irving's bungalow when she heard the news, thirdhand, from Ginger, who had shrugged.

"Did you know?" Laura asked, once one of Irving's fleet of secretaries had noiselessly shut the door. "Did you know he was going to do that?"

Irving took off his glasses and held them up toward the light. "In fact, I did."

"Gosh," Laura said, as she sank into the chair opposite his. She dropped her purse onto the floor. "I never took him for a soldier type. Or anything even close. I guess I didn't know him very well at all. I'm sort of impressed."

Irving stifled a laugh. "Oh, Laura." He got up and walked around the desk, toward the window that overlooked the lot. "I told Gordon Pitts that if he didn't get out of town, he would never work again. Not at Gardner Brothers, and not anywhere else." He fingered the blinds, peeking out into the world that he controlled. The Gardner Brothers water tower stood spitting distance from his window, the studio emblem painted ten feet high. You could see the water tower from anywhere in the lot, even from the cemetery on the other side of the lot's walls—you could see it from the studio next door. To see it out Irving's window reminded Laura that she was not the one in charge, no matter what she did.

Laura cocked her head to the side. "You made him go? To war?"

"Oh, they'll kick him around different training camps for months," Irving said, turning to face her. "He'll learn to shoot, to run. It'll be good for him. Who knows if he'll even see any real action. I'm not putting him to death, Laura, I'm not sending him to Hitler on a silver platter."

She was still working it out in her head. Gordon was gone—he wouldn't bother the girls, wouldn't ring her doorbell, wouldn't breathe his hot breath on her cheek. "You did that for me?" It was wrong of Irving, potentially lethal, and yet she was moved.

"You bet I did," Irving said. "I'd do it again too. That guy was a prick."

Laura laughed, but stopped herself quickly. "And Louis approved it? It's okay?" She tried to imagine Gordon in uniform, a real uniform instead of a costume, but realized she didn't know the difference. "Oh, God," Laura said, shaking her head.

"It's done, it's done," Irving said. "People will like Gordon more now. That's what I told him, and it's true."

Laura moved across the room to Irving. She held out her hands, and he took them, rubbing his thumbs over her knuckles. "Would you ever do it? Sign up, I mean?"

"Oh, they wouldn't take me. Too many childhood illnesses. Fluid in the wrong places. Hole in the heart. I'm like something out of a Victorian orphanage." And just like that, Irving confirmed everything she'd ever heard about him, as nonchalantly as if he were placing an order for dinner. Laura was glad he'd been a sick child: It meant that she could have him now, and keep him forever. He looked at her and smiled, as if amused at the expression on her face.

"And what about me?" Laura asked.

"What about you?" Irving sat on his desk and crossed his arms over his chest, amused.

"Shouldn't I do something too? Sell some bonds? Visit some troops?"

Irving shook his head. "Leave that to the Dolores Dees of the world. All you need to do is spend a couple shifts at the Hollywood Canteen. We need you *here*, my dear."

"Well, then," Laura said, and folded herself against him, her lips against his neck, then his cheek, then his mouth. "If you say so."

❧

Irving wanted to meet the girls, and to give them a proper tour of the studio, despite the fact that they'd been regular visitors on the lot the entirety of their young lives.

"Trust me," Irving said, and Laura did.

The plan was to meet in front of the schoolhouse at three p.m., when the girls were finished for the day. Florence was three and an excellent mimic, repeating back nearly everything she heard. Clara was five and quick on her feet, choreographing elaborate dance sequences that she then performed for her dolls. Laura stood in front of the schoolhouse building, her hands patting her thighs. It was a clear, bright afternoon, the only shadows cast by the buildings themselves, and by the trees. Laura wasn't used to going on dates with her children, or going on dates at all, really. Before they'd kissed, Laura had told herself that Irving was interested in her only professionally, as he was in all of his actresses. Surely he wasn't kissing them all the way he'd kissed her—Laura had kissed enough actors to know the difference between a real kiss and a manufactured one, kisses just for play. Irving rounded the corner from his bungalow, his small frame dipping from side to side as he walked quickly toward them.

"Girls!" Laura said. "Girls!" She scooted them in front of her and held their shoulders in place. Florence was too young to stand still for more than a split second, and was already rubbing her bottom against Laura's leg in a way that was embarrassing. "I'm sorry," she said, as Irving came closer. "She's still a baby, really."

"I'm not a baby!" Florence said. "Baby!"

Irving nodded hello to Laura and than sank directly to his knees in front of the girls, so that he was on their eye level.

"Hello, ladies," he said, and stuck out his hand for them to shake. They both giggled, and Clara curtsied, her elbow knocking into Florence's chest, which made Florence's face cloud over, with chances of showers ahead.

"Oh, no, no," Irving said. "There's no crying! We have too much to do! Come along, now." And with that he stood up and again held out his hand, this time for Florence to hold. Laura waited—Florence was a shy child, but good enough with strangers, from all her time on the lot. She wished that she could will her daughter into taking Irving's hand, and Clara toward his other side. Laura closed her eyes for a moment, and when she opened them, it was right there in front of her, the three of them pawed up like a merry little band of friends, starting their march down the sunny pathway.

❧

Six months later, Irving moved out of his modest house. The truth was, more often than not he slept in his office, which had a place to sleep and a private dining room, and so the house meant little to him. Louis and Maxine Gardner sent over a magnum of champagne, glad that Irving was finally taking a wife. He hired movers to come to Laura's house and pack anything she wanted to keep. She and the girls climbed into Irving's waiting car and drove to see the new house, where they would all live together. It wasn't in the neighborhood—Laura watched Ginger's house recede in the side-view mirror. Irving liked Beverly Hills, and so that was where they were going. The girls would have their own bedrooms, and a swimming pool. Laura supposed she'd always known that this was going to happen, and that it was the reason she'd never fully set up her household before. A girl needed a husband, a proper husband, to say whether or not he liked this lamp or that one, the sofa against this wall or that. And to manage the money, which Laura didn't like having to keep track of herself. So it was old-fashioned! *She* was old-fashioned. Laura couldn't do it all alone, and with the girls both running full speed across the wide grassy lawn, the new house seemed like a gorgeous, whitewashed opportunity.

The marriage took place in a judge's chamber at City Hall; it was the tallest building Laura had ever been inside. The service itself took less than five minutes. Ginger and Harriet acted as witnesses. Laura wanted to invite the girls, but Irving didn't think that was a good idea, too confusing. Irving's parents had died when he was very young, and Laura thought that it was therefore only fair that hers didn't come, either. It was family-free, efficient. The judge was brief and moved quickly through the state-issued phrases. Laura cried. She wore a cream-colored skirt suit that the chief costume designer, Cosmo, had created for the occasion, with draped lapels like sleeping lilies, and Ginger pinned some Queen Anne's lace into her chignon, where the delicate white fans stood out against her dark hair. When she looked at the photos later, Laura decided it was reasonable to think of it as her first wedding, because the previous one had been someone else. Elsa Emerson would never have been married in a courthouse, wearing a suit. Elsa Emerson wouldn't have known what to do with a man like Irving Green. Elsa and Laura, before and after. There were an endless number of things that Laura was going to do that Elsa never would, and she couldn't wait to find out what they were.

That evening, Harriet put the girls to sleep and Laura and Irving spent the night in the Biltmore Hotel. Their suite was larger than the house Laura and Gordon had lived in, with two rooms and a balcony. One of the hotel maids had used rose petals to draw a heart on top of the coverlet, no doubt at Irving's request. Laura excused herself and went into the bathroom to change—there were too many lights on in the room. She felt as if she were still on a film set, only this time she didn't want to be. One mostly pretend marriage was enough. The bathroom was mirrored from floor to ceiling, and Laura watched herself pee and then wash her hands and face. She thought about putting her makeup on again, but didn't. They were married—he could see her face. Without the dramatic eyebrows and painted lips, Laura's face looked so pale that she might fade away. It was the first time in days that Laura had seen her own freckles. It was almost summertime, and the sun had been out in full force. As a wedding gift, Ginger had given Laura a proper peignoir set, with peach-colored marabou feathers that hung off the sleeves. Laura unfolded the silky material and slid it over her body. She didn't need to go to Paris. All she needed was Irving. The thought of spending the rest of her life with him filled Laura with an actual, physical sense of relief, the same way that the cold water of Lake Michigan had been a relief on the hottest days of the year. The body of water was always there, winter or summer, wider and deeper than the eye could see.

Irving had turned off all the overhead lights, leaving only the bedside lamps illuminated. He was sitting up in bed, naked to the waist, with the top sheet falling loosely around his legs. His bare chest was speckled with brown hair, and his stomach receded behind his rib cage, concave against the sheet. His waist was as small as hers, and she'd never known it. Laura had a brief flash of all the things she still didn't know about her husband, and it filled her with both excitement and fear, like she'd just jumped out of an airplane with only a wedding ring. Irving still had his glasses on, and he adjusted them on his nose as Laura stepped out of the doorway.

"You look lovely, my bride."

"I don't have any makeup on," she said.

"Neither do I." Irving pulled down the sheet on the empty side of the bed. Laura walked quickly around the foot of the bed and climbed in, tucking her legs under the covers. Irving turned onto his side to face her.

"Are you nervous?" Laura asked. Her heart was a marching band, a polka band, a big band. Irving slid closer, and took her chin in his right hand, and led her face toward his. It wasn't anything like kissing Gordon, with his slippery tongue darting in and out like an archeological exploration. Irving was slow and persistent, his mouth strong and unafraid to seek out what it wanted. She could feel it in her belly button, in her spleen. Irving stopped and propped himself up on his elbows.

"You're the one who should be nervous," he said. "Once I take my glasses off, I won't be able to see anything. You could steal my wallet and I'll still be holding on to this pillow, telling it how nice it looks."

Laura chuckled. Her new husband reached up and pulled off his glasses. He folded them neatly and placed them on the nightstand. When he turned back to Laura, his face was brand-new. Everything looked bigger: his brown eyes, his Roman nose, his mouth. Laura cupped her hand around his cheek. Her entire body felt like it had been flooded with new blood, like her heart had decided to flush out every cynical thought she'd ever had about Gordon or love, and all she wanted was to have her husband as close to her as possible, forever. She crawled on top of him, not caring that the sheets were bunched up and in the way and then falling onto the floor. Irving's delicate hands slid her peignoir off her shoulders, and the silk felt like a sigh against her skin. When Laura felt Irving's mouth on her bare stomach, it was all she could do not to cry out, to shout to the world that something good had finally happened, something real. Then she remembered that her children were miles away, tucked safely into their beds, and no one would know or care if she did cry out, and so Laura did, over and over, until she and Irving were slick with sweat and panting for breath. When exhaustion forced them to sleep, they could hardly wait until morning to do it all over again.

4

THE STAR

Winter 1948

The polls were clear: Audiences wanted Laura Lamont either sultry or sad. After *The Ballad of Bayonets*, they swooned over her in *Girl Thief*, in which Laura crept around a hotel room on a remote Greek island, pilfering jewels and antiques. By the film's close, it was her heart that was stolen by a competing cat burglar played by Robert Hunter, whom everyone in Hollywood thought was a homosexual, and everyone in the rest of America thought was the handsomest bachelor in the world, both of which were equally true. The last scene of the movie showed them both wearing all black, standing outside a well-lit hotel, holding hands. They liked Laura most of all, however, in the role of Sister Eve in *Farewell, My Sister*. Sister Eve was a young nun who returned home to her family farm following the death of her twin. Sister Eve then fell in love with her dead sister's fiancé, resisted him, and turned back to God. *Farewell, My Sister* earned Laura an Academy Award nomination, as well as an endorsement from the

Catholic League of America, which included several young, good-looking politicians. Irving stayed by her side at every party, eyes narrowed at any dapper young man who had perhaps missed the lollipop-size diamond on Laura's left hand. When Laura put on the ring every morning, it felt gloriously heavy on her finger, as though all of Irving's tender love were riding on that single digit.

Louis Gardner himself called Laura to tell her to be sure to attend the Academy Awards ceremony, as if she would have missed it. Cosmo and Edna set to work on her dress, and Irving supervised all the fittings. Edna's first sketch was for a feathered cape, which Cosmo thought was gauche, given that so many of Hollywood's men were still overseas. Her second sketch was for a slinky black crepe gown with shoulders that jutted out, giving Laura the silhouette of an Amazon woman, larger than life and twice as fierce.

Cosmo and Edna brought the dress over to Laura and Irving's house, and set up a mini tailoring shop in the living room, to see how it moved.

"Don't you think the shoulders are a little large?" Laura said, tapping her fingers lightly against the elaborate black fabric draped over her collarbones.

Edna pulled the fabric tighter across her waist. "Which corset are you wearing?" she said in response. There were always at least a dozen pins held in between Edna's teeth, but she didn't seem to find them a hindrance. "No," she said, in answer to Laura's question.

"Irving?"

Her husband was standing by the door, at a distance, watching the way the gown moved. "Yes, dear?"

"What do you think?"

"I think you look like an Academy Award winner."

Edna applauded, and stuck in a few more pins across the back. Laura would rather have worn something more simply feminine—something satin, something that moved—but knew better than to argue. These were not her decisions to make.

Irving took the Academy Awards as an overdue opportunity to fly his in-laws and sister-in-law to California. Laura hadn't seen her parents in nearly ten years, since she was eighteen, and on the day they were due to arrive, Laura fussed nervously. She stood behind Harriet in the kitchen and questioned the thickness of the tomato slices she was cutting for the girls' lunch. At Irving's insistence, and despite Laura's protestations, Harriet was wearing a uniform, a stiff black dress with long sleeves and a white apron on top. Laura ordered Clara and Florence to change their clothes whenever a speck of childish filth appeared, as it often did, on their elbows or knees. Clara was nine years old, and always a mess. Her sister was slightly better, as she enjoyed playing outside less, and was more likely to be found under the bed playing with one of Laura's stoles that still had the face attached. Irving was not immune to Laura's critical eye, and was forced to change his tie three times, from brown to black and back again, and every time he coughed something into his hankie, Laura whisked it away into the laundry basket. Gardner Brothers sent a limousine to the airport, and Laura tried in vain to sit on the sofa with her ankles crossed and wait. Instead, she paced back and forth the length of the room, sitting for only a few seconds at a time before her body propelled itself up again.

The news of her second marriage had not been met with great

excitement. Laura was nervous to call, and had written a letter instead. John and Mary had written a letter back, though Josephine had telephoned to congratulate her, still no closer herself to a wedding. Though Gordon-from-Florida had been no one's idea of a perfect match, her parents had at least been able to set eyes on him before the blessed event occurred. That Irving Green was wealthy and powerful mattered little; he was an older man, and a Jew. How would he treat the Emerson girls, the erstwhile Pitts? Even thinking about her daughters, and the fact that they had not yet met her parents, made Laura's throat clamp shut and her head begin to throb. It was too much for one visit—she should have gone home to Wisconsin; she'd meant to, so many times. At first, Laura had been waiting for success, but when success arrived, she still didn't go. The Cherry County Playhouse was doing better than ever, due in no small part to her growing fame, Josephine had told her on the telephone. Laura could close her eyes and be in the barn whenever she liked, and the smell of the wood and hay never changed. It was almost too frightening to imagine the possibility that time had marched on in Door County as it had in California.

The doorbell rang, a simple *dong* that couldn't possibly contain all the notes it needed to. Laura was on her feet before she even realized she'd heard the sound, and halfway to the door in five seconds' time. She'd warned them about her dark hair, about her thin figure. She'd told them about Clara and Florence and Irving and Harriet and Ginger and everything else she could think of—the color of the walls, the shape of the house. There were no secrets waiting to be told (save, perhaps, Gordon's drinking and subsequent firing by the studio), but still Laura felt paralyzed with nerves. She had aged almost a decade. The room was too warm; they would surely think so. Laura wanted to hide in the bedroom and make Harriet answer the door—it was too much all at once, to just open a door and see them standing there, as though her parents were no different from the mailman. The doorbell rang again.

Laura twisted the knob and pulled the door open. Josephine stood in front, her thick finger still hovering before the bell. She'd cut her hair short, though not in the fashionable way Ginger recently had. Josephine's hair looked as coarse as straw, and stood on end. Laura wondered whether she'd cut it herself, but then remembered: Of course she had, just as Laura would have too, had she not left Door County. Her sister was standing at her door. It was almost too much to believe. Laura wanted to reach out and touch her sister's cheek, to know that what she was seeing was real.

"Elsa?" her father said. It was a shock to hear her old name pass so naturally through his lips, though of course Laura had expected him to use it. Josephine moved to the side and let him through. Before Laura could even take in the figure before her— white hair, sloping shoulders, soft belly—she was in his arms. When she closed her eyes, he smelled just the same. Laura briefly wondered why she had ever left home, when there was this much love there, this much warmth.

"Oh, Dad," she said. "Dad."

John pulled back, keeping his hands gripped tight around Laura's arms. Though his hair was all white, a downy shade the color of a pigeon's underbelly, her father did not look old to her the way her mother did. Mary stepped forward and stood at John's side. At the studio, the makeup ladies warned Laura not to smile too much, for fear it would give her wrinkles. Laura knew that her mother rarely smiled, but all the time she'd spent frowning seemed to have done an equally strong number on her face. Delicate, thin lines crisscrossed the skin around her eyes and mouth.

"Hello, Mother," Laura said, stepping forward to kiss her mother's cheek. Mary wrapped her arms around Laura and began to cry without the added histrionics of noise or tears. Her body jerked up and down for a few minutes, and when she was finished, she let go and straightened out her traveling dress. Laura pushed her hair off her forehead and led her family into her home.

"It's so garish," Mary said, looking around the room. "You must have spent a fortune on the lighting fixtures alone. Of course, it's not your money, really."

Laura brushed her finger against her own lips, as if it would soften her mother's words. In the center of the living room, Irving waited with his fingers knitted together at his waist. He looked so small, standing there all alone, so much smaller than her father, whose comforting heft she had forgotten. Laura hurried to his side, and saw the room as her parents did. The ceiling was high, as tall as the loft in the barn, tall enough for a family of giants. Covering the walls in a damask silk had been Laura's choice—she loved the way she could sink into the walls if Irving pushed her against them with his thin, taut arms, like they were always rolling around in bed, no matter where they were in the house. Surely her parents could see that on her face, that she'd become a sex-crazed harlot, a hysterical woman. The lights were too low—the whole room felt like a bordello. Thank God she hadn't chosen the red silk for the walls, as she'd considered. John, Mary, and Josephine shuffled into the room like herded cattle, their eyes looking everywhere except where they were going, which was toward Irving.

"Mom, Dad, Jo," Laura said. "This is Irving." She clung to his left elbow, both her arms wrapped around it like a human anchor. Irving stepped forward to greet them, and Laura stepped forward too, unable to let go. It was John who came to meet him first.

"Mr. Green," John said, "I'm a great admirer of your work."

"Mr. Emerson, please call me Irving." The men shook hands, and Laura wept, as she'd known she would. Harriet poked her head in from the hall that led to the girls' rooms, and Laura nodded at her—it was time to bring them in.

Clara and Florence appeared in the corner of the room, with Harriet's hands giving them a gentle shove onto the rug. Josephine saw them first. Laura was the family's only chance for grandchildren, for nieces and nephews; that was clear. There would be no first cousins, not on the Emerson side of any family tree. Hildy might have—Hildy would have, Laura thought—but Josephine was as likely to produce a child as she was to produce a Pegasus. There were words to describe women like her, Laura knew. There were actresses she knew at Gardner Brothers who kept only one another's company, who shared dressing rooms and beds and held one another tightly in the dark, just as she did with Irving. Laura didn't mind—what was the difference to her? Their parents had put it together over time, realized that Josephine wasn't going to marry one of the local farmer boys after all, but no one ever said a word. Hildy tried to say something to their mother once, the summer before she died. Josephine had just come back from a fishing trip in the bay, and was slick with watery goo, standing in the yard, gutting. Their mother had stuck a bar of soap into Hildy's mouth and clamped her hand over it. Elsa had watched in horror, and no one had ever mentioned it again.

The girls were holding hands. They were still as different as sisters could be: Clara was tall for her age—the doctors always said so—with full cheeks and a face like sunshine, always beaming at everyone at once. Florence was small, with long, thin limbs, and dark hair that hung down past her shoulders. She was whip-smart and, at six, could read to herself, which her older sister could not. Laura wanted to brag to her parents, to show off her beautiful children, but she didn't know where to start. Hadn't Laura asked Harriet to pin their hair back? She'd wanted them to look flawless, like two human diamonds, and instead they just looked like little girls.

"Sweeties," Laura said. "Come and meet your grandparents." The word meant nothing to them—how could it? It was like calling a truck a lorry, or calling gasoline petrol. It just wasn't how things were done here, assigning such clear names to people, and anyway, Clara and Florence had made it this far without anyone but her. The word *father* was tricky enough, with Gordon expunged from the record and Irving still fairly new. They called him Pop, or Poppa, at his request, but Laura wondered how long it would last, and what it was doing to their tiny emotions to throw such words around. She wanted the girls to love Irving as much as she did, of course, but one couldn't force such things into being true. He wasn't a natural with the girls, but he was trying, which was more than Gordon had ever done.

The limousine came at half past four to take them to the Biltmore for the ceremony: Laura, Irving, and her parents. They would be seated at a round table with the rest of the cast from *Farewell, My Sister*, with Louis and Maxine Gardner at the next table with Susie and Johnny, who weren't nominated for anything, and were sure to drink too much and embarrass the studio if left unsupervised. Laura had heard that Johnny had recently bought a ranch with half a dozen horses and thirty pigs, and was thinking about going into car racing professionally. Susie wore a sequined dress that surely weighed more than she did, and shook almost imperceptibly when there wasn't alcohol slipping down her throat. Laura tried not to stare, just as she noticed other actors and actresses at tables farther back trying not to stare at her. It was all a game—she could see that, even then, when it was all as shiny as a baby's toy. There was always someone new, someone fresh. Laura hadn't admitted to Irving how much she wanted to win, but she did, especially with her father at her side. She wanted to climb onto that stage and have every single eye in the room trained straight on her. It was the same feeling she'd had as child, when she first stepped out onto her father's stage and felt the audience's gaze firm upon her face.

Irving had been to the awards before, every year since they began, but everyone else was nervous and fidgeting with their buttons and purse clasps. Laura felt ashamed that her first panic of the day arrived when she realized she didn't know what her parents would wear—they didn't have the clothes for the occasion. But Cosmo and Edna had thought of that, and there was a suit in John's approximate size and a gown in Mary's, with Edna on hand to make any and all necessary adjustments. There were only the two extra tickets, but Josephine seemed pleased to stay home with Harriet and the girls, so they could all get to know one another better.

It helped that Mary didn't know who any of the stars were. Laura watched her mother squirm in her seat, flinching whenever addressed directly by the waiters. It was as if she hadn't been around actors her entire life, around directors and writers and all sorts of dramatic types. *This is your life*, Laura wanted to say, *only bigger!* But Mary was struck mute by the flashbulbs, the champagne glasses that were refilled whenever they even approached empty, the feathers. (Edna had been right; there were feathers everywhere, sticking off hats and off brooches and shoulders and shoes—instead of pretending to be somber in the face of war, almost everyone seemed to be celebrating the fact that *they* hadn't gone, that *they* were still here, and wasn't it their American duty to look glamorous, after all?) John was more gregarious than his wife, and complimented all the actors and directors on their fine work. He'd seen everything; Laura had forgotten how much her father cared. He'd seen every movie she'd ever made, not that it was such a staggering number yet, only six. They were sitting next to each other, with Irving on Laura's other side and Mary on John's. Even Laura wasn't used to seeing so many stars in one room—it wasn't just Gardner Brothers, it was everyone in Hollywood, the entire parade! Robert Hunter looked so handsome in his tuxedo that all the men and women in the room swooned simultaneously, as if his body had been engineered for that purpose alone, to walk across a room in a good-looking suit. Dolores Dee had somehow muscled her way in, and sat one table back, her seat pointing away from the stage, which was where they put people no one cared about anymore. Susie and Johnny looked like country bumpkins next to Hunter, too suntanned and noisy. Laura saw Joan Fontaine going into the ladies' lounge and nearly followed her in.

It was different being off the Gardner Brothers lot, where everyone knew Laura and saw her every day, working like everybody else. At the Biltmore, actors and directors from other studios came up to her as well, and congratulated Laura on her achievement. She so rarely left the house without Irving that Laura sometimes forgot that other people knew who she was, that her face belonged in the public domain. Every now and then she would go to the grocery store with Harriet, and the whole place would begin to move in slow motion, as necks craned around aisles in order to keep her in their sights, whispers spreading around the store like brushfire, hopping from one shopper to the next. Laura thought of it like hunting, when her father would sometimes let her tag along when she was a girl, how the world would slow to the pace of your own breath, and everything else would disappear. She didn't feel *hunted*, not exactly, just under observation. Irving and Louis kept close behind her, lest any producers try to whisper seductively into her ear.

Still, it was difficult to enjoy the evening when every time Laura looked at her mother, Mary's mouth was clamped in a tight knot, her face pointed at the tablecloth.

"How are the flowers this year, Mother?" Laura said, leaning over her father's plate.

Mary exhaled hard through her nose, like an angry bull. "This year?" she said. "It's the winter, Elsa. I suppose you've forgotten what Wisconsin looks like in the winter. I think you've spent too much time with the wrong kind of people, and you've forgotten where you came from."

Irving's head snapped back around, as did John's. "What was that, dear?" John said, clearly hoping to have misheard his wife.

"She thinks I've abandoned her," Laura said.

"I didn't say that, but I might have," Mary said. She crossed her arms over her stomach, the dress pulling at her shoulders. "All the money in the world only makes people greedier, you know."

"Mary!" John said.

"John, I can speak for myself."

Irving pulled Laura backward, so that the nape of her neck was flat against his mouth. "Don't listen to her," he said. "This is your night, not hers." Laura turned into his chest, and away from her mother. Mary wouldn't have admitted to being anti-Semitic; she supported whatever America supported, but damn it if she didn't agree that the Jews were trouble. That was her problem with Irving, Laura knew. She didn't want to think about what anyone at the neighboring tables might have heard, or whether any of the gossip writers were in the room, or whether even Irving, her dear, sweet Irving, would think differently about her now that he knew the truth. Laura *felt* wretched next to her mother, because it should have been Hildy here in Hollywood, and she—still Elsa, always Elsa—should have been at home, back in Door County, her entire world only as wide as the peninsula. It was all wrong; Laura knew that. She was a body double, and her mother was the only one who saw it. Her dress pulled tight across her hips—it wasn't made for sitting, not really. Laura wished that she could flutter her eyelids shut and open them on Cherry County Playhouse Road. Irving rubbed her left hand between both of his, his small palms moving briskly. He probably thought her mother was a total cow. He didn't understand, and there was no way Laura could tell him. Across the table, Mary turned her face away from the stage and stared into the crowd. Her mother was stronger and angrier than any of the people in the room, Laura knew, no matter how much she looked like a trussed-up turkey, no matter any of it. Mary had suffered more than they had, and Laura knew that the real problem wasn't with her, or with Irving. Next to her, everyone else in the room was held together with glitter and glue, with only Hollywood troubles, the kind that were solved by the end of the picture. Laura wiped at her eyes and focused on the stage.

Her category—Best Actress in a Motion Picture—was one of the last of the night, and so there was much clapping and nodding beforehand, though Laura didn't hear a single word. She tried to stay calm, and to pretend that her mother hadn't opened her mouth all night, and that everything was right as rain. All the other nominees in her category were in the room, and they looked beautiful, with the light from the giant chandeliers making everyone sparkle even more than usual. The actor announcing was handsome; Laura recognized him from his most recent film, a World War I drama in which he'd played a brave pilot, always with the wind whipping his scarf around his neck. Louis Gardner and Irving went to see every movie, or rather had everything brought to them, watching them in the screening room on the studio lot. There were rumors about poaching, but Laura didn't believe them. People came to Gardner Brothers when they were ready for something new, something better. It had nothing to do with Irving. She gripped his hand under the table as the actor read her name along with the others. He paused before opening the envelope, as they always did—these were actors, after all, and every moment in the spotlight was as precious to them as oxygen.

Though Laura very much wanted to win, it was absolutely true that both Irving and her father wanted it even more. She watched their faces as the syllables came out of the actor's mouth—Lore-ah Lah-monde—and the rest of the room, so full of applause, felt silent to her ears. All Laura could see or hear were the two men who loved her the most, now standing up to embrace each other over her head, their suit jackets flapping about her ears. Laura wedged her way between them and kissed her father on the cheek and then her husband on the mouth, being careful not to muss her lipstick. Mary remained seated, the only one at the table. Laura had a fleeting, uncharitable thought that people might think that her mother was crippled, which was better than their knowing the truth: that her mother was reluctant to stand up and clap. A young man who looked like some military-school dropout appeared at the bottom of the ballroom's staircase to help her to the podium and the microphone, where Laura blinked into the lights and said simply, "My parents are here," which was indeed what she was thinking at the time, but not nearly for the reason the giddy audience may have thought. When they'd quieted down, and she felt more composed, Laura thanked Gardner Brothers, and all the voters, though she could have said anything at all and not realized it, so amazed was she by the heft of the statue itself, eight pounds, nearly the same as Florence when she was born, and how delightful it felt in her hands.

Irving sent John and Mary home after the awards, and had another car take him and Laura to the Gardner Brothers' party, where everyone pretended to be overjoyed for Laura, whether or not it was true. Susie, who had never won an Oscar, marched straight up to Laura and grabbed her by the wrist. "I'm so *happy* for you," she said, her mouth a tight, cold dash of red without a hint of a smile, and then turned straight back around and walked away. When they got home late that evening, Laura woke up the girls to show them the golden man with her name on it. Florence wanted to sleep with it next to her, and Laura promised that she could win another one, maybe next year, so that she and her sister could each have one, and it would be fair. That seemed good enough for Florence, who promptly fell back asleep with her mouth wide open, as nonplussed as if her mother had won a Cracker Jack prize out of a cardboard box. Instead of tucking the golden statue in with Florence, Laura took it to her own bed and placed it on the pillow between her head and Irving's, so that they could both see it until they fell asleep. That night, Laura dreamed of the ceremony taking place in her parents' barn, with both her sisters at the next table, laughing and toasting one another again and again, and when Laura awoke, the sound of Hildy's laugh was still in her ears, so, so delighted. It was only a few minutes later that she remembered her mother's consternation, and wished that she didn't have to get out of bed.

⸺ ❦ ⸺

The morning after the ceremony, the house woke slowly, with everyone wanting not to be the first. Harriet, back in her usual clothes, made coffee for herself and breakfast for the girls, who clung to sleep more fiercely than usual, as if their bodies had absorbed the monumental shift in their mother's world, their eyelids still heavy when they lumbered out of bed and into the kitchen. Josephine had woken early and left the house on her own for a walk, which no one in Beverly Hills did unless they had a dog. Laura could feel the house beginning to move—whether or not it was real, she felt that she could hear all the familiar noises her parents had made when she was a child, but echoing now through her own walls and hallways. Her father grunted as he rose from the bed; her mother blew her nose once, and then again, with force. Laura held Irving's waist as he tried to get up.

"Don't leave me," she said, burying her face into his back.

"I'm not leaving you, I'm going to be polite to your parents." Irving had won awards before, for the studio, and didn't need the morning to recover. Laura reluctantly released Irving, who then turned around and kissed her on the forehead. "You won," he said, as if she could have forgotten. Laura watched him close the door behind him, and thought that he was wrong: Had she been a failure, this new creation, Mary would have reacted less harshly. Had she married another young actor with a less ethnic surname, Mary might even have been happy. And so Laura hardly felt that she'd won at all.

Once everyone was awake and accounted for, and Josephine returned from her predawn stroll, it was decided that a family outing was in order. The Emersons wanted to see the ocean, which Laura thought was because they didn't actually believe it was any bigger than Lake Michigan. Mary thought it sounded far away, and didn't want to put anyone out, but John insisted. They drove two cars: Irving at the wheel of his black Cadillac, and Laura in her maroon convertible. The children went with Irving, and the Emersons all climbed in with Laura, which made the zippiness she usually felt when driving the car vanish completely. Her mother and sister both insisted on climbing into the back, which was barely big enough for Clara and Florence, and her father's knees hit the dashboard when he sat down in front. Laura thought about calling out to Irving about swapping some passengers, but then the car started and pulled away. John ran his hand over his side of the dashboard.

"Nice-looking automobile, Elsa," he said, and caught himself. "Laura."

"You can still call me Elsa, Dad," she said. "You can call me whatever you like."

In the back, Mary released a small groan, an involuntary noise like being walloped in the gut, but shook her head when Laura turned around to face her.

"To the beach!" John said, urging the car to move with a raised fist. They rode the rest of the way in silence, Josephine's and Mary's heads hitting against the cloth top whenever the car went over a bump.

❧

Florence and Clara were already out of the car and dancing around the parking lot when they arrived at the beach, doing interpretive movements of the sea and the wind, their sandals clopping gently against the concrete. Laura loved when they were together and speaking their own little bodily language, two feral cats with no need for speech. The girls were wonderful sisters, truly a pair. Neither girl had worn her bathing suit, as it was too cold for swimming, but Florence was eager to play in the sand, and Clara was ready for a snack.

"Mother, I'd like an ice-cream cone, please," Clara said.

Mary shook her head, as though she'd never given her daughters a treat in their life. Laura wondered when it was that her mother has gotten so cold—when Laura was a child, her mother had seemed no-nonsense but still a mostly kind presence in the house. But then Laura identified the moment—*of course*—and moved on.

"When we get home, sweetie," Laura said, tucking Clara against her body, as if that would keep her from saying anything else that her mother would find distasteful. Irving leaned against his car and squinted out at the water. He was the only man Laura knew who liked the beach even less than she did; Irving had never been permitted to swim as a child because the chances of his taking ill were too great. She doubted he'd ever even seen a swimming pool before he moved to California. He'd probably never been in anything bigger than a bathtub. Seeing her husband so close to the sand, salty air whipping around his head, made her wish for a moment that her family had already gone home.

It hadn't occurred to Laura before that Irving reminded her of her father, but she saw it now. John was in charge of the Cherry County Playhouse just as Irving was in charge of Gardner Brothers studio, each one selecting scripts or plays from an endless stream of words and then putting those words into the mouths of their chosen actors. They chose women with bird-boned frames,

or women with bodies that filled their dresses; they chose men
with wide eyes or squinty eyes, men with shoulders the size of a
mountain range. They knew who could deliver which line, whose
lips were made to proclaim the words as if they were the truth.
When she was a child, Laura—no, *Elsa*—would sit at her father's
feet while he auditioned actors for the summer's productions, and
she would scratch her own notes into the floor with her fingertip,
invisible ink scrawled across the uneven floorboards. Was that really so different from what she did at home, when Irving would
come to her and tell her he was choosing between Peggy Bates and
Betty Lafayette for the second female lead in the new J. J. Rush
movie, deciding whether to go quirky or sexy? The only difference
was dollars in a bank account.

The money was tricky. Laura wondered whether her father
saw it as clearly as she did, or whether he was blinded by the
golden sheen of the light in Hollywood, the way every surface
seemed to glisten more brightly than the last. She looked down at
her clothes—even what she wore to bed was expensive. Her silk
pajama pants were tied tight around her hips, and the wind blew
them against her skin. She should have put on proper clothes,
something more modest.

Laura watched her father stare at the waves crashing against
the sand, some large and rough and some small, tightly curled as
lips ready for a kiss. When she was a little girl, Laura too had
imagined that no body of water could be larger than Lake Michigan, which seemed impossibly vast, the other shore well beyond
her line of vision. Some days she still felt that way, that the ocean
couldn't be that much larger, no matter what anyone said. How
did they know; had they been? Gordon might have known, she

supposed—he might have flown in a plane across the Pacific, look-ing out the window all the while. She didn't think of him often, but when she did, Laura felt a sharp pain in her stomach, as if that was where her conscience lived. It was her fault that he was gone, and whatever happened to him was, in some way, on her head. Irving didn't seem to believe in guilt, or in duty—he was a proper businessman, as straight as they came. The wind was picking up, and Irving moved toward Florence, who had sunk to her knees in the sand about ten feet away from the parking lot, her dark hair a nest behind her, going every which way. Sometimes Irving and Florence seemed so much alike, so much a pair, that Laura forgot that he wasn't her biological father. Irving had never once backed away from the girls, never once given them any less than a father should. They were his, and he was theirs. It was that simple.

"Mother," Laura said. She closed the gap between herself and her mother's back. Mary had wrapped a scarf around her head, and Laura mimicked her, so that the two of them were shielded together, as if that would help. Laura clutched the silk corners of the scarf under her chin, and repeated herself. "Mother."

Mary tucked her chin in toward her throat.

"I understand why this is all so distasteful to you," Laura said. Her mother still didn't turn, and so Laura stared at the side of her face, her flat profile. "But this is all for her, you know. All of it."

At this, Mary pivoted on her heels. "And to whom are you re-ferring?" Her eyes were tight brown slits.

"My sister."

"I don't see what that has to do with anything," Mary said into her shoulder. "We all make choices, Elsa. We all make choices."

"And you think I've made the wrong ones. I get it." Laura let the scarf blow off her head. She watched it sail down the beach. Florence started to run after it, but Irving called after her, and like a good daughter she stopped, silently agreeing to let it go. "And I don't appreciate the way you're treating my husband. In case you haven't noticed, the rest of us happen to love him."

"I remember the last one you said you loved too. At least then it seemed like you might come back someday." Mary hadn't always been so cruel: Laura tried to remember what her mother had been like when she was a child, when Hildy was still loafing around the house, every one of them so in love with her they could hardly speak.

"Mother," Laura said, reaching out to touch her on the arm. Now that she had Clara and Florence, she thought less about leaving and more about being left. It wasn't as easy as she'd imagined, getting away. There were roadblocks at every turn, always forcing you to circle back the way you came.

A wood-paneled wagon pulled up beside Irving's car, and a noisy bunch of teenagers spilled out into the parking lot. Mary moved a step closer to John. There were three girls and two boys, one too many for them to pair off and snuggle in the sand. Laura watched them paw at one another like a litter of puppies, and it was only when one of the girls looked up at her, eyes wide, that Laura realized she should have turned her face away. Sometimes Laura forgot that from the outside, other people couldn't tell the difference between Laura Lamont and Elsa Emerson, when she was so clearly feeling one way or the other. She'd been Elsa all morning.

"That's Laura Lamont, that's Laura Lamont!" The girl, a tall blonde with thick glasses—the fifth wheel, Laura guessed—

announced to her friends, who, seeing that she was right, and that the woman standing in the parking lot was indeed Laura Lamont, rushed to Laura's side, brandishing pens and scraps of paper torn from nowhere. The girls kept trying to touch Laura's clothing, as if one gentle hand against her sleeve would be something they could hold on to forever. The boys hung back at first, not wanting to seem like they cared, but in a minute's time they were crushing their bodies against their friends, trying to get as close as they could, to share a meaningful word.

Over the teenagers' bobbing heads, Laura saw her parents move farther and farther away, until they were halfway to the breaking waves, with her father pointed toward her and her mother pointed toward the water. Clara did clumsy pirouettes at Laura's side, her round face turned upward, toward the flurry of attention, just as Laura had done as a child. After a few minutes, Irving came around, Florence held aloft in his arms, and steered Laura to the front seat of his car. The teenagers hurried away, waving as they ran, their wool blankets flapping behind them. Laura and Irving watched John and Mary slowly make their way back across the sand, Mary's heels sinking further in with every step.

The Emersons left the following evening, after spending all day long with the girls and pronouncing them both wonderful. Josephine looked her sister in the face for a long time before saying, "You do look like a Laura now," and walking to the car. Laura ran after the car as it went down the driveway, blowing kisses like a lunatic, though she knew that neither her mother nor her sister

would have wanted her to make such a spectacle. Laura imagined
her father was twisting his body around in the backseat, trying to
catch every kiss she threw. She didn't know any of the neighbors
in Beverly Hills—if Ginger still lived down the street, she would
have run straight there. But Ginger lived too far away to go on
foot, and Harriet wanted to talk about what to feed the girls for
dinner, and Irving wanted time alone with his wife, and so Laura
turned around and walked back into her house, taking the smallest, slowest steps she could. She pulled her hair into two pigtails,
the kind of thing Susie was always doing in her movies so that she
could still play a teenage girl, as if no one had noticed the lines
forming around her eyes. When they arrived back in Wisconsin,
Laura's mother sent her a letter congratulating her on all her success, and saying that she was sure Laura wouldn't mind if she
wasn't in touch very often anymore, seeing as Laura was so busy
and they had so little in common. The letter went on to say that
Mary was sorry she'd been so stupid as to name her Elsa, as it
had proven an inferior choice, and that she hoped very much that
Laura's own daughters would never hurt her so deeply. It was the
longest letter Laura had ever received from her mother, and she
read it over and over again, crying more each time, until Irving
took the letter away and threw it in the fireplace.

⌒

It was Laura's twenty-eighth birthday, and they still hadn't gone
to Paris. Laura knew that Irving needed to be close to the
studio—the phone rang at every restaurant in town, and his secretaries always seemed to know when he was at the breakfast

table, awake and alert. There were stars who traveled with their children, taking over entire floors of expensive hotels, with rooms set aside for their dogs and parakeets, but Laura wasn't one of those. She liked to be at home with the girls, and to feel like they were as normal a family as possible.

Her birthday had never been Laura's favorite holiday, what with the focus trained onto her and off the girls, and it was her first birthday when she knew her own mother wouldn't call. Laura stayed home with Harriet, having nothing to do on the lot except wander around and have people wish her a happy birthday.

"I don't feel twenty-eight," Laura said. They were making an omelette for lunch, with fresh tomatoes cooked inside. "I feel a hundred and seven."

"Well, you look about sixteen, so you should thank your lucky stars," Harriet said.

"You don't look any older!" Laura swatted at Harriet's arm.

"I too need to thank my lucky stars, it's true," Harriet said, rocking her hips from side to side. She held out the pan and slid the omelette onto a plate.

The front door opened and closed with a decisive thud, and Irving's voice called out, "Hello? My love?"

"What is he doing at home? It's the middle of the day!" Laura quickly dried her hands on her skirt. "In here!"

Irving bounded through the kitchen doorway and kissed Laura on the cheek. "She all ready, Harriet?"

"Bag is by the door." Harriet did a little ironic curtsy at Laura and took her lunch toward the table.

Irving held up one of his ties. "Turn around," he said, and Laura closed her eyes as he secured her temporary blindness. "I promise not to let you walk into any walls."

Laura let Irving guide her through their house and into his car, and resisted the urge to peek during their drive. She didn't ask where she was going, but she imagined that Harriet had packed whatever gown Irving deemed necessary, along with the shoes to match, and some nice jewelry that she wouldn't otherwise get to wear. Irving kept one hand on her knee as he drove, and Laura thought she wouldn't have minded spending her whole birthday just like that, in a state of suspended anticipation. But soon enough they stopped—it didn't feel like they'd gone farther than Beverly Hills, or Brentwood, maybe.

"Ready?" Irving said.

Laura reached up and felt the contours of her eyes through the silk of the tie. "Ready." She pulled it down, so that the fabric was resting around her chin. Straight ahead of them, clearly visible through the windshield, was Beverly Bowl, the bowling alley. "Are you serious?" Laura said. The parking lot was almost entirely empty, with only two other cars parked close to the entrance. Laura swiveled in her seat, trying to look around. "Are we the only ones here?"

"All for you, my bride."

"You do know that I'm going to beat you. Girls in Wisconsin know how to bowl, Irving. I am not afraid to beat you." Laura leaned forward and kissed him, the tie still between their faces.

"Harriet picked out an outfit. I ordered you a pair of shoes. They're inside."

Laura clapped her hands and quickly climbed out of the car. Irving walked slowly around to her side, and they walked into the alley hand in hand, as elegantly as a couple of teenagers on their first date, wanting both to show off and to rub against each other as often as possible until they exploded. When they left, several hours later, Laura and Irving would smell like French fries, and hand sweat, and cigarette smoke, and Coca-Cola, and neither of them could remember a better evening out.

5

THE DEN MOTHER

Spring 1949

Irving didn't want another girl, but he'd never have said so—
after all, they already had Clara and Florence, who now
climbed all over him and hid under his desk and pulled on his
earlobes and called him Pop without a moment's hesitation. When
Laura got the news that she was pregnant again, Irving bought
cigars for the entire studio. Everywhere Laura went, guys on their
breaks from sawing wood or rigging lights or acting a scene were
puffing away, their mouths opening and closing around the cigars
like so many guppies. The air above Gardner Brothers must have
smelled like Cuba.

There weren't any roles for pregnant women—not few, none.
Gardner Brothers had a policy that female stars should vanish
from public view as soon as they were showing, and reappear only
once their figures had been regained. Laura was happy for the
break, and spent all day at home with Harriet and the girls. All
four of them would be in the kitchen to watch Irving gulp down

two cups of coffee and inhale a piece of cheese Danish before heading to the studio. Florence would wrap her body around one of his legs, and Clara would serenade him with a song. Clara was always singing, ready to be the next Shirley Temple, even though she already outweighed Shirley by two to one and was about as dainty as a Holstein. Harriet, always discreet, would turn her back when Laura leaned down to kiss her husband good-bye, as though some things were too intimate to stare in the face. Of course, Harriet had lived with them for long enough—almost five years— that there was nothing she hadn't seen. Her room was on the other side of the kitchen, facing the back of the house. She went to visit family a few times a year, and had weekends off, and Laura never asked where she went. It seemed rude to impose a friendship on a relationship that already took up so much of Harriet's time. The girls treated Harriet as their second mother, which she was, and Laura knew that their nightly whispered secrets and pledges of eternal love were the reason she'd stayed so long.

With the new baby on the way, Laura wanted the house to be perfect. The palm trees lining the long, wide streets in Beverly Hills seemed like such fun: She wanted some of those in their yard. In one of Susie and Johnny's latest films, *The Sunshine Kid*, a beachy romp with a subplot about a baby abandoned in a wicker basket full of snorkeling gear, Susie had sung a song from a white woven hammock—Laura wanted one of those too. The swimming pool was cleaned and treated on a weekly basis, the flowers trimmed and tended just as often. The new baby would have his or her own room, even if it meant the girls would have to share. They were sisters; they would understand. A baby needed to have his own space; that was what Irving said, and Laura agreed. She was nervous about the possibility of having a son; the idea seemed so foreign, like having a baby that spoke only Chinese. She was a girl from a family of girls, raising another brood of girls—surely there were things that had to be done differently. Laura sat by the pool and watched Clara and Florence splash each other, their long wet hair plastered to their small backs. She didn't know how to speak to a boy, how to raise one to be a good man. There were some books at the library, but Laura was too embarrassed to check them out, and made Ginger do it.

"This one's written by a doctor," Ginger said, rolling her eyes. She had new sunglasses with pinky-brown lenses. The pink clashed with the red of her hair, which Laura knew had to be the point. The Gardner Brothers had made a string of screwball comedies starring Ginger as an eccentric widow who solved crimes, always with her tiny dog in tow. The role suited Ginger, and she'd taken to dressing the part even off the set. The dog, fortunately, was a professional, and lived at the animal trainer's house. While Irving had been grooming Laura to be a serious actress, he'd put Ginger on a different track. Her comedies were now Gardner Brothers' most successful property, always beating Susie and Johnny at the box office. Laura liked to think that it was the film that they made together that had done it, which was true, because before that Ginger had been only an extra, someone pacing back and forth, pretending to walk down the street, or a lone face in a crowded market. It wasn't that Laura wanted to take credit for Ginger's success, not precisely, though she did like to think that her own acting chops had brought something out of Ginger that Gardner Brothers hadn't seen before. "Really, Lore, how different can it be?"

"I don't know about you," Laura said, lowering her voice, "but I didn't even *see* a penis until I was seventeen."

Ginger loved it when Laura talked dirty. She said it was like hearing a librarian shout. "Ha! Oh, you poor thing. Okay then. Page one . . ." Then she opened the book and pretended to read. Despite her claims to the contrary, Laura knew that Ginger felt as strongly about being an actress as she did, that she lived for moments like this, when she could feed off the breath and hush and warmth of her audience, even when it was just one person.

If the child was indeed a boy, Laura would teach her son to be chivalrous, like his father. She would teach him manners, and the power of stoicism. She would teach him that frozen custard was better than ice cream, even if no one in all of Los Angeles made it. Together they would explore Griffith Park and look at the stars from the observatory. That seemed like something a boy would like, didn't it? She didn't know. Clara and Florence were easy children, most of the time—Laura knew they couldn't all be polite, so good.

"Mom, look, Mom, look!" Clara was running at top speed along the slick wet concrete lip of the pool, which Laura had told her not to do a thousand times. Florence bobbed in the pool, clapping her hands with delight as Clara pushed off. She flung her thick little body off the ground, and then crashed through the surface of the pool, sending great plumes of water into the air.

"Bravo!" Laura said. She laid the open book against her stomach, as though her unborn child could read it himself through all the layers of tissue and blood. Clara was missing two teeth, right in front. She climbed back out of the pool and did a little shimmy for her mother and Ginger, her hands gripping her waist like a showgirl, her wet hair sticking to her swimsuit in thick clumps. If Laura had stayed in Wisconsin, if she'd never become Laura at all, Clara might have been just the same, sashaying across the creaking boards of the playhouse. Florence looked more and more like Gordon as she got older: the small frame, the dark circles under her eyes, as if her daily troubles were already wearing her down. She could sit alone and read a book for hours, until after the sun set and the room was dark, never getting up to switch the light on. Laura wasn't sure what to make of her, but as long as Clara was there to help, they were fine. What couldn't some bows and ribbons fix, for a girl? Laura always felt happy when there was a box to open, some shiny paper to tear. Her girls were the same way. It wasn't that they were spoiled: They were lucky to have her, just as she was lucky to have them. Laura was sure they knew the difference. When she went back to work, Laura thought she'd like to do something funny again, maybe with kids. Ginger wasn't the only one who was a cutup. She rubbed the space where her belly button used to be, now flush against the rest of her skin. Laura would talk to Irving about it when he got home.

The boy was born on a Thursday morning in February, and despite the fact that it was bad luck in the Jewish faith to name a child after a living relative, Laura and Irving named him Irving Green Junior. Irving loved gallows humor, and claimed he'd die young, and the name wouldn't be taboo for long. At Laura's request, the doctors gave her half as much pain medication, and Irving was allowed to stand in the hallway just outside the delivery room. Junior—that was the nickname they'd chosen—was a small baby, only five pounds, and his father could hold him with one hand, though Laura insisted he use two. The baby looked so fragile, his arms like plucked chicken wings, that Laura was afraid he would stop breathing. The nurses insisted the boy was fine, but Laura threw a fit anyway, and extra tests were run. Later she thought that her anxiety was the flip side of the relief of having the baby outside her body, where she would no longer be the only one responsible for his well-being.

Being a father suited Irving—being a father to a son. He dressed Junior in miniature baseball uniforms and toted him around Gardner Brothers on his hip. It occurred to Laura that her husband had suffered the lack of men in his house as she had in hers—with no brothers or sons of his own, Irving was as surrounded by women as Laura had been. He worked at a studio named for imaginary brothers, for God's sake! Laura would have left the baby at home with Harriet, but Irving insisted he come along whenever she made the trip in for dance classes and the like. She'd tie a handkerchief around her head and hold the baby on her lap in the Cadillac while a Gardner Brothers' driver drove the six miles to the studio at a whopping top speed of twenty miles an hour, as per Irving's strict instructions.

Ginger cried when she saw Junior for the first time. She and Laura were sitting outside the commissary, enormous sunglasses blocking the winter sun. Junior was asleep in his custom-built Gardner Brothers pram, which had almost certainly been bought as a prop and then painted quickly after his birth. On one side, it read, GARDNER BROTHERS PRESENTS . . . and on the other side, IR-VING "JUNIOR" GREEN, JR.! Laura found it all downright silly, if not frankly embarrassing, but Irving loved it, and she couldn't argue with that. Ginger had recently gotten engaged to a man she'd met on a ranch in Colorado, a rodeo rider named Bill Balsam, and she'd been crying even more than usual.

"It's just that he's so perfect," Ginger said, tugging a hankie out of her bra. But Junior wasn't perfect; he remained small for his age, and spent most of his waking hours wailing at the top of his lungs. Laura thought that Florence was becoming a tricky child, what with her cloudy moods, but Junior seemed content only when he was asleep. She worried about him more than she'd worried about the girls, who'd both been born when she was too young to realize anything could go wrong.

"You think so?" Laura asked. Everything about Junior made her nervous—if it was the girls who had come between her and Gordon, what if Junior drove Irving away? It seemed unlikely, what with the fanfare and the endless stream of coos that came out of Irving's mouth, but she could never be sure.

"Perfect," Ginger said. She reached into the pram and spread her palm across Junior's chest. Both her thumb and her pinkie touched the padding beneath him. Ginger wanted babies; she'd told Laura so. There had been a first marriage, in her twenties, to a guy back home. They'd tried and tried to have kids, but every time, something inside went wrong, and Ginger would miscarry. Laura had never known anyone whom it had happened to before: At home, no one ever talked about things like that. But Ginger told her all the details. The sore breasts and missed menses that marked the pregnancy's arrival, the first sign of blood a few weeks later, then the horrible days of cramps and bleeding that took it all away. It took only a week, Ginger said, for her body to go back to normal, but only if you were counting in actual human days. In certain ways, that week never ended, but just kept getting longer and longer, the week that her body decided what was best. Moving to Hollywood was supposed to change all that—not the fact that her body wouldn't cooperate, but the fact that she cared. Ginger said that being an actress was something people did when their ordinary lives weren't good enough. Laura had told her about Hildy; she couldn't disagree. Now Ginger was getting too old to have kids of her own, but Bill didn't mind. Laura had seen them together. Bill wore denim tuxedos, blue jeans and a matching jacket, like he was always on a horse, with a wide-brimmed cowboy hat and, sometimes, leather chaps with his name stitched down the leg in a loopy script. He looked at Ginger like she was a giant slice of strawberry shortcake. Laura approved. As soon as their engagement was announced, Irving decided he was going to put Ginger and Bill on television, give them their own half-hour show once a week, in which they would play themselves, more or less. Ginger would be a lovable goof, and Bill would rein her in, lasso and all. The audience was going to love them, Irving was sure, and he'd given both Ginger and Bill bigger dressing rooms to prove it, plus one for Bill's horse, Clementine.

"I couldn't have one now anyway," Ginger said, as if she could hear Laura's silent cataloging in her head. "Not with the show. My schedule is packed already. I couldn't take the time off." She looked up at Laura, her big eyes hidden behind her sunglasses.

"Well, it's not a question of *could*," Laura said, now annoyed in spite of herself. "Of course I should still be working. It's just that when you're a mother, you have to prioritize. Some things are more important than others." Laura missed working; she didn't mean to be cruel. There were certain territories she hadn't figured out yet with girlfriends. They weren't quite the same as sisters, not exactly, with hurt feelings always threatening a schism. She regretted the words as soon as they were out of her mouth.

"You're right," Ginger said, and got up and walked out the door. Laura wanted to follow her, but Junior would have awoken if she'd picked him up, and her ears weren't ready for his next hungry wail. Instead, she watched Ginger's bright red pile of hair get smaller and smaller as she walked down the alley between the soundstages toward the cities that didn't exist.

<hr/>

Ginger didn't stay upset for long—that was part of her professional appeal. Sometimes it would take as long as a few days for her to regain her cool, but when she came back around, it was as if nothing had happened. Laura thought that Ginger would have done excellently well in Wisconsin, where no one ever talked about anything unpleasant, at least not in the Emerson house.

When Ginger and Bill got married, they moved to a horse farm in the canyons, up in Calabasas, which was light-years away from Beverly Hills in spirit, and about forty-five minutes in the car. The girls loved Clementine, and Laura liked the idea of getting out into nature for the day. Irving had never liked the outdoors particularly, but he liked seeing the girls happy, and so off they went, Irving behind the wheel, with Florence twiddling the radio knobs, and Laura, Clara, and Junior in the backseat, all playing "I Spy" out the window.

The farm was called Balsam Acres, though Ginger had paid

for it. Bill was waiting for them atop Clementine at the gate to the property, and the girls squealed with glee. The house was back from the road a good distance, and down a bit of a slope, so that it was totally hidden from view, with fruit trees ringing the porch like Christmas decorations.

"This reminds me of where I grew up," Laura said to Junior's soft scalp, already so close to her lips.

"Mom, look, more horses!" Clara said. Both the girls were wearing cowboy boots, earlier presents from Ginger that somehow still fit.

"Yes, I know, but be careful, remember? They're bigger than you are. And watch out for your sister." The girls scrambled out of the car and hurried up to the horse, who, as a trained professional, didn't flinch.

There was a hooting off in the distance, and the clanging of a bell, and then Ginger came closer, waving a hat over her head, beckoning the stragglers—Laura, Irving, and the baby—forward.

"Yee-haw," Irving said, and put his arm around Laura's back.

❦

Clara was a natural on the horse—she held the reins loosely, and gamely let herself be bounced around by the horse's even gait. Florence preferred the ground, but quite liked feeding carrots and apples to the horses roaming the paddock. Laura watched as Florence's whole body tensed up when the animals' big, soft lips would search her palm for another morsel.

Outside with the girls—really outside, not just on a soundstage with a backdrop painted to look like the mountains—Laura sat on the porch swing with Junior on her lap. Irving had ducked inside to make a phone call, which he promised would be short, and Bill was with the girls. Ginger came out onto the porch with two tall glasses of lemonade, and sat down next to Laura on the swing. After a moment, they settled into an easy rhythm, forward and back, forward and back, their heels and toes working in tandem as if on a shared bicycle.

"Irving's still on the phone with Louis," Ginger said.

"The story of my life," Laura said, and rolled her eyes. Junior gurgled out a noise, a spitty laugh, and both Laura and Ginger turned their attention to his sweet round cheeks and thighs.

"Sometimes I forget that the girls aren't his," Laura said, tracing her finger around Junior's belly.

"They're his, all right." Ginger nodded her chin out toward the horses. Florence stood with her back to the house, her hands on her hips, shaking her head at her sister. Her tiny bones had no idea how small they were, how delicate. "That's him, don't you think?"

The screen door clattered open. Irving stepped out onto the porch, reflexively smoothing his hair. Bill and Clara had started to go faster, a gentle, rocking canter, and Irving walked forward to get a better look. He put his hands on his hips, his pointy elbows jutting out like wings. "Look at our girl go!" he said, turning to Laura, shaking his head with pride and amazement.

It was another six months before Laura was back to her prepregnancy weight, and even then she was cheating the numbers a bit. Even Clara got tired of telling her mother that she looked thin. She was eleven, and strong enough to help Laura get into her girdles, to pull strings tight.

Laura wanted to be loaned out. The studios were doing it more and more—swapping around their stars for an added boost at the box office. People were crazy to see Susie dance with someone who wasn't Johnny, and it wasn't only because Johnny was looking the worse for wear. There was a movie shooting across town at Pierce Pictures, and Laura wanted in it, whatever it was. After her maternity leave, she wanted to be something *new*. After all, every single one of her pictures had been made by Gardner Brothers. She begged Irving until he relented.

"It's about *what*?" Laura asked Irving for the third time that morning. She couldn't keep it straight in her mind—since Junior was born, she'd been getting headaches, brain crushers like the Emerson women had always gotten, and she sometimes lost entire afternoons to the darkness of her bedroom. She thought it had to do with Junior, but couldn't say so without upsetting Irving, and so she kept it to herself. Sometimes she had the strangest urge to cover his tiny body with a pillow and leave the room. Not suffocate him, exactly, but arrange things so that it might happen. But then she would be so horrified at herself for even thinking it—not thinking about *doing* it, but even allowing the image to exist in her mind—that she would do penance by baking four batches of cookies and making the girls pass them out in the neighborhood.

"Conquistadors, my bride, conquistadors." Louis Gardner had spoken to Mr. Pierce himself, who assured him of the film's credentials, and then Louis had passed the information on to Irving. According to Mr. Pierce, conquistadors were the most exciting, adventure-seeking warriors never before seen on film. According to Louis, conquistadors were Spanish explorers who wore big helmets and had mustaches. According to Irving, they were the next knight, the next gladiator, the next war hero. Laura would play a Mexican woman, the daughter of a Mayan shaman, and wear a lot of lace. The studio had already requested that her brown hair be darkened to black. Laura protested—the actor playing her conquistador love interest was also bringing smallpox to the Americas; how was that supposed to be romantic? She'd already done two movies in which men died in her arms. But Irving liked the director, the movie was to be shot locally, and Laura wanted so desperately to prove herself once again that she insisted the project move along as rapidly as possible. The deal worked out best for Gardner Brothers—they would continue to pay Laura her salary, and Pierce Pictures would pay them another, greater sum, with her home studio pocketing the difference. Laura didn't feel taken advantage of; after all, it had been her idea. She and Irving had discussed it: After a baby, it was important to build back up. One couldn't go straight back to the top; it simply wasn't possible.

A car came to the house every morning and drove Laura to Burbank, where an entire Mexican town lived inside the walls of Pierce Pictures. Mr. Pierce himself met Laura at the gate the first day, and introduced her around. All the young people turned to look at her as she walked past—if she'd been home at Gardner Brothers, Laura would have waved, but to wave at strangers seemed inappropriate, so she just felt their stares and looked straight ahead. It was hotter on the east side of town, and Laura had to dab her temples in order to keep sweat from dripping down her cheeks. No one wanted to see Laura Lamont perspire.

Mr. Pierce was older than Irving, older than Louis, even. He walked with a cane, and kept his sunglasses on even when they went back into his office. It was roughly the same size and shape as Irving's office, a large rectangle with a wooden desk and windows on two sides, and Laura felt as if she were inside a mirror image of her normal life, as if Mr. Pierce could have been her husband, if things had been different earlier on.

"Miss Lamont," Mr. Pierce said. She felt awkward not knowing his first name, but didn't know how to ask without seeming rude. He gestured for her to sit, and Laura sank into the leather chair opposite his desk. She crossed her legs.

"Mr. Pierce, my husband speaks so highly of your operation." That sounded too clinical, too businesslike. She was supposed to be a movie star, all volatile emotion. Susie was the only movie star who was ever as golly-gee sweet as her on-screen image, and even she'd been slipping in public lately. There were rumors about Susie and her new boyfriend: too much drinking in the afternoon, her eyes always bloodshot and red. Ginger liked to tease Laura by saying that Susie was Susie only on the outside, but that Laura was Susie on the inside, all sunshine and rainbows and cups of sugar. At the moment, Laura didn't want to be made of sunshine, she wanted to be made of steel. "I'm happy to be here." She crossed her legs the other direction, striking a pose. That was better.

Mr. Pierce started to explain the contract to her, but Laura waved him off. "It's all right," she said. "I've already discussed it with Irving. If he's agreed, then I've agreed. Now, let's talk about conquistadors!" She snapped her fingers over her head, the way she'd seen Spanish dancers do. Sometimes Guy had them Spanish-dance back and forth across the floor, stepping and snapping in unison. Part of her had wanted her first postbaby movie to be something fun, like in the old days, but that wasn't right. She put her hands back in her lap. If Irving had thought a comedy would be better, he would have said so. Without him, Laura would still be Elsa Pitts, overweight and miserable in a tiny house with a drunk. The people who said fairy tales didn't come true weren't looking at her, that was for sure.

Flowers for the Dead had problems from the first day of shooting. The director's assistant had to be replaced. The producers wanted more fight sequences, with horses. Laura wanted to get out of her lace corset at least twice a day, to eat something and to use the ladies' room, but her dressers always seemed to take their breaks exactly when she needed their help undoing the hundreds of buttons that ran the length of her dress. The actor playing her Spanish lover, Howard Powers (né Rosenblum), was so pale that he had to be covered in makeup all day, even more than Laura. If Howard had had a sense of humor, they could have compared to see which one of them was wearing more eye makeup, but Howard didn't seem to find anything amusing. Laura kept her mouth shut and tried not to move. It was hotter when she moved, and she found that if she moved, she usually discovered that she had to go to the bathroom.

Three weeks later than scheduled, the director finally called "Action" on Laura's first scene. By that time, she'd forgotten the story she'd concocted for herself about why this beautiful Mexican woman would find this plundering heathen so attractive. A heathen in mascara, no less! All Laura wanted to do was go home and put her ear on Junior's belly. She wanted to hear her daughters giggle in the next room. She wanted the children to be asleep and for Irving to dive under the covers with his glasses on the nightstand, his narrow body as slippery and quick as a fish. That was the key—the conquistador was Irving, an unlikely match. He was powerful and sexy, even though he wasn't whom her parents would have chosen. That was a start. But when she stepped onto the set, her long black lace dress dragging behind her across the sandy concrete, Laura knew that the movie was going to be terrible, and there was nothing she could do to help.

Ginger liked to come over in the early evening. Her husband had the sleeping schedule of a farmer—up before dawn, asleep by dark—and so her nights were free. *Ginger & Bill's Hoedown Happy Hour* filmed from nine until three, and because Irving was usually at the office, the women often had the house to themselves, with baby Junior as the only man around.

"They're making me act with a *monkey*," Ginger said. "It's this tiny little thing, yap, yap, yap." She yapped with her fingers, and then sighed. "At least it wears diapers. Better than that stupid dog. I can't tell you how many times that mutt peed on my shoes."

"I'm sure it'll be funny," Laura said sympathetically. They sat at the kitchen counter, a space no bigger than an ironing board, by far the closest quarters in the house. Their elbows bumped against each other every so often when they reached for their coffee cups. Sitting so near to another body that wasn't her husband made Laura think about her sisters. Laura missed her sister Josephine's solid physical presence, her steady breathing. There weren't many people in the world who could just sit together quietly without worrying that something was wrong. In her weaker, darker moments, Laura knew that Ginger was envious of her life, that she had both the jobs and the children, but she never would have spoken it aloud. It was getting harder to remember when they were just the same, both bad dancers with oversize dreams and no responsibilities. Laura imagined that Ginger felt the same way, that she'd trade all her fame for a child, though Laura never would have asked, not in a thousand years.

"Yeah, but who are we supposed to laugh at, me or it?" Ginger leaned her head back and howled. "Uh, what's the difference, though, between Johnny and some monkey, if you think about it. All grabby little paws, always climbing all over you. I'd rather act with the chimp."

Even when no one else was around, Laura still felt guilty about speaking against Gardner Brothers. After all, the studio had given her everything she'd always wanted, and Irving had always taken care of her, since even before they were married. She took a long sip of coffee and set her cup back down. "I'm sure they know what they're doing." The truth was that Gardner Brothers needed Ginger more than she needed them, and they both knew it. Nowadays when Irving came home and Ginger was still there, a thin coating of frost hung in the air between them, a professional barrier. Laura tried to pretend it wasn't there, but seeing Ginger often put Irving into a foul mood for the rest of the night, as if he were already bracing himself for when she packed up and left, taking her television show and all her fans with her. He wouldn't have been nearly as upset were Laura to leave, whether or not she was his wife.

Ginger balled her hands into fists and beat them in front of her chest. She stuck out her tongue. "Oh, well," she said. "I have to go to work."

"Oh, well," Laura said back, sticking out her tongue. One day she would have to choose between Irving and Ginger, and she would have to choose Irving, and until then, she wanted to be around Ginger as much as possible.

"Let's have a party," Laura said, stopping Ginger before she left.

"Okay," Ginger said. "But I'm not cooking."

It was Irving's idea to call the magazine. *Hollywood Life* would come over and cover the party—not what people were saying, but what Laura Lamont served, on what linens, to which guests. It was to be Laura and Irving, Ginger and Bill, Robert Hunter and Dolores Dee, recently engaged, a new Gardner Brothers writer named Harry Ryman, Peggy Bates, and the children, who were to appear briefly halfway though, looking adorable, and then be whisked back into their bedrooms. Laura wore a cream-colored gown that skimmed the floor and a diamond brooch over her left breast. The theme was "Nights of Spain," which meant that there were bulls embroidered on the napkins and chorizo sausages on toothpicks.

Laura paced nervously with Harriet before the guests arrived. She didn't have to do anything but welcome them—they'd hired caterers, a bartender, and a waitstaff, but still, they were both fretting, and Laura kept letting her cigarettes extinguish between her fingers because she'd forgotten they were there.

Peggy Bates arrived first, and golly-geed everything in the living room—"I love your curtains!" and, "Gosh, look at that lamp!

What is that, gold?"—until she'd run out of things to compliment. Then she ate two sausages and sat down in the middle of the couch, chewing and nodding, nodding and chewing. Irving brought her a martini with a Spanish onion at the bottom of the glass, and she poured it quickly down her throat. Laura forgot that Irving made people nervous.

Everyone else came late, all in a clump, as always happened at parties, like they'd been hiding in the bushes outside, awaiting some smoke signal. Robert Hunter and Dolores Dee hadn't been engaged long, only a week or so, and everyone in the room (including the reporter, who wouldn't have said a word) knew it was in name only. Still, they played it up, especially in front of Irving, patting each other gently on the rear. Ginger and Bill brought a cloud of noise in with them, always laughing and singing louder than anyone else in the room. The screenwriter slunk in unnoticed, and Laura nearly asked him to fetch her a drink before she realized that she was speaking to one of her own guests.

"You must be Harry," she said, and stuck out her hand.

"Miss Lamont, it's an honor," he said, bowing slightly at the waist.

"Where you from?" Harry Ryman was taller than she was used to, and she had to look up to make eye contact. Men around the Gardner Brothers lot hovered at the five-foot-seven mark, unless they were doing construction.

"Who, me? Chicago." He smiled at her. There were freckles on his cheekbones—Harry was young, probably only twenty-five.

"We're practically neighbors," Laura said. "Come, let's get you a drink."

The seating cards had been written by a calligrapher at the

studio, and had Irving at one end of the table and Laura at the other, with the rest of the guests separated from their dates and placed boy, girl, boy, girl. Harry was on Laura's left side, with Robert on her right, and the latter seemed as interested in the former as Laura was.

"What are you working on?" Robert asked, cradling his chin in his long fingers. Laura watched Harry watch Robert, calculating and recalculating everything in his head.

"Who, me?"

Robert nodded. He really was the handsomest man on the lot. Laura had heard rumors for years, but it was only a few months ago that Robert's proclivities for male companionship had gotten so obvious that the studio had had to step in and do something. Dolores didn't seem to mind—Laura watched as she put her paws on Irving's forearm as he talked, and leaned over so that her cleavage nearly spilled out of her dress and onto the table.

"I'm writing a picture for Irving. It's about a horse and a boy. . . ."

"Hey, Ginger! This one's got a horse movie for ya!" Laura called across the table, having fun.

"I like it already." Robert winked at him. "Giddyap."

"No part for me, then?" Laura said. Two could play this game. Acting was her job—she could certainly do it at home if she wanted. Laura raised an eyebrow, as if Harry were a camera pointed her direction.

"Well, yes, Miss Lamont, actually, Irving and I spoke about a part for you. It's the mother of the boy." The young writer didn't even realize that he'd said something wrong. Robert let out an oversize laugh, loud and mean. Irving turned away from Dolores's cleavage and toward his wife.

"Olé!" Laura said, smiling her brightest smile of the night. Though she herself was the mother of three children, it was entirely different to play a mother on the screen. Mothers were old, with unflattering aprons tied around their stout waists. There was always someone more beautiful than the mother. That meant that Laura had been demoted, and her picture with Pierce wasn't even out yet. It was as if Irving assumed it was going to fail, and had adjusted his own schedule to reflect it. The gaffe made its way down the table in an indiscreet game of telephone.

The screenwriter flushed, his cheeks turning from peach to scarlet. "I'm sorry, Miss Lamont, did I say something wrong?"

"No, dear," Laura said, her eyes trained on her husband. "Not at all."

Bill chimed in, sweet and daft, wanting specifics on the horses in question, and Laura was happy to have the attention shift.

The photographer from *Hollywood Life* trained his lens on the place settings, the actors, the bowl of punch. He photographed Dolores smiling at Irving, and Robert charming the hostess. Peggy Bates sat quietly in the middle of the table, talking to no one, and the children came and went as they were bidden. Laura made sure that no one at the party gave another thought to the slight, and carried on as though she were having a wonderful, wonderful time. She kissed everyone good-bye at the door, and then, once they were all alone, and the reporter had taken all his notes and vanished down the drive, Laura slapped Irving on the cheek and instructed him to sleep on the sofa.

Laura was right: Her movie was a flop, and Ginger's monkey picture was a smash, drawing crowds for weeks. *Flowers for the Dead* was her first real failure, which Irving swore meant only good things—it meant that it hadn't been her fault. Laura wanted to tell him that of course it hadn't been her fault; it had been his, for loaning her out like a moving truck, but she couldn't say that to her husband, and anyway, it had been her idea in the first place. She nixed the horse picture—if Laura could have, she would have sent the cute little writer all the way back to Chicago—and Gardner Brothers quickly pulled together a couple of projects to make the audience forget they'd ever seen Laura Lamont try to speak with a Mexican accent.

By the summertime, Laura was a trapeze artist in love with an elephant trainer, and in the fall, she was an impressionable young woman who fell in love with a dashing widower, the film set on a private island off the coast of Maine, filmed entirely on the lot in Culver City. Gardner Brothers printed massive posters—twice as large as life—and put Laura's face on the side of the building. It didn't help her mood. The movies were quick jobs, shot on borrowed sets, with story lines that hung together with costumes and lighting. Laura memorized her lines and the words tumbled out, rote and wooden. There wasn't enough time to sort out why the widower was a good match, or what made the elephant tick. The ground underneath her feet was soft, and she could feel it sinking. Despite what Irving told her, Laura knew that the public was fickle, and that one bad movie meant that people might not go to another. Since the dinner party, Laura could think only about all the meetings her husband had where her name was mentioned, or wasn't mentioned. She didn't know which was worse.

Her headaches had gotten worse, and the house couldn't be quiet enough: Laura thought about going to visit her family for a few weeks, but Irving couldn't be away that long, and she couldn't take Junior on her own. In any case, she hadn't been invited, and Laura felt sure that her mother would not have wanted her there. Harriet was a godsend and spanked the girls' bottoms if they made too much noise—Laura wouldn't have done it herself. When she was finished putting the girls to bed, Harriet would bring a tray of soup into the master bedroom and set it next to Laura on the bed. It was a Sunday, one of Harriet's days off.

"Why aren't you at home, Harriet?" Laura asked. She'd thrown a scarf over the single lit lamp, and the room glowed with faint red light. It was still too bright, and Laura squinted.

Harriet sat down on the edge of the bed. Her hair was twisted into two fat French braids, each one thicker than all of Laura's hair combined. Some of the people Laura knew had their maids and nurses wear uniforms, but Laura thought that was silly. She and Harriet were the same age, born only months apart. They could have been sisters. Laura missed her sisters. Her headaches brought everything back, both Hildy and the darkness in her wake.

"I wanted to make sure you were okay." Harriet's voice was low. She didn't want to make the headache worse. The only black people Laura knew were Harriet and her sister, whom Harriet had brought over when Florence was a baby. She'd never even seen a black person in person until her father took her to Chicago when she was a teenager. Door County was as white as stone.

When Harriet spoke to the children, as gentle and friendly with them as always, Laura's mother's face had hardened. It wasn't her fault, Laura thought, that she'd never been anywhere else, though it did make Laura sad. Aside from Ginger, Harriet was Laura's only real friend. She wouldn't have said so aloud, for fear that Harriet would laugh, but Laura felt that it was the truth.

"I'm fine, really," Laura said. She pushed some pillows behind her back to sit up straight.

"Better than that, Laura, better than that." Harriet stayed until Laura ate all the soup and crackers on the tray. It was hard to say no to Harriet, and Laura liked being told what to do. Irving always said that if he couldn't get Laura to agree to something (how ludicrous an idea! Did he not understand his wife, after so many years?), that Harriet would be his emissary. The two women sat in silence in the near-dark, the only sound the soft slurping of chicken soup.

The girls were old enough to go to a real school, not just the one on the lot—Helen and Millie, Louis Gardner's daughters, had gone to Marlborough, and Laura wanted Clara and Florence to go too. The school required knee-length skirts and loafers, as well as white collared shirts. Laura loved the idea of an all-girls' school: all those ponytails thwapping back and forth as they ran around the track, all those small hands raised in class. It was supposed to be the best way for a girl to learn, and Laura wanted her girls to have every chance she never had. Irving was charmed by the whole idea, and didn't mind footing the bill. He was their father, pure and simple. No one had heard from Gordon Pitts in years. After the war, his contract with the studio had expired, and unlike most lapsed actors, he didn't come forth and beg for another round. The last Laura had heard, he was living with some other men in a hotel by the beach. Ginger said she'd heard he'd lost a tooth, one of the obvious ones. Laura believed anything Ginger said—she was so busy now, with her show and with her husband, that Laura didn't get to see her nearly as much as she wanted to. She knew that there were negotiations happening between Ginger and the studio, but no one wanted to tell her what was going on. It was easiest to assume that everything was going to be all right, the way she would comfort her children, by telling them easy lies about the goodness of the world.

Clara was nervous on her first day: She refused to come out of her bedroom until Laura, Harriet, and Florence were all begging. It would be worse to be late, Florence finally said, and that did the trick. Sisters knew what buttons to push: the trigger points. Laura felt awash with guilt on her sister's behalf, out of nowhere, like a rogue wave on an otherwise calm ocean. There was a school bus, and it was the girls' idea to take it, even though their father would have been happy to have one of the Gardner Brothers' cars take them to and fro. Clara was in the seventh grade, Florence in the fifth. Junior cried all day after his sisters left, inconsolable. It was hard to be so much younger than your siblings; Laura knew that firsthand. He was only two, and wandered bowlegged around the house, searching every room. When he and Laura were alone, she let him wear her shoes, the lowest heels, and it was only then that he would smile for her, his broad face the spitting image of his father.

6

THE DAUGHTER

Fall 1953

That fall, Ginger and Bill took their show next door to Triumph, a smaller studio just over the Gardner Brothers' wall. *Ginger & Bill's Hoedown Happy Hour* was the same as it had been, and starred Ginger and her husband as only slightly fictionalized versions of themselves. The set was built to look like a ranch, with hitching posts, and hay strewn about the floor. The hairdressers at Triumph dyed Ginger's hair an even brighter shade of red, saying that it had to look darker to really read as red on a small screen, despite the fact that Ginger had always been happy with the way she'd looked on the small screen before. They painted her lips outside the lines with deep red lipstick, and arched her eyebrows even more than normal.

"I look like a clown," Ginger said when Laura called. Irving was still angry at Ginger for leaving, and Laura had to call when he was at work.

"You look hysterical," Laura said, not disagreeing. That was the idea, and Gardner Brothers had sold it over and over again: Ginger was the housewife gone mad.

The show was wackier on the other side of the studio wall—it had slapstick scenes and serious ones. There were intimate moments with Ginger and Bill curled up together on a blanket, and scenes of Bill singing and playing the guitar by a fake campfire. But then there were the moments they really let Ginger fly, things she wouldn't have been allowed to do at Gardner Brothers because they were too ridiculous: mishaps at the swimming hole, when Ginger's hair dye turned the water pink; the time Ginger pretended she could speak French and mistakenly agreed to host a two-hundred-person wedding in their living room. It was one of the only shows Laura would let Clara and Florence watch, and only after they were finished with their homework and field hockey practice, and only if their father wasn't home. They'd rush in, step out of their cleats, and throw their sweaty bodies on the sofa. Clara had just turned fourteen, and her body reminded her mother of a horse, all muscle and motion. The girls would howl with laughter, their throats open wide with unguarded amusement. Florence never laughed that way around her mother, not unless Ginger was involved.

It was while they were watching the *Hoedown Happy Hour* that Josephine called to tell Laura that their father had died. Josephine's voice was calm and even, which made it seem to Laura like she might be making the whole thing up, playing some kind of sick practical joke. But Josephine persisted, and when Laura hung up the telephone, the girls were staring at her with wide eyes. She hadn't realized she was making any noise, but when Laura saw the look of horror on Florence's face, she heard the wailing and realized it was coming from her own throat. Clara called their father, and in turn Irving's secretary called the airline and booked tickets for the first flight out the next day.

Laura had always intended for the girls to know Door County, to know where she came from, and it seemed impossible to her that this would be their first trip. It was September, still high season for tourists, and the playhouse would be in full swing. It had been a few years since John and Mary hired on professional help with managing the theater, and though the stage would be dark for the days immediately surrounding the funeral, there were no questions about what would become of the playhouse. Lawyers were involved, and arrangements had already been made. The land went to Josephine, who deserved it, and the theater would remain in operation. Laura hadn't seen her childhood home for fifteen years. She counted on her fingers twice, sure she'd done the arithmetic wrong.

She hadn't thought to be nervous about the airport itself. They hadn't even made it to the gate when the first person tapped Laura on the shoulder.

"Excuse me, aren't you Laura Lamont?" The woman was polite, and so how could Laura not be? She nodded, dipped her neck like a swan, signed a paper cocktail napkin from the lounge. After the first, there were always more. Irving and the children were yards ahead, just watching. Laura tried to catch Irving's eye for him to make it stop, to make everyone go away in a poof of magical movie smoke, but he had all three children and was only one man. The crowd tightened around her, all the strangers breathing on her face as she bent over to scrawl their names—*H-E-L-E-N, M-A-U-R-I-C-E, for my father, thanks, golly*—and it wasn't until a voice came over the loudspeaker announcing their flight that Laura felt she could break free. She hurried through the crowd toward her family, her cheeks burning scarlet.

It was the children's first flight, and only Laura's third; the first two had been to New York and back as a docile ward of Gardner Brothers, during the lead-up to *Farewell, My Sister*. She strapped herself into an aisle seat, with the girls and Junior across the way and Irving in the seat beside her. The long-legged stewardess pinned small metal wings to Junior's jacket, a gesture that made Laura's eyes water. There was no kindness that went unnoticed. She was glad when they were all in their seats and facing forward, with something concrete to feel nervous about. The plane rattled from side to side as it zoomed down the runway, with the stewardess smiling daftly at Laura the entire time, as though she were sitting in a dark movie theater, her stare that steady. Laura closed her eyes and clutched Irving's hand with both of hers as the nose tipped upward, into the blue sky. He held her hands tightly for all six hours, until they were back on the ground in Chicago. It didn't matter that scientists swore that airplanes didn't simply fall out of the sky—Laura thought that today would be the day, if it was ever going to happen, and she was glad that Irving understood her enough not to let go.

There were so many reasons it seemed impossible that her father was dead: John's size, his booming voice, his command of Shakespeare, the letters he sent the children on their birthdays. Those things couldn't just vanish into the ether. Laura fell asleep in the rental car on the way north to Door County, and she dreamed about Hildy for the first time since the girls were little. In the dream, they were sitting in Hildy's bedroom, which was overflowing with water. It poured through the windows and slid in under the closed door. The room was going to fill, and they were going to drown, and no one would save them. Laura knew this for a fact: She and her sister were going to die together in that room. Hildy and Elsa. She woke up just as the water started to lap at her neck. Junior was looking at her, his eyes narrowed in concentration.

"Hi, sweetie," Laura said.

"You were making funny noises," Junior said. He already wore glasses. Laura never knew they made such small pairs, the prescription lenses only an inch and a half wide. He had a small toy airplane, and ran it back and forth across his lap. Junior was a good boy almost all of the time, as well behaved as a loyal hound at his mother's heel, but when something set him off, his crying fits could last for days. Laura never knew what would push him over the edge.

"I'm sorry, sweetie," she said. Out the window, the afternoon sun shone through the trees and painted the farms beside the highway with an ever-changing pattern. Cows lounged by the side of the road, taking turns swatting the flies away with their tails. It was impossible that her father was gone, impossible that she would never see him again. Laura wanted there to be a button to go back in time, back far enough so that there was never any insurmountable space in between them, back far enough so that she could have visited every summer and moved the girls into the house and sat in the audience, just like anybody else. Laura wanted to push that button and be Elsa Emerson again, and to be alive with Hildy and Josephine, the three of them all together in the same place for as long as it took to bring her father back. Laura Lamont was as much a stranger to the place as Irving and the children. She patted Junior on his narrow thigh—*grandson*. How had she kept her father's only grandson away? Elsa would never have done such a thing, no matter how busy. Elsa would have picked up her child and stomped home through mud and snow and rain. Junior kept staring at his mother, instead of looking out the window, as if he understood that there was more happening inside her head than in the passing scenery. Irving was in front with the driver, talking Wisconsin politics, which her husband knew nothing about.

L aura could have given directions with her eyes closed and her mouth shut, just by the feel of the road. She was sure of it. But Cherry County Playhouse Road came sooner than she expected, before she was ready. There were other cars parked in the drive, and outbuildings that Laura didn't recognize. In her mind the house was a castle, so full of hiding places and secret passageways that it was almost too big to fathom, but now that she was out of the car and standing in front of it, the roof looked like it needed to be redone and the windows cleaned. Her parents were modest people, and had built the house themselves. How big could it have been? How many square feet did children need, when there were the woods and the lakes and the wild, wild universe just out the front door? The roof needed mending, and Laura wondered whether her parents—her *mother*—had the money. But of course no one was going to talk about the roof.

Josephine was standing in front of the house with her hands on her hips. She looked so much like their mother that Laura paused, as if to make sure she knew the difference. Her hair had grown in a bit, and it hung from her middle part to just below her ears.

"Hey, there," Josephine said, coming down the drive to meet them. Laura felt like a lunatic, bringing all three kids plus a husband her family didn't understand, as if she'd brought all of California with her on the airplane, and they were waiting around the corner for an opportune moment to pop out and sing.

"Josephine," Irving said, holding out his hand. Of course he'd reached her first; there was nothing for him to wade through. Laura stood still and watched as the rest of her family made their way to the front door. Junior was the last one through, the sweet boy, and Laura urged him in with a jut of her chin. She would go in too, when she was ready. She just didn't know when that would be. Laura hugged her arms across her chest. The house was so much smaller than she remembered. The entire trip seemed like a cruel joke, orchestrated by another studio. If someone were going to write a movie about Laura's life, they would have to start here. There would be panning shots of cherry trees, the round red fruit hanging delicately off the thin stems. It would be the story of a girl and her sisters and their father. Laura turned away to face the road. Cars drove past more frequently now. Were they looking for her? She was wearing a plain cotton dress, but the cut was too good, the darts too precise—she was too put-together for Door County, everyone would say so. But, oh, like a punch to the stomach! Laura hated herself for thinking she was the center of the story. This was not about her. Slowly she made her way toward the screen door.

With the exception of a refrigerator in the icebox's place, the kitchen was unchanged. The same patterned wallpaper clung defiantly to the walls, and the same wooden cabinets sloped away from the ceiling. Laura stepped in slowly, letting her eyes adjust to the darkness. Josephine was at the stove, fixing the girls what smelled like grilled cheese sandwiches. Irving had settled into one of the worn wooden chairs at the kitchen table, and the girls were next to him, their backs to the windows, their three bodies taking up half the space of three Emerson bodies. Without the heft of the studio and a good night's sleep behind him, Irving looked smaller and more sallow than usual. Junior had found a spot on the floor, and zoomed a toy car back and forth, revving its tiny engine with a whisper. He understood what Laura needed: space, quiet. Her son was a sensitive boy, and Laura was grateful for that.

"Where's Mom?" Laura asked.

Without turning around, Josephine said, "Upstairs, resting."

"Should I go say hello? Tell her that we're here?"

"I wouldn't." Josephine turned, holding a sandwich aloft in front of her on a wide spatula.

Laura slid the sandwich onto a plate and cut it in half. The bread was soaked in butter and browned on the outside, with white, melted cheese oozing out of the middle. She hadn't eaten anything like it since Clara was born, since before she had a figure to maintain. Florence took one look at the sandwich and slid the plate over to her sister, who inhaled the grilled cheese in a minute flat. There was grease on Clara's chin and flecks of bread wedged in between her teeth. Laura's stomach made watery noises; she hadn't even realized that she was hungry. Being in one's childhood kitchen made all food look and smell as if it were made from memories alone, as if each taste were capable of transporting you back into your younger self, when things were better, simpler, and more delicious.

"Will you make me one too?" Laura said. She waited for Josephine to turn around again, to look her in the face. There was something hard about her sister that Laura wanted to see soften. It was the Door County winter and the miles of frozen ground and water and snow. Laura walked around the butcher-block island until the heat of the stove was warm against her legs. Josephine stared at the skillet, patiently pressing down on the next grilled cheese. Laura slid her arm around her sister's thick waist. She didn't care whether Josephine had to elbow her out of the way, or that she started dripping with sweat, and felt the liquid collecting at the backs of her knees and notch of her throat. She could have stayed there all day, feeling her sister's ribs expand and contract underneath her arm. Laura ate her sandwich standing up, not caring whether there were grease spots on her sleeves.

When everyone was fed except for Florence, who was a picky eater and had the scrawny figure to show for it, Josephine led them upstairs to show them to their rooms. Laura didn't want to ask, and so she didn't. Let her family decide; that was what she thought. Josephine showed Junior into the cubby that had been Laura's bedroom. At some point, her parents had made it into a proper room, carving space out of the neighboring walls to make space for a bunk bed. Junior quickly scrambled up to the mattress on top, and pulled a comic book out of his back pocket, happy as could be. Laura half wanted to sleep beneath him, to listen to his sleepy snuffling. They could whisper until they fell asleep. Irving would be fine on his own. But that wouldn't do, Laura knew, and so she kept following her family as they trudged along behind Josephine. Their parents' bedroom door was closed—Laura would have bet a hundred dollars that her mother wasn't sleeping, just putting off seeing her. Josephine had won. It wasn't quite fair to put it that way, she knew, but that was how it felt. Hildy was dead and Laura was gone, so Josephine—quiet, steady Josephine—had won the silent contest for her parents' love. No matter how much money Laura had, or how many people looked at her when she walked down the street, her mother wouldn't want her to climb into her bed and let her face rest on the same pillow. Irving would have told her that it wasn't a competition, but he'd never been a sister.

Laura and Irving were to stay in what had been Josephine's room—it looked out over the front of the house, onto the driveway. Of course she wasn't using it—she lived nearby, a three-minute drive down the road, in a house that Laura had never seen. It hadn't even been built yet when she left. The room was small but tidy, with an iron bed and a patchwork quilt that Laura recognized. It was reassuring that some objects remained.

"I thought the girls could stay in the cabin," Josephine said. "Or they could stay with me."

"Cabin," Florence said quickly. "That's here, isn't it? Right outside?"

Josephine nodded, no doubt relieved. Laura couldn't imagine her interacting with adolescents. She'd hardly been one herself. "All right then," she said. "This way." Josephine turned around and started walking the girls back downstairs, and through the kitchen. Clara paused at the top of the stairs, waiting for Laura to follow, but Irving waved the girls on, and then they heard the *step-step-step, step-step-step* of their feet on the stairs, and then the creak of the screen door, and they were gone.

Laura walked over to the window. There were two cars parked behind their rental: neighbors, maybe, or actors. She was glad that there were still players wandering around. Josephine must have kicked someone out of the cabin for the girls' sake, someone important, in the scheme of the playhouse. Laura remembered when the Cherry County players were the only actors she knew. In some ways, acting on the stage still seemed more real to Laura than acting for the screen—she couldn't imagine Susie and Johnny treading the boards, or Dolores Dee, actors who could live on close-ups alone, who had never sweated through their costumes because the night was warm and there was no alternative angle. Irving opened their suitcase on the bed and started hanging his suits in the small, empty closet.

"How are you?" He spoke without turning around. Laura closed her eyes and listened to the soft thumps of the clothes hitting the bed, and then the small scrapes of the wire hangers against the clothing rod.

"I'm glad that the girls didn't have to sleep in Hildy's room." It was the first time Laura admitted it to herself, her fear that she would have to watch her daughters' sleepy faces vanish behind that closed door. She'd tried not to look as they walked past it, as though even a simple glance would have made Josephine offer it up faster.

"Oh, Lore," Irving said. He looked up at her. "Or do you want to be Elsa here?" It was a practical question. Irving adjusted his glasses on his nose. It was still mild in September, and none of the house's rickety fans seemed to have made it into Josephine's room. Laura's skin felt warm, and her dress stuck to her legs as she moved.

"No," she said, though her voice belied the word that had just come out of her mouth. "Let's just see, okay?" But Laura did want to be Elsa, if not forever then for the foreseeable future, certainly for the length of the visit. There were more people on the lawn now; they couldn't all be actors. Laura hadn't even thought to ask which play had been halted. It would have been what her father wanted her to know. Her father would have wanted his baby girl, his *Elsa*, to walk down the stairs and talk to the actors, get to know the voices he had chosen. Instead, Laura backed away from the window and sat down on the bed. "Will you sit with me for a minute?"

Irving sat down beside her. The bed sank nearly to the floor. Laura heard the suppressed groan in the back of Irving's throat, and loved him all the more for swallowing it. The bed would be bad for his back, and bad for his sleep, but Irving wouldn't complain. They would curl their bodies against each other as though it were the middle of winter and they needed the warmth to survive.

The memorial service and the burial were the following day. Laura woke early and left Irving in bed. She tiptoed downstairs, past all the closed bedroom doors, but found Junior and her mother awake in the kitchen. They were making pancakes.

"Good morning," Laura said.

Mary turned around slowly, as if she half expected not to find Laura standing in the doorway. "Good morning," she said, looking Laura up and down. "Sleep well?"

"Sure," Laura said. If they'd been at home, Harriet would have been cooking, and Laura felt self-conscious, as if her mother could sense her own lack of familiarity with measuring cups and spoons.

Junior scampered over and wrapped himself against her waist. Other boys his age had already started to distance themselves from their mothers—she knew because Harriet had described the pickup scene at Junior's school, when all the girls flew into their mother's waiting arms, and the boys only kicked their schoolbags and battled one another with sticks. Laura wanted to talk to her mother about the wonders of raising sisters, but then realized that she couldn't—what could Mary say, having lost one girl to death and another to California? Josephine could not have been enough. And so Laura kept her mouth shut. It seemed rude to even think about saying something that would make her mother even sadder. And she was not that kind of daughter, not here.

"We're making pancakes with blueberries in them," Junior said. He moved constantly—his shoulders, his hips. Even in his sleep, her son was never perfectly still.

"Delicious," Laura said. "And maple syrup, I bet, too."

Junior nodded. The kitchen smelled like melted butter, and he licked his lips.

"Can I help?" Laura knew what the answer would be.

"No, no," Mary said. "You just sit." And so Laura slid in against the windows and watched her mother and her son make breakfast. The service was in the early afternoon; there were so many hours to fill before then, Laura wasn't sure what to do. Irving had the right idea, staying asleep. The Gardner Brothers doctors had given him some sleeping pills, and Laura some antianxiety medication. There was no reason to suffer unnecessarily. Laura had packed the drugs with her toothbrush and perfume, and now she wished she had the bag beside her. It wasn't just that her father was dead; it was that she was still alive, and the house was still standing, and that her son wanted pancakes, and her husband was still in bed, everyone everywhere functioning as if the world were normal and nothing were wrong. If her father had been in the room, he would have hoisted Junior up onto his massive shoulders, or held him upside down by his ankles, the kind of roughhousing that Junior never got at home. Laura felt her breath shorten in her throat. She wanted the world to stop and take notice before hobbling forward, forever changed. The problem was that no one seemed to be changed but her.

"I'm going to check on the girls," Laura said, rising to her feet, which felt wobbly beneath her. She was out the door before either Junior or Mary could respond. Laura walked the short distance from the house to the cabin and knocked on the door, still breathing quickly. She heard them squealing inside.

Clara opened the door. She had stripped down to her underwear and camisole. It was warm inside—they hadn't opened any of the windows. Without Harriet, maybe they couldn't figure out how.

The girls loved the cabin; they said it reminded them of being at the studio, which was code for make-believe. Sometimes, when they were on the lot and Irving was feeling playful, they would find a stage that wasn't being used and he would follow them with a spotlight, the yellow light bathing their dances and skits in fatherly love. In the cabin, Clara and Florence shared the full-size bed, which they didn't seem to mind. The girls were used to sharing a room at home, and the novelty of being in a separate house, surrounded by trees and strange animal noises, was nearly too much fun.

"We need a cabin at home, we decided," Clara said. "We love it." She pushed her hair out of her eyes. Clara's body was bigger than Laura's in every dimension—she was taller when they were both in bare feet. Her breasts were larger, her thighs rounder, her cheeks fuller. Clara looked like every girl in Door County: raised on cream and butter. It was no wonder she would feel so at home. Sometimes Laura felt aware of Clara's size at home in Los Angeles, when they went shopping at Saks Fifth Avenue. She would watch Clara try to squeeze into dresses that would have glided over her own frame. Zippers got stuck, shoes pinched in the toe. If Clara had been an actress, Louis Gardner and Irving would have put her on a liquid diet for three months, but she was his daughter, and so he passed her the ice cream instead. It amazed Laura how different the girls could be: She knew that Florence thought no one noticed how little she ate, how she considered every morsel of food that went into her mouth. Laura would never bring it up, never mention it to Irving. Instead, Laura just watched as Florence's bones rose to the surface of her body like driftwood in the ocean, plentiful and pure. Sometimes she worried that one daughter was getting too fat and one was getting too thin, but Laura thought a mother's voice might push them both farther toward the edges—wouldn't it be better to let them sort it out on their own, their tender hearts mending as they got older? Sometimes Laura worried that she was a bad mother for keeping so quiet with the girls, for giving them so much space on both the inside and the outside, but it was exactly the kind of thing her own mother would have railed against, and so she thought it was the best way.

The cabin seemed smaller also, which didn't surprise Laura. Everything she'd seen and touched as a child was going to have shrunk in her absence; she was expecting it now. The planks of wood that made up the ceiling and walls had weathered with age, and there were holes here and there from when actors had hammered things in over the years. Florence and Clara had strewn their clothes around the whole place, though they'd been there only a night, and Laura had to step gingerly in between the items on the floor.

"This is a mess," Laura said, though she couldn't muster the disdain needed.

"Oh, we'll clean it all up," Clara said, flouncing back and forth. She seemed to have forgotten that they had come to Wisconsin for a funeral, and that their mother was likely to be sad, and that the flouncing should be kept to a minimum. Laura felt her anger rising closer and closer to her throat. No one yelled at the Cherry County Playhouse except for the actors on the stage; if she raised her voice, her mother would hear it in the kitchen. The trees would sway and fall. Irving would pick up his son and go. It might not have been true, but Laura believed it.

"We're leaving at one o'clock," Laura said. She wanted to add, "For the memorial service," but found that her tongue was too heavy to form the words. Without the windows open, the air was stuffy and thick with the bodily smells of two teenage girls. Hildy had been a teenage girl in this room too, and had stripped down even more than Clara had, until she'd had nothing on at all. Laura didn't want to think of her sister naked inside these walls, that lumbering creep moving on top of her, crushing her delicate bones into the mattress, but it was too late. She began to cry softly, and covered her face with her hands. The girls didn't know about Hildy, not really. They knew that she was beautiful, and vivacious, and they knew that she was dead. Their brains were too busy to process more than that, to understand that she had been their mother's *sister* as they were each other's sisters, that Hildy had been as real as they were, as alive. By the time they were old enough to know the truth about her death, Laura felt like it was too late. She had died in an accident; that was what they were told. Was it a car? A horse? Laura couldn't remember. They were small, and hadn't asked questions. Now all that they remembered was that she was gone.

"We'll be ready, Mom," Florence said. She was sitting cross-legged on the bed, her knobby knees pointing to either side of the small room. An open book lay in her lap. The eighth grade at Marlborough was reading *The Adventures of Tom Sawyer*, a book that Laura herself had never read. There were so many things to be sad about at once, Laura didn't know which to choose.

"Thank you," she said, and tiptoed back out the front door. Laura kept walking away from the main house until she found a felled tree close to the ground. She lowered herself down until her head rested on the tree trunk and her body was on the forest floor. The sun was on the other side of a thousand leaves and branches, just poking through here and there to reassure Laura that it hadn't gone away. In Los Angeles, the sun was always right overhead, perkily asserting itself. It was nice to remember that there were places in the world that were harder to reach. Laura closed her eyes and let the rustling of the wind be the only sound she acknowledged. Her own breath ceased to exist; there was only the sound of air in motion, a sound that no one could touch.

⸙

The memorial service was held at the Trottman Funeral Home in Egg Harbor, the only full-service mortuary on the peninsula. Laura rode with Irving and the children, following her mother and sister in Josephine's truck. Florence and Junior were quiet, and stared out the window at the passing scenery, which mostly meant cows and docked boats and houses much like Laura's parents', only smaller. Clara was gushing, suddenly, about a classmate's older brother named Theodore with long eyelashes and a dimple in his chin.

"And then *he* asked *her* about *me*!" Clara said to no one.

Laura couldn't summon the energy to pretend to follow along, as she sometimes did when she'd had a long day, *mm-hmm*ing at every pause in each of Clara's lilting sentences, even when she wasn't sure whom the object of Clara's affection was. Her first-born daughter was pure Los Angeles, conceived under the aegis of Hollywood's hope and glamour, weaned on sequins and sunshine. Laura wondered how different her family would be if she had taken the girls and raised them in Wisconsin, whether their laughter would be different, their dreams, their hearts.

"Marjorie told me that Theo's been telling his friends that he's going to ask me to the homecoming dance. She says it's for sure, a hundred percent. He said that he already has his license and everything. That's okay, right, Poppa? If Theodore takes me to the dance? Florence would be there too, and everybody else from school. We wouldn't be alone at all, and I'd dance with other people too, so it's really more like it would just be calling it a date."

Irving coughed into his shoulder, silencing Clara, and then reached over and took Laura's hand. The funeral home was a fifteen-minute drive, but Josephine was driving twenty miles an hour, even on the stretches of road that were completely empty.

"Isn't this supposed to be how we drive from the service to the cemetery?" Laura asked in a low voice. "I think Josephine is trying to drive me insane. I honestly think that my throat is going to close up and my eyes will fall out of my head if this takes a minute longer. I'm so sorry, my love, for making you come here." She started to breathe heavily, as if she'd just run up seven flights of stairs and was going to vomit.

"Here," Irving said, letting go of Laura's hand and shoving it into his coat pocket. He pulled out two small pills: the blue ones, for anxiety. "Take these."

Clara remained completely silent long enough to watch Laura drop the pills into her mouth and swallow them dry. There was a brief chalky taste in her throat, but then it was gone. By the time they arrived at Trottman's, Laura was able to smile at her mother and sister, and the hard edges around their faces began to blur. The three women walked into the funeral home together, their arms linked like debutantes. When people started to approach them, Laura realized what she had to do: pretend it was all happening to someone else, to Elsa Emerson, who'd loved her father to pieces and had never left Door County. Laura Lamont floated away, up toward the ceiling, and needed neither food nor drink nor a bathroom break for hours and hours. Strangers kissed her on the cheek and she kissed them back, thanking each one profusely for coming in her family's time of need. Laura was aware, vaguely, that her children were still present and accounted for, and when she saw Clara slink off with a group of boys, her daughter's soft body slouching playfully against one of them, she didn't make a stink. Elsa Emerson was a wall of kindness, and nothing would make it fall. When Laura heard someone tap her fork against a glass in anticipation of a speech, she was surprised to realize that it was her own fork and glass, and that she was able to say several words about her father without once bursting into tears. Irving stayed as close as she would let him, his thin frame coming in and out of her peripheral vision. "We're going to need some more of those little blue pills," she said, patting him on the arm. It didn't matter what anyone in Door County heard her say: She wasn't Laura Lamont here, even if people were staring, which they were. Every word that came out of her mouth would be buried with her father. That was how it was done here; it was called respect. The casket was closed, and sat at the far end of the long room.

Laura shook off whoever was holding her elbow—it was Irving, of course it was—and staggered in the direction of the casket. Her father had wanted it closed; he must have said so. Josephine probably had stacks of legal documents saying exactly what her father wanted to happen to his body. He wouldn't have left it up to them, the three women still standing. No, John had always been good at making decisions. Laura ran her hands over the smooth wood of the casket. It was nearly as long as the width of the room, but even so, it seemed too small to hold her father's entire body. Hadn't they shown the body before it was closed? Surely her mother and Josephine had seen him. It wasn't as though John had suffered from an illness for many years and everyone had seen his body shrink down over time, as the cells on the inside ate up the ones on the outside. No, his death had been sudden. A heart attack, simple and decisive. Laura supposed it happened all the time. She'd heard about a man who worked for the studio—a big guy, a gaffer—who'd fallen dead while walking down the street. Her father had been lucky that way, if death could ever be lucky; it had happened at home, in the barn. A few of the actors had seen it happen: Laura could guess which ones they were, huddled there on the folding chairs, still in shock. One of them had run into the house for the phone, and to find Mary. By the time the ambulance came, it was too late, but they'd hooked up all the wires just the same. Perhaps every profession required a bit of acting, just to make sure the grieving wife didn't have to be grieving just yet. Was it so wrong to give people hope?

Laura let her hands run down the side of the casket until her fingers gripped the lip of the lid. The wood was heavy and dark. She turned to look over her shoulder; Irving had his eyes trained on her—she could feel it, accustomed as she was to his watching her most minuscule movements—but no one else was paying attention. Josephine was the sister everyone wanted to console. She and her housemate, the nurse (was it the same nurse? Laura didn't think so—Josephine had gone through a few already), sat at the far end of the room, greeting mourning neighbors and friends as they came in. The housemate wasn't as dowdy as Josephine. She had sturdy bones but a pretty face, with her hair pulled back into a neat braid. They held hands, as primly as two girls could. How stupid everyone in Door County was! Laura couldn't believe it. Josephine could parade around, rubbing her lesbianism in everyone's face, but her mother didn't want to talk to *her*? The daughter who had given her three grandchildren? The one who'd won an Academy Award? Laura laughed. Her father had always loved her best, even counting Hildy. Laura gripped the lid tighter and flexed her arm muscles. In one great push, Laura hoisted the lid of the casket until it was all the way open and leaning against the wall.

Her father's eyes were closed; the Trottman brothers had done that. They'd also put him in his best suit, the one he'd worn to the awards ceremony. His hair had been combed and his cheeks daubed with rouge. He looked as if he were taking a nap. There were rustling noises behind her, but Laura didn't turn around to see who was whispering. For almost a full minute, Laura stared at her father's clasped hands. Her mother hadn't taken his wedding ring; why was that? Laura wanted to wear it on her thumb, to have the metal rub against her skin. The absence of fear, of anxiety, felt like skating on fresh ice. She could have looked at him forever.

A tall man with broad shoulders—a Trottman, she guessed—came up behind Laura and eased the lid of the casket back down.

"I'm sorry for your loss, ma'am," he said, now holding Laura firmly on the wrist, as though she might try it again. "But this is a closed-casket service. It's what the family requested."

"Ha!" Laura's voice rang out; she could tell she was being too loud for the room, but it was too late. If they'd been on a set— some sad film about a dead father, a weepie—the soundproofed walls would have absorbed the sound of her voice, softened its jagged edges. She pulled her wrist out of Trottman's grip. "This is my father," she said, no longer sure whether she was speaking as Elsa Emerson or Laura Lamont, or both. She'd come down from the ceiling, and the only thing floating in the air above her head was her too-loud voice, still ringing.

"I'm so sorry, ma'am. But the ceremony is closed-casket. If you'd like, we can arrange for another viewing after the service." The man's eyes were small and blue, two more little pills. He'd had to do this before.

"Of course," Laura said. Her limbs felt heavy. "Irving?"

Her husband was already behind her, moving through the crowd. Josephine had corralled the children in the hallway, out of earshot. No one wanted to see their mother this way. Junior peered through the still-open doorway, his eyes wide and frightened behind his glasses.

"No!" Laura said. She kicked her legs and thrashed her arms, moving everything at once. The Trottman now had her father's face, and he was moving her quickly toward a door she hadn't seen before. Of course they had a room for things like this, a room to put people who were being disorderly. Irving shoved her from behind, his small hands firm against her back, and then shut the door after them. Laura sank to her knees on the floor.

"I'm sorry, honey," she said. "I just wanted to see him. I didn't think anyone would mind, isn't that crazy? I just didn't think anyone would mind." Irving stood with his back to the door. His own father had died when he was a child, both of his parents gone by the time he turned twenty. She never thought about that—why? It seemed so central to his person now, the idea that he'd been orphaned. The room was small and dark, with two upholstered chairs and a dank, sinking sofa. Laura pulled herself up onto the sofa, panting. Her forehead was damp with sweat. Irving handed her his handkerchief and sat down beside her.

"I know, Lore," Irving said. He took off his glasses and rubbed them with the hem of his jacket. Irving Green was not supposed to be in a tiny, damp room in northern Wisconsin. He was supposed to be in his office in Los Angeles. Laura tucked herself under her husband's arm and closed her eyes. If she waited long enough, the feeling would come back, and she'd be floating again, above it all, connected to her body like a balloon on a string. On the other side of the door, someone began to sing a hymn. Laura hadn't even remembered to think about God. Her father had been a Lutheran, more or less, from a family who cared about such things, and prayed even on the six days a week they weren't in church. Laura had left religion in Wisconsin, and was surprised to find it still so healthy and robust in her absence. She pulled herself back up onto her feet and slowly opened the door. Two men and two women were standing beside her father's casket, each of them plainer and doughier than the last, and the sounds coming out of their mouths made Laura hold her breath. It was a simple song— no more than three or four lines repeated. She stood in the doorway and listened as their harmony floated up over her head to the rafters, where the sound gathered and turned into something else, something she hadn't known she needed: beauty. Laura took her husband's hand and walked to the back of the room, where even the people hovering by the door had damp faces.

The cemetery was quiet: At Mary's insistence, only the family was invited, which meant that Laura and her brood outnumbered everyone else. Mary wasn't interested in seeing any Hollywood lookie-loos, anyone with a notepad or a camera. In addition to Josephine and Mary, one of John's frail and blue-haired elderly aunties was in attendance, as well as Mary's bachelor brother, a sturdy chap who'd driven up from Green Bay for the occasion. The girls stuck together as closely as if they were Siamese twins, hanging back toward the edge of the plot. Mary kept turning around to look at them, as though she thought they might at any moment begin dancing on someone else's grave, which Clara might very well have done. Junior stood solemnly at his mother's side, as still as he'd ever been.

The Lutheran priest spoke slowly. John was with Jesus, where he would remain until the second coming of Christ, at which time his good deeds would be recognized, and he would once again return to his body for celestial eternity. Laura held Junior by his shoulders to keep him from squirming around and asking questions. It didn't matter that she didn't believe what the priest was saying; her mother did, and Josephine too. Laura had never given more than a moment's thought to Jesus, not since she was a girl and used to pray for things like ponies and shooting stars as proof of his existence. How they could believe, still, after Hildy and now her father, was beyond Laura's understanding. Instead, she thought about other things, while the priest's even voice droned on. She thought about how her father's voice had always made her feel well looked after, and that without him, she never would have guessed that people could choose to be actors, just like that, as if it were choosing to be a postal clerk or a checkout girl at the grocery store. Laura thought that her father would have been pleased to see her back on Door County soil, and she was sorry not to have come back sooner. The priest said something about Jesus rising again, and Florence made a zipping sound with her tongue, and then crossed her braids in front of her mouth like a horse's bit, a nervous habit. It was like nothing her daughters had ever heard—no one in the movies talked about religion. The movies *were* their religion, the whole town's. Laura wasn't sorry for the choices she'd made, for moving so far away. There were pieces of her father that she would always have with her, pieces that couldn't be taken away. They were in Clara's curvy charm and Florence's quick mouth. They were in Junior's concentration, his devotion. Laura raised a gloved hand to her face and wiped away tears as they fell. Junior leaned back against her legs, and Laura loved him so much, her whole family so much, that she could hardly stand.

The drive back to the house was silent. Even Clara kept her mouth shut. The plan was to return to the house, stay the night, and drive back to the airport first thing in the morning. Mary would not be sorry to see them go, but Josephine seemed fond at least of Florence and Junior, whose quiet demeanors she found more relatable.

They returned home to find a small colony of covered platters and Tupperware containers waiting on the front step. It reminded Laura of the morning after her Academy Award win, when the living room was filled with congratulatory flowers, a proper swarm, a thought she kept to herself. Everyone had come and left food, enough for the family to eat for a week or more. Laura and the girls helped pick up the dishes and carry them indoors. At Josephine's insistence, Mary went upstairs to bed.

"What *is* this?" Florence had peeled back a corner of aluminum foil and was peering at a brownish stew.

"It's hotdish," Josephine said, bustling in and taking the heavy tray out of Florence's reluctant grip.

"Oh," Florence said, and gripped her elbows. There was no such thing as hotdish in California, and Florence seemed unconvinced that she wasn't peeking into a casserole filled with poison. "I think I'll go back to the cabin."

"Go ahead," Laura said. "Clara, you go too. We'll finish up."

The girls didn't have to be told twice, and banged out the kitchen door. Laura watched them through the screen door, Florence's sharp elbows waving in and out as she hurried to keep up with her sister. Irving and Junior were in the yard, conducting some sort of experiment on one of the trees. It was strange to see Irving so far outside of the studio's walls—in all the years they'd been together, Laura had never seen her husband interact with nature for so long. He was probably thinking about ways to suspend trees from an unseen sky, about backdrops of orchards and creaking wooden barns painted red.

"Are you just going to stand there?" Josephine held the front door open with her bottom, and reached down to pick up another plate of food—cookies.

"Yes, sorry, I mean no," Laura said, hurrying back. She squeezed through the open door and picked up a bowl with each hand. It took several trips to bring everything inside, and when they were through, the kitchen table and cooking island were both covered. Laura leaned against the stove while Josephine began to peek under each sheet of foil to see what needed to be refrigerated.

"It's so strange to be back."

"Yeah?" Josephine said, not really listening. She was arranging the dishes by size, sliding them onto the already crowded racks of the refrigerator.

"I wish Hildy was here," Laura said.

Josephine stopped what she was doing, with one hand on the refrigerator door handle, her face pointed away from her sister. "Sure you do," she said, and let the door close with a quiet thunk.

"I don't know how you can be in this house so much," Laura said, "and not think about her all the time. Every day. I think about her every day, and I'm on the other side of the country."

"Did it ever occur to you that it might be *because* you're so far away?" Josephine spun around. Her face was taut and hard.

Laura stared down at her fingernails. They were painted a pale pink, almost so pale that they hardly looked painted at all. She wore her wedding band and a diamond ring Irving had given her after Junior was born. She wished she'd left the diamond at home. "I miss her, Josie."

"Of course you do," Josephine said. She began to rub her hips, exactly the way their mother did, with her fingers on the front side of her body and her thumbs poking into her back. Laura wondered how much she would have absorbed if she had never left, if their mother would have loved her more. "You were so young, you didn't really know her at all."

Laura was sure she had heard her sister wrong. "You can't mean that."

"You were a kid, Laura, only a little bit older than Junior. How much do you think he understands of the world?" Josephine put her hand over her eyes. "All I mean is, Hildy wasn't perfect. She wasn't perfect, okay?"

Laura pushed herself away from the stove and walked the width of the room until she was staring out the front door. Their rented car was sitting in the drive, just waiting to be driven away. "I know that," she said. "I knew everything."

"What did you know?" It was a real question. Josephine was testing her, and Laura didn't want to fail.

"About Cliff," Laura said. "I knew about Cliff."

"Oh," Josephine said. "And?"

"We were very much alike," Laura said, not wanting to hear anything else that Josephine had to say. There was nothing she didn't know about her sister, and she resented the implication. No one had loved Hildy more; that was a fact. Josephine was on the very edges of Laura's memories from her childhood, a peripheral figure, whereas Hildy was the absolute center. Behind her, Laura heard Josephine move back into action, shifting the dishes so that they would be out of the way when their mother decided to come downstairs. Laura stayed put until she heard Josephine's heavy feet walk out of the room.

❧

That night, Irving curled his body along the far edge of their bed. The girls were jittery but fine, content in their own private cabin; Mary fed them buttery potatoes and corn, and Laura watched Florence demolish two whole ears, so grateful to finally be fed something she recognized. Though Laura wanted to stay longer, to just sit in the house, Irving had to get back to work, and the children had to get back to school. They were leaving for California in the morning, first thing. Laura scootched her body closer to her husband's, but he shrugged her off.

"What is it?" Laura asked. "Are you all right?" The house was so dark at night, with no streetlights or passing cars. She'd be happy to get back home. The house wasn't the same without her father in it, not remotely. The only noises she could hear were ghost steps, her father's feet on the floorboards, her father's large body moving around the kitchen. Every time, Laura's body would give a start, a synapse firing falsely, telling her that he was still there, still alive. The moments that immediately followed, when the reality would slowly sink back in, were excruciating, and Laura was glad to have the blue pills by her side. If she thought that the pills would have taken away all the pain at once, without any consequences, she would have swallowed the entire bottle.

Irving turned onto his back. "I'm sorry about the movie," he said, meaning the boy writer's horse picture, or *Flowers for the Dead*, or maybe both.

"It's not your fault." Laura waited, sensing that Irving wasn't finished.

"And I'm sorry about your father. I don't even remember mine, not really. Nothing more than what I've made up." They rarely spoke of Irving's life before Gardner Brothers, his mysterious childhood in New York, his dead Russian family, just as they rarely spoke of Laura's. There had been nothing wrong in Irving's childhood, nothing more painful than poverty. But that was enough to keep him from ever mentioning it.

"She was a really good mother, my mother." Irving was holding his tongue.

"Of course she was," Laura said. She sat up straight, her body the only thing moving in the dark, silent house. "What do you mean by that?"

"Nothing. I don't mean anything. I was just thinking about how hard it's going to be for your mother to be alone. My mother was alone too. There were five of us."

Irving had never mentioned his siblings, not once. Laura had always assumed that her husband was an only child. The four phantom siblings—all girls, Laura knew at once—floated around her, transparent as ghosts. He turned back onto his side, but at least he was facing her again. Laura stroked the top of his head.

"You didn't do that to her, Irving. You didn't leave her alone." She wriggled back under the covers, until their noses were almost touching. Laura wanted Irving to stop talking, to press his nose against hers until they were breathing each other's breath and half-asleep.

"Of course I did," Irving said. "I was seventeen when I left home to come to California, and she died the next year. Who was supposed to take care of her, my sisters?"

"She had her daughters." Laura didn't understand the conversation she was having, didn't understand why it felt as if she were lying on a bed made of quicksand, with no rope to climb out.

"Just like your mother," Irving said. "Daughters, grown and absent. Only my mother didn't live."

"Are you trying to make me even sadder?" There were so many reasons to feel miserable on any given day, so many slights to absorb.

Irving sighed, and his breath slid over Laura's cheek. "No," he said. "I was just thinking about her, that's all."

Laura hated to think that coming to Door County had made Irving unhappy in a way she hadn't anticipated, that being around her sadness had made him remember his own. That was what love was, though, wasn't it? Holding each other's misery as close as your own? They had a good life together, a good marriage. Laura thought that anyone on the Gardner Brothers lot would have said the same. Still, no matter how good, Hollywood marriages were fickle things, like gusts of wind in a broken sail, with disaster always likely around the bend. So far their marriage had been built on love and luck, but luck didn't last. Laura wrapped her leg around Irving's waist and drew him closer to her. No matter the weather, she wanted to tell him, no matter the past, this was for good.

7

THE WIDOW

Winter 1958

There were socks missing and juice stains on the rug, and Laura loved it all. The years following her father's death were busy with everyday tasks. Laura stayed home; she tried to learn to cook, much to Harriet's amusement, and drove the children to school in Irving's Rolls-Royce, waving at their friends' parents through the window like a queen in a passing parade. The world was a different place without her father in it, and Laura wanted nothing more than to love her family and to keep them nearby. The girls chafed at their mother's close attention, claiming that she counted their fingers and toes in the middle of the night, which was creepy, and also sometimes the truth. Laura had dreams about building a fortress somewhere deep in the countryside, maybe in Wisconsin, a place big enough for all the children and even her mother and sister, if they wanted to come. It would be big enough for everyone, with enough bedrooms for her unborn grandchildren, and maybe their children too.

The audiences didn't seem interested in Susie and Johnny anymore, and it was Irving's job to find the next smiling faces to fill the vacuum. He stayed late on the lot poring over scripts and photographs of teenagers, and pretend teenagers, who were often even better than the real thing. Pierce had taken a shot on a young European actress, Bernadette LaFarge, who was smoldering across every screen in the country despite having only a tenuous grasp of the English language. Irving had seen her and passed—she was too obviously sexy for Gardner Brothers—and now he was paying the price. Every studio in town was looking for someone with an equally kissable pout, an equally outrageous figure. It didn't matter whether they could talk; that was what the box office numbers said. Irving stayed late every night, sure he could find the right face for the next decade.

"Have you checked all the pregnant women?" Laura asked him in bed.

Irving took her chin in his hand and kissed her on the cheek. "That was only you, my dear."

"What about this one?" Laura picked a photo out of the pile— a gloomy-looking blonde with a mouth the size of Pittsburgh. Irving shook his head. She picked out another one—a tall brunette with light eyes and a mole in the middle of her cheek. Irving shook his head even more strongly.

"I wish it could just be you," he said.

"Susie transitioned from child star to bombshell," Laura said, though not in protest.

"It has to be a new face." Irving took off his glasses and set them on the nightstand. He rubbed his eye sockets with the palms of his hands. It was late, almost one, and he hadn't slept well in days.

"I know, my love." Laura fanned out the photographs on the bed and began to sift them into piles: the young, the glamorous, the foreign, the strange. Bernadette was the latter, not an average beauty. Her face was more angles than curves, with eyes disproportionately large for her other features, and with a body as twiggy as a young boy's. She wasn't Irving's type, and so he had missed her. Laura tapped all the strange photographs on her knee, so that they were all lined up properly, and began to leaf through her selections. Olga Kalman was all chin; Jean Baxter had eyes that seemed to stare off in opposite directions; Ruth Reed had a squarer jaw than Robert Hunter. Laura reached toward her side of the bed and took a blue pill.

"Headache," she said to Irving, who had flung his arm above his face and was staring at the ceiling.

He reached over and put his hand on Laura's thigh, holding it there until she had wriggled under the covers next to him, sending all the photos sliding onto the floor.

"I wish I could find you over and over again," he said. Laura set her ear against his chest and listened to his heartbeat.

"Me too," she said. Everyone in the house was asleep, everyone in the neighborhood. The only people awake in Los Angeles were the ones who were still after something, and Laura was glad she wasn't one of those. She shut her eyes and held on tight.

⤜

The first signs were small: more coughing in the night, Irving's cheeks sunken farther into his face. By the New Year, there was no mistaking that something serious was happening inside

Irving's cells. The doctors were vague, or at least Irving was vague when he relayed their messages. Nothing was the matter—it was the same problem he'd had since childhood, a rheumatic heart. Laura was not permitted to accompany her husband into the office, and instead sat in the waiting room, her hands folded in her lap, an unread magazine open underneath them. It couldn't be *so* serious, whatever was wrong with Irving. Her father's heart had been enormous, the size of a giant's, too big for a simple human chest. That was what Laura always imagined, that her father had arteries as large as hubcaps—*that* was the problem, and it physically couldn't last forever. But Irving was different, as slim as a pencil. How hard could it be to keep the blood moving in a space so compact? Laura decided to take matters into her own hands.

Irving had never taken a sick day, not one, despite his medical history, and those days had accrued: An entire month of days, at the very least, was at his disposal. Laura counted them off with the secretary, and then had the girl book two tickets to Mexico. There was a healing center on the beach several hours south, in a town so small there was only one flight every three days. Laura didn't wait for Irving to agree.

The center was small, with six bungalows for patients and their families and then a central building with treatment rooms and an office. It reminded Laura of Gardner Brothers, with different costumes. The other patients—all of them older than Irving by thirty years, with white hair and slowed gaits—were polite enough, or simply old enough not to notice that someone famous was now in their midst. The doctors—they were doctors, of a sort—used herbal remedies and steam baths and massage and yoga and hovered magnets over his body. They adjusted Irving's qi, which had some-thing to do with his energy. When he was being treated, Laura sat in their room and cried.

On days Irving was feeling healthy, they would walk along the beach, Laura supporting Irving's diminishing body with his arm slung around her shoulder. She told him things that he already knew about her childhood in Door County, stories that he liked: the fresh cherry pies, the fish boils, skipping stones. She told him details that she couldn't believe she'd never told him before: about Hildy's laugh and Josephine's unflappability. On days when he was feeling bad, they rested inside in the dark, Irving on the bed and Laura in the wicker chair beside him, the sunlight peeking through the blinds only enough to draw yellow stripes on the floor. On the days he was feeling worst of all, Irving sent Laura out into the world without him, and she sat on the sand, feeling far away from everything she loved in the world, as if he were already gone, and there would be no going back to the life she'd had before.

They stayed three weeks, until the Mexican doctors—were they doctors?—told Laura to take her husband home. Sand was in every corner of their suitcases, clinging defiantly to the soles of their shoes. Irving closed his eyes on the airplane home and Laura worried, not for the first time, whether he might not open them again. When Harriet opened the door for them at home, the look on her face told Laura that the treatments hadn't gone as well as she'd thought. Nevertheless, being in Los Angeles brightened Irving's mood, and he was soon back to worrying over box office numbers, and asking after Florence's and Junior's days at school. Some days he would forget that Clara had already graduated, and ask her whether she'd done her homework, to which she would roll her eyes affectionately and say, "*Pa*-pa," which meant, *I love you, don't leave*.

❧

There had been rumors, but Laura didn't believe the news until it was in *Variety*. Louis Gardner, a man who had sent all of her children presents on their birthdays for their entire lives, had fired Irving Green; it said so right there in black and white. *Ouster at Gardner Brothers Studio Leaves Green Out in the Cold*. Bernadette LaFarge had been the last straw, though as far as Laura could tell, she was also the first. Everyone in town knew that Irving had done all the work, that Gardner himself was little more than a bankroller and a figurehead. The ideas, those belonged to Irving. The stars were loyal to him, not to Gardner Brothers; it was absurd to think otherwise. Now the doctors came to their door, and Laura could think of no loyalty except her own.

The day was bright, still morning. Irving lay quietly in their bed, the skin on his closed eyelids so thin and purple it looked like he had two black eyes.

"I've decided," Laura said, the folded-up newspaper still in her hands. She read him the trades on days when he wanted to hear the news. "I'm going to leave too. They can't expect me to stay after what they've done to you."

Irving wet his lips but didn't say anything.

"Did you hear me, sweetie? I'm going to quit. My contract's up next month, and I'm going to leave. Screw them if they think they can do it without you. Louis Gardner? I'd like to see him produce one-tenth of what you've made."

Irving nodded and pulled his mouth into a shallow smile. Above them, the ceiling fan spun in circles, its blades circulating the stale air in the room. All around them, the noises of the world persisted: squawking birds, the radio in the kitchen, airplanes flying overhead. But Laura couldn't hear any of it; she could hear only the light swinging on its chain, the electric buzz of the fan, and her husband's labored breathing. She would quit as soon as possible. There was no other solution. There was enough money in the bank, Laura was sure—Irving had worked his entire life, and never spent a penny before he married her. She didn't worry for a moment about her decision, though she did take a pill, just in case. And then it was done.

Florence was still at school, but Harriet and Junior were on their way home. Laura heard the horn honk when Harriet pulled into the driveway, announcing their arrival. It wasn't unlike a movie set, when certain noises set other actions in motion—before the director called "Action," the extras were already moving, the world already brought to life. It had been decided—Laura had decided—that Junior shouldn't see his father when he was ill, despite the fact that Irving was now at home. Junior had always been a dreamy little boy, often content to entertain himself. Laura had imagined that things might change when he started school, and hanging around with other boys. As it was, Junior had only his older sisters, and other girls who lived in the neighborhood, always gussying one another up with their mothers' makeup. More than once Laura had come home to find him sitting alone on the front stoop with lipstick and blush on, a forgotten practice dummy. He never complained, even when Irving spanked him. Of course, that hadn't happened for months, or even a year. Irving was too weak to say more than a few words, let alone lay a hand on him. Harriet would wash the makeup off Junior's face, but the lipstick was clingy and a ghost of it remained on his face for days. The girls were big, so big they hardly needed anyone, but Junior, he was still a child, only eight years old.

Harriet knocked once and then opened the door. "In his room. It'll be fine," Harriet said, and then pulled the door shut again. Laura believed her, because the alternative was worse.

"Come on, honey, let's take a bath," Laura said, her steady voice coming from some hidden recess, some part of her throat that believed what Harriet said was true, and that everything would be all right. Before her sister died, which was to say for the first nine years of Laura's life, she might have really thought it was the case, that all things worked out in the end, and that the world was a benevolent place, but she knew better now, and had to fake it.

Not even the lawyers tried to stop Laura from leaving Gardner Brothers. She wasn't the only one who was jumping ship: Actors and directors were going all the time; Johnny had ripped up his contract and was being his own one-man band in Las Vegas. For the first few days, Laura had Harriet answer the home telephone to make her appointments, and after that she brought in Jimmy Peterson, a second cousin of Ginger's, who was twenty years old and wanted to get his foot in the door in Hollywood. Laura cleared out one side of Irving's home office and set up two small desks, one for her and one for Jimmy, who was a very sweet boy and who had nearly fainted when she offered him the job. After all, she still had to work. Laura knew that some women in her position would stop entirely, but she found that she couldn't. Irving's illness and firing from the studio were two sides of the same coin: Had he had the job to go back to, Laura felt sure that his health would have improved. She worried that the same was true of her: that if she went too long without working, all of Hollywood might pick up in the middle of the night and move to Boise, Idaho, without telling her, and she would be left alone, without a sister or father or husband *or* job. She wasn't ready to give everything up at once. Yes, there were the rising medical bills, but Laura was confident that there was more than enough to cover the expenses and then some. Surely there was enough until she went back to work.

The tasks were simple: Jimmy was to answer the telephone, find out what the callers wanted from Laura. Make appointments: breakfast meetings, lunch dates, dinner dates, drinks. Call the directors and producers who had slobbered all over Laura's hands when she was with Gardner Brothers, tell them she was free, as if *free* meant something other than "unable to leave the house." Jimmy had blond hair that crested in a short wave over his forehead, and always looked Laura in the eye when she talked. It was like having a Labrador who could use his thumbs. Florence liked to say he looked like Wally from *Leave It to Beaver*, which was not a compliment. She was a senior in high school and was reluctant to offer praise to anyone excluding her brother, on whom she doted, but only when she thought no one else was paying attention.

Jimmy wasn't the only one with a new job. After graduation Clara, a quick typist, was hired by Triumph Studios. She worked as a secretary for Ginger and Bill's show, fixing up the scripts for the writers. She had a desk with a small brass plate that had her name on it, which she would polish with her own spit and a corner of a handkerchief. Clara loved being in an office, and would come home at night and clatter back and forth across the kitchen floor, still in her heels, pretending she had important work to do that couldn't wait until morning.

"You do know that you're only a secretary, don't you?" Florence asked from her spot on the sofa, where she had tucked herself into a little ball. She was having crackers for dinner. Laura was too fraught with worry to notice. The girls pretended not to notice how sick Irving was, at least when they were in the same room. They were old enough to visit with him, and would kiss him on the forehead at least once a day, sit in the chair beside his bed and talk about their day. Laura couldn't help but envy the easy way that they took for granted that their father would recover, though she knew it to be false. One morning, before school, Laura heard a loud noise in the bedroom and ran in, her pulse already dangerously quick, her finger ready to dial for an ambulance, and found that it was just Florence's laughter. When Laura walked in, they both turned to look at her, the warden who'd come to ruin their fun. She'd shut the door, walked down the hallway to the bathroom, locked herself in, and cried.

Clara smacked her sister on the back of the head. It was a Friday afternoon.

"Hey!" Laura said. She and Jimmy were finishing up for the day, and had exited their office just in time to see the smack. Clara was still in her work clothes and shoes, which she would usually kick off the moment she walked through the door.

"Flo has her feet on the sofa," Clara said, by way of an explanation.

Florence unfolded herself and put her socked feet on the rug.

"Have you two met yet, sweetie?" Jimmy was new, and Clara was often at work until after dinner. Florence hoisted her elbows onto the back of the couch and tucked her hair behind her ears, anxious to watch the introduction.

"Why, no." Jimmy stuck his hand out. "I'm James. Your mother, er, Laura's assistant. Jimmy. Please call me Jimmy."

"What else would she call you, Frederico?" Florence rolled her eyes. She'd seen enough and slumped back down, leaving a trail of her long, dark hair thrown over the back of her seat. Irving's illness was showing up in funny places—Florence's attitude, Clara's appetite, Junior's eyesight. They were all taking it on wherever they could, little pack animals preparing for winter. Perhaps they thought that fathers came in waves, for indeterminate periods of time, and had never admitted to themselves that they might get to keep one for good. Laura wanted to talk to her daughters about what was happening, but couldn't find the words. She would often leave the room, only to find she'd left every room in the house and was sitting on the front steps.

"So nice to meet you," Clara said, taking Jimmy's hand in her glove. "I'm Clara."

Watching them bat their eyelashes at each other was like watching a car accident that was about to happen. Laura stood still and hoped she was misunderstanding the signals. Of course she was—clearly she had never *correctly* understood a single signal in her entire life. That made her feel oddly better about the whole situation—knowing that she was probably wrong, because she had terrible instincts, and if she felt like something was happening, well, then it was most likely the opposite.

The master bedroom no longer had enough room for Laura, despite the fact that Irving's body was taking up less and less room in their bed. Beside the bed, the nightstand now held half a dozen small white pill bottles, a half-empty glass of water, Irving's glasses, and a book he was never going to finish. Laura sat with him most days, from six in the morning until it was dark outside and she could no longer keep her eyes open. She often fell asleep sitting upright, her head resting against the arm of the chair. The doctors and the girls and Harriet came and went, dispensing food and drugs on trays. Laura kept a small bottle of the blues in her pocket and chewed them like candy, the bitter taste no longer a deterrent. It seemed only fair that she share some of the physical discomfort, as if fairness were something that existed anymore. Junior stayed in his room, or in the living room. He wasn't allowed to see his father every day, only when Irving was feeling good— Laura felt powerless about so much in her life, but she could control the last time Junior saw his father's handsome face. Laura herself could barely stand to look at her husband, with the fact of his vanishing now so clear. It seemed impossible that Irving could be gone, as swiftly as a season, when he was still her only, best love. Laura wrote letters to her mother and didn't send them, but stacked them up on her desk, tying them together with ribbon before the stacks fell over onto the floor, the letters slipping out and spreading like tarot cards on the rug, each one saying only Death, Death, Death. This was being a wife and mother, being a witness to the fullest spectrum of human horrors and unable to stop them. If she were to cry out, Junior would come running, and if Junior came running, he would see his father's chest barely moving up and down, and he would know—too young, too soon—the truth about the human body, how quickly everything could fall apart.

It was a few days before Christmas, Jimmy and Clara off from work, and no doubt off somewhere together. Ginger and Bill came over to see the children, but more to do their part as professional actors: Bill brought in the tree and set it up in the stand, his silver spurs jangling all the while. It didn't matter anymore that Irving had been angry at Ginger for leaving the studio; he wouldn't see the guests anyway. Triumph had made Ginger more famous than ever, more famous than Laura and Robert Hunter, more famous even than Susie and Johnny, and Laura herself felt starstruck, as if they hadn't been friends since the beginning of time, the beginning of her life as Laura Lamont, which seemed as old as the glaciers, and she was embarrassed how much it meant to her to have Ginger in her living room. Fragrant pine needles scattered from the tree like snowflakes, and Laura tried to follow them for a pattern, a secret message from the great beyond. Ginger unpacked ornaments from a large box and hung them one at a time on the branches of the tree, always asking Junior whether she should go higher or lower, left or right. Laura, Junior, and Florence sat rapt on the sofas, watching the performance. After the tree was sufficiently decorated, Ginger led the group in a game of charades, which everyone loved, even Florence, who pretended to despise the game until it was her turn, and then gamely became Roy Rogers or Rin Tin Tin, barking silently at the twinkling tree. Laura had to hide her face while watching Florence, because it was just too much to watch her daughter's sweet bravery, her willingness to try to behave as if the world were still a benevolent, normal place. Irving, the good American that he was, had always loved Christmas best of all the holidays, perhaps because he'd never celebrated it until he was an adult. There was no Jesus, of course, only singing and presents and Santa Claus, a holiday made of tinsel and magic, perfect for Hollywood.

The nurse, however, didn't care about Christmas, or was paid enough to pretend not to. She was large and thick, like so many of the women Laura remembered from her childhood, capable of lifting Irving out of bed and carrying him into the bathroom with no help whatsoever. Laura did her best to look away, as Irving had instructed. Someone was always with him, day and night. The doctors themselves came every other day, scratched notes on their little white pads, and left Laura with ever more prescriptions. She'd started to take twice as many blue pills as she was supposed to, but who was going to notice? It was Irving's pulse they were always taking, Irving's heart that concerned them. Laura stood still, as if she and her husband were in the eye of a storm, and if they didn't move a muscle, their house would remain intact, with only the water sucked out of the pool and the leaves torn off the trees.

The next morning, Laura helped Irving into the tub to take a bath. His body was smaller even than when they met, when he already seemed to Laura the size of a woodland sprite. His bones were pressing against his skin, forcing her to sponge new knobs and connections where before there had been flat expanses, or even gentle bodily slopes and curves. Laura dunked the sponge again and again, always making sure the water was neither too hot nor too cool. Irving leaned forward and back as directed, letting the warm water run from Laura's hands to his skin.

"What do you want me to get you for Christmas, my love?" Laura asked.

Irving laughed a very small laugh, though it clearly pained him.

"Surely you must want something."

Irving gripped his knees with his hands, pulling himself as upright as possible. His glasses were in the bedroom, which always gave his face that slightly faraway look that Laura remembered so well from her wedding night, as if he no longer needed to see in order to know what he was looking for.

"I would like a thousand more nights with you," Irving said. "For a start."

Laura dropped the sponge into the tub with a small splash, and wrapped her arms around her husband, the cool porcelain of the tub between their bodies.

There were only a handful of moments Laura could think of, in the span of her entire life, when she was unable to identify the seam in between what she felt and what she said or did, moments during which all of the selves that she'd ever been lined up perfectly, with no cracks in between. When she found her sister's body, when Florence was born, when Clara first smiled, when Josephine called to say that their father had died, when she saw Irving hold their son in his arms for the first time, when she kissed Irving for the first time, when she and Irving first saw and touched and kissed each other's bodies for the first time, when they were married, and when she knew she was his, forever, forever, forever. And now this moment was added to the list.

"I think we'll need more than that," she said, her mouth on his shoulder, on his collarbone, on his unshaven cheek. Water had splashed out of the tub and onto her robe and Laura wished that it were ink, some physical proof that her husband had loved her so much, and that she had held on to him as long as she could.

I rving died in the middle of the night on Christmas Eve, with Laura and the sturdy nurse standing beside his bed, both of them having been roused from their half sleep by a series of unusual noises coming from Irving's bed. Laura clutched the nurse's hand with her right hand and Irving's hand with her left, her eyes still adjusting to the dark. She reached for the lamp switch, but the nurse steered her hand away—it would be a shock to Irving's nervous system to have a bright light turned on, she thought; better to let him slip from darkness to darkness. Laura's ears were filled with the quickened pace of her own heart, which rushed and pumped as loudly as the ocean. Laura squeezed the nurse's hand as hard as she could, while Irving's fingers only twitched in her palm. She spoke to him quietly, trying to calm him as she had calmed the children when they were babies, whispering promises that she didn't know whether she could keep, platitudes her Irving would have laughed at, had he been well. They were more for herself than for him, she knew, but what could Laura do but try? Her husband was dying, and she had things to tell him. It was over in a minute, and Irving's body relaxed into silence. Laura moved the nurse aside and switched on the light, wanting to see her husband's face again before it turned into something else, something frozen and hard, the way her father's had been. She rested her hand against his cheek, feeling the bones in his face, his skin still warm. Laura felt as if a camera were watching them, recording every movement. She thought of Hildy's face, full of blood and anger, and her father's sorry mask of day-old makeup. At least Irving still looked like her husband. In the film, the wife closed her husband's eyes; the wife knelt on the floor beside her husband's bed and wept. She saw herself through the twin lenses of a camera, at once upside down and right-side up, the edges of the frame flickering as they moved past, quicker than the eye could see.

I rving Green was laid to rest at Hollywood Forever Cemetery, at a plot directly in line with the Gardner Brothers water tower, which was visible over the shared wall. He had chosen the plot himself well before the end, and Laura thought it suited him. Irving had told her once, on one of their first dates, the story of the cemetery. The cemetery had owned the land that Gardner Brothers sat on, owned the entire lot, but had rented it to the studio. It must have seemed like a lark to them, to the serious people whose business was death, to see a film studio set up shop in their backyard. They'd always assumed they would get the land back—what was more reliable, burials or movie stars?

The doctor's final pronouncement had been pneumonia, which anyone could get during a particularly bad cold, but which Irving's weak heart and lungs could not fight off. Louis Gardner insisted on paying for everything, and despite her daughters' protestations, Laura did not refuse him. It was to be a private service, but all of Hollywood had been invited, and attended. Laura sat with her sunglasses and a black veil in the front row, right before the coffin, her three children flanking her. Clara cried most of all, dampening Laura's crepe de chine dress with her muddled whimpering. When Louis Gardner rose to address the assembled crowd of actors, directors, and other Gardner Brothers employees, Laura blew her nose into her hankie so loudly that he would get her message. The giddy friendliness she'd felt when she arrived in Hollywood was gone, and in its place was a wooden box. The answer seemed as simple as this: If Laura loved anyone too much, they would be taken away. She held on to her children more tightly, their arms and hands grabbing at one another as if they were dangling from a skyscraper made of grief. Junior sat on her left, his legs swinging above the ground, Florence's arm wrapped around his shoulder as tightly as if their chairs were fifty feet in the air. Laura half started out of her seat, afraid that he might fall, but realized that everyone was looking at her, and instead just reached out, as if her hand could hold on to all of her children at once.

Laura looked over her shoulder and saw Ginger and Bill sitting right behind her. Her mother hadn't come, but Josephine was two seats over from Ginger, having flown on her own dime, as soon as she'd heard. She stared straight ahead, steady as a mermaid on the prow of a ship. Louis Gardner and his family were in the third row, and Susie and Johnny, and after that Laura couldn't bear to look. Everyone was watching her face, as if trying to gauge her misery. *Yes*, she wanted to shout, *yes, my husband is dead*, but she couldn't. It didn't feel real, all the flowers filling the house, all the people in black sitting behind her. Laura wanted to wake up in her bed and have Irving next to her, reading a script or writing notes furiously on his next project. She wanted Junior to have a father, and the girls—they were all in the same boat now, Laura and her children, all fatherless and bereft.

The service went on too long—after Louis, several actors got up to speak, including Johnny, who had put on thirty pounds and seemed to be wearing a toupee. Ginger spoke, which made Laura as happy as she could possibly be, as if there were a tightrope strung between the past and the present and Ginger was on it, walking backward. There was no mention of God, or heaven, only the glamorous universe Irving had helped to create, the heaven that could outlast everyone present, which was just how he would have wanted it. After it was over, Laura stood in place and let herself be embraced by hundreds of people, many of whom she had never met. This was a role she had played before, and it wasn't until Junior said that he was hungry, and Josephine pushed her way to the front of the line, that Laura agreed to be taken home. Clara glared at Laura when it was time to go, as if in leaving they were saying good-bye to Irving for good. Laura wanted to tell her daughter, her sweetest and eldest, that what was gone was not at the cemetery and not at the house but in their hearts forever, but she couldn't, because she missed her husband too much to make up something that sounded better than agony.

⌇

Some people called; some sent notes. Peggy Bates sent a hand-written poem in girlish purple ink (*Though buds do fall / and boughs do break / so do our hearts / for you*), and Dolores Dee sent over a garishly large bouquet of lilies. Laura sifted through all the letters on the floor of the office. It was impossible to remember whom she had already written back to, and who was still waiting for a response. She found herself so easily exhausted: While Junior and Florence were at school, and Clara was out at work, Laura most often wanted to sleep the day away. She would tuck her knees into her chest and fall asleep in a little ball on the carpet, an over-grown puppy at no one's feet. Harriet would cover her with a blan-ket and close the blinds, always wanting to defer to her boss's judgment, even when it was so clearly clouded by misery.

Laura awoke to the sound of keys in the door—the drapes were drawn, though it was still the middle of the day. The clock on the wall told the unfortunate truth: It was hardly even the af-ternoon. Laura pushed herself up to sit and felt the grooves on the side of her face from using her hands as a makeshift pillow. She heard laughter coming from the living room—Clara, who should have been at Triumph. Laura crawled over to the door of her office and rested her ear against the keyhole. The living room was a long hallway away, but she could hear well enough, with the rest of the house perfectly silent. Clara wasn't alone.

"I *promise*," she said to her unseen companion. "Don't be such a baby."

Clara and her friend—it was a man; Laura could tell by the sound of her daughter's voice—sat down on the sofa. It was funny, Laura thought, that she knew the sound of every object in the house, without even realizing it. She could have been blindfolded and still identified every piece of furniture just by its individual groans and creaks. Every object in the house belonged to her and Irving together, and Laura wanted the house to mourn in silence too. They were on the sofa, not talking. Laura put her hand on the doorknob and turned it quietly. Though she was straining to hear every noise coming from the living room, no one was listening for her, and so the noises kept coming as she pulled the door open and began to crawl down the hall.

She'd made it halfway to the living room before she could really tell what was going on. Once it was clear, Laura wondered how she could have mistaken the sounds for anything else—an impromptu lunch date, a visit with Mama? Or a burglary? By her eldest daughter? No. Of course not. But Clara had managed to make some things disappear, nonetheless, and in record time. The straight line between the front door and the lip of the sofa was now polka-dotted with Clara's clothing.

Her red skirt was closest to the door—it had come off first. Then the matching jacket, and the blouse underneath it. One kitten heel, then another. Laura stayed frozen in place, on her hands and knees. Clara's back and head were visible, pointing the other direction, toward the kitchen. She still had her bra on, Laura was happy to see, but no, there were hands reaching around to unclasp it. Clara had always been a good-time kid, kissing neighbor boys until they ran off home, and shutting her little friends in the closet if they didn't want to play. Laura watched a section of Clara's soft blond hair detangle itself from its pins and fall against her bare back. It was too much. They were laughing, and kissing, and Clara folded in half so that she was nearly out of view, resting her torso against her unseen partner.

Laura couldn't take it anymore. She pressed all of her weight into her palms and straightened her legs, tilting slowly until she was standing all the way up. She'd never put much thought into the sexual lives of her children. She wasn't a monster—it was better for them to be normal and have urges and live full lives than the alternative—but to see the urges undressed in her living room would have seemed a touch over the line on the best of days.

From her normal height, it was easier to see everything in the room: her daughter's mostly naked body and the person beneath her, his eyes closed in dreamy reverie.

"Jimmy," Laura said, loud enough for him to hear it. She picked some dust motes off her pajamas and strode into the living room. It was *her* living room, after all.

The boy opened his eyes, his lips still attached to Clara's face. His pale eyelashes couldn't have blinked faster if they'd been on fire. Jimmy rolled Clara off him, sending her crashing to the floor.

"Mom!" Clara said, and crossed her arms over her chest. Jimmy scooted backward on the sofa, until he was as far away from Laura as he could get. An apology tumbled out of his mouth, an incomplete sentence on an endless loop, as if it would explain away his lack of clothing and good timing.

"Laura, I'm so sorry, we were just . . ." was how he began.

"Enough." Laura shielded her eyes with her hand. "Clara, get dressed. Jimmy, get out." She waited. Under the edge of her palm, she could see Clara's legs—wearing only her stockings—scramble to the other side of the sofa to retrieve her skirt.

Jimmy's shoes came into view, his brown loafers just opposite Laura's own bare feet. Laura let her hand drop. Jimmy's face was nearly purple.

"Am I fired?" He spoke facing the carpet.

"No, Jimmy." Laura sighed. "Just go home."

"Thank you," Jimmy said in a very quiet voice. He quickly walked over to the door, where Clara was still putting her clothes back on. It always took more time to put things on, Laura thought; it was true. She could remember when the house was new and she and Irving could hardly make it through the front door without undressing each other. Jimmy smoothed his hair with both hands, just like Irving used to do, which gave Laura a jolt. He then jerked toward Clara, kissing her awkwardly on the cheek. She slapped at Jimmy's arm and pushed him out the door.

The room hummed. Clara let her arms drop to her sides. Her blouse was still unbuttoned, and hung open like a pair of sorry drapes. Laura hadn't seen her daughter in such a state of undress for years, since the girls were truly girls and not young women.

"I thought you were out with Ginger," Clara said.

"Well, I'm not," Laura said.

Clara shrugged, and then buttoned up her blouse. "It's not like you never did it," she said. "Everyone knows that."

"I was married." Laura rested a shoulder against the wall of the hallway, bracing herself up. Clara looked so much like an Emerson still, with her sturdy hips and face tight as a sailor's knot. "I was married to your father."

"But you were still married to Gordon when you started sleeping with him, weren't you? That's what everyone says at Triumph." Behind Clara's head, the light flickered. Laura would have to remind Harriet about it, remember to change the bulb. There were too many things falling apart at once. She hadn't slept with Irving while she was married to Gordon, but she'd thought about it, imagined it, wished for it, and that made her guilty enough. There was lipstick on Clara's cheek, a red line drawn with Jimmy's cheek.

"I'm going back to bed," Laura said, unable to stand any longer. She wanted to sink to her knees and crawl back to her spot on the floor, but knew that she couldn't, not now. So she held her chin up and pivoted on her bare feet, walking as slowly and carefully as if she were walking across a stage. Just before she reached her bedroom door, she stopped. "Don't do that again," she said without turning around. Clara could hear her well enough. After locking the door behind her, Laura climbed into her bed and swallowed three blue pills, enough to let it all sink away. When she let her head relax against the pillow, her body felt as if it were floating on the surface of the ocean, soft and lethal.

8

PANTHERESS

Fall 1959

The first job Laura took after her Irving's death was a feat of new technology—some of the studios were experimenting with three dimensions. 3-D, that was what they called it. The movie was about a woman who turned into a panther when she got angry—*Pantheress*. Susie and Johnny had made a couple of the 3-D films, but they never did more than toss bananas toward the camera during a scene at the market. They hadn't *used the technology*—at least that was what people were saying to Laura.

A new studio was making *Pantheress*—the producers were young and frankly awed that they got to be in the same room with Laura Lamont, always wringing their hands and tapping their feet. She liked that they were nervous. It had been a long time since people had tried to convince her to be in their movies, and it felt somehow welcome to be unsure of the future. The kids making the film were only a few years older than Clara and Florence. Someone was funding them, somebody's grandmother with oil-deep pockets. They wanted to start filming immediately, and Laura said yes without even having read the script. She couldn't bring herself to read a single page without Irving beside her in bed. Jimmy had said he liked it, that he would go see it in the theaters, and that seemed like enough. If the movie was wretched, who was going to notice?

The idea was this: Penelope, Laura's character, was a librarian, still single after all these years. She lived alone in an apartment above her landlady, and cooked meals for one on a hot plate every night. She wore glasses, and had her hair in a bun, stuck through with a pencil. One night, Penelope was late leaving the library, and a couple of guys were lingering around the exit, barely visible in the shadows. Penelope hurried, keeping her keys in her hand, ready to attack, and the men trailed her, whistling catcalls. One of them came so close that he grabbed the hem of Penelope's skirt and ripped the skirt off. Another man pushed Penelope to the ground and started to attack, forcing himself on her, when out of nowhere, a giant *wwwwrrrrrrrroooooooaaaaarrrrr* came out of no-where. The men turned and looked in horror at the giant black panther that had just landed beside them. Penelope kept her eyes closed tight, and once the men had run away, the panther began to lick her body, starting where the men had touched her. Penelope woke up in her own bed, her wounds healed, thinking the whole thing had been a dream.

"So the love interest is a jungle cat?" Laura wanted Jimmy to explain it to her after the meeting. She'd been taking a lot of the little blue pills—the prescription was in her name now, and Laura had already refilled it twice, from two different pharmacies. There were so many doctors in Los Angeles, it seemed silly to have only one. It was easier to pay attention after she'd taken her medicine. It made her nervous to imagine having only a single bottle left, let alone running out entirely. Before Irving died, Laura had been self-conscious about her need for the pills, but now there was no one to feel self-conscious in front of. Harriet had her own room, and so did the children, and Jimmy was far too polite to ever follow Laura into the bathroom.

Jimmy looked down at his notes. They were sitting in their office, which overlooked the pool. Laura had been thinking about redecorating, but that was as far as she'd gotten—thinking about it. She thought about eating meals too, but had largely forgotten to do so.

"Not exactly," Jimmy went on.

When Penelope awoke, she found she no longer needed her reading glasses. Even without any of the library lights on, she could read the smallest print without any trouble whatsoever. She shelved books on the highest shelf without needing a ladder— she just scampered on up. Things were changing in Penelope's body. When she showered in the morning, there were a few short black hairs in the drain, along with the usual long brown ones. It wasn't until she was again leaving the library at night, and again was followed, that Penelope discovered what changes were afoot inside of her. This time, instead of having a panther come to her rescue, Penelope herself morphed into a giant black pantheress. She ripped the men to shreds and then leaped into her own window, curling up like a house cat on her bed.

"Oh," Laura said. She stared out the window. Her body felt creaky and cold, as if her joints were filled with ice. It seemed likely that she had forgotten how to act, as one forgets a foreign language if it isn't spoken. Laura felt that she could barely act like herself, let alone someone else. When Irving was alive, it had seemed important to her to keep working, and now she couldn't remember why. The neighbor's palm leaves slaked off onto her grass, giant discarded husks. The surface of the swimming pool was clear blue, like a child's painting of the ocean. With Clara at work and Florence and Junior in school all day, the pool was almost always empty. The breeze blew the inflated plastic beach balls back and forth across the otherwise smooth surface of the water. She had already forgotten what Jimmy was talking about.

"And it goes on like that, with her turning back and forth. She gets revenge. She prevents crimes. She's really a very strong female character." Jimmy sounded as if he were trying to convince himself.

"So I'm playing a cat," Laura said. The next-door neighbors had small children, much younger than Junior, and no pool. Laura thought about inviting them over, but she'd never spoken to them before, though she waved whenever she saw them. They might find her too strange. It wasn't everyone who wanted to swim in a stranger's pool. She would call and ask. Laura wrote herself a note. *Pool*, it said. Even as she wrote it, she knew she wouldn't remember what it meant. Since Irving's death, the days had been full of such half-remembered memos and thoughts. One night, Laura had a dream that lasted for at least two hours—she was sure of it—and within the dream she kept reminding herself, *Remember this, remember this*, because she was with her father and Irving on the night she won the Academy Award, and they were sitting together in the living room, just talking, as natural as could be. When she woke up, she wrote down *Living room*, but by the time she brushed her teeth, the rest was gone.

❧

The budget was small: smaller than that, even. The budget for the entire film was less than what the Gardner Brothers would have paid for Laura's dresses alone. Laura missed her old dresses, the silk that slid along her skin, the rich wools, the crepe de chine. She'd never felt fabrics like that before she started working for Gardner Brothers, never knew the difference. Of course, it wasn't really the dresses themselves that she missed; it was the way she would walk out of her dressing room, the sky over Hollywood warm with twilight, and walk down to the soundstage, the material sliding back and forth over her hips as she moved. Irving would have been close; he was always close. He could have been watching her out his office window. That was it: She'd always felt as if he were watching her, and that in his eyes, she was the most beautiful creature on the lot. Laura was only thirty-nine. That was still young enough to be beautiful, wasn't it? It was difficult to concentrate on the present when so much of what Laura loved was in the past. She thought about her sister and her father and her husband, all gone, all gone. Losing Hildy had been hard enough to make her split in two, and now Laura worried that there weren't enough parts of her left to split, that she had divided too many times, until there was nothing left, nothing left but what was missing.

At Jimmy's insistence, he accompanied Laura to and from the

set every day. The shoot was short: only four weeks. Laura was glad for the company, as much as she could feel gladness. There were brief moments of the day when she was talking to Jimmy that she would forget her grief; he was from the Midwest, which she liked. When she told him that she'd grown up in Door County, he didn't believe her, and Laura began to cry, so distraught that all traces of Wisconsin had been expunged from her biography that the idea was so far-fetched. Once she'd taken another little blue pill and calmed down a bit, she and Jimmy had had a long conversation about different flavors of frozen custard, which would have made Laura giddy if she hadn't felt so tired. She wanted to tell Jimmy all about Josephine's job at the custard shop, but she couldn't quite recall the name of the shop. She would tell him later. Jimmy had been talking to Clara on the telephone at night, as regular as a rooster. Laura could remember that: that when the phone rang at half past eight, she had a feeling deep inside her gut that it was Irving calling from the lot to say he would be home later than usual, but by the time someone answered, the truth would have come back to her, as sharp as ever.

Laura's memory had never been a problem before, but now she was having trouble with her lines. Even as a child, she found there was a place in her brain that was always just the right size for the words she had to say, as if they were written on the back of her tongue, and would spill forth on command. The first time she flubbed a line, the director told her not to worry about it. Laura thought she saw him make a face to one of his grunts. But it wasn't Shakespeare. Laura discovered that any approximation of the line worked just as well. There was something funny about the movie—whether or not it was intentional Laura couldn't discern—and she hadn't been in a funny movie since she was a girl. It felt like several lifetimes ago that she and Ginger were poking those umbrellas at each other, doing their tap steps up and down those stairs, their hands holding bunched-up layers of petticoats. Ginger would be glad to see Laura doing something entertaining, if Ginger ever called. Gardner Brothers was old-fashioned, and Laura was glad to be rid of them. She stretched a paw toward the camera. She was tickling the audience's heads, lapping up their attention. When she wasn't on the set, Laura sat in her trailer and stared at the mirror. She was sure that if she stared long enough, her eyes pitched just over her left shoulder, where the door was, eventually Irving would walk in. She couldn't even picture him doing it without starting to cry, her anticipated relief was so great. All he had to do was come back. In a funny way, it made it easier to imagine now that she was filming again. It was so clear to her now: He hadn't felt needed. With the girls so close to being out of the house, and Junior a grown boy, why would they need him there? Laura shook her head slowly, without taking her eyes off the mirror.

❧

Ginger thought it was a good idea to get out of the house, and disagreeing sounded like more trouble than it was worth, so Laura acquiesced. She hadn't been out to dinner in six months, since before Irving died. Ginger and Bill had a table at Pierre's, which sat a few hundred feet above Hollywood Boulevard and overlooked downtown Los Angeles, the kind of place that tourists dreamed about, always crackling with fresh ice cubes. Dinner would be just the two of them, just the girls. When Irving was alive, they always had to decide whether their dates would be single or double, but now that he was dead, having dinner as a threesome was too depressing for words. Even though Ginger and Bill rarely seemed as happy as they'd once been, when they wore leather jackets with each other's names stitched on the back in a gentle rainbow, even watching them glare at each other and pick tiny fights was excruciating.

The restaurant clung to the side of the hill, and one had to make a series of hairpin turns around the hillside in order to reach the overstaffed driveway, where men in vests waited to properly park your car. The inside was just as precarious and overdecorated, with framed photographs of famous patrons hung on every available wall, and a photo of Ginger beside the entrance. The owner, a Frenchman who'd lived in Los Angeles longer than Laura, kissed Ginger on both cheeks and then led them to their table. Everyone in the restaurant turned to look as they walked by, squeezing their way between tables. Laura sat first, and waited for Ginger to finish talking. A decade earlier, Laura would have known every person in the room, but she recognized only the faces in the photographs on the walls. It seemed like generations ago that Laura had been the more famous of the two.

"Did you see that writer?" Ginger said as she sat, lowering her voice.

"What writer?" Laura looked around the room. She recognized everyone and no one—it was a typical crowd, with women in dresses tailored tightly against their waists, no matter that they were at a restaurant and not a cocktail party, and men in dark suits slim against their shoulders, their hair always so neatly cut. She could have been in a room full of extras playing diners. Laura was too tired to pretend to be anything more or less than what she was, heartbroken and exhausted by the simple act of leaving the house after dark.

"The one who came to your dinner party. For the magazine. Harry, I think, or Henry. He's at the bar, see?" Ginger spoke without turning around. She knew what it felt like to have strangers looking at her, knew how easy it was to detect a stare from across the room. Laura craned her neck.

Sure enough, Harry Ryman was sitting at the bar, alone. Laura hadn't seen him since the dinner party he'd come to so many years earlier, and he'd aged since she saw him last. His thick blond hair was now thinning at the crown, and his broad shoulders had filled out a bit. The horse picture had never gotten made, not by Gardner Brothers, and not by anybody else. Laura felt a pang of guilt— it had been her doing, the picture getting buried, all because she didn't want to play somebody's mother. As if she didn't have three children, as if she had a choice whether or not to get older.

"I wonder how he's doing," Laura said. It had been a long time since she'd wondered about anyone but herself and the children. Harry was drinking a martini, and Laura watched as he tipped the glass and poured the rest of the liquid down his throat in one long swallow. "I'm going to go say hello—do you mind?" Ginger started to say something in response, but Laura was already up and moving across the room.

Laura watched Harry recognize her. She'd aged too, she supposed—certainly her face was not as elastic, as creaseless, as open. He recovered quickly, and smiled broadly as she approached.

"Laura Lamont," he said.

"How are you, Harry?" Laura perched herself on the empty stool next to him, sliding up the smooth oxblood leather. Ginger could wait.

He chuckled. "I'm just fine." A sudden thought flashed across his face, *Irving*, and Harry's smile vanished. "I'm so sorry about Mr. Green. I thought about writing, but I didn't think you'd remember me."

It was refreshing to be out of the house; Ginger had been right. Laura looked back at her friend, on the far side of the room. This was the idea: Break the pattern. There was too much death in Laura's life, too much silence, too much solitude. She wanted to be surrounded by other people, to hear their stories, to lose herself in someone else's life.

"Why don't you join us for dinner?" Laura motioned for the waiter before Harry had a chance to respond. She pointed at Ginger's table, and by the time she and Harry had made their way back across the room, arm in arm, another place had been set. For the rest of the night, Laura laughed at every single one of Harry's jokes, whether or not they were funny. Ginger watched with a fish eye, unsure of what was unfolding, but Laura didn't care, and when Harry offered to drive her home in thanks for the dinner, she said yes. The three of them stood outside, throats vodka-soaked, waiting for the valets to fetch the cars. Ginger's boat of a Cadillac arrived first, and she hesitated before getting behind the wheel, clearly conflicted about leaving Laura snuggled up against a man who was nearly a complete stranger. But eventually Ginger drove off, and they were alone. Laura didn't wonder until later why Harry hadn't minded leaving his own car at the restaurant. She was happy to have someone else at the wheel, and lolled her head against the back of the seat, closing her eyes and humming along to whatever song was on the radio.

The house was dark when they pulled into Laura's driveway. It was after ten, and Harriet would've put Junior to sleep hours ago. Florence was likely in her room studying, and there was no telling where Clara might be. She'd been staying overnight at a friend's house, which Laura took to mean that she'd been spending nights at Jimmy's. Laura wouldn't have disobeyed her mother for a boy, not ever. She thought about the last summer she spent in Door County, and the way she and Gordon had talked to each other for hours in the grass behind the barn. Their voices would have carried to the house, or they wouldn't have, but Laura thought that if her mother had ever listened, she wouldn't have heard anything so horrible. She would have heard two kids who'd never seen the world talking about what it might be like, two blind men describing the color of the sky. Clara seemed to have a more concrete understanding of the romantic universe.

"I'm sorry if I got in the way of your movie," Laura said. She rested her hand on the back of Harry's head, feeling his thin hair, and the smooth scalp beneath it. In front of them, the house looked as perfectly kept as a doll's house, with straight trees growing on either side of the front door, and the Spanish tiles so neat along the roof. She hadn't touched a man like this for years, a man other than her husband. Laura closed her eyes and pretended that it was Irving's head beneath her fingers. That was all she wanted: to touch him again, to have his full, healthy body beside her, smoking and talking as if they had all the time in the world left.

Harry lit a cigarette and exhaled a plume of smoke out the open window. His head nearly brushed against the roof of the car. It had been so many years since Laura lived with a tall man that she'd forgotten what their bodies were like in space, how their knees jutted up when they sat down, how the ceiling always seemed lowered around them, like they were another wooden beam holding the earth and sky apart. She let her body slump against his, arm to arm, thigh to thigh, not worrying about her dress getting mussed against the seat.

"Don't worry about it," Harry said. He was staring at the house. Laura lifted her bottom off the seat and smoothed the hem of her dress with her free hand. When she settled back down, Harry put his arm around her shoulder and held her tightly against him. Laura felt Harry's ribs expand with each breath, and she slowed her own breathing to match his. She wanted to feel another body moving close to her, and she didn't. Laura let her lips fall against Harry's lapel. She arched her neck backward so that she could see him better, and then shut her eyes and waited for contact. If she didn't move, then it wasn't really her doing, Laura thought. Through her closed eyelids, she pictured her husband, alive and able, his strong hands and lips waiting to touch her.

When Harry finally realized what he was supposed to do and leaned down to meet Laura's face, she slapped him quickly on the cheek.

"That was for Irving," she said, already pulling Harry close again, wanting her heartbeat to speed up so fast that her chest would crack in half, turning her inside out. Laura slid backward until Harry was on top of her, undoing his buttons as fast as he could, his cigarette abandoned in the car's ashtray. Laura watched the smoke continue to curl out the open window as Harry began to push her dress up to her waist. She wanted to pretend that her body belonged to someone else, someone ravenous and carefree, someone whom loss had never touched. Harry began to make noises, soft little moans, and Laura wrapped her arms around his back. "Sssh," she said, "sshh." When he was through, Laura told him to wait in the car as she called him a taxi from inside the house. She tiptoed in, her shoes in her hand, and leaned against the back of the door like the world's oldest teenager, her wishes and regrets all pooled together into one soggy mess. She might have cried if she didn't think it would wake the children.

Party invitations began to arrive more frequently—or maybe they'd always been offered, but Laura had never cared enough to take note. Now that she knew there was relief to be found in the world outside her body—or rather, by moving her body through the outside world—Laura said yes to nearly every invitation.

Junior, who had always been an introverted child, seemed to take his mother's sudden interest in nightlife to heart, and had stopped sleeping.

"Sweetie," Laura said, sitting on his bed one night. "Is everything okay at school?" Junior was in the third grade, and the smallest, weediest boy in his class. He wore glasses with small round frames, and Laura often thought that he looked like a nervous owl, his eyes wide and unblinking behind the lenses.

"I guess so," Junior said. He was sitting up in bed, his legs covered by a thin quilt. Irving had tried so hard to make Junior's room a proper boyish space, with Brooklyn Dodgers baseball pennants hung on the wall, but the room had never shaken the feeling of his older sisters, as if their whispered conversations had clung to the walls, even through the coat of blue paint. "It's the same as always." He stared at her, his back starkly straight against the wall.

"Aren't you sleepy?" Laura ran her hand back and forth over his shins. Junior shook his head. "Do you have a book?"

Junior produced a flimsy paperback from under the covers—he loved books, and was proficient enough to read books that Clara hadn't read until she was twelve.

"Mommy has to go out for a little while, so why don't you read your book until you're tired enough to fall asleep, okay?" Laura leaned down and kissed Junior on the forehead.

"What if I'm still awake when you get home?" he asked, as Laura began to back out of his room.

"Then I'll kiss you again," Laura said. She flicked off the overhead light, so that the only area illuminated was a small yellow circle around Junior's pillow.

"Okay," Junior said, dubious. He watched her shut the door, and Laura was sure as she walked to her car that he was watching her still.

⁓

Harry Ryman was friends with Joe, who was friends with Dotty, who had the best parties. Dotty lived in Villa Valentino, an apartment complex off Sunset with lots of other actors, some of them young and all of them broke. Her apartment was on the ground floor, at the back of the building, and in order to get to it, one had to walk through a gate and then around the neglected swimming pool. Laura stayed close behind Harry, though when he tried to hold her hand, she swatted it away. She still wasn't sure whether she liked to be around him, but she knew that she didn't like spending her nights alone.

A crowd of partygoers stood outside the entrance, making the narrow doorway nearly impassable. The smell of reefer wafted through the air, sweet and sour as a skunk. Harry turned sideways in order to squeeze through the people and get into the apartment, and Laura reluctantly followed. At every step, she considered that she was too old and sad to be at the party, though she was not nearly the oldest in attendance, and that she ought to be home with her children. Something wasn't right with Junior; a mother could tell. The problem was that Laura and Junior were fighting off the same disease: loneliness. How could she rescue her son from the depths when she herself was sure they hadn't yet hit the bottom? Harry was several steps ahead, and Laura hurried to catch up.

They made their way into the small kitchen, a glorified corner of the main room, which was empty except for two ratty sofas and some milk crates that men were using as ottomans. Young women in various stages of undress pretended not to recognize Laura, and went back to necking with their gentlemen friends along the walls. The tile floor was dirty, and the open cabinets were largely empty. Laura felt overdressed in her silk dress, and didn't want to lean against the lip of the stove, the only available spot, so she leaned against Harry for a moment, was surprised by his sturdiness, and then stood up straight, floating in space.

"Who lives here?" Laura whispered backward, toward Harry.

"Dotty. You'll like her, you'll see," he said, but Laura wasn't convinced.

"Which one is Dotty?"

Harry gently pushed Laura aside and checked the refrigerator, where he found two cold bottles of beer. He opened them both and handed one to her. "In the pink."

There was a young woman wearing a pink blouse in the far corner of the room. She had her hair tied up in a scarf, as if she were in the passenger seat of a convertible, already sixty miles out of town and headed for Big Sur. Dotty, Harry told Laura, was a poet. Laura had never met a poet before. She watched Dotty adjust a lamp shade, tilting it one way and then the other, so that the dim spotlight moved back and forth across the floor. It seemed like a poetic thing to do.

To her dismay, Laura had to use the bathroom, which Harry escorted her to, promising to wait just outside the door. She felt sick to her stomach, treating this man she barely knew like her boyfriend, but the idea of going back to nights spent curled up on the rug alone was too awful to bear. Laura flushed the toilet and looked at her reflection in the small mirror. The glass was dingy, and the room was dingier, with a tub that looked like it hadn't been cleaned in years. Laura washed her hands and slowly pushed the door open.

More people started streaming in from the courtyard, packing into the apartment like sardines. Two young women—hardly older than Clara—came up to Laura and clasped her by the hand, each on one side.

"Miss Lamont, you're the reason I became an actress," one said.

"Miss Lamont, you're the reason I came to Hollywood," said the other.

"Are you twins?" Laura asked. She wanted to ask them where

they lived, and whether they wanted her to take them home to their parents' houses, but then they were off, giggling and blushing and tickling each other's waists. Laura felt silly for even trying to talk to them, or anyone.

"Harry," she started, and looked around to see that Harry had disappeared. Laura scanned the room and saw him sitting beside Dotty on the sofa. Excusing herself as she went, Laura stepped carefully across the tacky hardwood, keeping her face turned toward the floor so as to avoid any more errant compliments.

"Harry," she said again, now standing in front of the sofa he was sitting on. Dotty sat beside him, her scarf knotted under her chin. She held a cigarette between her fingers and picked the loose tobacco off her tongue with her other hand.

Even in the dark, Laura could see that Harry's eyes had glazed over, and were struggling to stay open. "Mmm?" he said.

Laura crouched down beside him and took his chin in her hand. "Harry, what's wrong? Are you all right?"

Dotty laughed. Up close, she looked older, her skin covered by too much makeup. Dotty's eyebrows were a penciled-in fiction, arching skyward, though her eyes themselves were only half-open, which gave her the disconcerting look of a clown whose circus had left him behind.

"Excuse me?" Laura turned her attention away from Harry, who seemed to have fallen asleep.

"He's fiiiiiiine," Dotty said. She pitched herself forward so that her elbows rested on her knees, just inches from Laura's face. "He's just hiiiiiiiigh, movie star."

The room was too warm, like the air just before a thunderstorm, thick with moisture. Laura had been around drugs before—

she'd taken a little blue pill before leaving the house, and would take another before she fell asleep—but that was different, she told herself, different. Harry's eyes were open, but he was asleep—or something like asleep. It wasn't like any kind of high Laura had ever seen, and it frightened her.

"He'll be all right?" she asked Dotty, knowing that the question would be met with more derision. Sure enough, Dotty laughed again, opening her little mouth wide enough that Laura could see her bad teeth, browning all the way to the molars. She pushed herself back up to stand and squeezed through the crowd until she was in the courtyard again. The air in Los Angeles never felt like the air in Door County, but that night Laura was so grateful to be outside that she hardly noticed the difference. The water in the swimming pool was speckled by moonlit beer bottles floating on the surface, and Laura wished that she were already home in bed. She wished that Irving would be there when she got home, and that he would tell her how to proceed, and how to get their son to sleep through the night. Laura wrapped her arms around her own waist and leaned her face toward the moon, a half circle, clean as an apple cut in half. Other people from the party were standing nearby, starting to stare. Laura walked out without turning around, wishing Harry luck under her breath, knowing that he would need it as much as she did.

❦

Harriet usually did the grocery shopping at Sale's Fulton Market on Mondays. On busy days, she would just phone it in, and the delivery truck would bring Junior's Jell-O and Laura's milk and sugar and Florence's fruit in syrup, but it wasn't such a far drive, and Harriet liked to go herself.

Laura stood by the door with her gloves and hat already on.

"I'll go with you," she said.

Harriet nodded and put on her hat. "All right," she said.

The women walked out in the sun and Harriet locked the door behind them. Junior and Florence would be fine on their own for an hour or two, and Clara's purse was sitting by the door, so she was home too. Laura took a deep breath, a momentary satisfaction filling her lungs—a full house. They rounded the corner and turned toward the garage. When they'd made the turn, Laura noticed two things: Someone had dropped off a bouquet of flowers in front of the garage door, where they were currently freezing to death, the large white blooms wobbling in the breeze, and beside the flowers, there was a man who seemed to be asleep, with his head pressed against the garage wall. Harriet stuck her hand out, as if to wave Laura back toward the house, but they both kept walking forward, taking smaller and smaller steps. The sleeping figure didn't start up as soon as the women approached, but roused himself languidly, as though he were in his own bed, with nowhere in particular he had to be. It was only when he sat up and shifted his hat to the back of his head that Laura realized she was looking at Gordon Pitts.

Ginger was right: He'd lost a tooth, maybe more. Gordon tried to straighten up as Harriet and Laura approached, their steps almost imperceptibly small now. Oh, yes: There would be a smell. "Stay here," Laura said to Harriet, and Harriet stopped in her tracks, clearly grateful not to have to move any closer.

"It's Mr. Pitts," Harriet said.

They were now standing only a few inches away from Gordon's feet. He slowly rolled his eyes open, saw Laura, and smiled widely.

"There's my girl!" Gordon said. "Came as soon as I heard."

Laura slid back, colliding with Harriet, who grasped her shoulders but didn't say a word. *This is your mess*: That was what Harriet's silence meant, but she didn't retreat.

"Gordon, what are you doing here?" Laura didn't want to get any closer. In addition to the missing teeth, which punctuated his smile like exclamation points, Gordon was missing the ribbon around his hat, a proper shirt, socks. He sat up and leaned against the garage door, nearly knocking the flowers over. Harriet moved a hand forward to catch them. He fingered the card, as if thinking about opening it to see who had been so thoughtful.

"Heard about Irving. Came to pay my respects." Gordon nodded and then seemed to lose himself to the nodding for a moment, as though all he had to do to be asleep was close his eyes.

"The service was months ago. You've missed it, I mean. You really didn't have to come." Laura didn't want to move any closer, but she knew that sooner or later, the girls would be up and clanging around inside the house. Junior would wonder where she was and come outside to sit in the dirt until she returned. Laura had to move Gordon somewhere the children wouldn't be. "Let's go out by the pool, Gordon, all right? I think we'll all be more comfortable out there."

"Ssssure," Gordon said, letting the world slip slowly out of his mouth. He pushed himself up to stand, and waved back and forth like a scarecrow.

Laura hurried toward him, nudging Harriet to come along.

They each threw one of Gordon's arms over their shoulders and escorted him back down.

"I love this," Gordon said. "Heel, toe, heel, toe." He waggled his hips back and forth. Harriet pinched her nose with her free hand. Gordon smelled like he'd been sleeping in a bus station for a month. Laura heard the front door slam behind them. She tried to think of a way that she could erase this moment from time, from the girls' memory. It wasn't supposed to happen like this: Gordon wasn't supposed to come back. She'd told them nothing— one doting father was enough. Clara's voice was louder: "Who *is* that?"

They walked in tandem around the back of the house to the pool. Harriet bore most of Gordon's weight, which wasn't much. How was it that so many hours of Laura's life of late had been with one arm tucked around a man's waist, holding him up from hitting the ground? She wished herself into another scene, another movie, something happier, with talking cars or dogs and a Ferris wheel.

"Fucking amateurs," Gordon said, as Laura and Harriet set him down, bottom-first, onto a metal recliner.

Laura ignored him. "Where did you come from, Gordon? Are you all right? You really look terrible, you know."

Gordon took off his hat and set it down beside him. His hair had thinned to a small tuft near his crown and a stringy half circle around the base of his skull. Laura felt as if she were watching him through a scrim. There was nothing in his features that reminded her of the man she married. He wet his lips with his tongue. "Laura Lamont. Look at you."

Harriet crossed her arms over her chest and made a sharp

noise, like a popping balloon. "Can we help you with something, Mr. Pitts?" The love that Laura felt for her grew to twice its size.

Gordon picked up his hat and attempted to twirl it on a finger. The hat flew off and skidded to the ground. "I remember you," he said, looking at Harriet with one eye closed. "Well, I did think that such loyalty might be rewarded. After all, those are my two girls out there, ain't they?"

"You're asking for money?" Laura tried to remember the circumstances of the agreement. No, she knew them—Gordon had signed away his rights to the girls, and he'd never had any claims on her money. Laura had always belonged to Gardner Brothers, just like Gordon had. Irving's money had nothing to do with her, and anyway, there wasn't any more where that was coming from. Gordon had been married to Elsa Emerson, a person who existed only in the moments between when Laura woke up and when she opened her eyes. With all the pills she'd been taking, Laura couldn't remember the last time Elsa had shown her face in the mirror.

"I'm not *asking*," Gordon said, putting on a shameless grin. "Isn't it worth *something* to you that I'm here? For your *husband*?" He spit out the word. "Irving always did like me, if I remember correctly. Don't you remember, Elsa?"

The door that led from the house to the pool swung open— Clara.

"Mom?" she said, her torso leaning through the doorway. "Maybe you should come inside."

Gordon turned back to Laura, his head still wobbling on his neck, as if poorly attached. "I always knew I liked that crazy broad." She had no idea whom he thought he was talking about.

After Gordon bathed in the guest room shower and put on some of Irving's clean clothes, which Laura told herself she would burn afterward, he sat at the kitchen table and made himself comfortable. Clara and Florence stood with their backs against the island, staring. Gordon lit each cigarette from the one before it, tapping off the ash before there was a chance for any to accumulate. Laura felt sick to her stomach, and made Harriet do all the talking.

"So, Mr. Pitts, what have you been doing since you left Los Angeles?" Harriet spoke with zero inflection, like a policeman who'd just stopped a weaving car.

Gordon laughed awkwardly. "Since Irving tossed me out, you mean?" He looked at the girls and shook his head. They moved closer together, until there was no space between their bodies. "Been here and there. I got a job in San Francisco, doing a play, but . . ." His voice trailed off. It was easy enough to imagine what had happened when this Gordon Pitts presented himself for the job. Laura would have fired him on the spot too.

Florence's eyes never moved off Gordon's face. Laura could understand why—Clara looked as though she'd been cleaved whole off of Laura's body, like Eve out of Adam, two parts of a whole. Florence looked far more like her father, with her thin wrists and eyes that slanted like a hungry alligator's. Out of the three children, Florence was the only one who'd had no human mirror. In Gordon, she could see what she might become. Laura felt proud of her daughter for not leaving the room in tears, as she surely would have done at Florence's age, and very much wanted to at her own.

"So you're Clara, and you're Florence," Gordon said. He looked the girls up and down like new car models on the lot. They nodded, docile and stunned as lambs. Laura wanted to scream. Everyone waited for Gordon to say something else, to follow up his identification with some mildly paternal line of questioning, but he didn't. Instead, he lit another cigarette and nodded, turning his attention back to Laura.

"Are you still acting?" Harriet was so patient. It was a tiny trial: Gordon was on the stand; Harriet was the inquiring lawyer; the girls were the two-headed judge. It was like an episode of *Ginger & Bill* gone off the rails, where the laugh track had been stunned into silence and there would be no happy resolution, no cozy snuggle. Junior was in his room, and Laura wished the imaginary camera would follow him instead, to capture anything but this. Gordon hadn't been so bad, not in the beginning. The army could have straightened him out, but didn't. If she could go back, Laura thought, she would still have married him.

Gordon shook his head. He leaned back and shut his eyes, a half-smoked cigarette still clamped between his lips. "You give me the part, man, I could play anything."

The kitchen was too small to hold both the past and the present, and it was the past that needed to go. Gordon meant nothing to the girls, even if he had once meant something to her—how could he? Even once the filth and booze on his dirty clothes was taken away, there was still a haziness that made Laura uncomfortable. There were other men on the set who'd started to look this way, with paler skin than California allowed, and scabs up and down their arms. Gordon had on long sleeves, and Laura was glad not to be able to see his marks.

"Girls," Laura said, without taking her eyes off Gordon, "go to your room."

Clara and Florence scooted sideways, their grown bodies having reverted to childlike movements, leaving the room as quickly as they could without turning their backs. Laura waited for the sound of their footsteps to stop before speaking.

"How much do you want?" Laura was thinking about herself as a teenager, about Gordon's slippery body inside hers, about the way his mouth looked like Florence's, with the corners turning down toward his chin. It was all too much, and she needed him gone. It didn't matter how much money he wanted, she was going to give it to him. That was what Gordon held over her head, and he knew it: Gordon had been married to her before she'd changed her name, when everything was still ahead of her. But no! That wasn't it at all. Gordon had been married to Elsa Emerson, the girl who hadn't been quite good enough for Hollywood, who would have done anything to make her name, even change it. In some basic way, Gordon had been married to the real her, while Irving—her love, her sweet Irving—had been married to a fantasy. Harriet put her hand on Laura's arm, but she couldn't stop her. It didn't matter whether she was giving him all the money she had in the world—Laura wanted Gordon out of her kitchen.

Gordon didn't seem to mind being talked about. He smoked his cigarette and picked at a fingernail, seemingly oblivious to the anguish he was causing. "I hear you've been spending time with my friend Harry. You know we're friends? I bet he didn't even mention it. But he mentioned you to me, boy, he sure did. Mentioned the front seat of your car and eeeeeeverything." Gordon flicked a piece of dirt from under his nail onto the kitchen floor and then looked straight at Laura, malice oozing out of his every pore.

"Five thousand dollars," Laura said. "I'll give you five thousand dollars. For you to never come anywhere near my children ever again." Her jaw was hard, set. It was one thing to be a drunk. But it was clear that Gordon was doing something else, ingesting a worse poison, and yes, Harry was doing it too. Laura had a momentary panic that the drugs could have been transmitted to the girls genetically, but no, that didn't make sense. The girls were all right, or at least they would be when they recovered from the shock of seeing him.

Gordon rubbed his eyes and appeared to ponder the proposition. When he looked up again, he smiled widely, the black spots where his teeth had been displayed in all their empty glory. "Well, okay," he said. "If you insist." It had all been a wager for Gordon; Laura was sure. There was no money coming from anywhere else, so why not test the familial waters, just to see? Even Harriet, whose steady face hardly ever betrayed a truly unpleasant emotion, looked disgusted. He slid out from behind the table and tipped his hat back on his head.

"I'll send you a telegram, let you know where to wire the money," Gordon said, walking jauntily now. Laura half thought that his decrepitude had been part of his scheme, but no, Gordon stumbled on his way to the front door. Laura watched him walk to the end of the driveway and turn onto the road, his small hips wagging from side to side, like he knew she was watching.

⌒

It was June, and a steady seventy-five degrees. Laura gave Jimmy the day off and sent Harriet on a long list of errands, and had the whole house to herself, just as she'd wanted. She put on her bathing suit and walked out to the pool barefoot. It was a mostly sunny day, but not so warm that most people would be swimming. Laura glanced down the sloping hill to her neighbors' house, and remembered that she'd wanted to invite them. Not today. Florence and Junior were at school; Clara was at work. As a child, Laura never would have imagined she'd have a swimming pool in her backyard, but, of course, Laura had never actually been a child at all. Elsa Emerson wouldn't have needed a pool; she would have gone to the beach and let the rough sand slide in between her toes, let it cling to her clothes and hair, her naturally blond hair. It would be darker now, probably, the color of wheat instead of the color of sunshine, but that was almost nicer on a grown-up woman. It was so hard to picture herself that way—Laura was almost forty, a widowed mother of three. A *widow*. Laura couldn't even say the word.

The morning had been hard; Laura'd woken from another dream about Irving, the third night in a row. In it, he'd been sitting in the corner of the room, just watching her sleep. Some nights he was smoking, some nights just leaning forward, his hands woven together under his chin. In the dreams she slept on, unaware of Irving's presence, and so when she woke up, her first thought was to check the chair to see if he was still there. He never was.

Laura had taken four of the blue pills instead of her usual two, and the outside edges of her body were already feeling fuzzy and soft. She put one foot in the shallow end of the pool and found that the water was only a little bit cold, and nicely bracing. Once her whole body was in, she wouldn't even notice. Laura remembered that from summers in Lake Michigan—the water was cold only when you got out and your wet skin met the air. As long as you stayed in the water, you weren't cold at all. She stepped her other foot in and walked a few feet farther, until the water was over her knees, and then up to her hips. There was barely a breeze, but the tops of her thighs were prickly with goose bumps as the water moved back and forth.

The idea was not to drown. Laura loved her children, and Junior in particular was so young. She thought of the heartbreak she'd felt at her own father's death—no, Laura would not do that to Junior, not until she had no other choice. But she couldn't rightly say that the thought of drowning hadn't occurred to her, either. If Gordon knew about what she'd done with Harry Ryman, then who else knew too? Maybe Clara was right, and she'd been that kind of girl all along. Laura wanted to let the water come in through the windows and doors and through her mouth and nose and ears until there was no oxygen left, only water. She walked farther into the pool, until she was on her tiptoes. The water closed around her neck, all the way up to her chin. She opened and closed her mouth like a fish, moving the water in and out, in and out. It was Irving's idea to get a house with a pool. Laura loved bodies of water as they were found in the wild: lakes, rivers, oceans. A swimming pool said something else: *We can afford to bring the water to us.* And so they did, trucking out mounds of dirt and rocks and filling the hole with gallons of treated water. Though Laura wasn't sure what they could afford anymore. Was it to make Clara and Florence love him more? They'd never had any other choice, or known any other father. Laura wasn't sure whether Clara remembered having Gordon around—she hoped not. His toothless smile came to her some nights, when she couldn't sleep. She would turn over and face the empty side of the bed, Irving's side, and there Gordon would be, his yellow eyes open and his gaping mouth pulled into a wet, sickening smile. In her dreams, Gordon was always laughing at her. It was he who drove Irving away, who had made him sick—the complication of her life before him. Laura thought she was crying but couldn't tell—her entire face was already wet. Had it started to rain? It rained so infrequently in Los Angeles that the girls acted as if the rain were made of bleach, and ran for cover when it started to fall. They knew no other way, which was Laura's fault, just like everything else. Junior's softness. His father's death. Gordon's addictions. Each one seemed like something that Laura could have prevented, if she'd been trying harder. She swallowed a mouthful of water and pushed herself forward into the deep end.

Laura opened her eyes underwater, which she had always liked to do. Hildy had been afraid to, complained that her eyes stung, but Laura—*Elsa*—had always enjoyed it. The bottom and sides of the pool were painted blue, as if another color would have made the water seem less inviting—better to pretend they were in the ocean, with the sky reflected and an entire world hidden beneath the surface. A palm leaf from next door had slunk all the way down to the drain, and Laura thought about diving down to retrieve it, but didn't. If she were to make a list about what she needed to do in life, Laura would have started like this: Go back in time. Go back farther. Go back to the beginning. Water was starting to slip up her nose, and Laura turned her face so that her mouth was again above water, and she gulped a few large breaths, dragged the air down deep into her lungs. If there were two of her, one Elsa and one Laura, each half as sorry as the other, which one would stay underwater? Which one would rise to the top? Laura wished that her life could be as static as a still photograph, all the players well lit and handsomely dressed. Sometimes Laura thought of herself as having had three sisters: Josephine, Hildy, and Elsa, with Josephine the only survivor of their shared childhood.

Harriet had been going around the house, shutting all the windows, which the girls always left open, as if they wanted every fly and pest in Los Angeles to move in. She had grown up in California, just like Clara and Florence, in a house that could have fit into two rooms of Laura's, but that didn't matter. The girls were her responsibility, as Laura was her responsibility, and the house too, all of it under her careful watch. Harriet's father had died when she was a child, no older than Junior, and she knew the mess that Laura was in, and how long it would last. The least she could do was make sure the rain didn't get in and ruin anything, that a soppy rug wasn't added to Laura's miseries. It was when she was closing the window of the living room that Harriet saw Laura facedown in the swimming pool. She told Laura later that she felt like she had an electrical current running through her body, starting at her feet and going straight to her brain. There were a thousand thoughts at once, but they were all the same: *Get to her. Get to her now.* Harriet let go of the window frame and ran to the side door, not thinking about getting wet, or her hair, or her clothes. She threw her body into the water, even though she was a poor swimmer herself, and dragged Laura to the shallow end by her outstretched arm, her body resisting. Laura's body, usually so light and thin, felt dense with water, and too heavy. Harriet's and Laura's bodies struggled together on the lip of the pool—Laura felt as if she were being dragged down by her darkest thoughts, and Harriet was trying to rescue a drowning woman who hadn't been drowning at all, only wallowing. Laura's skin was puckered and faint, with her dark, soaked hair like a bloodstain around her head.

"I'm fine," Laura said.

"What the hell are you doing?" Harriet asked, panting. Water dripped from her chin.

"I was swimming," Laura said. She knew she didn't sound convincing.

"What the hell were you doing?" Harriet asked again.

"I don't know." Laura rolled onto her side and tucked herself into a fetal position. She felt Harriet's weight on top of her, and let herself be pulled in toward the soaked cotton of Harriet's dress. "I miss them," she said. "I miss all of them."

"I think you've had enough of those pills," Harriet said. She put her arm underneath Laura's, helped her inside, sat her down at the kitchen table. Puddles formed at their feet while Harriet picked up the telephone and spoke. "Operator," she said. "I need a doctor."

The ambulance arrived just as Junior was coming back from school. Laura tried to argue with the men that she didn't need an ambulance, or a stretcher, or to be taken away at all, but they wouldn't listen. All she could think about were her children, and her husband and her father and Hildy, and how they were all going to feel as though she had let them down, let them *down*, as if that were an adequate description of her halfhearted betrayal. The yellow bus usually stopped right out front, but it double-parked a few houses back and waited for the ambulance to depart. Junior was standing in the front stairwell of the bus as his mother was wheeled out to the ambulance on a stretcher, and he was so stunned that he found he could not cry out for her, which was something that he regretted for the rest of his life. He told his mother on his fifteenth birthday that if he was ever given any moment in his entire life to live over again, it would be that one, when he could have raised his voice and shouted loud enough for her to hear him. He would have shouted loud enough that she would have heard how much he needed her. But as it was, Laura went to the hospital alone, and Harriet and Junior followed soon after, leaving a note for Clara and Florence that told them not to worry, though the note was written in such haste that the girls could not help but panic, and nearly forgot to lock the front door on their way out.

The hospital was discreet. Laura was in a private room with large windows that overlooked a courtyard with benches and graceful little stone paths. From the bed, she could see the tops of palm trees and the other wing of the building, the happier side, where women went to deliver babies. It wasn't so unusual to have a building divided that way. Laura thought of her parents' house, and Hildy's room, always shut away behind a closed door, and of her own house, with her bedroom that had become a mausoleum. She couldn't imagine that anyone would use the swimming pool again, at least not for a long while. There were parts of her brain like that too, sections that she'd tried to wall off, like a bombed-out eyesore: her happy years with Gordon, her mother's hurt feelings. That seemed harder to do.

The nurses never left. One of them was always in her room, even if just sitting in a chair by the door, looking slightly dozy, or doing her knitting. Laura didn't want to talk to the nurses, and they didn't seem to want to talk to her either. But they were always there, no matter what time Laura woke up and opened her eyes. The second thing Laura noticed was that it was *hard* to open her eyes—not just the physical action, but to keep them that way. She wanted to sleep all the time, even at the brightest hour of the afternoon. The doctors would cycle in every few hours and rouse Laura long enough to ask her questions about how she was feeling, always the same questions with the same answers. The doctors seemed not to communicate with one another very well, or else they thought they might trip her up eventually and get a new answer. But no, Laura said over and over again, she wasn't trying to kill herself, not really. It was the "not really" part that they always repeated back to her. One of the doctors was a handsome man, probably Laura's age if not a few years younger, and she hated it the most when he asked, because his big brown eyes were so round and clear, like two perfect marbles. She thought he might cry, and she felt so ashamed of putting him in such an awkward position.

"When you say 'not really,' what do you mean?" The follow-up questions were even worse. The doctor's name was Baker. In her whole life, Laura had never met a doctor in a social situation. She knew scores of actors and writers and directors and even lawyers but not a single doctor. Maybe they never left the hospital, and slept in the hallway closets, lined up like so many winter coats. No one in Los Angeles had any real need for coat closets, but they kept building the closets anyway.

"I mean that I wasn't really trying to kill myself," Laura said. She was wearing a nightgown that Harriet had brought from home, but even with the heavy hospital sheet over her legs, she felt exposed, and her body gave an involuntary shiver. The room was cold, and she felt her nipples push against the thin cotton of her nightgown. She crossed her arms over her chest.

"And how many of the barbiturates did you take before getting into the pool?" Dr. Baker crossed his legs just like her father had, with one ankle hooked over the opposite knee.

"Hmm?" Laura turned and stared out the window, as if she hadn't heard him. She didn't like talking about the pills. They had always been her little secret, and it wasn't anyone else's business. It wasn't that she *needed* the pills, it was just that they made everything easier. Talking to a doctor about her blues was like dancing naked in the middle of Sunset Boulevard. She just wasn't prepared to do it, and certainly not without taking a few pills first. She'd taken a small number—two or three, no more than five—every day since Irving died. Her blood pressure was starting to rise, and there was a growing feeling in the back of her throat, halfway between thirst and anger. Laura wanted the doctor to stop talking, to go away, to back his way slowly down the hall. It sounded so much more shameful when he said it out loud, so much more shameful than she'd ever let herself believe.

"We found a large number of barbiturates in your system, Miss Lamont." Dr. Baker was going to be patient with her, she could tell, but still Laura found herself unable to turn away from the window. On the other side of the hospital, women were being handed their babies for the very first time, and hearing those squawking cries. Laura didn't want to be in the hospital; she wanted to be at home with Junior and the girls, all of them curled together like a litter of puppies on the living room rug. She didn't know what Harriet had told the girls. Even if she'd told them the truth, it would only have been *her* truth, anyway, and not the real story, though Laura wasn't sure what the real story was. The doctor didn't know about Irving, not really. No one knew anything more than they'd read in the tabloids, and that wasn't them at all. Laura blinked back the tears that were forming behind her eyelids. She wondered whether anyone had called her mother.

"When can I go home?" Laura asked, turning back toward the doctor at last.

He looked down at the clipboard in his lap, her facts and figures written so plainly in black ink. "In a couple of days," he said. "Get some rest." Dr. Baker stood up. He was tall, with broad shoulders, and his white coat skimmed his body like a raincoat. In another life, he could have been an actor, a proper leading man. Laura opened her mouth to tell him so, but then thought better of it and didn't. He paused by the door. "If you need anything," he said, and nodded, leaving the rest of the sentence hanging there like a string of lights around a Christmas tree. Laura started to make a list of all the things she needed, but in the end, it was only three items long, and impossible for anyone except Orpheus, and even he had failed.

❧

Laura asked Harriet to stay with the children while she was in the hospital, but when Junior wouldn't stop screaming in the middle of the night, and was wetting his bed besides, which he hadn't done since he was a baby, Harriet took the three children back to her house instead. In the nearly twenty years that they'd known each other, Laura had never once been to Harriet's house, nor did she know precisely where it was. There was a public bus that Harriet took to Beverly Hills in the mornings, on Mondays, and a bus she took home on Friday nights. She lived with her sister and their mother, somewhere to the south, but that was all Laura knew. Once she'd overheard Harriet telling Florence a story about roosters waking her up by crowing in her bedroom window. Laura had laughed—there had been roosters in Door County, noisy pests, and she'd always hated them.

"In Los Angeles?" Laura had asked, incredulous. The look on Harriet's soft, relaxed face had changed in an instant.

"Yes," she'd said. Harriet stared at her hands. The lights were off in Florence's room, but Laura could see Harriet well enough.

"Oh, no," Laura said, "I didn't mean anything by that. I miss those sounds, now that I don't hear them anymore." Laura had lingered in the doorway, waiting for Harriet to resume her story, but after a few minutes, Laura realized that Harriet was waiting for her to go, and so she did.

It was going on a week at the hospital. Dr. Baker had smiled at Laura a total of four times, including once when he thought she was asleep. Only Florence came to visit. Everyone decided Junior was too small to see his mother all trussed up like a turkey, and so he went to school, or stayed home with Harriet.

Laura was staring out the window when Florence knocked. She turned toward the door and saw her daughter's head poking through the narrow slit of the doorway.

"Come on in, sweetie," Laura said, shifting her body so that she was sitting up straight. The most jarring part of being in the hospital for so long was being separated from her makeup. Laura couldn't remember when she'd gone without lipstick for longer. Of course, now she had no one to wear it for. The same was true of all her jewelry, and the dresses made for her body alone. She didn't deserve any of them anymore, no more than she deserved her beautiful children. Of course, she probably wouldn't be able to afford such things for very long, either.

Florence tiptoed across the room, as though afraid of rousing some invisible roommate. She slid her body onto the plastic visitor's chair without making a noise.

"How are you feeling?" Florence's hair hung down almost to the middle of her back. Laura's own mother would have cut it off herself, with Florence sitting in a kitchen chair, a towel draped around her neck, but Laura didn't mind. The hair covered up some of the knobbier parts of Florence's body—she was still scrawny like a child, as narrow as a pine needle. Sometimes, especially at night in the hospital, when she was all alone, Laura wondered whether other mothers had those kinds of thoughts, thoughts about the vast, unknowable parts of their children's brains, or whether other mothers knew the insides of their children's minds as intimately as the contents of their own sock drawer.

"I'm fine, sweetie. How are you? How's Harriet's house? How's school? How's your brother?" Laura felt her eyes well up. She held her hands together in her lap and stared down at them. All she'd wanted was for Irving to come back, one simple, impossible thing, and instead she'd driven everyone else out of the house too.

"I'm okay. School's fine. Harriet's house is small. Her sister is always cooking. Sometimes it smells weird. But we're having fun— Harriet's sister and mother are really nice." Florence pulled her purse onto her lap, and Laura realized that it was in the middle of the school day, and she didn't know how Florence had gotten to the hospital. The children all had pocket money, but taxis were expensive. Laura had a flash of Florence with her thumb out on the side of the road, her long dark hair whipping around her face, but blinked the image away.

"And your brother?" It was possible that someone had driven her, or sent a car. Laura didn't think that Louis Gardner had been talking to the girls, but she'd been out of the house for days. Surely the tabloids knew where she was, and if the tabloids knew, so did Louis. Sure, she was no longer on the Gardner Brothers payroll, but it seemed odd that no one had sent flowers. Did no one think she'd had a horrible accident? Laura wanted to call Josephine and her mother; she wanted to yell until someone gave her the benefit of the doubt. But, of course, she didn't deserve it. And Florence, her beautiful Florence, as narrow as a reed, was right there in front of her. It was more than she deserved.

Florence screwed up her face. "Well," she said, clearly in possession of some information that she didn't quite know how to dispense. "He's been getting into a little trouble."

"Junior? Your brother?" When Laura went to sleep, she imagined her son in a bed beside her. Sometimes she pictured it so perfectly—his tiny glasses on the hospital tray in between them, his white sneakers on the ground, laces all whipped up together like a couple of tango dancers—that she could almost hear his chest moving up and down with his sleepy breath. She put her hand to her throat. "What are you talking about?"

Florence tugged at a pleat on her skirt, pulling the gray fabric down toward her ankle, then stopped abruptly. She looked up at her mother. "He's been wetting the bed."

"Yes, sweetie, I knew that." Laura's heart swelled with sympathy for her son. At least Clara and Florence had never known Gordon to be a good man or a reliable father. There were no illusions to break. Junior had more to miss.

"And he set something on fire. In Harriet's yard." Florence's cheeks were pink.

"Something?"

"They think it was a squirrel. Or a small opossum. It was hard to tell, as it was running away. There was definitely a tail." Florence swallowed hard, as if she could take the words back, take everything back. "I wasn't there."

"I see," Laura said, though she didn't. She could picture a front yard, its untended grass drying in the sun, and she could see her son kneeling down, and she could see a small wild thing running in circles, thankful for finding a fallen nut, but she couldn't see a box of matches in Junior's hand, or a flame, or the moment of connection. She couldn't see that part at all. Florence didn't say anything after that, but sat next to her mother in silence until it was time to go.

＿＿＿＿ ᒂ ＿＿＿＿

All told, it was two weeks. Ginger came to take Laura home. She had her car waiting out front, with a driver at the wheel and Bill waiting at the door, like a bellhop dressed for the rodeo, complete with cowboy hat. Ginger had her arm around Laura's waist. It was the first time in years they'd actually touched—Laura couldn't remember the feeling of anyone's arm around her waist, let alone Ginger's. She'd had to argue with the nurses about not using a wheelchair. Of course, the nurses all loved Ginger's program, and she flashed her kooky smile at each of them in turn, and there weren't any problems after that about what Laura could or couldn't do.

"They like you more than they like me," Laura said. This was a fact. Nurses and lab technicians and orderlies and custodians who hadn't so much as batted an eyelash at movie star Laura Lamont were tripping over themselves to get a look at Ginger. One young nurse was gearing up to ask for an autograph before a coworker smacked her arm back down.

"I'm in their living room," Ginger said.

"I suppose that's true." They reached the sliding glass doors that separated the inside of the hospital from the outside universe— Laura watched cars drive by, always in a hurry. Life in Door County never moved so fast, not even when something was on fire. Laura thought of what Florence told her about Junior—no, it couldn't be true. He was a moody boy, sure, but who wasn't moody as a child? It didn't mean anything.

The day was bright—Laura wished she'd packed her sunglasses, but then she remembered that she hadn't packed anything at all. Dr. Baker had prescribed some milder anxiety pills—that was what he called them, mild. Louis hadn't sent flowers to the hospital or to the house, and he hadn't come to visit. Even Ginger had only phoned, and hadn't come upstairs. Laura felt like her entire life with Irving had been an elaborate fantasy, in which she had both success and love, like people had in the movies. The only thing she cared about was getting home and seeing her children.

Bill was waiting at the curb. "You look beautiful today, Laura," he said, lying through his teeth. The yellow overhead lights at the hospital had made Laura's skin sallow and sickly. She needed to dye her hair, as her light roots were starting to grow back in, the gap between Laura Lamont and Elsa Emerson beginning to widen. Laura put her hand to her scalp.

"You don't mean that," she said, and tried to smile. He was trying to be charming, and she appreciated the effort. Bill did a funny little bow at the waist, and opened the back door of the car. Laura took one look behind her at the hospital and saw a small cluster of nurses pointing her direction. "Oh, Ginger," she said, and tucked herself deep into the belly of the car without another moment's hesitation. Laura kept her face against Ginger's shoulder until the car stopped again, and they were home.

Harriet had Florence and Junior waiting in the living room. The boy looked spit-polished, with his brown hair shellacked into place behind the ears. The moment she saw him, Laura knew that

Florence had been wrong—there was no way that her beautiful son had done anything so heinous in his life, nor would he. His hair was getting long in the back—Laura could see that all the way from the door. She wanted to put her face there and breathe in nothing but her son's neck, the perfume of soap and sweat and cotton. He stood up, expectant.

"Hello, Harriet, kiddos," Ginger said, pushing Laura in toward her children, and pulling Harriet into the kitchen. Laura knew that Ginger and Harriet must have spoken, arranged this moment. They had decided together that it would be good for Junior to see his mother walk through the door, without any makeup on, without her nice clothes. Laura couldn't imagine why. She hadn't been thinking about Junior when she got into the swimming pool. She had been thinking only about herself, about the person she used to be. Laura was so angry at Irving for leaving her alone that she'd forgotten she wasn't the star of a romance, but a family drama, and a farce, and a tragedy. It seemed impossible to fit all the people she'd ever been into a single body, let alone a single moment: Maybe Elsa had wanted to die, but Laura hadn't, or Gordon's wife, or Irving's wife, or Junior's mother. She looked at her son. In a few years, he would be a teenager. A few years after that, he would move out, and live on his own, maybe not even in Los Angeles. Children did that all the time, just picked up and left, just as she did, without looking back. How could she not have thought about him? Laura watched as Florence gripped her brother's shoulders. She had made them worry. It was all upside down.

"How are you feeling, Mom?" Junior's voice was smaller than she'd ever heard it. He sounded as if he were speaking across a thousand miles of telephone wires, crackling in the distance.

Laura couldn't see his eyes behind his glasses, just the shining, reflective panes.

"I'm feeling much better, love. Just swallowed some water, is all. They were just keeping me there to make sure it was all out of my lungs." Laura spoke as though the lines had been written for her—she didn't know what was true, or what was appropriate, but she spoke with as much conviction as she could muster. All she wanted was for her son to never look at her again the way he was looking at her now, like she might vanish into thin air without leaving so much as a mark on the rug. Florence leaned down and whispered something into Junior's ear. He nodded and, without looking back up to his sister, crossed the living room floor slowly and steadily until he reached Laura's body. The top of Junior's head almost reached Laura's chin, and she tucked him into her chest as if she would never let him go. Florence watched silently from across the room, nodding every now and again in approval. *Something with a tail.* Whatever had gone wrong with her sweet son, it was Laura's fault. Even though it seemed impossible that he had done what Florence had said, her daughter wasn't a fabulist. Elsa Emerson had been a better mother than Laura Lamont, and Elsa was the only one who could fix it.

The phone rang and rang in Laura's office. Jimmy was off for the day, and Clara was likely still at work, though Laura imagined that if Ginger wasn't in, there wasn't much reason for anyone else to be, either. But Clara was a sensible girl, or at least heading in that direction, Laura hoped. Her eldest child seemed too corporeal to worry about, too rooted to the earth. Laura let the telephone ring, afraid that if she let Junior go, he would wriggle out of her arms and never find his way back.

9

THE HOSTESS

Spring 1963

It was only after the accountant's sixth message that Laura called back to make an appointment. Dobsky & Dobsky, CPAs, were on Beverly Boulevard near the Silent Movie Theatre, a father-and-son team of the old-world variety who had managed Irving's money for his entire professional life. They had called every so often, and Harriet reported higher and higher frequencies in their voices. *We need to speak with Miss Lamont,* the messages read. *This is urgent.* Harriet handed over the slips of paper without comment, her eyes wide, and then, unable to help herself, she added, "Laura," which alone said all it needed to.

The office itself was comfortably shabby, with worn Persian rugs and stacks of files on the desk, all of it illuminated by the low light of two green glass banker's lamps. Arthur Dobsky gestured for Laura to sit in one of the cracked leather chairs, and then sat down beside her. Arthur's father, Leonard Dobsky, was a man of nearly eighty, and half stood on the other side of the desk, supporting himself on the arms of his chair. He looked happy to collapse back down once Laura was seated.

"Thank you for coming in, Miss Lamont," Leonard began.

"Thank you for getting back to us," Arthur continued.

"As you know, we worked with your husband for many years," Leonard said.

"He was a wonderful man," Arthur said. "A very prudent spender."

"Is there a problem?" Laura asked.

Arthur turned his face toward the rug and kneaded a bald spot with his toe.

"In fact, there is," Leonard said. "This is why we've been trying to get in touch with you. The problem is one of supply and demand—you know what that means? Supply is the money coming in, and demand is the money going out. Right now, you've got all demand and no supply. You see what I'm saying to you? There's no money coming in, and all the money's going out." He opened a manila folder on his desk, pulled out a sheet of paper, and handed it to Laura.

"What is this?" Laura asked, though she recognized the name of the bank from her checkbook.

"That is your bank statement. An overview. You see the number in the upper right corner? That's the amount of money you had in the bank when your husband died. Now see the number in the lower right corner? That's the amount you have now."

Laura tracked her finger down the column on the right side of the page, watching the number decrease. There was the five thousand dollars she'd given to Gordon, Harriet's salary, the school tuition, the groceries, the pharmacies, the hospital bills, the gasoline, the restaurants, Jimmy's salary, Clara's shopping trips, all of it. "Oh, God," she said, as she reached the number at the bottom. "Oh, God!"

Arthur and Leonard nodded appreciatively, glad that Laura had finally seen the approaching train, now speeding violently down the track.

"What about Irving's money? That's all gone?" Laura gripped the sheet of paper with both hands, as if that would make the number increase.

"I'm afraid your husband's portfolio was smaller than he may have led you to believe, Miss Lamont. Mr. Green's salary from Gardner Brothers was handsome, but he didn't enjoy the stock market, and he didn't like to save." Leonard looked at his son. "We tried to speak with him about that."

Arthur chimed in. "The other issue is with the insurance." He looked almost giddy with anticipation. This was what accountants lived for, Laura thought: proving their worth after the fact. "As I'm sure you know, Mr. Green's heart condition prevented him from ever purchasing life insurance, and the health insurance he did have was through the Gardner Brothers studio. At the time of death, Mr. Green was not insured, and so there are still some rather large bills to pay."

Laura tried to remain composed. She laid the sheet of paper back down on the desk, and held on to the armrests on her chair. "And what do you suggest I do? I have three children, you may remember."

Arthur finally looked up from the floor, and mopped his forehead with a handkerchief. "Respectfully, Miss Lamont, we suggest that you get a job."

Laura rose slowly, shook their warm hands, and walked to the parking garage with as much dignity as possible. If Irving had been there, he would have rubbed his hands together and had a plan before the key was in the ignition, but instead, Laura was alone, and stared at the keys in her lap for a few minutes, wondering what to do, what to do, what to do.

The wedding was small but extravagant—Clara wanted to gild everything in sight, including the hotel silverware. She and Jimmy had chosen to hold the ceremony at the Bethel Lutheran Church on Olympic Boulevard, and the reception in the small ballroom at the Roosevelt Hotel. Laura tried to explain that proper Lutherans were understated, modest people, but Clara was having none of it. She whooped with laughter in the church, and made everyone throw buckets of rice afterward. Laura was picking the grains out of her shoes and hair for the rest of the day. At the reception, there were gold chargers at every setting, and wine goblets that could easily hold an entire bottle each. Laura sat at the long table at the front of the room, with Clara and Jimmy in the middle, Florence and Junior beside her, and the pale, bewildered Petersons on the other side. It was either this or tell the girls that they were broke, and Laura would rather go out with a bang—a gilded bang—than ask her children to wear burlap and eat beans on toast until the next paycheck arrived.

The dress that Clara chose for the wedding was high necked and short sleeved, with a beaded sash around her waist and a train that dragged several feet behind her. On her head she wore a satin bow that spanned eight inches from one side to the other, like a deranged Minnie Mouse. All the guests approached Laura with the same two lines: "Congratulations!" and "That is quite a bow." She thanked each of them in turn.

Florence was the maid of honor, which meant that it was her job to ensure her sister's happiness on her wedding day, a task that required she smile more than usual. She and Laura wore dresses in the same shade of pink, the soft blush of a magnolia blossom. Or, as Florence pointed out to her mother, the exact same color as Pepto-Bismol. All the popular wedding designs for the year were equally offensive to Florence, and she wouldn't have been truly happy unless she had been permitted to wear black. Her kohl-rimmed eyes were the bane of Clara's day, and Laura tried her best to keep the girls apart, or at the very least to keep Florence behind Clara, holding her train, where her eyeliner would be out of sight.

Mr. and Mrs. Peterson clutched each other's elbows as they made their way around the room, offering limp handshakes to anyone who asked. Mrs. Peterson wore a fur wrap around her shoulders, having forgotten that March in California was no different from June in Illinois. She was shy around Laura, and whenever they were face-to-face, Mrs. Peterson opened her handbag to forage around for mints. It was unclear whether she was shy because Laura had once been a movie star or because Jimmy had told her about the pool incident. Laura found that it was often hard to tell the difference between bashfulness and shame.

The hired band—Stevie Dean and the Starlight Orchestra—played their standards on a small stage along the left-hand side of the room, leaving ample room for the dance floor. Clara and Jimmy bopped around, bending their knees and wiggling their bottoms, two giant chickens. Laura's weddings had both been small, with hardly any fanfare, and she enjoyed watching Clara dance in her floor-length white dress, her bow flapping in time with her movements. Clara looked happy to be married to Jimmy, and to be the center of attention. Laura felt a twinge of envy for her daughter's happiness, and for the Petersons' slow and steady togetherness. Weddings were for the parents, she now understood; no matter what the bride and groom thought, they were one stop on the continuum, birth to death, a milestone that meant you were closer to the end than to the beginning. Jimmy's parents looked thrilled, in their quiet Midwestern way, as if they were dipping their toe in the coffin and deciding that it felt quite nice after all. Laura just wished that Irving were next to her, dancing. She might not have minded it at all had she not been alone.

"Mom," Junior said, his voice high and sweet. He was having one of his good days, one of his sunny days, and was bouncing off the walls. Teenage boys were different from girls, all volume and bravado. "Dance with me!"

Laura followed him onto the dance floor. Junior loved rock 'n' roll, Elvis Presley most of all. He'd taken to slicking his hair back with pomade the way his father had, the grease giving his soft, downy hair a reflective sheen. Laura's hair was darker—the girls at the salon made sure of it—still the color that had made her famous, but Junior's look was all his own creation. Sometimes Laura wondered what her life would have been like if she'd stayed a blonde, if she would have had better luck. Clara was as fair as they came, and blissfully ignorant of any of her faults. Maybe that would have been better.

Junior swung his hips from side to side, his eyes shut tight behind his thick-framed glasses. Clara spotted her baby brother through the crowd and came dancing over, spinning him around and around. Laura clapped in time to the music and watched them go.

"Isn't this the best, Mom?" Clara shouted over the band.

Laura watched her son and daughter giggle together, so amused by the shapes of their bodies, the bumps and angles, the hilarious biology of it all. Laura sometimes worried that she'd ruined everything for the children, especially Junior, that life had been as unfair to them as it had been to her. They were happy, though, at least for this moment, with one another and the universe outside their cellular walls, and Laura felt nothing more acutely than a sense of relief. Even if she was never happy again, not for the rest of her life, Clara had danced with her brother at her wedding, her white bow stuck in place with a thousand bobby pins and an entire can of hair spray, its little satin wings threatening to fly away. "It's the best," Laura said back. "The best."

❧

Ginger was sorry to miss the festivities, but she was eight months pregnant and unable to go anywhere without causing a traffic accident.

"I'm a whale," she said.

"You're gorgeous," Laura said.

Ginger ran her hands back and forth over her belly. "I'm a gorgeous whale."

They hadn't even been trying—Ginger's uterus was, as she liked to say, famously inhospitable—but then she was pregnant, just like that. She was already four months along when she went to the doctor for the first time, sure that her lack of a regular period was the first sign of menopause. She'd cried for three days straight when she found out, and then she'd called Laura. It was a secret until Ginger was too big to fib about a sudden interest in boxy clothing.

The columnists were ready to strike—Ginger was the first female studio head, having taken the reins at Triumph from the men who'd stolen her away from Irving, and reporters were placing bets on when she would quit after having the baby. The greatest odds were in the one-to-three-week range, postdelivery, with one to three weeks predelivery a close second. If Laura had placed a bet, she would have bet that Ginger would work in the delivery room, the recovery room, and every day following, no matter what. Since the pregnancy, Bill had found more of a reason to be on the rodeo circuit, getting back to his "rodeo roots" was what Ginger said. Laura thought the whole thing sounded suspicious, but it wasn't her marriage to worry about.

"Listen, Ginge," Laura said. They were sitting on the patio of Ginger's new house, the only Italian villa in Bel Air. She'd imported marble columns, marble floors, and a bathtub big enough for a Roman orgy. Bill and the horses seemed to stay mostly back in the canyon. Laura didn't think the spurs would sound very good against all that stone.

"Hang on, I need more ice." Ginger swiveled her neck sharply. "Hello?"

One of her butlers scurried out from an unseen corner. He bowed almost imperceptibly. "Yes, Mrs. Balsam?"

"More ice, please. It's a thousand degrees out here."

Laura wasn't warm at all, but she remembered what it was like to have another human being living inside your body, with all the extra blood pumping and whooshing through your veins. She lit a cigarette and felt the smoke travel down into her lungs.

"So, listen," Laura started again. "I was thinking you might be able to find something for me. At Triumph."

"You know we don't really do movies, Lore, they just don't make money like they used to," Ginger said, waving the idea off like a bad smell.

"I don't care if it's a movie. Anything." Laura hadn't worked in years, not since *Pantheress*, which she'd never actually seen. The reviews had been bad enough for her to stay away. Some afternoons Laura sat on the front step and waited for Junior to come home from school, pretending that she was sitting in her dressing room on the lot, just waiting to be called, wondering how she would pay to send Junior to college. Laura wanted to work, and needed to. The Dobskys called once a week, and Laura had stopped answering the telephone.

"Well," Ginger said. "We are putting together a new show. One of the game shows, you know, only a new one. *Will You or Won't You* it's called. The host is this kid who used to be at MGM, looks like a politician and talks like Jerry Lewis. Hilarious. The idea is that every show, a contestant gets paired up with a celebrity, and they both have to decide whether or not they're going to do something—you know, pogo for a minute, bob for apples, say all the states in order. The team either does it or they make the other team do it. If the team can complete the task, they win money. Simple."

Laura pictured herself with wet hair, lipstick smeared against the skin of an apple, her dignity waving good-bye, along with all the mystery she'd ever had, and the romance, and the adoration. She thought about the Academy Award sitting on her desk, which only made her think of Irving. He would have been appalled.

"I'll do it," she said.

Ginger grabbed Laura's hands and pressed them against her belly, hard. "Feel," Ginger said. "She's kicking. I think I'm going to have a feisty little bugger."

The set of *Will You or Won't You* was built on stage four of the Triumph lot, which meant that Laura had to drive straight past the gate to Gardner Brothers on Marathon, a street she'd been avoiding since Irving got sick. The driver pulled up to Triumph's lone entrance and announced Laura's name and destination. In the old days, when she drove herself to Gardner Brothers, or when Irving or Louis sent a car, Laura sailed through, waving at everyone she knew, Miss America on her float. This guard dutifully took her name and then turned his back to check it against his list of drive-ons for the day. Laura faced forward, unwilling to be humiliated. There would be plenty of that to come.

The soundstage itself had already been transformed from a cavernous box into the home of the game show. Three walls with an orange Art Deco pattern were in place, as well as three wooden consoles—one for each team, and one for the host. Laura hadn't been on a soundstage in years, and she'd missed the way the high ceilings felt dark and endless before the lights turned on. Big, burly men in overalls clomped around, and the air was thick with sawdust—nothing was ever finished on time. Laura had missed those men too, and the hours she'd spent in her dressing room learning lines or gabbing with whoever else was around. But it was different now.

Instead of a proper dressing room elsewhere on the property, they'd built a narrow hall of tiny, coffin-size rooms right on the soundstage—one for Laura, one for the host, Phil Mayweather, one for the visiting celebrity guest, and a shared room for the two contestants, who wouldn't need to change their clothes unless they were soiled during an episode or they were filming two in a row. Laura wandered around the set until she found a door with her name on it, and then went in and sat down. She was the regular, the fixture, the ones that fans would tune in to see. At least that was the idea.

The walls were made of single sheets of plywood, which were about as soundproof as sheets of paper. Laura stared at herself in the mirror and listened to the conversation next door.

"But what am I supposed to do with her? See if she can *act* like a person with a sense of humor? Or if she can *act* like a person who can hula hoop? Come on, Pete, this just isn't gonna work and you know it."

The other voice, Pete, offered a grunting laugh in response. "She's going to be fine, Phil."

Laura sat perfectly still and watched her reflection as she moved her head from side to side. She had not been their first choice, as they had not been hers. Laura loudly cleared her throat once, and then again, before pushing herself back up and walking to the next room over to introduce herself.

The show moved quickly: With only a week of rehearsals, which were mostly for the host and the cameramen, they were ready to film. Pete Hollowell, the director, ran Laura through the paces. Though it would seem to the audience that the contestants had a choice about whether or not to participate in a certain stunt, it was all worked out beforehand, and written in a script that would be held beside the camera in the form of cue cards. Laura was not to wear any of her own jewelry on set, for fear that it might be damaged. The costumer put Laura in demure skirt suits, as if she were auditioning for the role of a bank teller.

The scripts were easy to remember: Laura never had more than a few phrases per episode, and most of them were along the lines of "Gee whiz!" and "I think we're gonna pass on that one, Phil." Physical gestures were important. Laura was supposed to wink, to elbow, to wring her hands, but in a *funny* way. Game shows were comedy, life with a laugh track. Sometimes people had to be told when they were allowed to laugh, especially when they were watching Laura Lamont try to hula hoop while holding a pineapple in each hand. It was a strange part to play, oneself. Laura tried different approaches: a warm mother of three, a widow, a younger sister, a kook, Ginger. In between takes, she sat very still and concentrated on whatever she was going to try next. Eventually she settled on the kook, a wild-eyed cross between Hildy and Junior and Peggy Bates, who had long ago made the shift to television. In thirty minutes, gestures could be big and broad—they would still be forgotten.

The first episode featured Laura and an insurance salesman from New Jersey on one team, and a very tan young actor named

George Wells and a housewife from Delaware on the other. It was all sorted out in advance: Laura was going to win the first episode for her partner, and George would win the next. Before the filming began, Laura and her insurance salesman stood behind the set's walls.

"It really is a pleasure to meet you, Miss Lamont," he said. The man was no more than twenty-five, a baby. His suit was cream colored, with gray checks. Laura wondered whether he bought it especially for the occasion, whether he and his pretty young wife—weren't they always pretty?—had gone shopping together, with her sitting outside the dressing room, her pocketbook on her lap.

"You are very sweet to say so," Laura said. They were waiting to have their names called by Phil, when they would trot out with big smiles and take their places behind their console.

"You're my mother's favorite actress. When I told her that I was coming on this show with you, she nearly had a heart attack." The insurance salesman was beaming, so sure he'd made Laura's day.

"Please tell your mother I say hello," Laura said, and turned her face back toward the short, dark passageway they would walk through to reach the set. The theme music—a nonsensical, bubbly tune—began to play, and Phil welcomed the whirring cameras and imaginary audience to the show. His voice had more energy than Laura had felt in years, and the sound of it, so zippy it seemed full of helium, made her want to take a sleeping pill, or better yet, slip one into his drink when he wasn't looking. But no: Laura had to remember Phil was in the right. She would have to match his energy and enthusiasm. She was the stranger here.

A producer blinked his flashlight at Laura's feet, indicating that it was time to move. Laura affixed a wide smile to her face and tugged at the hem of her jacket. "All right," she said. "Here we go!"

⌖

The first *Will You or Won't You* stunt of the day was a double-header: the three-legged race, followed by the egg-and-spoon balance. Laura and the insurance salesman passed, sending the easy challenge to George and the housewife. Laura watched, clapping in time to the music, as they hobbled and spun around, giggling all the while. She wondered whether George had taken the housewife into his dressing room, given her the grand tour. The woman was blushing like mad, and squeaked when she dropped her egg, which wasn't really an egg at all, but a painted piece of wood. The whole thing was too stupid to be believed. When it was their turn, Laura and the salesman had to build a house of cards while wearing Indian headdresses. She was glad there weren't any mirrors on set, but then realized that television was its own mirror, that the children and everyone else she'd ever known would just have to flip on their sets to see Laura Lamont make a total and utter fool of herself. They won—Laura and the salesman—just as they were supposed to, the cards were coated with rubber cement and had notches snipped into their sides. Laura graciously shook George's hand, and the housewife's, before waving to the camera as it slid backward and the little red light went dark. Phil Mayweather whispered in her ear, "You'll get it, don't worry," and then patted her on the back, too low to be a friendly gesture, too high for her to actually complain.

Pete Hollowell spoke to Jimmy, who spoke to Laura. They were concerned. Jimmy came over to the house. He and Clara lived nearby, almost close enough to walk, but not quite. Laura wouldn't have wanted to live that close to her own mother, so she didn't mind, though if she had her way, Jimmy would have just moved in, and they all would have lived together, happy as a bunch of hermit crabs.

"The issue, as far as I can understand it, is that you don't seem comfortable," Jimmy said.

They were in her office, with the shades drawn. No one wanted to look out at the pool, not even Jimmy. They'd finally moved Irving's desk, and bought more furniture, so that the place seemed inhabited again. Laura didn't need any help imagining ghosts.

"Have you been reading the scripts? In the last episode we filmed, I had to make a batch of pudding and then eat it, Jimmy. The entire batch. I thought I'd be sick." Laura crossed her arms and leaned against the wall. She'd spent too much of her life sitting down, waiting for her name to be called.

"I understand," Jimmy said. "But that's the nature of the show. It's goofy. It's fun!"

"It's humiliating," Laura said. "Isn't there anything else?"

Jimmy was a good son-in-law, and Laura could see how the truth of the situation pained him. He wanted so badly to say yes. "No," he said. "There isn't."

"Well, okay, then," Laura said. She crossed the room and pulled the cord to open the drapes. It was sunny outside, a flat yellow sheen. Laura used to think that California made everything golden, but now she could see that it was merely the sunshine play-ing tricks on the eye. Nothing stayed golden forever.

⤶

They'd filmed only five episodes when Ginger came on set. The baby (Petunia, after Bill's first horse) was only a week old, but Ginger wasn't breast-feeding, and they'd hired two nannies, one for the days and one for the nights. The bags under Ginger's eyes were the only sign of the new arrival. Pete scurried over and bowed slightly, as one would before a foreign leader, where one wasn't quite sure of the customs of the country. Phil hung back, clearly unsure of what to say.

"How's Petunia?" Laura said, greeting her friend warmly.

Ginger proceeded, all business. "Pete, could you give us a minute?"

He backed away without a word.

"What's going on, just coming to visit?" Laura asked. She turned around so that she and Ginger were facing the same direc-tion, both looking toward the set. The orange wallpaper looked dull without the lights on, like someone's unfortunate kitchen.

"We need to talk," Ginger said.

"Is it Bill? Babies are so terrifying when they first arrive, aren't they? Like tiny little aliens. What's going on?"

Ginger sighed. "It's not the baby, Lore."

Laura turned her head. "What is it?"

"I have to fire you." Ginger lowered her voice. "Come here," she said, pulling Laura by her elbow toward the dressing rooms. Neither woman spoke until they were shut inside the narrow space, and despite what Laura knew about the thickness of the walls, she began to cry as soon as the door was closed.

"Laura, listen," Ginger said. She had her usual lipstick on, and her red hair was curled and piled on top of her head like a wedding cake. Laura thought about the girl Ginger had been when they'd met, funny and sweet and dying for good news, always. "You knew this was a stretch."

"I can do it," Laura said. "I can do it, I swear."

"You're better than this," Ginger said. She gripped Laura's shoulders and held her close enough that Laura could smell her breath.

"Then don't fire me," she said.

"I have to." Ginger let go. "I'll stay while you get your things together." She sank down into Laura's makeup chair.

"Don't bother," Laura said. She unhooked her coat from the rack and walked out before Ginger could follow.

⁓

It was better to tell them sooner rather than later, Laura thought, although it had already been a week, and Laura had been leaving for the set as usual and just sitting in various parking lots around the city, waiting out the clock. She, Junior, and Florence were about to have Harriet's famous spaghetti, which Laura was fairly sure came out of a can, but was still the best spaghetti they'd ever had. They sat around the table in the kitchen. Florence had already poured glasses of wine for herself and Harriet.

Laura waited for everyone to be at the table, already reaching over one another for the rolls or the salt or their forks, before she began.

"The good news is that I don't have to be on that awful game show anymore," she said, as if already in mid-conversation. Harriet, Junior, and Florence all turned their attention away from dinner and onto Laura's face. This too was a performance. "I got fired."

Florence dropped her fork with a clank. Junior had just ripped a roll in two, and held both pieces in his hand, as if he were about to perform some secret ritual to raise the dead.

"What happened?" Harriet asked.

"Fired by *Ginger*?" Florence said, having regained the power of speech.

Junior threw both halves of the roll against the wall, where they ricocheted without a sound. "How could she *do* that?" he said, his body tense with anger. Laura hated to see her son upset, because it was always bigger and darker than it should have been, no matter the reason. Junior had an internal well of disappointment and fury that was always full and threatening to bubble over.

Laura raised her palms, as if calming a spooked horse. "It's going to be fine, everybody. Ginger is the boss, and if it wasn't working, it wasn't working."

"That is total BS," Junior said. He skidded his chair backward along the floor and stormed out of the room, sending his napkin fluttering to the floor, which made Laura sad with pity that he wasn't even frustrated properly, but always too soft, just skirting the edges of his bad feelings.

"You two start, I'll be right back," Laura said, and followed

Junior down the hall to his bedroom. Florence and Harriet didn't move.

Junior had gotten under the covers without turning on the light, so all Laura saw was a shadowy lump on the bed. She sat down next to him and ran a hand back and forth over his spine. After a minute, Junior unpeeled the blanket and stuck out his face.

"How could she do that to you?" His voice was high and strained.

"Sweetie, it's complicated. It was a business decision, not a personal one. You don't have to get so upset."

Junior bolted up, nearly knocking Laura off the bed. "That's the thing! It is personal. She's your best friend!" He threw himself forward so that his head rested in Laura's lap, folding himself neatly in half. Since he'd hit puberty, Junior had been like this: up and down, slap-happy and inconsolable. The girls watched from a careful distance: Florence was still the most likely to sweet-talk Junior for hours, to lure him off whatever high branch, and Clara had her own family to watch over now.

"It's just that if Ginger could do that to you, and I don't even have a friend as good as Ginger, then *anyone* could do that to me, you know? I don't think there are real friends in the world, at least not here." He looked up at her, his eyes wet. "If someone could be that mean to you, your best friend, and I don't even have a best friend, then what does that say about me? What's the point of even having friends?"

"Junior, my love," she said, "we'll be fine." He panted softly, like an overheated animal, his breath quick and ragged. Laura petted his hair, her sweet, worried son, and traced her finger around his ear, feeling its gentle slopes and turns. It was still surprising to have a full-grown person who had lived inside her, who spoke and ached and cried. Laura sat with Junior until she heard the clattering of plates in the kitchen, and Harriet and Florence cleaning up, and longer still, until Junior's breath had returned to normal and he had drifted off to sleep.

Jimmy was right: There were no offers, zero, zip, zilch. But sometimes the casting calls were for smaller parts, played by older women. Laura didn't ask Jimmy whether it was a good idea; she just went. Sometimes there were crowds of ladies waiting at the gate, a gabby mob, and sometimes there were crowds of ladies standing around a large room, as if waiting for a doctor's appointment or a tardy bus. When it was the former, Laura kept her sunglasses on and stood still, ignoring the chatting around her. Inevitably one woman would recognize her, and then the game of telephone would begin, until all Laura could hear was her own name whispered over and over again. Eventually the chatter would stop, and everyone would turn their bodies slightly so that they had a better look. Laura often thought that she could have taken a job as a statue in any park in the city, so practiced was she at being the object of someone else's gaze.

The auditions were the kind she remembered from her youth: One by one, or in groups of three, the women would file into a room with casting directors seated at a table, not unlike the banquet table at Clara's wedding. Each of the auditioning women would slide her headshot and personal information across the table, and the casting directors would look her up and down, barely making eye contact. Laura hated the moment before she slid her picture over most of all, because as soon as the casting director saw Laura's name, his features would contort in confusion. *It couldn't be*, he would think, and yet it was. He would look up and see her face, and Laura had to smile at his wrinkled brow, his sorry expression. The worst of all was when the casting directors let slip a whoop of a laugh, a sound wholly made of surprise.

"No," one man said, holding the photo of Laura in both hands. "Really?"

Laura curtsied and backed up a few feet. The casting director and his friends were still laughing when she began to read her lines. That was the easy part, once she opened her mouth and began to speak; when that happened, Laura was far, far away, and only her body was still in the room. She had read a book about astral projection, and acting seemed like a version of that—one could travel anywhere, to Egypt, or the cherry orchards of Wisconsin, or back in time; she had only to believe it. When they called later to offer her the part (a shop owner with three scenes and a fake mole), Laura pretended to be surprised. She wasn't happy to audition, but she was happy for the work—the other women were sad for her, felt sorry for all that she had been through. The brave ones even said so. But to Laura, auditions were a humiliation with promise—if the right person saw her, he would hire her, and if the right person hired her, then she could act again, over and over again, until she could pay all of her bills, and until the world woke up and saw what it had been missing.

10

THE COMEBACK KID

Fall 1970

Selling the house was the only thing to do. Laura wept as she walked the real estate agent through room after room, pointing out details that Irving had insisted upon: the glass doors that led out onto the yard, the chandelier he'd ordered from France, the damask wallpaper designed by someone important whose name Laura could never remember. Harriet cried too, although she'd already found another live-in job as a nanny for a television actress with blond curls and a smile like a jackal's. They held on to each other's elbows, pointing out the few pieces of furniture and fixtures that Laura would take with her. The real estate agent made sharp notes on a pad of paper, and Laura was terrified to think of what she was writing down. The house was beautiful, but perhaps it seemed old-fashioned now. All the young stars wanted houses made of hard angles and shag rugs, somewhere James Bond could roll around in bed with a woman wearing full makeup but no clothes. Just thinking about being without clothes made Laura begin to sob, and she buried her face in Harriet's shoulder, but the familiar smell of her shampoo and face cream only made her cry harder. The agent stalked her way around the two women, avoiding them as well as she could, her high heels like ice picks through Laura's heart.

The bungalow at the Beverly Hills Hotel was already paid for—it had been one of Irving's investments from before they were married, though he'd essentially used it as a place to stash stars in mid-divorce or to host executives visiting from New York. It was a large bungalow, as bungalows went, two bedrooms and a small sitting area with a reduced kitchen. Laura had to pay a monthly fee, for the maids and the gardener and the linens and the wash, but it was far less than the house, and so they were moving. Florence took one bedroom, Junior took the other, and Laura herself would sleep on the pullout sofa in the living room when both children were in residence. It was rather a step down, but no one from the lifestyle magazines was knocking on her door to take photographs of her nonexistent dinner parties anyway.

The first night, the three of them sat in silence on the sofa, their hips all touching, unsure of how to proceed. Junior was twenty, and should have been in college. Laura wanted so badly for him to be, but he'd proved less studious than he'd seemed as a boy. He loved to read, and often carried around a bent paperback book in his pocket, but Junior couldn't seem to concentrate on more than one subject at a time. Laura understood—it was hard for her to be more than one thing at a time; why should she expect more of Junior? The only class he'd ever enjoyed was a costume design course in high school, where he helped make dresses for the actresses in the school play. He would never bring home a girl; Laura had known that for years. She loved her son desperately, and would have been happy if he'd brought home anyone, but he never would. There were boys, from the neighborhood and from the school, boys who seemed never to go home. Each one would be at the house every day for a month and then vanish. Laura tried to learn their names, but was always making mistakes. When she called one by another's name, Junior sank so far into the recesses of his bedroom that she was sure he'd never forgive her. She never saw him kiss one of the other boys, not even give one of them a soft touch that might imply that they were touching more when the door was closed, but she imagined that was what was happening. The boys were usually polite, and always quiet as mice when they saw her. Some of them came over because of her; Laura knew that, and so did Junior. It was harder for him than it had been for the girls. When Clara and Florence were in school, people had heard only good things about their mother. It was different for Junior; there was more of a story there. Despite moving across the country, and choosing a wildly different life for herself, Laura had ended up with exactly the same fate as her mother: no longer a wife, with only one of her three children acting the way she'd expected. She supposed it served her right for thinking that she deserved more, that her fate would be any different.

Florence came and went. After spending most of her twenties in and out of the classroom—she'd been an art major, a poet, pre-med—Florence was finally a full-time student at UCLA, and loved sitting alone at the university library, her spine hunched over a book. She often slept at Clara's house, where there was an extra bedroom, taking the bus the short distance back and forth to the hotel if Clara or Jimmy didn't have the time to drive her. Laura had traded in her Packard for an even smaller model, and the car felt flimsy, as if she were driving down the road in an oversize soup can. But most of the time she didn't drive anywhere at all. During the day, Laura moved around the hotel—from the pool to the breakfast bar to the Polo Lounge and back to the pool. The waiters were patient with her once they understood that she wasn't going to order more than hot tea and toast. If she kept her sunglasses on outside, everyone ignored her, which Laura thought was lovely and polite, though it occurred to her late at night, curled up on the sofa bed, that they might not have said anything because they hadn't recognized her in the first place.

❦

Jimmy called with great excitement, and for the first time in several years it had nothing to do with the children. Someone—Christos Contogenis, Laura had read his name in the papers—was interested in funding a project. He'd called Jimmy, who had long since moved out of the home office and into a small but clean office space on Wilshire Boulevard. Before she'd had her two children, Roy and Leslie, sweet towheaded kids who would have fit in on any farm in Wisconsin, Clara had worked as his secretary and office manager, but it had been years since she'd done anything but stay at home with the kids, making lunches and occasionally sneaking pieces of their candy when she thought no one was looking. Luckily Jimmy had other clients: the actor who played the captain of a boat that never went anywhere on a television show, a female comedian even older than Laura who cackled and spit her way through game shows, a trained gorilla.

There were many things that Laura missed about working regularly, so many things that she could hardly do anything else all day long except miss parts of her life that were gone. Laura missed having a dressing room more than she missed having a bedroom, in particular the lightbulbs that surrounded her face and made her skin glow. She missed learning her lines, speaking the same words over and over again until they formed pathways in her brain so deep that they couldn't be knocked loose. Laura missed the camaraderie of players, the kinship she had known her entire life. Actors were different from other people, more acutely sensitive to words and gestures, always absorbing new emotional landscapes. Why would anyone do anything else? Laura didn't know how. She was always ready to go into Jimmy's office, always prepared to meet with anyone. She wore sunglasses half the size of her face, and wound a scarf around her shoulders. Her arms weren't as thin as they had been, and other parts of her body had started to lean slightly out, as if testing the boundaries of her flesh, but when she had to, she could still look like Laura Lamont. In April she would be fifty years old. It was always a surprise to Laura, the number. It just kept rising, no matter what she did or didn't do in any given year. One year, Laura told Florence that all she wanted was a button she could push to pause her age, just for a little while, a few years, while she got used to the idea. Florence had thrown her head back and laughed, and Laura gamely tried to laugh along, though she hadn't been joking.

Jimmy was waiting for Laura in the hall, as he always did. She wondered whether that was what he thought of her, that she was so prematurely dotty that she might get lost, despite having been to his office dozens of times before. He was a good son-in-law, and the only one she thought she'd ever have. Florence was no closer to getting married at twenty-nine than she had been at twenty-five, and seemed content being single. She was better at school than her siblings, and was working toward a degree in psychology, that mysterious study of the mind. Florence was going to be a doctor, she said, the good kind who never gave you shots but always asked what was wrong. It would have made her father weep with pride, Irving having had nothing more than a tenth-grade formal education.

"Hiya, Mom," Jimmy said. He lightly held on to Laura's arm and kissed her on the cheek. She liked that he called her his mother—Jimmy's parents, like Mary, had never gotten over his decision to be a part of the Hollywood galaxy. Laura was sure that they had never liked Clara, that they would swap the whole family for a normal one, if they could. "How was the drive over?"

Though Laura didn't think of Jimmy as her son—the bonds were different, conditional on marriage, which she knew didn't last forever—she did love him as much as she loved her other children, and she did lump him in with the motley group. Jimmy was her Josephine, her steadiest ally. Clara bored easily and was always wandering off in the middle of conversations, and Florence picked everything apart. Junior either kept his mouth shut or never stopped talking, making it nearly impossible to get a word in edgewise, talking so fast it was hard to follow what he was on about, but Jimmy would talk to Laura for hours on end about the movies. He'd seen everything, almost as devoted to the industry as Irving had been, rabid in his enthusiasm. Laura liked to ask what he'd seen lately, which felt like winding up a toy and watching it careen across the room. Out of all her children, Jimmy was the only one who seemed to care that Laura was an actress, *was still an actress*, that she wasn't finished yet. Maybe it was that Jimmy had come from somewhere else, out of another woman's body, that made it possible for him to view her as a woman in addition to his mother-in-law. Laura wasn't through, and Jimmy knew it.

"Fine, fine. Now, what's the story?"

Jimmy ushered Laura into his office through the open door. The suite was small but sparse, with modern furniture placed at careful angles. That had been Clara's influence; she was always so interested in life looking like a home decorating magazine. Every time they'd come over to Laura's house with the children, Clara complained that the furnishings were too old-fashioned, the fabrics too dark. But Laura was happy to let things be. She sat down on the edge of a white leather chair, and Jimmy sat opposite her. Outside, the traffic on Wilshire honked and zoomed, with everyone jostling for first place in a race that went on all day.

"Greek shipping family. Tobacco money, and oil. Very interested in Hollywood, and in the golden age." Jimmy put his right hand over his heart. "And you, of course, are his favorite."

"His favorite what?" Laura took off her sunglasses. Her son-in-law still looked boyish, with his blond hair cut short like Steve McQueen's.

Jimmy laughed. There were a few wrinkles around the corners of his eyes, which made Laura want to put her sunglasses back on. If Jimmy had wrinkles, Laura shuddered to think of what her own face must look like. "His favorite movie star."

Laura shook her head, pursing her lips. It felt almost like teasing. Her Academy Award now felt like teasing too. Laura kept it in her office at home, a room she avoided for weeks on end. Every now and then she happened on it by chance, catching Oscar's golden eye, and would then have to retire to her bed. If the statue was real, it meant that her marriage had been real, and not just a fever dream she'd concocted and sold to the children. More than anything, Laura wanted to be given lines, to be given the outline of another human being to pour herself into. She felt almost ashamed of how badly she wanted to be back on a soundstage, the lights warm on her bare shoulders, a crew of hundreds waiting for her to speak. Sometimes, when she was sitting by the pool at the hotel, she pretended that it was a scene in a movie, with the director hiding in the palm leaves, capturing her smallest movements. She wouldn't dare say it out loud, not even to Jimmy.

A loud knock on the open door startled them both. A stocky man with white hair and heavy, black-rimmed glasses poked his head in. "Mr. Peterson?" he said in a deep, lightly accented voice.

Jimmy stood and hurried to the door, hand outstretched. What he lacked in business acumen he made up for in earnest friendliness, a quality seldom seen in Los Angeles. "Mr. Contogenis. So glad to meet you. Please come in."

Laura stood and waited to be introduced. She held her hands loosely in front of her body, with her fingers touching. Jimmy shook Mr. Contogenis's hand vigorously and then turned back to face Laura and the otherwise nearly empty room. Laura wished she'd thought to have the meeting in the bungalow, where the lights were dimmer and she might look more comfortable. She was wearing an outfit that Florence had picked out, a swingy tunic with pants to match. Her first impulse had been to wear a dress, but Florence had insisted. Now she just felt awkward, like someone's grandmother (which she was, whether she liked it or not) trying to look young and with-it. Laura felt her cheeks flush.

"Mr. Contogenis, allow me to introduce Ms. Laura Lamont," Jimmy said, shifting his body out of the way.

"Christos," he said, and reached for Laura's hand, bringing it to his lips.

"Well," Laura said, taken aback. "Hello." No one had kissed her with anything but maternal affection in ten years. In ten years, women went from ingenues to wives, from wives to matrons, from matrons to hags. The skin on her knuckles began to tingle and sing. The idea of a love affair was better than the thing itself, and Laura let her mind careen forward: her skin, his skin, her mouth, his mouth, his glasses on the floor, everything else forgotten for as long as it took. It was as clear as the morning she'd sat with Gordon at her parents' picnic table: Laura would follow this man when he left the room, no matter what Jimmy arranged. She recognized a spark when she saw it, and wanted to hold it tight against her chest, a blinking signal shouting in all directions.

Christos had booked a table for lunch, and they rode together to the restaurant in the back of his limo. They held hands in the car and he whispered into her ear. He wanted to make her a star again, because he'd always loved her the most. Did he mention that he loved her? He did, over and over again, until Laura's head was spinning with hope and the champagne that Christos kept pouring into her glass. The clouds outside the limousine's sunroof were compliments, the salty peanuts were kisses on her earlobe, the bottle of chilled champagne pulled from a concealed compartment was a promise of more to come.

The dining room was in a small but beautifully appointed hotel on the beach in Santa Monica, and overlooked the ocean. The room was blue and white, and felt to Laura like the inside of a giant boat. Susie and Johnny had made a movie on a ship once, *Anchors Up!* They played young lovers whose parents were trying to keep them apart. They danced up and down glowing staircases, with life preservers swinging around their waists like hula hoops. Laura hadn't spoken to either of them since she left Gardner Brothers, but she'd heard the rumors. No one could stay young and cute forever. The word was that Susie shook like a leaf without a fifth of vodka in her belly, that she'd had her face pulled taut too many times, that she was leaving all her money to her Pomeranian. The news on Johnny was even worse: pornography, young men, a club in the basement of a hotel where you could pay for anything. Laura didn't want to know more.

A waiter pulled out her chair, and Laura slid in, tucking her legs under the table. It was the best seat in the house: She stared out the glass wall at the waves of the Pacific. Laura had a sudden panic—why hadn't she raised her kids on the beach? Clara could have bopped around in her bikini, and Florence could have studied the shells and rocks, and she and Junior could have hidden themselves under an umbrella with a couple of books. This was why people moved to California. Without the ocean, they were just choosing to live like coyotes, in the underbrush. The next time someone handed her a big check, Laura thought, she would buy a house on the beach.

Christos set his napkin on his lap, and then stuck a finger in the air, which prompted more champagne.

"I can't drink this much," Laura said. "Well, maybe just one more glass." She was laughing at nothing, at the idea that she was finally back on track, after all this time. He wanted to put her in a movie. The financing was in place! Laura knew that was the trickiest part nowadays, with everyone so plumb sure that they could do everything themselves, without the studio's pocketbook and expertise. She was glad she'd left when she did, when quality was high and movies were still pieces of art, every inch designed and thoughtful. Christos wanted to go back to that, to make a real picture.

"You don't think I'm too old? For people to want to see me be romantic?"

Christos looked at her with a lascivious gaze, the only appropriate answer. "I think you're perfect," he said. "Even when you were playing a nun, I wanted to get you in bed."

"Oh," Laura said. "Thank you."

Christos motioned for the waiter to come back, and ordered for both of them—hanger steak and Caesar salads. When the waiter was gone, Christos scooted his chair closer to Laura's and put his hand on her knee under the tablecloth.

"So when do you think we'll start filming? Is there a good script?" Laura crossed her legs, knocking Christos's hand away. She liked feeling admired, but this was business. Business came first.

He seemed not to notice. "What's that?"

"The movie," Laura said. "When do you think we'll start?" She looked down at herself. The outfit Florence had picked out wasn't so bad, even though it could have been ironed. "I should probably go on a bit of a diet, don't you think? Maybe I should skip the steak."

"Oh, we'll see," Christos said. He leaned back in his chair and ran his hands up and down over his large belly like a pregnant woman.

"What do you mean, 'we'll see'?" Laura tilted her head to the side, checking to see whether a different angle might change the answer. "Who do you have on board?"

"On board?"

"ADs, hair, makeup. I'd love to hire Edna, if we could. I miss those dresses. Edna is at Gardner Brothers, and she is really the best in the business." Laura paused, already so many steps ahead. "Do you mean I'm the first person you approached?"

Christos leaned forward with a groan. His nose was lumpy, with pores the size of potholes. "I'll get to it," he said. "We're not in a rush, are we?" Laura thought he might reach over and touch her arm, just to let her know that he was going to do whatever needed to be done, but instead, he reached for his glass of champagne. "Next year," he said. "Let's talk about it next year."

"Next year?" Laura said, realizing that the project was as likely as an iceberg in the Gulf of Mexico. "Enjoy your steak," she said, and pushed her chair back from the table before the waiters had a chance to help.

Junior was waiting in the bungalow when Laura got home. It was only just the afternoon, but all the shades were down and all the lights off, which made the living room feel like midnight.

"We were supposed to have lunch," he said from the middle of the darkness, his voice thick with repulsion. "After your meeting. I called Jimmy to see why you were taking so long and he said you went on a *date*."

Laura flipped on the overhead light, which made Junior scream, and so she turned it off again and felt her way over to the sofa.

"Not really," she said, already wanting to pretend it had never happened, that she'd never entertained the idea. "It was a mis-understanding. I thought he was going to give me a job." Laura found Junior's knee with her left hand and squeezed it. The truth was so simple when she said it out loud, that what she'd really hungered for was the work and not the love, at least since Irving.

"But you would do that?"

The bungalow was silent, without even the gentle humming of a lamp. Cars drove by, and there were faraway splashes in the hotel pool, but the air inside the room itself was perfectly still.

"I'm sorry, love," Laura said. "I had to try."

"You didn't even think about me, did you?" She could feel his body stiffen.

"Of course I did."

Junior shook Laura off and got up, his thin legs making creaking noises, as if he hadn't moved in hours.

"How long have you been sitting here?" Laura asked, but Junior didn't answer. Instead, he walked in the dark into his bed-room. Laura stayed on the sofa for a few minutes, unsure of what she could say. She and Irving had rarely fought, and had never come to blows, never done any of the things that were bad news for children to witness. If anything, they had been too absorbed with each other to pay proper attention to all three children on a daily basis. Laura had a quick flash of all the times they'd locked a whimpering child out of their bedroom to keep that space for themselves. It was hard to think of Clara as a mother the same way that Laura herself was a mother, hard to imagine that the two experiences were at all the same. Laura certainly felt no such common ground with her own mother, who had hardly shown her any affection even before Hildy's death, and certainly not after. She was thinking of her sister so often lately, at the oddest moments. Pouring a cup of coffee in the morning, clicking off the hotel lamp at night. Hildy was there all day long, just waiting in the shadows.

"Junior?" Laura said into the empty room.

The door to his bedroom was slightly ajar, letting Laura slip in without knocking. Laura heard the toilet flush, and then the shower turn on—Junior was in the bathroom. She pressed her face gently to the door and spoke into the wood.

"Sweetie, can you hear me?"

On the other side of the door, Junior made a grunting noise.

"Is that a yes?"

There was the unmistakable sound of breaking glass—the mirror. Laura's hand moved to the doorknob, which she couldn't turn. She knocked on the door again, hard. "Junior, please open the door. What are you doing in there? Please open the door."

She could hear motion, and the constant beating of the water, but nothing else. There was nothing interrupting the flow of the shower, no irregularity of water hitting skin, hitting the tub, hitting the curtain. Junior wasn't actually taking a shower at all. "Open the door. I'm serious—open it right now, or I'm calling the front desk, and they'll open it for me." She threw her body against the door, over and over, but the wood didn't weaken beneath her weight.

There was a louder crash and the sound of porcelain shattering. Laura watched as the lock turned, and the door slowly pulled open from the inside.

Junior was on the floor, the shower rod sitting in between his legs. The wet cloth curtain was spread around him like a petticoat. Behind Junior's back, the shower continued to beat against the tub.

"What happen—" Laura began to ask, but then she saw—attached to both Junior's neck and the shower rod was his blue nylon belt, a sturdy thing she'd bought for him at a sailing shop in Malibu. *Indestructible*, the label had boasted. Laura dropped to her knees and began to pull at the curtain, trying to detach the rod from her son's body. Junior was gasping for breath, his chest pumping in and out in shallow heaves. Of course Junior looked just like Hildy—how had Laura not seen it before? The full, berry-stained lips, the short, soft nose, the pretty eyes. She had to shake her head to knock the image loose, Hildy's swinging body in her bedroom. This wasn't that—Junior was alive, not dead. She had come in time. Her relief was the ocean, the galaxy—it was too big to be contained by her body, or the hotel, or all of Los Angeles. Laura thought that if someone was listening hard enough, they could hear her exhale all the way in Door County.

"No no no no no no," Laura said, the words spilling out with neither thought nor effort. She unwound the belt from Junior's neck, a deep red stripe marking its place. He was starting to breathe normally again, but refused to look her in the eye, staring at the corner of the tiled floor instead.

Laura wrapped her arms around her son's shoulders and

rocked him back and forth, with the water from the shower still beating steadily behind them. It didn't matter that the floor would get wet, or that their clothes would soak through. Laura didn't care whether the shower flooded the entire Beverly Hills Hotel. She would stay there as long as Junior needed her to. There was a knock on the door to the bungalow, and Laura kicked the bathroom door shut, keeping her foot taut against the lip of the door. If it was in or out, then Laura had already made her choice.

The doctors explained what Laura had always known: that Junior went up and down as quickly as a yo-yo, his moods swinging because of a chemical imbalance in the brain. Laura's first thought was of her sister, and her second thought was to finally say, "Yes, yes, there is something wrong, but we can fix it."

The psychiatric ward looked much the same as it had when Laura was a patient, though with newly refinished floors and more comfortable chairs in the rooms. The walls were painted a salmon pink, which Laura thought did seem comforting, in a certain way, as if they were all swimming upstream. She wore her sunglasses in the elevator, taking them off only when she approached the desk and gave Junior's name, though she knew where his room was, because she'd come in with him two days before.

"Irving Green, Junior?" The nurse repeated. Hearing his name from someone else's mouth felt like a hole through Laura's lung.

"That's right."

"Follow me."

The nurse led Laura through the common area filled with people playing board games and watching television, and down a well-lit hall. It was Laura's fault that her only son had ended up in a place like this; she could admit that to herself. She tried to keep her breath steady. Someday Junior would forgive her. The nurse stopped in front of a glass-paned door, and Laura saw Junior sitting in a chair by the window, looking out onto the courtyard.

"This is the hospital you were born in, you know," Laura said, stepping over the threshold.

Junior turned around, his narrow face wan. "Mom," he said, standing up. He was wearing borrowed pajamas; Laura had brought his own in her bag, along with a robe and some slippers. She remembered that about staying in the hospital: It was funny to get dressed when you knew you weren't allowed to leave. Better to turn it all into a big slumber party.

"Love," she said, walking briskly across the room until he was in her arms, his narrow rib cage rising and falling with quick, short breaths. He smelled like hospital soap. Someone had cut his hair. "Oh, love," she said again, over and over again, until Junior knew for certain that his mother would do anything for him, for the rest of his life, for even longer than that.

⌖

Jimmy, the dear, had been on the phone all day, updating everyone who needed to be updated, a one-man phone tree. He'd called Josephine right after he'd called his wife and sister-in-law, and she was in Los Angeles that night. When Laura came home from the hospital, when visiting hours were over, her sister was already curled up on the sofa in the bungalow underneath a thin cotton blanket. Laura set her keys and purse down quietly by the door and walked to the side of the couch, where Josephine's bent knees poked out.

"Hey," Laura said, wiggling her hips into the available space. Josephine sleepily raised her feet to let Laura in, and then set them back down on her lap. Laura ran her hands over her sister's socked feet. No one in Hollywood had ever complimented Laura on her feet—no costume designer, no smarmy actor, not even Irving. Laura had Emerson feet, just like Josephine's—as wide as they were long, and flat as flapjacks. It was nice to be in such close physical proximity, even though they hadn't spoken in months, and only via cursory birthday cards and the like. In the end, it didn't matter. Sisters were sisters.

"Is he okay?" Josephine asked. She stayed lying down, her face turned toward the coffee table and the dark square of the television.

"He will be," Laura said. "I'm glad you're here."

Outside, some hotel guests were taking a midnight swim, and Laura heard the splashing of a cannonball, followed by peals of laughter. The watery sounds filled the living room, and both Laura and Josephine stayed quiet, appreciating the liveliness so nearby.

Josephine rolled onto her back and inched backward until she was sitting up. In the relative dark—the only light in the room came from the floor lamp beside the sofa—Josephine's features seemed not to have aged at all. Intellectually, Laura knew that her sister was sixty-three years old, but even with her blond hair now gray, she didn't look old to Laura.

"Me too," Josephine said. She had lost some of her middle-aged weight, and now just looked sturdy.

"How is Helen?" Helen had been Josephine's roommate for the last decade. They were both retired, and Laura knew that they were happy together by the look on Josephine's face when her name was mentioned. Laura imagined a woman in her twenties, a slim, modest beauty, the way Josephine's girlfriends had looked once upon a time. "I'd like to meet her one of these days."

"That would be nice." Josephine held her kneecaps, one in each hand. "Listen," she said, as if Laura were doing anything else. They both sat in silence, preparing for whatever Josephine was about to say. "I know you think you know everything about Hildy, and I'm sure this brings it all back for you." She paused. "But you don't."

Laura licked her lips and then swallowed. "Okay." She both wanted Josephine to hurry, to open her mouth wider and let the words stream out, and for her to take it back, to take it all back, to never have to walk into that bedroom ever again as long as she lived. *One at a time,* Laura thought. *I can only take one thing at a time.* But she didn't move, and so Josephine continued.

"You remember Cliff?" Light fell on only half of Josephine's face, and the other half remained in darkness. There were still sounds coming from the pool, happy, joyful noises, but Laura could hear only her own heart, which was beating faster, and somewhere around her ears.

"Of course." Laura nodded.

"And you know they were together?"

She nodded again.

"Hildy was pregnant. She was pregnant when she killed herself, Else." Josephine put her hands flat against her cheeks and slowly moved her fingers over her lips, until her hands were in prayer position, resting at her chin.

"Really?" Laura pictured their parents' house, and Hildy's room, back when it was a living thing, and not a neglected museum. She could hear the sound of the staircase at night, when Hildy came in late, and the sounds that Hildy would make when she and Cliff were alone together. Laura didn't know what her parents would have done if they'd known Hildy was pregnant. Or maybe they did.

"Did Mom and Dad know?"

Josephine shook her head vigorously. "No," she said. "No. Just me."

Laura was still in Hildy's bedroom, sitting at the foot of her bed. Her sister was still alive, still beautiful. Hildy's hair was long and brushed, a thick braid hanging over her left shoulder. Laura was close enough that she was sure she could almost touch her sister, almost hear her voice. Hildy looked so young—for the first time, Laura saw her sister as a child, a teenager, a girl barely on the cusp of everything.

"Do you think that's why she did it?"

Josephine winced. "I don't think so. Maybe. I think it would have been something, if it wasn't that. She was sick, Else, you know? Like Junior. She was sick."

Laura felt her body bristle with the discomfort of understanding that her sister was right. The shiver ran through her arms and legs and heart and spine before it landed, gently, on her tongue. "I wish I could have helped her," she said.

"I know, sweetie," Josephine said, finally pulling the blanket off her knees and sliding next to her sister. She wrapped her arms around Laura's shoulders and pulled her close, until their torsos were flat against each other. Laura thought that if they had tried to fuse their bodies together precisely at that moment, they could have, so unified were their feelings, so in sync. If they had tried to conjure Hildy out of thin air, they could have, brought her back to life with nothing more than their love and sorrow and regret. Both Laura and Josephine cried the way they had cried when they lost her the first time, each wetting the other's shoulder with tears. When they were finished, Laura invited her sister to sleep in Florence's room with her, and so they slowly made their way down the hall and climbed into bed, their bodies side by side and completely still until morning.

The day that Junior was to come home from the hospital, Laura got dressed and stood in front of the mirror in the bungalow's bathroom, which had been replaced. It reflected her only from the belly button up, and showed her hair, which needed to be washed, hanging straight to her shoulders. She'd been spending so much time with Junior that she often forgot to shower for days, or to feed herself anything that didn't exist in the cafeteria, unless Josephine or Florence reminded her. Junior would be healthy; that was all that mattered, and Laura deeply believed that it was true. He would recover, just as she had recovered. There were broken parts inside each of them. No parent could keep her child whole; that was the truth. All she could do was to show up every morning with a smile on her face and something new for him to read. Laura quickly brushed her teeth and splashed some water on her face. It would be better when he was home.

11

THE SHOPGIRL

Winter 1975

Edna's Custom Gowns and Hats was a small, elegantly appointed salon on the second floor of a building on Dayton Way, just north of Rodeo Drive. On the far side of the room, by the windows, there were three-way mirrors and a small felted box on which ladies could stand while their dresses were being pinned. To the left, Edna kept all her fabric swatches and supplies, her scissors and measuring tapes. To the right were two dressing rooms, each with its own heavy curtain on brass rings. It was Laura's job to greet the customers when they came in, and to walk them through the process of having a gown custom-made. She went over the possibilities, the necklines and the hemlines and everything in between. For the first two years, Laura had only answered the telephone and made appointments for Edna and her assistant, but Laura loved being around the dresses as they were made and tweaked, the feeling of the silks she could no longer afford, and she found that having a place to go every day made her happy. Junior said it made her look younger, which made Laura wrinkle her nose in embarrassed pleasure.

Sometimes the women wanted something modern, a pantsuit made out of polyester, and Edna would tighten her lips and give her head a short shake. She didn't make those kinds of things. Laura loved to watch Edna work. It wasn't just film stars who came in, needing a dress for an event, it was also regular women, housewives and members of the working world, women with paychecks and birthdays and children and bodies that didn't agree with off-the-rack dresses. There were women with enormous breasts or no breasts to speak of, women with hips three sizes larger than their shoulders. Edna wasn't just making dresses, she was making women feel better about themselves. Laura saw their faces as they walked out the door with the dress bags over their arms, so careful not to muss them on the stairs. For most of the day, Laura sat at the small desk by the door and watched Edna work. In some ways, it felt to her as if she were back at the studio, waiting to be called to perform. The job paid her only slightly more than Gardner Brothers had paid for her first contract, three hundred dollars a week. That money, along with the sums contributed by Junior and Florence from their part-time jobs, was enough to pay the hotel maintenance bill on time, almost always.

No matter how much she enjoyed herself at work, the best part about having a job were the days off—Laura had Sunday and Monday to herself, when the shop was closed. Florence had moved into her own apartment, and so Laura had the master bedroom to herself, with a desk against the shared wall that she used to write her letters. Laura missed Harriet terribly, but felt it was rude to intrude too much on her position. She'd left the jackal-faced actress for a director's family in Malibu, and Laura sent letters on a weekly basis. She called Ginger at the studio, and was put on hold for so long that she hung up. Ginger had Petunia written into the show, and so the two of them were always together, two redheads, the perfect Hollywood family, in color. Bill had never been as popular with the viewers, and no one seemed to miss him when he left for the ranch life elsewhere. Things were moving in the right direction, the only direction they *could* move. It wasn't healthy to think too much about the past. All of the good days that Laura had ever had were gone, as were the bad ones. She could think only about the future.

Laura wrote a letter to her mother with all the news she could muster. She wrote that Clara's two children, Roy and Leslie, were still charming little blondes, and looked straight out of Door County. She asked after Josephine, whom she was more in touch with, but it seemed the polite thing to do. A phone call would have been easier, she supposed, but her mother wasn't likely to answer, and if she did, she was even less likely to stay on the phone long enough to hear everything that was spilling out of Laura's mouth. She hadn't spoken to her mother for more than five minutes at a time since her father's funeral, but she'd written a dozen letters, each of them pages long. It was almost better that her mother never wrote back—this way Laura could pretend she'd never sent the letters at all, and her mother had never rebuffed her. It was possible that the letters had never existed, but just vanished into thin air as soon as she'd slipped the sealed envelopes through the mailbox slot.

Junior knocked on her bedroom door.

"Hi, sweetie," Laura said, and pointed to the bed. Junior's hair was long, tickling his shoulders, and the glasses he wore were the perfectly round ones, like John Lennon's. Junior's job was at a natural-food store, where he unpacked boxes of avocados and tomatoes and different kinds of granola. He seemed perfectly content, even when the trucks were late and he had to sit in the store after dark, the smell of carob and sourdough bread clinging to his cotton vest.

"What are you doing?"

"Writing a letter to your grandmother." Laura signed her name—*Elsa Laura*—and folded the pages, tucking them into the waiting envelope. She gave it a timid lick.

"Isn't she pretty much an asshole?"

"Junior!"

"Well, isn't she?" Her son moved a pillow so that it was behind his head, and lay back. He closed his eyes for a moment, and then opened them long enough to make sure that Laura was paying attention. Once assured that he had his mother on alert, he curled up into a ball. Laura thought he slept so much because of his headaches—just like that, they'd shown up, the Emerson girls' worst enemy, as bad as Hildy and her mother had ever had them.

"She is not, and don't say that word." Laura narrowed her eyes at her son. "Your grandmother likes to keep things simple. California just didn't agree with her, that's all."

"You mean Dad." Junior's feet were bare, and his soles dusty from walking around the house.

"My father loved your father. It's true that my mother didn't quite understand him."

"Because he was a Jew." Junior sat back up. He took off his glasses, cleaned them with the tail of his shirt, and put them back on. Sometimes he looked so much like his father that it poked a hole straight through Laura's heart, as precise and deadly as an arrow. Even with the straggly long hair, Irving was right there, staring back at her.

"Because he was older than me. And Jewish. And, I don't know, different than they expected."

When she was a little girl, Laura would have conversations with her father in the barn, with him on the stage, or on the benches, and her in the hayloft above him. There was a safety in that, in being able to say whatever she wanted without having to look him in the eye—just like writing her mother letters that might go unread was easier than calling and having a difficult conversation. Junior wasn't like that—he wanted to see the expression on his mother's face when he said something difficult.

"And it wasn't like that with Clara and Florence's father."

"First of all, their father is your father—you know that—but yes. Of course it's different. It's very different." Laura didn't want to say too much. She didn't want to say anything at all. She half wanted Junior to forget he'd ever had a father, and herself to forget she'd ever had a husband. It wasn't that hard to play a part, once you understood the role. Maybe she needed another name, another skin to slip inside. She was a new woman now.

"That's what I thought," Junior said, satisfied.

It was Laura's birthday, and at her request, no one was allowed to say the number. The party was at Ginger's house, and everyone was invited. Clara came over early with Jimmy and the children to help set things up, though of course Ginger had hired people to do everything, and so Clara just mimed helping for a few minutes and then accepted a glass of champagne and sat down. Despite the aforementioned catering, Harriet brought her famous chocolate cake, and Laura cried when she walked through the door, looking slender and beautiful.

"I'm so terribly fat," Laura said, but she was in truth only a bit rounder than she had been ten years previous.

"You are a drama queen," Harriet said. "Same as ever."

Clara scooped a heap of icing off the top of the cake with her finger and plopped it into her mouth before the thing had even been served, and no one said peep.

When Laura married Irving, she thought that he was rich because he was the head of a studio, but when she met Christos she understood that she had not begun to see what money could mean. It wasn't the studio; it was the city block. It wasn't the cigarettes; it was the tobacco. It wasn't the fancy cars; it was the gasoline that powered them. Ginger was like that now, in the stratosphere. And so when Junior's spiritual guru told him that he should learn how to surf, Ginger offered to close the beach for miles. When Leslie, Clara's youngest, wanted to paint, live models were brought in for her and Petunia to sketch. There were no limits. Ginger gave Laura's children what they wanted, and never asked for anything in return. She was their benefactress, except for Laura: Laura would never let Ginger give her a job again, no matter how badly she wanted it. It was more important for her to have a friend.

"This really is something, Mama," Clara said. She was wearing a royal blue dress made out of some stretchy new material that clung like Scotch tape to her wide hips and large breasts. Laura had a newly critical eye for fabric and cut, but she wouldn't criticize her daughter, either in public or in private. Clara had had her blond hair curled, and it bounced around her head. Laura didn't like to think uncharitable thoughts about her daughter. Maybe it was the burden of being first, and always having to be the one to plow forth into uncharted territory. Before Clara, Laura had been a girl herself, and she supposed that some part of her had always blamed her daughters for taking her youth away. It wasn't a fair thought, and it made Laura sad to think it, but it was true.

"Yes, my dear," Laura said.

Clara stuffed a cocktail wienie into her mouth. While she was still chewing, she pulled two cigarettes out of her purse and held one toward her mother. Laura shook her head—she'd been trying to stop, especially around the children. But that didn't stop Clara, who was clicking open her gold lighter and exhaling smoke over the top of the cake and the rest of the food already laid out on the table. "You know, not all of us are as lucky as you are."

Lucky. Laura had never thought of herself as lucky, not since Irving had spoken to her at that party a thousand years ago, not since she'd shed the skin of Elsa Emerson and become this other, more glamorous beast. For that was how she thought of herself: the snake that had lived inside the body of a kitten. What was it for? Laura thought of Hildy, her beautiful sister, the one who should have been adored. It was Hildy who had wanted to be a movie star, whose face had called out for cameras to follow her every move, whose body begged to be watched—even as a teenager! It was so hard to understand that Clara and Florence and even Junior were now all older than Hildy had ever been, and would ever be. Laura was lucky, then; she was lucky to have lived when Hildy had not. She was lucky to have three healthy, beautiful children. And she was lucky that she could get to choose what happened next.

Jimmy was across the buffet table, his blond hair now almost all gone, except for around his ears. He looked like a teenage athlete who had gotten tired and decided to swallow the basketball. "No, my love, you're the lucky one," Laura said, and meant it. Jimmy looked up at his wife and winked, piling his plate full of macaroni salad, the love on his face as clear as it was when they were teenagers. Laura squeezed Clara's elbow. "You really are."

Clara's son, Roy, and Petunia threw a football back and forth in the back. There were patio chairs set up in the small grassy area beside the pool, and Laura could see Ginger sitting there, watching the children. It had happened late for Ginger, motherhood. She and Bill hadn't even been trying; it was too late by all the standard biological markers. Ginger had long since given up on having children of her own, and then, out of nowhere, a baby. It didn't even matter that she and Bill had split, or that Ginger worked as much as she did. It was the baby who'd brought Ginger back to her, Laura knew, the baby who'd helped bridge the gap between them. Laura watched Ginger watching the kids, her big red mouth open wide with laughter. Petunia made her happy—it was that simple; she was happy. All of the hard things in her life had prepared her for this happiness with her daughter. She'd been wild; she'd been bad; she'd been famous; she'd been powerful. Now she was this: still funny and so *happy.* Laura thought that if she spent the entire party just looking at Ginger, she might be okay.

Florence came in late, squeaking on the tiles. Northern California agreed with her. She'd cut her hair, which now swung just below her shoulders.

"You look like a giraffe, like a beautiful doctor giraffe," Laura said.

"Thanks, I think," Florence said, letting herself be embraced by her mother.

"How was the drive?" Laura pulled back so that she could look at Florence better.

"Not bad. How about *you*, Mom? Happy birthday!"

"Ms. Lamont?" It was one of the catering staff, waiting patiently behind Florence with one arm wrapped around a giant bouquet.

"Yes, that's me," Laura said, and moved to take the flowers out of his hand.

The caterer nodded and turned back to polishing the silverware.

"Who are they from?" Florence asked, peering into the papery cone.

"Oh, lilies," Laura said. "I love lilies." There was a small white card pinned to the paper, and Laura plucked it off. "Hold these, will you?"

Florence took the flowers in her arm and waited for her mother to open the card.

Dear Laura, the card read. *Yours were always my favorite films to make, and I would like to make more. I will always regret the way things ended with Irving. Please call. Yours, Louis Gardner.*

"Well, who are they from?" Florence tapped her foot, impatient.

Laura tucked the note back into its envelope, and then slipped the card into her pocket. Ginger wouldn't notice another bouquet of flowers, or want to know where they'd come from. Laura would ask one of the staff to put them in water, and they would blend in with all the rest. "They're from Louis Gardner," Laura said. Her eyes were wet. She couldn't go back to Gardner Brothers, couldn't and wouldn't. How could she walk down those streets, watching younger women fall in and out of love? She had already had her chance, and it had worked like a charm. Laura put her arm around Florence's waist and walked back into the party as if she were walking on a frozen lake, each step lighter than the last. She would have a piece of cake as big as Clara's, and spend the whole day smiling at anyone who dared look her way. No one could tell Laura Lamont what to do; she was too old for that. Let them come and look at her, let them try to swallow her up into their old-fashioned story lines. Laura was going to sew herself into the shape of happiness all on her own.

The shop was busiest on Saturdays, but the women with the most money came in during the week. Laura sharpened her pencils quietly while Edna spoke with a pair of women who needed bridesmaid dresses for a wedding. Edna looked at the clock and then hurried the women along, her tiny foot tapping as they prattled on about sea foam versus peach. When they were gone, Laura said, "Are you in a hurry, Edna?" But then the doorbell rang, and before Laura even had a chance to reapply her lipstick, Peggy Bates was standing in front of her, handing over her purse.

Laura tried to do the math but couldn't. The last time she'd seen Peggy in person, they were both under contract at Gardner Brothers, and Irving was still alive, and Peggy was one of the studio's perma-teenagers, a woman who couldn't look thirty if she'd worn a gray wig and a pair of granny glasses. The rest she knew from the trades: drugs, a handful of marriages, and then a miraculous second life on the small screen. For the last five years, Peggy had played Pixie, the titular character on *Pixie's People*, a half-hour sitcom about a magical fairy who lived with a normal family in the San Fernando Valley. Pixie was famous for sprinkling fairy dust over someone's head and then whispering, "They'll never know the difference!" Laura was shocked to see Peggy dressed in normal clothes, instead of Pixie's regulation chiffon.

"Peggy!" Laura said, too surprised to pretend to be otherwise.

"Laura Lamont?" Peggy said, and withdrew her handbag. The women hugged awkwardly, Peggy's leather satchel wedged between their bellies. "What are you doing here? I haven't seen you in *ages*."

Laura cleared her throat and gave her jacket a little tug. "Actually, I work here, with Edna. I work here." It happened every so often, the awkward encounter with someone from her past life. Customers recognized her all the time, almost every day, but that she was used to. It was her peers who threw Laura off, the actresses.

Peggy opened her mouth so wide that Laura could see the white spots on her tongue, bad breath waiting to happen. "You don't say!" She smacked her purse against Laura's hip. "Laura Lamont the shopgirl!"

Edna hurried over and stepped between them, kissing Peggy

on both cheeks. Edna's trademark dark glasses and severe hair-cut were exactly the same as they had been at Gardner Brothers. It was both reassuring and alarming to be in the presence of a woman who was immune to change. "All right, all right, all right," Edna said, removing Peggy's coat. "Enough of that. We're doing the dress for the gala today. I already have the fabric pulled. Come look." She passed Peggy's coat to Laura, who hung it up and then tried to vanish into thin air.

"Laura? Can you come take notes as we talk?" Edna was already unrolling a bolt of crimson silk.

"Sure, of course," Laura said, and grabbed her notepad. She wrote down everything both women said for an hour, her fingers moving quickly so that her brain didn't have to.

When Peggy had her coat on again and was walking out the door, she turned around and said over her shoulder, "You know, Laura, it was really good to see you." Laura agreed that it was, and shut the door gently behind her. After the sound of Peggy's heels on the stairs was gone, Edna crossed her arms over her chest and said, through the pins in her teeth, "Fuck her."

Jimmy called the bungalow on Monday night to say that there'd been an offer—a Japanese perfume company wanted to fly Laura over to shoot a commercial.

"A commercial? As in, an advertisement?" Commercials were for the blond and the buxom, for those who could credibly pass for young mothers with a new mop, a frozen chicken, a kissable pout. "Do they know what I look like?"

"They want to fly you there, Mom. They'll pay for everything. It's just one ad, and no one you know will ever see it."

Laura was sitting in the living room. She could hear Junior's stereo playing softly in his bedroom. It was one of the bands she didn't understand, with fifteen-minute-long songs and no discernible melody. She thought that Irving and Junior might have talked for hours about music, about jazz and psychedelic rock and roll, and the Elvis Junior had loved as a teenager. They would have locked themselves in a room full of records and needed to come out only for meals.

"Will they pay for Junior to come too?"

Laura had never learned to enjoy flying, and she felt jittery as soon as she buckled herself into her seat.

"Honey, would you get me a drink from the stewardess? I just need to use the ladies' room."

"We're about to take off, Mom. I don't think you're allowed to go yet." Junior didn't look up from his book, but he did place his left hand on his mother's wrist, holding it flat against their shared armrest. "It's going to be okay."

Laura exhaled loudly. She should have said no. No to this commercial, no to everyone but her children. Edna had given her the week off, but the whole thing felt like a fever dream, like she had fallen asleep and woken up in a different place in her own life. She should have stayed in Irving's house forever, until the weeds grew up to the roof and the police had to knock the door down. She should have had pets—why had none of the children ever gotten a puppy for Christmas? It seemed an oversight of the highest magnitude, only a smidgen behind total neglect on the scale of abuses. The flight to Tokyo was just over ten hours long. The Japanese stewardesses bowed and cooed over Laura just as they bowed and cooed over everyone else in first class, but they stared at her longer, were more solicitous of her strained smile. Laura's glass of whiskey wasn't empty until she fell asleep, her face pressed against her son's bony shoulder.

An escort from the perfume company met them at the airport, holding a handwritten sign that said LAMONT in large capital letters, with something written in Japanese beneath it, as though Laura might be likely to recognize her name in another language. The man bowed at Laura, and again at Junior, and they both bowed back at him, confused by the daylight outside the terminal building.

The set of the commercial was simple: Laura stood in the middle of an empty stage. She sprayed her neck and wrists with the perfume—Hollywood. Then, behind her, dancing girls appeared, kicking their legs like the Rockettes. The director, a Japanese man only slightly older than Junior, stood beside the camera. The dancing girls wore sequins and top hats as they made their way across the stage, and Laura had to look into the lens and say, "Smells like Hollywood." All Laura could smell was the alcohol in the perfume, the hair spray in her hair. Junior was somewhere in the room, but she couldn't see past the bright lights pointing in her direction. It seemed so implausible that her career would flame out so spectacularly. Even if what Jimmy said was true, and no one she knew ever saw the ad, Laura would still know it was out there, floating around in the ether. They'd dressed her in a beaded evening gown and elbow-length white gloves, fancier even than most of the dresses that Edna made, and the heavy fabric felt like an anchor around her throat.

It was all done in a few hours, the length of time it would take to shoot a single complicated scene. Laura tried to think of the commercial as a scene from a film, but she couldn't imagine the part she was supposed to be playing—every possibility was more depressing than the last. She was a nightclub owner, a has-been actress, a madam in a whorehouse. The makeup was thick on her face, and every time Laura reached up, bits of her foundation rubbed off on her white gloves. Someone snapped a number of photographs of Laura with the dancing Japanese girls, with the director, with the executives from the perfume company, and then the escort took her and Junior back to the hotel.

A woman at the front desk waved Laura down and handed her a message, which read:

> *Laura—Thought you should be back under the lights. Hope you don't object to my recommending you for the gig. I did an advertisement for them six months ago. The Japs do love us old dames.*
>
> *—Peggy Bates*

Laura bowed in thanks, and quickly turned toward the elevator. Junior chuckled at his mother's obvious mortification. He read the note and said, "I thought she was supposed to be one of the nice ones."

"She is. I mean, she was. I guess she is? Oh, I don't know," Laura said. "It was generous of her to think of me." They walked into the elevator and leaned against the far wall.

"*How much* did they pay you for that?" Junior asked.

"Fifty thousand dollars."

"For *that*?"

"Yes, my love." Laura turned the note in her hand, watching the light reflect off the paper. "When we get home," she said, "I'm going back to Edna's. It's better to be normal, I think."

Junior nodded. He looked so much like Irving, hair so dark brown it looked black in the low light, eyes hooded and deep. "That sounds good, Mom."

Laura missed her husband. She rested her palm against Junior's cheek. He had a few days' worth of stubble, but still looked handsome to her, always handsome. There were home movies from when Junior was a baby, movies that Irving had had the studio make, and she wondered where they were. Boxed up in the film archives along with everything else. Laura wanted to show her son the way they had all looked as a family, how happy they had been. She could never adequately describe the look Irving had had when Junior was born, the look he'd had when Junior took his first jerking steps. Laura wanted all of it back, every moment, so that she could live it all over again. She let her hand rest against her son's face until he felt embarrassed and pulled away.

12

THE PLAYER

Spring 1980

It was never good news when the phone rang in the middle of the night. No one ever called in the middle of the night to tell you that they loved you—it couldn't have been Junior; he was at home. Something must be wrong with her mother, or Josephine, or one of Clara's children. Laura rolled over and grabbed blindly for the receiver.

"Hello?" Laura cleared her throat. Her heart was beating so quickly that she could hardly believe she'd been asleep just a few moments earlier. Hearts shouldn't speed up that quickly, she thought. That was how people got killed. "Hello?"

"Ms. Lamont?" The voice on the other end of the line was tinny and measured, a professional person. There was no hurry there.

"Yes?"

"Ms. Lamont, this is the Los Angeles Police Department. I'm

afraid I have some bad news for you. We've just picked someone up, and we need you to identify the body."

"The body?" Laura could suddenly make out everything in the room—the paperweight, the ashtray, the chair legs, the open closet, the door to the bathroom. Her body hummed with adrenaline.

"I'm afraid it's your husband, Ms. Lamont."

"Irving? What happened to Irving?" Laura sucked in sharply, as if she'd been struck. When she was woken in the middle of the night, there was only one person who'd ever truly held that title. Once her breath returned, Laura felt her midsection wobble in and out, like a dog panting in the sun, an involuntary movement her body was making in order to regulate her temperature. She needed to know what had happened.

"Uh, no, ma'am. The person in question is Mr. Pitts? Mr. Gordon Pitts? I'm sorry, ma'am, but you were listed here as his wife."

Laura let out a loud, involuntary noise that started somewhere around her gut and made its way out her throat.

"Ma'am?"

"I'm sorry," Laura said. She exhaled, a nervous sound that she knew made her sound like a harpy. "Yes, I was married to Gordon Pitts. What's happened to him?"

The detective coughed. Laura could picture him: a young man sitting awake all through the night, having to make these kinds of calls. She felt sick to her stomach for her reaction.

"It seems to have been an accidental overdose, ma'am. Are you able to come into the station to identify the body? We're at the Central Community police station on East Sixth Street."

"Of course," Laura said. "I'll be there in an hour." She hung up the phone, but didn't move for several minutes. Laura kept her hand on the phone, as though holding it down would take back everything she'd felt in the few moments that she'd thought that Irving was still alive, somehow brought to life by the phone in the middle of the night. She stayed as still as possible, waiting for her breathing to return to normal, and then Laura stood up and slowly got dressed. She slipped out quietly, careful not to wake Junior in the next room.

Gordon had been found on a bus stop bench. The women who found him, two housekeepers at a nearby hotel, had at first thought that he was sleeping and kept their distance. One of the women had finally noticed that Gordon wasn't moving, and spoke to him. When he didn't speak back, she spoke louder, and when the woman approached Gordon and gingerly put her hand on his hand, she found his flesh cold and hard. The women ran to the nearest pay phone and called 911. The police relayed the information to Laura without any extra sugarcoating—the gentlemen understood that she was not distraught, and so just gave her the facts straight. Gordon had overdosed on heroin. He had been dead on the bench for at least a few hours, and all evidence seemed to indicate that he had been sleeping outside for much longer than that.

It was necessary for her to visually identify the body before the conversation progressed. Laura felt as if she were on a field trip in school. There were many parts of the police station she had never imagined—secret hallways, bright overhead lights despite the late hour, cold metallic surfaces. When the officer led Laura into the room with Gordon's body prone on a table, she held her breath, both for fear of the smell (there wasn't any) and for fear of what she might see. The officer unzipped the body bag far enough to show Laura Gordon's head and shoulders. There was no doubt that the person before her was Gordon Pitts, and yet Laura felt so distant from him, and from her life with him, that she could not be sure that he was he and she was she and that they were not perfect strangers. His cheeks were caved in, and Laura was sure there wasn't a tooth left in his mouth. Not only did Gordon not look like Florence anymore, he didn't even look like himself.

"I see," Laura said. "And what happens to the body?"

"Well," the officer said, suddenly looking down at his shoes, "I'm afraid that's your responsibility. Mr. Pitts had you listed as his wife. It took us a while to find you. That was until . . . Well, my mother is a great fan of yours, and that's how we were able to locate your whereabouts." The policeman was Florence's age, or younger. He seemed nervous. Laura was sure that no one ever got used to doing this kind of thing. She put her hand on his arm and steadied them both.

"Oh," Laura said. She forgot how affecting celebrity could be, forgot that her own face could matter to strangers. Her life as an actress felt like it had happened to someone else, someone young and lucky, Elsa Emerson's ghost. "I see." The officer zipped Gordon's face back up, away from view, and led Laura out of the room.

There were several options: Laura could pay for Gordon's burial herself; she could send him to a pauper's grave; she could cremate him and scatter the ashes somewhere meaningful, as if such a place existed. Then she could tell the children, or she could pick one option and never tell anyone. In the end, Laura decided it would be best to pay for a grave somewhere nearby, in the same cemetery as Irving. That way the children could visit if they wanted to. She made the arrangements by telephone from the police station, and then drove herself home in the early morning light. As Laura turned back off Sunset Boulevard, the smells of car exhaust and freshly mowed lawns coming through the car's open windows, she felt herself begin to hiccup. She wasn't crying for Gordon, not exactly. She was crying for the children, and because even if she hadn't loved him the way she loved Irving, Gordon was the reason she was in Los Angeles. Without him, she—*Elsa*—might never have left Door County. She might have gone to Chicago, or New York, or Paris. Laura pulled the car over to the side of the road. Only the gardeners were out this early, and the pink dawn light was just starting to cling to the roofs of her neighbors' houses. Laura rested her elbows on the steering wheel and leaned forward, until her forehead rested against the wheel too. She stayed there until cars began to drive by with more frequency, which meant that Junior would be awake soon, wondering where she was.

It was Harriet who saw the notice in the paper. Laura had given up reading the trades and the glossies and watching the local news—it was better to be in the dark.

"Laura, did you know about this?" Harriet said, holding up a section. She'd come over for Sunday brunch prepared by the Beverly Hills Hotel, and the two women sat at a table in the coffee shop. Laura had to put on her glasses to read it, but the large photo was instantly recognizable—Gardner Brothers Studio. The black-and-white photo showed the tall main gate, the studio's name in large letters looming overhead.

"What is it?" Laura asked. It must be Louis, the old man himself finally gone, she thought. What else would make the papers?

It wasn't Louis Gardner, but it was a death. The whole studio had been bought by an outfit called the TransMedia Corporation, and there was going to be an auction right there on stage twenty-seven in Hollywood. There were twenty thousand items being auctioned off during the month of May, everything that wasn't bolted to the ground. Even though Laura hadn't been under contract at the studio for more than twenty years, she could still see every piece of that lot in her mind, feel the chumminess of the canteen, the whole lot like an office building without any walls, with girls tap-dancing down the fake streets. From where she sat, Hollywood was a happy hallucination, old-fashioned as a dinosaur. It would be easier to think she'd made it all up. Laura thought about all those things up for sale—the dresses she'd worn, the umbrellas she'd twirled, a pair of Irving's glasses, a pile of scripts she might well have tossed into the wastebasket—and wished them luck out there in the universe, with no one like Louis or Irving to look out for them. It was as if all of them—the actors, the directors, the grips and best boys—as if *they* were up for auction too, just waiting for someone to make a bid, to say, "You know, I bet that old bird's still got life in her yet." The proceeds would go to a brand-new TransMedia hotel in Las Vegas, a shining tower in the middle of the desert, with enough rooms for everyone who was a member of the Screen Actors Guild.

Laura put the newspaper down and asked the waitress to hand her the telephone. She dialed Ginger's number with one finger.

Ginger & Bill's Hoedown Happy Hour was still in reruns every day, despite the fact that they hadn't filmed a new episode in ten years. Suddenly it was quaint to have a television show in black-and-white, and children younger than Clara's, who were no longer children, after all, watched it daily after school. When Ginger's housekeeper answered the telephone, the dogs were yapping in the background, all four of Ginger's white toy poodles. After a moment, Ginger came to the phone.

"It's over. Did you see?" Laura knew she wouldn't have to explain.

"Are you going to buy anything?"

"What, like a souvenir?"

"I almost want to go buy all my old lipsticks. Ha! As if there's any left. No one can say I wasn't thrifty." Ginger's full-throated laugh made Laura feel like she'd just drunk a giant mug of hot chocolate.

"I wouldn't want to be seen there," Laura said. "After everything."

"Sweetie, let me tell you something. Hollywood loves a comeback."

Now it was Laura's turn to laugh. "Do you know how old I am?"

"In fact, I do. Here's what I want you to do, Laura Lamont. You probably saw every play known to man when you were a kid, right? With your parents? I bet you knew all the parts, right? I want you to write down all your favorite parts for old ladies, even ladies you think you're too young to play, and then you find somewhere to play them." A dog yapped. "The puppies agree."

Laura couldn't help it: The car seemed to drive there by itself. She didn't tell anyone where she was going, and didn't even know it herself until she found the nose of her car at the front gate of Gardner Brothers.

The studio was larger now than it had been, having taken over the neighboring Triumph after Ginger's exit. She'd gone to the hairdresser and put on a smart-looking dark suit, the kind of thing she might have worn to a funeral, which was what it felt like. The guard at the gate recognized her and pointed toward the employee lot.

As her heels clicked down the alley in between Louis Gardner's office and the building that had once housed her dressing room, Laura felt short of breath—it was too much, being back and alone. She should have convinced Ginger to come along, or Junior, though she didn't want to put him in a stressful situation. It felt like walking back onto the set after decades away, as if she were playing the part of Laura Lamont in a film that had taken her entire life to write. She was a character! That made it easy to walk quickly, to ignore the stares from the older crew members and the ignorance of the young ones. Stage twenty-seven was one of the largest, and deep inside the belly of the studio.

The soundstage was overflowing. It reminded Laura of a swap meet, an endless yard sale, only the yard was full of costumes, of furniture, of things that had spent a moment on the silver screen. Some lots were labeled (*Sled used in Susie and Johnny's* Holiday on the Slopes*!!*) and some were not, just slumped over the back of a chair like a load of dirty laundry. Laura slowly made her way through the vast room. Where was Louis Gardner? She hadn't heard anything in years, and suddenly wondered whether she'd missed his death. No, that wasn't possible. He was probably old and weak, no longer able to run his own body, let alone an entire studio. Laura knew how that felt.

Other people milled around in between the large lots—the furniture, the flattened backdrops and hollow pillars—and the small ones, encased in glass and put on small velvet cushions like the royal jewels. Laura kept her eyes down. There was Dolores Dee's red dress, cut so low her bosom had nearly spilled out in every scene of *The Devil's Mistress*. There was Robert Hunter's tuxedo and top hat. There were filing cabinets in the corner, and Laura climbed over a small hill of children's costumes to reach them. She pulled open the first one—scripts, some of them marked up in Irving's hand. She rifled through, incredulous. What were they auctioning off? Didn't they understand? It was in the second filing cabinet that Laura found the script for *Farewell, My Sister*. Irving's notes were to her; they were to her! *LL: more of a pause here, remember to face left, otherwise we lose the line.* Laura sat down on the closest chair, a lion tamer's stand from a circus film, and read. All around her, people dug through clothes and papers and looked at the listed prices and laughed, but Laura didn't move until she was finished reading the entire script. She'd forgotten the details: It was the nun's dead sister whom the man really loved, not the nun herself. At the time, Laura had thought it was a love story between the nun and her suitor, but now she realized that the strongest love on the page was between the nun and the sister she'd lost. That love was so steadfast, so immutable, that the nun truly thought she would be able to give up God for her sister's happiness. It was a trade, a bargain out of O. Henry.

Laura could remember the need to leave Door County, and the desire to see herself on the screen. Rather, she remembered *Elsa's* need for those things. Elsa Emerson: She'd been so quick to throw it all away, to swim inside a new body and a new name. It was true that she had always loved to act, loved to pretend, but it was Hildy whose face should have been on the screen, her cheekbones projected, her beauty marks copied. It had always been for Laura's sister, this slipshod career. Elsa had done everything for Hildy, until Elsa got so lost inside the machinery that she could no longer speak. Laura sat still, afraid that if she moved, her entire body would break apart and scatter on the ground, just another thousand souvenirs. She stayed until the light outside began to change, until the bidding closed, having neither placed a bid nor returned the script to the cabinet, but instead tucking it inside her bag, knowing that no one would ever miss it.

After so many years on hiatus, Jimmy was glad to be put back to work for Laura. A producer in New York was mounting a Broadway production of *The Royal Family,* and was delighted to hear that Laura Lamont was interested in the theater. The pay was standard union, the conditions standard Broadway: eight shows a week, with Mondays dark. It was to be a limited run, only twelve weeks.

"Which part?" Laura asked. There was only one right answer.

Laura heard Jimmy rustling through his notes on the other end of the phone. "Fanny Cavendish," he said. "Isn't that what you said you wanted?"

She didn't hesitate for more than a split second, long enough for her chest to expand, and to speak the word *yes*.

The producers set Laura up in an apartment near the theater, walking distance from Central Park. She arrived at the airport at seven in the morning, and a waiting car took her straight to the building, which was taller than most buildings in downtown Los Angeles, unapologetically big and white, with air conditioners dotting every other window. The apartment itself was a one-bedroom on the twenty-second floor, clean and anonymous, and the smallest place Laura had lived since she was pregnant with Clara. The pullout sofa was for Florence, or Junior, or for anyone who wanted it, but the bedroom was just for Laura. Now that he was on medication, Laura didn't feel anxious about leaving her son alone. His sisters checked up on him every day, his own personal fleet of nurses. He was in no better care when she was at home. Laura unpacked her small suitcase—she'd had Jimmy send some boxes ahead, with heavier things like sweaters and coats, so that she wouldn't have to struggle with all those cases in the airport.

As Laura stood at the window and looked out at the busy city, she realized a number of things in quick succession. It was the first time Laura had been to New York City in nearly forty years, after a brief press tour for *Farewell, My Sister*. It was also the first time she'd ever lived alone. Not only did she not have a husband, she didn't even have one of her children to keep her company. Laura thought about calling Ginger or Harriet, but it was only five o'clock in the morning at home in California, and neither of them woke up that early. And so Laura simply stood at the window, with her forehead pressed against the glass, and stared down at the street. The yellow taxicabs flooded the roads, zipping and jerking their way across the avenue. People walked their dogs and their children and one another. Laura was afraid that she would get lost if she tried to walk anywhere by herself. Central Park was in the distance, a few blocks north and a few blocks east, but she wasn't sure she could find it by herself from the street. Laura took out a map that Florence had given her at the airport and unfolded it on the small kitchen table. Manhattan was a grid, not like Los Angeles, which curled and waved like a dancer, its long streets full of their own ideas of where they should lead. It was nine blocks total to the park—at home she would have driven. Laura washed her face in the small sink and looked at herself in the mirror. Her skin looked so pale against her dark hair, the rich chocolate color of which seemed more and more of a fallacy every day. The director of the show wanted it to be gray; Jimmy had told her that later, after she'd already agreed. *Gray hair.* At first, Laura didn't even understand what he meant—a wig? Some baby powder, like schoolchildren used? But no, of course not. The director wanted Laura to look her age, all sixty years of it. She would have to have the color stripped out, and see what was left behind. Jimmy, nervous about this part of the contract, had stuttered out, "W-well, you can always d-dye it back," but Laura knew an opportunity when she saw one. The hairs growing along her part had been gray for many years, a decade, even.

It was late September, and outside, the world couldn't decide whether to be summer or fall. Laura had been warm in the taxi on the way in from the airport, but the people-dots below her were wearing coats and scarves. Florence had helped her pack, and there was a sweater in there somewhere. Laura slipped her arms into the sleeves, wrote down her new address on a slip of paper, and tucked it into her sweater pocket in case she got lost and needed to ask for directions.

It was true what people said about New York City. Even Ginger claimed that she could walk down Broadway without being mobbed, that the ordinary people left the famous people alone. Laura wore her big sunglasses and wrapped a scarf around her head, and no one batted an eye at her for all nine blocks. At first, Laura nervously watched the sidewalk whenever she passed anyone old enough to recognize her, but the closer she got to the park, the bolder she felt. By the time she reached the park, with a line of horse-drawn carriages across its southern edge, Laura felt so light, so *independent*, that she practically danced through Columbus Circle, despite the fast-walking students and cluster of panhandlers. It was the longest walk she'd taken by herself since she was Elsa Emerson, and no one cared one way or the other what she was up to. When she hit the east side of the park, she kept walking, until she finally looked at her watch and realized she'd been out for nearly four hours. It was only when she stopped walking that Laura noticed her shoes had begun to pinch, and so she hopped into a taxicab, suddenly flushed and exhausted, and went home.

A reporter from the newspaper met Laura at the theater for an interview. It was *human interest*; that was how Jimmy described it. No one had cared about Laura for so long that somehow she was a story again. The reporter was a young man with blue jeans and a necktie. They sat in the last row, with cups of tea from backstage fetched by one of the helpful young things who always seemed to be running across the stage like mice, duct tape attached to their belts, clipboards cradled in their armpits.

"I understand that your parents ran a theater in northern Wisconsin. Is this your first time onstage since you were a child?" The reporter was a child himself, no more than twenty-five years old. He was wearing glasses with thick black frames, similar to the ones Irving had worn decades ago. Laura wondered whether he'd ever interviewed anyone before, but then decided that that was awfully rude of her, and that she should take him more seriously.

"It is my first time onstage since I was a teenager, yes," Laura said. She loved being in the theater during the daytime, when she could see the worn spots on the velvet chairs, the dust gathered along the baseboards. Even the most beautiful theater in New York City was always crumbling a bit—that was what made it so lovely. Laura wouldn't have wanted to be in a new theater, like some of the shows down the way, with gleaming aisles. There was something powerful in the layers of performance preceding her. "It was this play, actually." She laughed. "I was acting a different role, of course."

This got the young man excited. "Really? And what seems different about this staging?"

Laura laughed again, more loudly. Onstage, two young actors were rehearsing, and one of them shot a look her way, softening when she saw where the sound was coming from. Laura had forgotten that about people in the theater—no one in the movies was ever deferential, not unless you were the one signing their checks.

"Well, I don't plan to marry my costar. My father isn't direct-ing. There are quite a number of differences, I'd say."

"Oh, really?" The boy checked his notes, and scribbled some more. "So, then, um, what do you think your second husband, Irving Green, would have to say about this, your return to the stage?" The boy didn't know enough to feel shy about asking.

Laura paused. It was funny to think about Gordon and Ir-ving being on equal footing, two marriages, as if anything were that simple.

"I think Irving would be absolutely overjoyed," she said finally. "I only wish he were here to see it. Luckily, I have three gorgeous, healthy children, and they will be here in his stead."

"What would you say you've learned about acting in the years since your days at Gardner Brothers?" The young man held a small tape recorder between them, level with Laura's chin. Un-derneath her, the chair squeaked, and she wondered whether he'd include that, the sights and sounds and smells of the room itself. She hoped he would. The intimate truth of bodies—spit, breath, reddened cheeks—it arrived in the theater whether or not it was invited. That was what Laura loved the most. Irving was there too, in the distance between the proscenium and the front row.

"It's better to work than not to work," she said. "But it's even better to know why you're working. When I was young, I made movies because people told me to, and hit my marks, and spoke my lines. I made *Farewell, My Sister* without knowing what was going on most of the time. I did what I was told." She paused. "I chose this," Laura said, "but I chose everything else too." Laura nodded, agreeing with herself, and then leaned over and gave the boy reporter a kiss on the cheek. She probably reminded him of his mother, or his grandmother, even.

"Um, thank you," he said.

"You're welcome, my dear," Laura said, and walked slowly back to her dressing room. She wanted to talk to Florence on the telephone, and there seemed no reason to wait. She wanted to tell Florence everything she'd just said, and more, and for her brilliant, smart psychotherapist of a daughter to tell her what it all meant. Of course, Florence always claimed it didn't work that way, but Laura thought she'd break down sooner or later and give her poor mother all the answers she was looking for.

The night before the show opened, Florence and Clara and Junior and Jimmy all flew in. Roy and Leslie were with the Petersons, and would come on their own later in the season. The apartment was completely silent before they arrived, and Laura switched from the chair to the sofa to a perch by the window like a one-woman relay race. The apartment wasn't much—the walls were painted a creamy white, with only a few framed reproductions, all innocuous flowerpots and such. Laura wished she'd thought to redecorate a bit, so that when the kids came in they would look around and see how happy she was, how well the space suited her. The doorman called to announce their arrival, and Laura squeaked out, "Yes, send them up, send them up!" and then waited in the open doorway. Her hair was gray now, which she'd warned them about, but she was nervous for them to see it in person and not in the play, to know that their mother really was old enough to have gray hair, that it wasn't part of the act. She adjusted her simple black headband over and over again, the way Clara had when she was in grade school.

Junior was out of the elevator first, and before he'd taken three steps, Laura rushed down the hall, leaving the door open wide, inviting the world in. He was wearing suspenders, which made him look young and serious, like an old-fashioned bank teller. He smelled like an airplane, but Laura didn't care.

"Mom! Your hair looks amazing! You look so beautiful," Junior said, his mouth so close to her ear. She hugged him tighter, filled with relief.

Clara was next, humping the bags clumsily out of the elevator, with the door trying to close on her over and over again, which turned out to be Florence hitting the button on purpose. They were with their mother, and so they were acting like children. Laura let go of Junior and shooed him toward the apartment, and then waved both Florence and Clara into her arms at once. The girls were tall, like her, taller than their father had been, her sweet, small Irving—and just then she realized she hadn't told the girls about Gordon. Laura's breath caught in her throat.

"You okay, Mom?" Florence said, pulling back. She righted her suitcase, which had fallen over onto its side. Clara too let go, and they stood there in a lopsided triangle. Jimmy was behind Clara, waiting his turn, all of them quiet except for Junior, whom they could hear all the way down the hall, exclaiming about the view.

"Your father died," Laura said. It came out so clumsily, but she didn't know what else to say.

Clara gave a little laugh. "Yes, Mom, we know, it was twenty-five years ago."

Then it was Laura's turn to laugh—at the number, as if time mattered, when she had thought of Irving every day since, when he was still her one and only. "Gordon Pitts," Laura said. "Gordon died. Just before I came to New York." She grabbed their hands and held them in a big pile in the middle of the triangle between them, like at a basketball game. "I'm so sorry I didn't tell you."

"Um, it's okay, Mom," Florence said. "But are you okay?" As she was talking, Florence ran her fingers through Laura's hair. "It's so shiny," she said. "I love it. Come on, we'll talk about it more inside." With that, Florence darted through the open doorway.

Jimmy took two steps forward, so he was now the third corner of the triangle. "He really was so good in *The Ballad of Bayonets*."

"You actually have seen them all, haven't you, my sweetie," Laura said, and kissed him on the cheek. Jimmy nodded.

"Here, Clara, give me your bag and I'll take it in," Jimmy said, and did, so that then it was just Laura and Clara standing alone in the hall.

"It's so nice to have you here," Laura said. She put her palms on Clara's cheeks. Now that Laura's hair was light again, they looked alike—perhaps it had always been so. "I missed you guys."

"We missed you too, Mom," Clara said, her eyes starting to crinkle at the edges.

"Well, come on in. We can order some Chinese food, just like real New Yorkers. How does that sound?" Laura put her hand on Clara's back and led her toward the door, letting her cross the threshold first, the way Irving would have done. When she got to the doorway, Laura stopped and rested her hand on the frame. The living room looked smaller when it was full of people, but so much warmer too. Laura looked from Clara to Jimmy to Florence to Junior and remembered something Ginger had told her ages ago, when the children were babies: that acting was what people turned to when their own lives weren't good enough, and she knew it wasn't true. Her family was healthy and gorgeous and alive, and she wanted to show them what their father had seen so many years before: that there was something special that she could do.

"Laura Lamont," Jimmy said, beckoning her in. "What are you waiting for?"

On opening night, Laura stood offstage, watching the heavy curtain from behind in the dark. All around her, people were wishing one another broken legs. There were legs breaking all over the place, and hers the oldest legs in the building. The children were there, all four of them, in the second row. She peeked out from behind and saw them, Florence on one side, Jimmy and Clara on the other, Junior in the middle.

Her son fidgeted with the program. He curled it up and smacked it against the back of the seat in front of him, which was still empty. At Laura's insistence, they were early, with no possibility of missing a single word. They were passing a box of candy back and forth, like they were sitting in a movie theater. Laura watched as Florence tipped the box into her cupped hand. The girls—they were women now, but Laura could think of them only as girls, as her girls—looked happy and expectant. Jimmy craned his neck around to see the other people coming into the theater, and waved hello to someone whom Laura couldn't see. She had a brief, fleeting thought that it was her father, though of course

Jimmy had never met her father, and he'd been gone since the girls were children. But there was always the balcony. Laura took a step back from the curtain until she could see the underside of the balcony, a sturdy Art Deco shelf floating in the middle of the room. Surely her father was there somewhere, along with Hildy and Irving and even poor Gordon, all of them watching from far enough back that she wouldn't be able to make out their faces, no matter how hard she squinted into the lights onstage. Even if she held her hand in a ready salute, Laura wouldn't be able to see them, but she knew they would be there, laughing and delighted. Was it possible that she'd finally gotten old, when she had always been the youngest? Laura supposed that anything was possible. All her lines for the evening went zipping through her brain, the words so ready to be spoken that they tumbled over one another with excitement. In the house, the lights dimmed, and she heard everyone in the lobby hustle into their seats. Laura Lamont took a deep breath and exhaled through her mouth, slow and steady. She stepped out onto the stage in the dark, feeling the wooden floor under her shoes. Once she hit her mark, Laura stood still and waited for the curtain to rise, and for the applause to begin.

ACKNOWLEDGMENTS

My boundless, ceaseless gratitude to Megan Lynch, Geoffrey Kloske, Ali Cardia, Claire McGinnis, Jynne Dilling Martin, Melissa Broder, Tiffany Yates Martin, Hal Fessenden, and everyone at Riverhead Books, for making my wildest dreams come true.

Profound thanks also to Jenni Ferrari-Adler; Christine Onorati, Stephanie Anderson, and Jenn Northington of WORD; Mary Gannett, Henry Zook, Zack Zook, and Chad Bunning of BookCourt; Lauren Cerand; Sophie Rosenblum; Kate Harvey and everyone at Picador UK; Anvar Cukowski and Birgit Schmitz at Berlin Verlag; Stuart Nadler; Julie Klam; Dan Chaon; Lorrie Moore, the University of Wisconsin–Madison MFA program, and the Wisconsin Institute for Creative Writing; Courtney Sullivan; Claudia and Eve Rose Gonson; the Sackett Street Writers Workshop; Megan Branch; Bethanne Patrick; Alexander Chee; Jennifer Gilmore; Elliott Holt; Jessica Francis Kane; Edan Lepucki and Patrick Brown; Rae Meadows; Michelle Wildgin and Rob Spillman of *Tin House*; Cathrin Wirtz; Adam Wilson; Alex Shepard; Michele Filgate; Andrea Walker; Cal Morgan and Carrie Kania;

Caitlin Roper; Corinna Barsan; Jason Diamond and Tobias Carroll of Vol. 1 Brooklyn; Karyn Bosnak; Lauren Groff; Maris Kreizman; Erin Kottke and Marisa Atkinson; Rachel Fershleiser; too many delightful, warm, and wonderful friends to name. Rest assured, I'm talking about you.

And thank you most of all to my very patient and encouraging family, cats included.

I would also like to acknowledge the fabulous Margaret Herrick Library in Los Angeles, where I did much of my research. If you need to learn anything about Hollywood, they will take excellent care of you.

Emma Straub is from New York City. She is the author of the short story collection *Other People We Married*. Her fiction and nonfiction have been published in *Vogue*, *Tin House*, the *New York Times*, and the *Paris Review Daily*, and she is a staff writer for *Rookie*. Straub lives with her husband in Brooklyn, New York.

Also available from

EMMA STRAUB

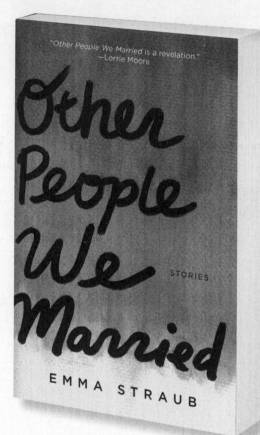

"*Other People We Married* is a revelation."
—Lorrie Moore

Other People We Married

STORIES

EMMA STRAUB

"Emma Straub is worthy of our adoration. These stories
are wise, surprising, hilarious, and unforgettable."

—Karen Russell, author of *Swamplandia*